The Crown and the Cross
THE LIFE OF CHRIST

FRANK G. SLAUGHTER

The Crown and the Cross
THE LIFE OF CHRIST

Published by eChristian, Inc.
Escondido, California

CHECK OUT

The Galileans, A Novel of Mary Magdalene

ALSO BY FRANK G. SLAUGHTER

Contents

Acknowledgments

It would be impractical to list here the large number of books which have been consulted in developing this picture of the Life of Christ. Certain volumes, however, have been especially valuable. Foremost among them are: *A Harmony of the Gospels for Students of the Life of Christ*, by A. T. Robertson (Harper & Brothers); *The Heart of the New Testament*, by H. I. Hester (William Jewell Press); *Sacred Sites and Ways*, by Gustaf H. Dalman (The Macmillan Company); *Daily Life in Bible Times*, by Albert E. Bailey, (Charles Scribner's Sons); *The Life and Times of Jesus the Messiah*, by Alfred Edersheim (Longmans, Green and Company); *The Beautiful Land*, by Henry C. Potter (Thomas Whittaker); *In the Days of Christ*, by Alfred Edersheim (Fleming H. Revell Company); *Life and Customs in Jesus' Time*, by Joseph L. Gift (Standard Publishing Foundation); *A History of New Testament Times in Palestine*, by Shailer Mathews (The Macmillan Company); *Christian Beginnings*, by Morton Scott Enslin (Harper & Brothers); *The World Christ Knew*, by Anthony C. Deane (Michigan State College Press); *The Dead Sea Scriptures in English Translation*, Theodore H. Gaster (Doubleday Anchor Books); *The Meaning of the Dead Sea Scrolls*, by A. Powell Davies (New American Library of World Literature).

All words spoken by Jesus Christ in this book have been taken from the King James Version of the New Testament, published by The World Publishing Company. In converting the Biblical phraseology to dialogue, it has been necessary to adapt slightly some portions of the original King James text. In most cases these changes are merely in forms of the pronoun, and in punctuation. In no case has the original meaning been changed in any way. No edition other than the King James Version of the Bible referred to above has been consulted in the production of this work, and any similarity to such versions is completely accidental.

I also wish to express my gratitude to The World Publishing Company for asking me to retell this most wonderful of all stories. Though it began in a manger in Bethlehem nearly two thousand years ago, it has never ended but has grown more thrilling as the years have passed and men have sought to understand more fully the meaning of the crown of thorns which identified Jesus of Nazareth then and now as the King of all who love God, and the meaning of the cross upon which He gave His life for the sins of mankind.

Frank G. Slaughter
Jacksonville, Florida
October 6, 1958

About the Author

(FROM THE ORIGINAL 1959 VERSION)

Frank G. Slaughter was born in Washington, D.C., in 1908. At the age of only fourteen he entered college and graduated from Duke University in 1926 with a Phi Beta Kappa key. Four years later he graduated from Johns Hopkins Medical School, an "M.D." at the age of twenty-two. For many years, both as a civilian and then as a major and lieutenant colonel during World War II, Dr. Slaughter devoted himself to the practice of medicine. During these years he also began to write and upon his release from military service at the end of the war, he decided to devote himself full time to the career of an author. Since the publication of his first book in 1941, Dr. Slaughter has become one of the most prolific men of letters of any century. In less than nineteen years he has produced twenty-eight books, drawing his inspiration from fields as diverse as modern medicine, Renaissance history, and the timeless and unlimited sources of the Bible. In his own country and abroad, books such as In a Dark Garden, The Road to Bithynia, and The Mapmaker have given pleasure to more than 20,000,000 readers.

Dr. Slaughter is also well known as the author of novels dealing particularly with Bible times, such as *The Galileans*, *The Song of Ruth*, and *The Thorn of Arimathea*. His interest in spiritual affairs extends to on occasion filling a church pulpit in the pastor's absence. From this background of research and activity, *The Crown and the Cross* has been written.

Publisher's Preface for
The Crown and the Cross

This best-selling book was originally published by Frank G. Slaughter in 1959.

This version of the book still contains the well-crafted characters of the original version—a mixture of men and women described in the Bible as well as fictionalized characters developed from Frank Slaughter's imagination. The author has taken some license with various people and events. It all adds up to create a compelling story of what might have happened.

We realize that the average Christian reader today has access to much of the study material about Jesus' life, and the resources Frank G. Slaughter refers to in his acknowledgements may now have been replaced by more recent scholarship. So we have adjusted portions of this book accordingly.

Our hope is that you enjoy this old book with new eyes and that it sends you back to read the firsthand accounts of this time period as recorded by the Gospel writers.

All revisions to this text come from the publisher, eChristian, Inc. Although Frank G. Slaughter is no longer alive to give us his approval, his two sons have graciously given us permission to bring new life to this best-selling book.

Joseph also went up from Galilee, out of the city of Nazareth,
into Judea, to the city of David, which is called Bethlehem.

Luke 2:4

In the long line of travelers approaching the city of Bethlehem from the south this winter afternoon, none was more certain of his own piety and righteousness than Elam, the Pharisee. Although only a little over thirty, the age at which Jewish men were considered wise enough to sit upon the village councils and give opinion upon matters under discussion, Elam was already a ruler of his synagogue in Hebron and well known to the Pharisees of Jerusalem. His robe was of rich material and he rode upon an ass, as befitted a wealthy man.

On foot, leading a second animal heavily laden with bales, came Elam's servant Jonas. Jonas was only slightly older than Elam, but the great hump on his back and his leathery skin, the result of working in the sun and wind, made him look much older. Jonas was weary and his back ached, for his master was in a hurry and all afternoon had been urging the ass he rode.

The bales upon the pack animal contained fine cloth woven on the looms of the weavers of Hebron. From it Elam expected to make an important profit in the fine shops of Jerusalem, and, being a pious man, he would use a part of the gold for the purchase of a sacrifice for the temple. Nor would Elam's be any ordinary sacrifice. Only the best was proper for a man of his wealth and station, a plump lamb purchased in his name alone, not shared by others to decrease the cost, as the Law allowed. Its burning flesh would make a sweet savor unto the Lord and, it was hoped, bring the giver good fortune in his business transactions over the coming year.

Jonas had no such pleasant prospect to ease his weariness, but he was happy nonetheless, even though the cold wind penetrated his worn clothing and sent a deep ague into his bones. Hidden in his robe where Elam could not see it, Jonas was taking his own gift to the temple, something far more valuable than the lamb his master would deliver so ostentatiously to the priest on the morrow.

Actually, the servant's gift was only a length of cloth. But what a fine piece it was! Nothing in Elam's bales could approach the softness of the fabric or its pure whiteness. The wool he had picked up from scraps thrown away, carefully separating the rich white portion from the dark and using only the best. Then he had carded and spun the thread, after giving to his master the full day's work required of all servants by the Law of Israel as set down in the Torah. The weaving Jonas had done himself also, working at night with a little loom he had fashioned. For light he had used candles made from wasted tallow, since Elam did not furnish lamps or oil to his servants.

On many a winter's night long after darkness had fallen, Jonas's gnarled fingers had drawn the shuttle of the loom back and forth with loving care, setting each thread patiently until the whole fabric was of a smooth and even texture. All the while he had been constantly ready to douse the candle if he heard Elam approaching. Then he pretended to be asleep, with the small loom and the wool hidden under the meager coverlet that supplemented his bed of straw. More than once Jonas had nearly been caught, for Elam watched his servants closely to see that they did not cheat him, but each time he had managed to hide the precious cloth in time.

Actually the Pharisee had no right to the cloth, but Jonas knew how small and avaricious was the soul behind his master's pious front. Elam would instantly recognize the value of the fabric and would certainly find something in the Law to serve as a pretext to seize it for himself.

All the way from Hebron Jonas had carried his precious gift inside his robe, carefully wrapped in a meaner cloth so no moisture from his body would stain the fabric. It was a relief to know that, with Jerusalem now only a few miles away, he could take it to the temple tomorrow and turn it over to the priests.

Jonas even dared to dream that the high priest himself might accept the cloth as a fit covering for the highest altar of all, next in importance to the Holy of Holies. Such a thought was sweet indeed to one who was virtually a slave, but Jonas did not allow his hopes to rise very high; he knew how rarely the dreams of slaves came to pass. But he could at least be sure that the Lord would know what was in his heart. And even the beating which Elam would undoubtedly give him afterward for having outshone his master, although in the service of the Most High, could not dim the pride Jonas would feel tomorrow in the temple when he handed over the cloth as his own special gift.

Busy with his thoughts and weary from leading the pack animal all day, Jonas stumbled over a rock in the road and grasped at the bales on the ass's back for support. The animal grunted from the extra weight and Elam looked back and frowned. The merchant, too, was tired and anxious for the comforts of the inn at the town of Bethlehem just ahead. The inn, he knew, would be a mean one, for the town was small, but if they went on to Jerusalem today they would arrive after dark. And since at night large cities and the roads leading to them were notoriously unsafe places for travelers with goods and money, Elam was only being prudent in stopping before sunset.

"Take care, Jonas!" the Pharisee scolded him. "If you soil the goods, they will not bring the best price. Remember, a part of it goes to the Most High."

"I will be careful, master," Jonas said humbly, for the Law was strict about a servant being respectful and obedient. Elam really was a good master, Jonas reminded himself as he plodded on, always scrupulous about obeying every word of the Law, although very careful never to give any more than was absolutely required.

II

It was hardly mid-afternoon and the air was still warm, although at this season the sun already hung low over the hills and the broad expanse of the Great Sea to the west. The dark blue fruit of the olive trees in the groves along the hillsides had long since ripened and been picked. Now the leaves, their pale green color somewhat lighter in winter than in spring, were curled up as if to protect themselves against the cool, often frosty, nights. The fig trees and the vines were bare, although occasionally a pomegranate bush in a protected spot showed yellow foliage. Against the sere death of winter creeping downward toward the valleys from the tops of the hills, only the leaves of the carob-bean trees remained bright green and glossy.

The road that wound southward from Jerusalem to Bethlehem, Hebron, and the border of Egypt was always heavily traveled, but especially so today when many who had been born in Bethlehem a few miles away were hurrying there to be counted in the Roman census during the remaining days allotted for it. The stream of movement brushed past a small procession that was keeping to the side of the road. The body of the woman riding upon the mule was awkward with child, and she appeared to be near her time for every now and then she caught her breath and bit back a cry of pain. The man leading the mule glanced back often and tried to smile reassuringly as he guided the animal carefully so as to jostle her as little as possible.

He was older than his wife, being in his forties while she was in the early bloom of young womanhood, but the men of Israel usually married women several years younger than themselves, marriage even with a girl of ten being not at all uncommon in this land. The clothing of these two was ordinary—the man's neither fringed nor sumptuously dyed as were the garments of the Pharisees who passed them with only a disdainful glance for the *am ha-arets*, the common people, whose piety could never equal theirs. Yet it was of good serviceable fabric, woven on home looms by hands accustomed to give good measure whether in passing the shuttle, pouring grain, or wielding the hammer and chisel.

The man carried himself with a certain pride for he was an artisan, a maker of fine cabinets and a builder of sturdy buildings. And certainly neither husband nor wife had cause to be awed by any of those going by them, for both were of the line of David, the great warrior king of Israel who, more than any other since Moses led the twelve tribes out of bondage in Egypt, had united the worshipers of the one true God whose name must not be spoken, and made the Children of Israel a great nation. Every loyal son of Israel yearned for the great days of David's kingdom now that his nation consisted of only a few provinces subjected to Rome.

There was a further difference though between this and the other families hurrying to reach the shelter of the public caravansary at the edge of Bethlehem where all travelers might pause to rest free if they arrived while there was still room. It lay in a look of certainty, of selection for an honor known only to herself, in the eyes of the young mother-to-be. She was lovely, like thousands of the daughters of Zion, but the strength of character and a certain quiet pride evident in her face, twisted periodically now with the beginning pains of approaching childbirth, set her apart.

"Joseph." She spoke as the mule reached the hilltop. "If I could—could rest a little—"

"Of course, Mary." Guiding the mule away from the road, he helped her to dismount and find a seat upon a flat rock near the very top of the hill.

Mary looked eagerly southward toward the white-roofed city of David that was their destination. And as she did, she thought once again of the strange yet thrilling things which had happened lately and were to culminate in the birth of the baby who now stirred in her womb.

She had been like any other happy young woman in Nazareth, the small town of southern Galilee where she had grown up. Betrothed to the man she loved, Joseph the carpenter and builder, she had been making plans for the time when she would enter his household as his bride. Joseph was a respected member of the community and its synagogue, and highly skilled in his trade. His ancestors had been woodworkers before him, and although, like Mary herself, he was proud of his blood kinship in one of the noblest lines of Israel, he would expect the sons she bore him to learn his trade, for a builder and worker in wood was always held in high regard.

It was true that Joseph was approaching middle age. But for Mary to marry a younger man and go to live in his father's household would mean becoming practically the slave of an older woman. Mary was looking forward to having her own home. She did not consider the difference in their ages as a stumbling block to a happy marriage; as she was growing up in Nazareth, she had observed Joseph's solid virtues, and she had been flattered when this worthy, capable carpenter had approached her father to arrange for the bride price, or *mohar*.

Mary had seen no reason to be frightened when, some ten courses of the moon previously, a stranger had appeared at her home in Nazareth and spoken to her. His bearing was regal; few such as he stopped in Nazareth. Still she had not thought of him as being other than mortal.

5

"Rejoice, highly favored one," the stranger had greeted her courteously, even reverently. "The Lord is with you. Blessed are you among women!"

Awed somewhat by the visitor's language and manner, Mary had not answered. Besides, it was not fitting for a young unmarried woman to speak to a complete stranger.

"Do not be afraid, Mary," the visitor had continued, "for you have found favor with God. Behold, you shall conceive in your womb and bring forth a Son, and shall call His name Jesus. He shall be great and shall be called the Son of the Highest, and the Lord God shall give to Him the throne of His father David. He will reign over the house of Jacob forever, and of His kingdom there shall be no end."

Mary could not remain silent any longer. "How can this be," she said, "since I do not know a man?" For she was as yet only betrothed and still virgin.

"The Holy Spirit shall come upon you, and the power of the Highest shall overshadow you," the stranger explained. "Therefore the Holy One who is to be born shall be called the Son of God. Behold, your cousin Elisabeth has also conceived a son in her old age; and this is now the sixth month with her who was called barren. For with God nothing shall be impossible."

By now Mary had come to see that she was in the presence of no mere human being but of an emissary from God. She grasped only faintly as yet the greatness of the honor for which she had been selected, but she said obediently, "Behold the handmaid of the Lord! Let it be to me according to your word."

The angel had then disappeared, leaving her filled with wonder and something of fear also. It was true that she was of the bloodline of David, from which the ancient writings said a king, or at least the great spiritual leader to be called the Messiah, would one day come again in Israel. But she was the daughter of an artisan of meager means in Nazareth, and betrothed to a man of no great riches, a man not even well known except to the people who used his services and the products of his skilled hands. Was it not unthinkable that any son born of her should ever become king of Israel?

Her first impulse had been to tell Joseph what had happened, but she instinctively realized he would have had difficulty enough in believing the story even had he seen the angel and heard him speak. And, indeed,

Mary herself could not help wondering now whether the man who had appeared to her had not been a creature of her own imagination rather than an angel sent by God to reveal the future to her.

She had gone about her duties with a troubled mind during the next several days. Nothing had happened to her body that she was able to detect, certainly nothing to give her reason to feel that she had conceived. Logic almost convinced her that the whole thing had been a dream, although the scene was as vivid in her memory as on the day when the stranger had appeared, and she still could not forget his convincing manner, or the reverence and respect with which he had greeted her.

Finally, knowing she must answer for herself the question of whether she had really seen an angel, Mary decided to do the one thing that, she was sure, could settle her doubts once and for all. The angel, if such he were, had said that her cousin Elisabeth had conceived. If Mary were to make the several days' journey to Hebron where Elisabeth lived with her white-haired priest-husband Zacharias, and there found her kinswoman pregnant, as the visitor had stated, she could be sure this strange experience had been no mere fantasy.

As she thought about it, Mary remembered rumors that had been going about of a strange thing happening to Zacharias while he had been serving with one of the priestly "courses" as the groups assigned at intervals to help with the ritual of worship in the temple were called.

Temple service was an honor coveted by all priests of Israel and regular processions of them journeyed to Jerusalem periodically to fulfill the holy office. Zacharias, Mary had heard, while serving in the temple had been selected to burn incense on the altar in the Holy Place. His instructions were to bow down in worship as soon as the incense was kindled upon the coals, and then to withdraw in reverence. But that day, rumor said, Zacharias had remained overlong in the room which contained the altar. When finally he had emerged to take his allotted position at the top of the steps leading from the porch to the Court of the Priests, he had been unable to speak and could only beckon to the others instead of leading in the benediction.

No one doubted that Zacharias had had a divine vision in the Holy Place, but the old priest had been able to reveal nothing of what had happened and had departed to his own village immediately his offices in the temple were completed. There he had remained, still not able to speak.

Mary was able to make the long trip to Hebron in company with a party of friends who were going from Nazareth to Judea. As she trudged along the road with them, she had wondered whether there could be any connection between the strange thing which was said to have happened to Zacharias and her own experience with the angel. Her questions were answered at once when she reached the home of her kinswoman. For Elisabeth, in spite of the fact that she was beyond the normal age of childbearing and had been barren for many years, was far advanced in pregnancy.

Elisabeth's greeting had confirmed the thrilling promise of the angel who had visited Mary. "Blessed are you among women, and blessed is the fruit of your womb!" the older woman had said. "But why is this granted to me, that the mother of my Lord should come to me?" Mary told Elisabeth of what had happened in Nazareth and of her own doubts, and how even though she was sure now that her senses had not betrayed her, she could not understand how she, a lowly daughter in the line of David, had been chosen for so high an honor.

It was a question that Elisabeth had not been able to answer. Before her visit was ended, however, Mary's body had confirmed what the angel had revealed, that she, though a virgin, was indeed to bear a child. The fact of her pregnancy being certain beyond doubt now, Mary straightway traveled back to Nazareth to tell Joseph the story of how she had been selected by God to become the mother of a king.

Several months later, Elisabeth had sent word to Mary that she had given birth to a strong boy who had been circumcised on the eighth day, as was required for all male children born in Israel, and named John. Immediately after the ceremony, Zacharias had found his tongue again and had told how an angel of the Lord had appeared to him in the temple as he stood beside the altar of incense and revealed that his wife would conceive and bear him a son who would, in the words of the messenger, "Go before the Lord in the spirit and power of Elijah, to turn the hearts of the fathers to the children, and the disobedient to the wisdom of the just; to make ready a people prepared for the Lord."

Few believed the story of the old priest, choosing to think that he had dozed as he waited before the Holy Place to burn the incense and had only dreamed a vivid dream. But Zacharias and Elisabeth were happy now. It had been many hundreds of years since a true prophet had arisen in Israel, and they were both proud that here in their house lay one to whom the Most High had promised the spirit and power of Elijah.

III

Mary had told all these things to Joseph when she returned to Nazareth. With the signs of her pregnancy already beginning to be evident, she was concerned about the talk that would follow when she bore a child which obviously had been conceived before she and Joseph were legally man and wife. Through it all Joseph had been gentle and kind, thinking of her before himself, as he did even now.

After seating Mary comfortably upon the rock beside the road where she could look across the valley to Bethlehem, he tethered the mule loosely so it could graze upon some small patches of dry grass between the rocks. From the pack that contained his carpenter's tools, he took a small waterskin and, after Mary had drunk from it, relieved his own thirst.

Toward Bethlehem, whose white rooftops were now plainly visible in the afternoon sunlight, a broad ridge gradually rose to form a hill that extended almost in a north-south direction for some distance before turning slightly to the southwest to parallel the road to Hebron, along which the dust kicked up by travelers approaching the city from the south was plainly visible. The back of the ridge was irregular in shape and to the east a lesser slope ended in a small plain between two valleys. Almost atop the ridge, on the lowest of its three elevations, lay Bethlehem.

From where he stood, Joseph could see the gates of the town, where he had played as a child, the northwestern one leading toward Jerusalem, only a few hours' walk distant for a vigorous man, and the western gate leading toward Hebron. To the south and east smaller gates were also cut into the winding wall that encompassed the town, but they were of little significance since no highroad traversed them.

Turning, Joseph looked to where Mary sat upon the rock, resting her back against the rough stone with her eyes closed. He saw her body suddenly grow tense and her face tighten in a grimace of pain as her hands pressed down upon the rock beside her. Her womb had begun to contract with the pains of oncoming labor about an hour ago and before the night was over, he was fairly sure, the child she carried would be born.

As he looked toward Bethlehem and remembered the promise of the ancient writings that a king of Israel would be born there, Joseph thought again of the story Mary had told when she returned from her visit to Elisabeth and Zacharias. He had wanted to believe her then, but it was all so strange he could not force himself to do so. Loving Mary as he did, he had felt no desire to make an example of her, though what had happened obviously made continuing their betrothal impossible.

He had decided therefore to break the betrothal privately. Though the letter of divorce that was required to sever the betrothal had to be public, it could legally be given to Mary in the presence of but two persons, thus avoiding having to bring her before a court of justice with all the scandal inevitably involved. And yet Joseph had hesitated, for, however unbelievable the story she had told of being pregnant by the Holy Spirit with a child destined to be Messiah and king in Israel, his love and respect for Mary would not let him cause her pain.

Three things had been regarded since ancient times as signs of favor from the Most High, "A good king, a fruitful year, and a good dream." So when the third of these came to Joseph one night, he took it as the voice of the Lord speaking to him, although with the tongue of an angel.

"Joseph, son of David," the voice in the dream had said, "do not be afraid to take Mary as your wife, for that which is conceived in her is of the Holy Spirit. She shall bring forth a Son and you shall call His name Jesus, for He shall save His people from their sins." And Joseph, on waking from his dream, had found himself convinced that if the Most High God had chosen his espoused wife as the vessel by which a Savior was to come to Israel, his own duty was manifestly clear. He must cherish and protect her and her child, counting it an indication of the Lord's trust and favor that so great a charge had been given him.

Joseph and Mary both loved the hill country of Galilee, but they were both from the line of King David and so had to return to their ancestral family city in order to be registered for the census decreed by Caesar Augustus. Bethlehem, where Joseph was born, was the City of David, the greatest king in Israel's history. A hallowed place, it was eminently suited to serve as a cradle for Him who, Mary had been assured, would one day reign over God's own people. God had long ago revealed through the prophet Micah that His Son would be born in Bethlehem, saying, "But you, Bethlehem Ephratah, out of you shall He come forth the One who is to be the ruler of Israel; whose goings forth have been from of old, from everlasting." So it was that in Mary's final days of pregnancy, they took the required journey to Bethlehem. Joseph took Mary and his few possessions with them, thinking to remain for a while at least to see how he might fare there in his trade.

Engrossed in his thoughts, Joseph did not notice, until the sudden coolness of the approaching winter night penetrated his robe and made him shiver, that a cloud had obscured the face of the sun. As he went to get the mule and bring it to the rock where Mary sat, he glimpsed far to the eastward, through a valley that divided the hills, the metallic-looking surface of the Sea of Judgment, in whose waters which had swallowed up sinful Sodom and Gomorrah there was no life. And a little to the south, on the highest peak in the gradual descent of the hill country to the flat wastelands of the desert, where no man could live without carrying water, stood the great castle which Herod had built and furnished for himself.

At once fortress, luxurious palace, and reminder that an alien instead of any son of David ruled there, the grim ramparts of the Herodeion, as the castle was called, were symbols of an authority based on murder, suspicion, and greed, exemplified in the wily Idumaean who was now king of the Jews. And yet of the child Mary was to bear, perhaps before the sun rose over the hills to the east again, the angel had said, "He shall be great and shall be called the Son of the Highest, and the Lord God shall give to Him the throne of His father David. He will reign over the house of Jacob forever, and of His kingdom there shall be no end."

And she brought forth her firstborn Son, and wrapped
Him in swaddling cloths, and laid Him in a manger,
because there was no room for them in the inn.

Luke 2:7

The yard of the inn at Bethlehem, where Elam and Jonas arrived with their pack animals just as darkness was falling, had already filled with travelers and their animals. Most of them were humble folk who had made the journey to Bethlehem only because the Emperor Augustus in Rome had decreed that every man must be listed by the census takers in the place of his birth—recorded for purposes of taxation by both his *nomen* and his *cognomen*—and now the period allotted for the census was nearly past.

Naturally no one stood in the way of Elam as he strode importantly into the building and shouted for the proprietor. Jonas followed his master unobtrusively to learn what place in the stable would be assigned to him as quarters for the night.

"I told you I have but one couch," the innkeeper was saying when they entered. "The price is two shekels, nothing less."

Looking at the traveler who was dickering with the innkeeper, Jonas knew at once that the man was not accustomed to taking lodgings, let alone paying any such price as two shekels for them. His robe of rough homespun was almost as torn as was Jonas's, and the strips of cloth wrapped about his ankles against the cold were stained with mud and torn by the horny bushes that lined the rough paths. Usually travelers such as he did not frequent inns but slept by the roadside under the shelter of the trees wherever night caught them or in the public caravansaries outside the towns.

"I am only a carpenter of Nazareth," Joseph said with quiet dignity. "But my wife is great with child and her time is near."

For the first time Jonas noticed the young woman sitting in the corner upon a bale. The quietly radiant beauty in her face made it shine, he thought, like that of an angel. Then she gasped from a sudden spasm of pain and her hands grasped her swollen body.

The look of pain on his wife's face seemed to resolve the carpenter's hesitation about the price asked by the innkeeper. "I will pay what you ask," he said quickly, reaching for the flabby and worn purse at his belt.

Just then Elam spoke loudly. "Did I hear you say you have a couch left for the night, landlord?" he demanded.

The innkeeper's quick appraising glance noted the Pharisee's rich robe and his air of wealth and authority. "I have only one, noble sir," he said, "and this man—"

"I will pay you four shekels for the use of the couch," Elam interrupted importantly, taking a bulging purse from his girdle.

The landlord's face brightened. "Certainly, sir," he said respectfully.

"But you contracted with me for the couch," Joseph objected. "I was opening my purse to pay." He did not speak loudly; the *am ha-arets* did not thrust themselves forward in the presence of a man of such obvious importance as Elam. But his tone was firm nevertheless, showing that he was accustomed to standing up for his rights and was well acquainted with them.

"No money changed hands," Elam pointed out.

"My purse is open."

"You have not paid the landlord," Elam said sharply. "Do you claim that you did?"

"No, I had not paid him," Joseph admitted.

"Then there is no contract under the Law, for no money has changed hands," Elam said triumphantly. "The couch is mine for the price of four shekels."

The innkeeper was not without pity. He, too, had seen the young mother's grimace of pain. Besides, it was considered good luck when a birth took place at an inn. "You were here first," he told the carpenter. "If you can equal the price of four shekels, the couch is still yours."

"Two would have emptied my purse," Joseph admitted. "The Pharisee is right about the Law; rent him the couch."

Elam was counting out the four shekels importantly, making certain everyone had a chance to see how fat his purse was. "This pays for a place in the stable for my servant, of course," he added.

"The very best space, beside the manger," the innkeeper assured him. "All the others are already filled."

"See that the animals are well cared for, Jonas," Elam directed. "We must leave very early in the morning."

The carpenter had gone to where his wife sat on the bale and was now helping her to her feet. "We will find a place somewhere, Mary," Jonas heard him tell her as he followed them outside into the inn yard.

The woman tried to smile, but just then another spasm of pain made her cry out. Moved by pity, Jonas said to Joseph, "My master purchased space for me in the straw of the stable. Your wife may have it if you wish."

"But you will have no place to sleep."

"I am used to faring for myself," Jonas assured him. "Besides, one of the other men will probably share his place with me."

Joseph was still doubtful and Jonas could understand his concern. A stable was a poor place for a child to be born, but at least it was a shelter and a measure of protection from the biting wind. Nor were they likely to find anything better tonight, with so many people on the road.

"The pain is great, Joseph," the young mother said. "I am not afraid to bear my child in a stable."

"We accept your offer then," the carpenter said gratefully. "But you must let me pay you."

"The poor stand together, friend Joseph," Jonas said with a smile. "I have slept in many stables and the space beside the manger is always the best. Secure it quickly now for your wife and let no one argue with you about it."

II

The child was born about midnight. Through it all, the mother bore her suffering with quiet courage, not once crying out even in the final agony of birth. The baby was well formed and strong, and when Jonas saw the look in the mother's eyes as she held it close to her body, he felt well repaid for giving up his own space beside the manger to her, even if he got no sleep for the rest of the night.

There was no heat inside the stable, and with the wind seeping beneath the eaves the temperature had fallen rapidly with the coming of night. Now it was only a little warmer inside than out, and those who had rented space to sleep burrowed into the straw for warmth and cover. Joseph and Mary had not expected the baby to be born so quickly upon their arrival at Bethlehem, they told Jonas, and had not had time to purchase swaddling clothes in which to wrap Him. Few of the other travelers carried more than the clothing they wore on their backs, and even if they had, the rough fabric would have been far too coarse for the tender skin of the newborn babe.

Mary was trying to warm the child with her own body but, worn out from the ordeal of birth, had little warmth to give it. When Jonas came to look at the babe and receive her thanks for giving up his place, he saw that her teeth were chattering and her lips blue from the cold.

"We need a blanket to wrap the child in," Joseph said. "Is there anything in your master's bales I could buy, Jonas?"

Elam carried only rich cloth for making fine robes. Jonas knew the carpenter would not be able to afford even the smallest piece and, with the markets of Jerusalem so nearby, there was no point in asking the Pharisee to reduce the price. But there still was a cloth in which the baby could be wrapped, a fabric far softer and warmer than anything the carpenter could buy. Jonas was carrying it, there within his own robe.

His brief conflict with himself ended when the baby began to cry. As he drew the cloth from his robe and removed the coverings from it, he did not dare feel the smoothness and softness of the fabric with his fingers or look closely at its snowy whiteness lest he weaken and decide to keep it for the temple tomorrow.

"Wrap the baby in this while I make a place for it in the manger." Jonas handed the cloth to Joseph. "The wool will keep him warm and we can use the straw to cover your wife."

Joseph rubbed the cloth between his fingers. "This is a fine piece—"

"It was not stolen," Jonas assured him. "I wove it with my own hands from scraps of wool that had been thrown away."

"You could sell it in Jerusalem for a good price, much more than I can pay."

"The cloth was to be a gift for the temple, but your child needs it more than the priests. Wrap him in it quickly before the warmth from my body is lost."

"Yours is the first gift to the baby," Mary said gratefully as she wound the soft cloth around the child's body. "Surely it is the worthiest of all He will ever receive."

With the excitement over, the other people in the stable began to settle down for the night. Finding no place to sleep among them as he had assured Joseph he would and thinking to lie down outside with the animals and gain a little warmth from their bodies, Jonas went out into the courtyard.

At first he thought it must be the light of the full moon that was bathing the inn and the town around it with such a warm glow. Almost blinded by the brilliance, he looked for its source and saw that the light seemed to come from a star hanging low in the sky above the inn, a far more brilliant star than he ever remembered seeing before.

Instinctively feeling himself in the presence of some power not of earth or man, Jonas dropped to his knees and his lips moved in a prayer he had learned as a child. He did not pray from fear, for the light seemed somehow friendly and warm—like the smile of the young mother in the stable as she had looked down upon her child.

"You there, little man!" A rough voice close to Jonas's ear startled him. "Why are you saying your prayers here in the middle of the night?"

Jonas stumbled hurriedly to his feet. Two men stood near him, travelers who obviously had been sitting late in the wine shops of the town and were now loud of voice and unsteady upon their feet.

"The—the star," Jonas stammered. "I was blinded by the star."

"The sky is full of stars!" the man said roughly. "I see no star that would blind a man."

Jonas looked up quickly, thinking the star might have grown dim while he was praying. But it was still there, its warm brilliance undiminished.

"There it is," he said pointing. "Hanging in the sky over the inn."

"Leave him alone, Asa," the second man urged. "The poor fellow must be possessed by an evil spirit; he sees things that do not exist."

"The star is there!" Jonas cried. "I can see it!"

The men hurried toward the inn. Everyone knew, when a man was possessed by a demon, the evil spirit could escape into the body of anyone who came near.

Jonas felt a chill colder than the winter night settle upon him. Madmen, he knew, often saw things others could not see. There were such in every village, shunned by the people lest they send the devils who possessed them to trouble others. If the men who had just left told of seeing a little man kneeling in the courtyard and babbling about a star no one else could see, everyone would think him a madman. Elam might not take him back home to Hebron and he would be condemned to wander through the countryside, seeking shelter, wherever he could find it and with nothing to eat except what he could steal or whatever scraps kindhearted people might throw him.

Jonas decided he would say no more about the star to anyone. And since the men would hardly mention his peculiar behavior before he had departed early in the morning with his master, no one else need know. Feeling somewhat better, now that his secret did not seem likely to be revealed, he lay down on the ground beside the animals.

Strangely enough, he felt the cold no longer, for the soft radiance of the star seemed to bathe his body in a warmth like the rays of the sun.

Once he was almost certain he heard faint music like the sound of harps and voices coming from some place in the sky. But he kept that to himself, too, and enveloped by the soft, warm, protecting mantle of the star's light, he soon slept.

III

E lam was up early for he was anxious to reach the bazaars of Jerusalem with his bales of cloth soon after the shops opened for business. Later in the day, when more merchandise had come in, prices would be lower, but since it was only a few miles to the Holy City, he planned to be among the firstcomers and thus be sure of a good price.

Word had gone through the inn that a child had been born in the stable during the night. With a good night's rest behind him and the prospect of a handsome profit on the sale of his goods, the Pharisee was in a good humor when he stopped by the stable to give his blessing to mother and child. But as he looked at the sleeping baby, he gave a muffled exclamation of surprise. Reaching down, he took a corner of the swaddling cloth between his fingers and for an instant a look of astonishment showed in his eyes, to be quickly replaced by a crafty gleam.

"This fabric is too fine to be wasted as a swaddling cloth," he said casually to Joseph. "I will give you a good price for it."

"I cannot sell the cloth." Joseph glanced quickly at Jonas, who had come in to tell the family good-bye before leaving.

"Why not sell it?" Elam demanded of Joseph. "You could not bid against me for the couch last night. You must be poor."

"We have no other swaddling cloth for the baby," Joseph protested.

Elam shrugged away that objection. "The shops of the town will soon be open. With what I will pay you for the cloth, you can buy another and still have money to spare. Hurry and name a price, man. I must get to Jerusalem early."

Joseph shook his head. "The cloth was a gift, the first gift to the baby. It is not for sale."

"A gift?" Elam's eyes narrowed and he looked quickly around the stable. Obviously no one there could afford such a gift. "Who gave it?" he demanded.

"I—I cannot say, sir."

"You mean it was stolen, don't you?" Elam seized upon the advantage Joseph had given him. "Then it is my duty to impound the cloth and hold it for the rightful owner." Elam knew that if the carpenter did not divulge the name of the owner now, the cloth would probably never be claimed and in due time it would become his property at no cost.

"Joseph did not steal the cloth, master," Jonas said. "I gave it to the child."

"You!" Elam wheeled upon his servant. "Where would you get such a fabric as this, Jonas?"

"I wove it myself. Nights, after my work was finished."

"You stole the wool from me, then."

"It was made from scraps that had been thrown away. I carded and spun the wool into thread myself, and wove it upon a loom I made with my own hands."

"You were going to sell the cloth in Jerusalem and keep the money for yourself!" Elam accused him.

"No, master." Jonas realized fully that he was inviting harsh punishment at Elam's hands for contradicting him. "It was to be a gift to the temple for an altar cloth."

"If it was intended for the temple, why did you let such a valuable fabric be used for swaddling a baby?"

"The child—it was cold," Jonas stammered. "I thought it needed the cloth more than the priests."

Elam snorted indignantly. "You were a fool to soil such a fine piece of fabric. Especially as it belongs to me." He turned to Joseph. "Unwrap the child and give me the cloth. I am a generous man, so I will still pay you enough to buy another, though this one is mine by right."

Joseph shook his head. "Jonas has explained to you that he wove it after his day's work was finished, from wool that had been cast aside. The cloth was his to do with as he chose."

"The work of a servant belongs to the master," Elam insisted. "That is the Law."

"You Pharisees speak much of the Law when it is to your own benefit," Joseph said firmly. "Let us take this question before a judge and see who is right. These men here in the stable will witness that you covet a cloth which Jonas gave the child and seek to get it for yourself."

"I will gladly be a witness for Jonas," a burly fellow bystander offered, glowering at Elam. "It will be good to see a Pharisee feel the weight of the Law on his own neck for a change."

When several others pushed forward to offer themselves as witnesses, Elam hesitated. If he took this dispute before a judge, the ruling would probably be in his favor, since it would be the word of a wealthy man against his servant. On the other hand, much of the "Oral Law" governing the conduct of the Jews was not set down in writing, and each judge could interpret it according to his own conviction. If the ruling should go against him, Elam would not only lose face—an important thing to a man of his sort—but he would have failed to reach the shops of Jerusalem early and might be forced to hold his bales until tomorrow's market.

Characteristically, the Pharisee turned his anger and frustration upon one who could not resist. "Strip to the waist," he ordered Jonas and, going to the wall, took down a leather strap hanging there. Elam had no fear that anyone would try to keep him from flogging Jonas, for the right of the master to punish a servant was undisputed.

Jonas's face was pale as he dropped the upper part of his robe, baring his back and shoulders. He flinched as the strap fell upon his unprotected skin, but he did not cry out. The Pharisee was skilled in punishing servants, laying on the leather with enough force to cause pain and raise an angry red welt which would be exquisitely tender for days, yet not enough to break the skin. Skin wounds could mean inflammation and even death, and a servant was too valuable a property to be destroyed simply to satisfy the owner's anger.

Soon Jonas's back was a crisscross pattern of red welts. The pain was excruciating but the little man bit into his lip and did not beg for mercy. Finally, though, a blow brought a slight stain of red, and then Elam, almost exhausted, tossed the leather strap aside.

"Get the animals ready while I refresh myself with wine," he ordered curtly. "We will leave for Jerusalem at once."

Jonas pulled up his robe and started for the courtyard where the animals were tied, but Joseph was there before him. "I should have felt the strap instead of you," he said humbly as he loosened the tether of Elam's pack animal for Jonas and tested the thongs lashing the bales upon its back.

Jonas managed to grin, although his back was a throbbing mass of agony. "The pain will go away. I have been flogged before."

"And will be again, if I judge that master of yours right," Joseph said grimly. "He was humbled in pride and purse, both tender spots for a man such as he."

The pain lines were gone from Mary's face when Jonas came to bid the little family farewell. Her serene beauty reminded him of the star that had shone over Bethlehem last night, and the sleeping child, too, seemed to have a radiance of its own.

"Jonas!" Elam's sharp voice sounded in the doorway. "Stop wasting time, unless you want another beating!"

The little man hurried to pick up the tether of the pack animal. To keep the rough cloth of his garment from scraping against his tender skin, he tried to walk stiffly erect. But even that little relief was denied him, for Elam at once kicked the ass he rode into a near trot, so anxious was he to get to Jerusalem by the time the shops opened, and Jonas was forced to hurry on behind him.

Busy with his own misery while he tried to urge the reluctant pack animal along, Jonas was paying little attention to the road ahead when he heard his master's voice ring out sharply.

"You there!" Elam called. "Don't block the road."

Three men, shepherds by their dress and the fact that one of them carried a crook made from the gnarled limb of a small tree, stood aside for Elam's little procession to pass. Jonas remembered seeing other such men when traveling near Jerusalem. The flocks in this area near the Holy City and its great temple were for the most part dedicated for sacrifice upon the altar, and the shepherds who guarded them were set apart and treated with respect by all who met them.

Elam now recognized the men and pulled the ass to a stop. Jonas, plodding behind with the lead rope of the second animal, also halted.

"Are you not the shepherds of the sacred flock?" the Pharisee asked in a more pleasant tone.

"One of us is keeping the flocks today so the rest of us can come to Bethlehem," one of the men said.

Elam frowned. Some landlord and owner was being cheated if shepherds were allowed to roam the countryside or go into the town for a cup of wine while their flocks were left poorly guarded in the field. Elam knew that many rich men in Jerusalem owned land and flocks in this area. No doubt some one of them would reward him well for discovering the shortcomings of his shepherds.

"Would your masters be pleased if they knew of this?" Elam demanded.

The taller shepherd who seemed to be the spokesman answered. "Last night something happened," he explained. "A thing so strange that we felt it should be reported in Bethlehem."

"What was that?"

"We were abiding in the field as is our custom when a bright light shone around us and we were sore afraid. But we heard a voice say, 'Fear not, for behold, I bring you good tidings of great joy, which shall be to all people. For to you is born this day in the city of David a Savior, who is Christ the Lord.'"

As an educated man, Elam knew what was written concerning the coming of the Expected One, the Messiah who would rule over Israel and free her from domination by others. He doubted strongly that so momentous an event would be announced to ignorant shepherds; it would be the high priest in Jerusalem who would be the first to know of it—if it really had occurred. If it had, though, and the temple authorities had not heard . . . Elam was shrewd enough to realize they would pay well for information about it . . .

If he were to be the bearer of such good tidings, he had best press on and say no more about it here. "No doubt you were dreaming," he said in a disparaging manner calculated to make the men doubt the value of what they had seen, if indeed it had any value. "Your dream has led you on a fool's errand. The Savior of Israel would hardly be born without notice." And kicking his mount, Elam directed it once again along the road.

Jonas did not follow at once, but beckoned the shepherds to come nearer. "Did this voice say how you would know the Christ?" he asked in lowered tones.

The tall shepherd nodded. "The angel said, 'And this shall be a sign to you: You shall find the babe wrapped in swaddling clothes, lying in a manger.'"

A great light burst in Jonas's brain, almost as bright as had been the star last night. But first, he knew, he must make sure the shepherds did not intend to harm the babe.

"Why do you seek the child?" he asked them.

"We would worship Him, for when the angels finished speaking there was a multitude of the heavenly hosts praising God and saying, 'Glory to God in the highest, and on earth peace, goodwill toward men!'"

"Are you sure the voice said the child would be found in a manger?"

The tall shepherd looked at him keenly. "Why do you ask? What do you know of this?" he demanded.

"A child was born in Bethlehem last night, in the stable of an inn where we stayed," Jonas explained. "I myself gave it the swaddling cloth. There was no cradle, so the baby was placed in the manger."

"That is just as the angel described it!" the tall shepherd said excitedly. "You say you gave it the first gift?"

Jonas nodded proudly. "A swaddling cloth of finest wool, woven with my own hands!"

"Then you are more honored than we can ever be," the shepherd told him. "But if we hurry, we will be able to worship Him too!"

"Hurry, Jonas!" Elam's querulous voice floated back along the road. "I must sell the goods early, so I can make my gift to the temple today!"

Jonas left the shepherds and followed his master, but he no longer noticed the pain from his flayed back. Nothing Elam could do would be able to hurt him now. For by some strange miracle which he did not even try to understand, he had been singled out for a great honor, for a privilege greater than had been given any man—that of making the first gift to the Son of God.

Now when the days of her purification according to the law of Moses were completed, they brought Him to Jerusalem to present Him to the Lord.

Luke 2:22

Before leaving Nazareth for Bethlehem to list himself and Mary with the Roman census takers, Joseph had decided he would remain in the City of David for a while to see if there were not a better market there than in Galilee for fine cabinet work. So leaving Mary and the baby in the stable of the inn, early that morning he went to seek a dwelling place for them.

Some notice had been attracted by the arrival of the shepherds, for when they found Mary and the child still in the stable, they spread the story that they had recounted to Elam and Jonas. A few who heard it marveled, but they could see that the child and the mother seemed no different from anyone else, except, perhaps, in the beauty of both. The husband, too, was obviously an ordinary man, for he spoke of setting up a carpenter's shop in Bethlehem to ply his trade as he had in Galilee. Many therefore thought the shepherds' tale nothing more than a dream.

Before nightfall Joseph was able to find a house which, though small, would serve to shelter his family. Since both he and Mary were of the line of David, they had kinsfolk in the city and so experienced little trouble in establishing themselves, Joseph taking up his usual trade of carpenter, cabinetmaker, and builder.

It was written in the Law of the Lord that every firstborn male child should be called holy to the Most High and accordingly must be redeemed from a priest for a token price. The earliest time this could be accomplished under the Law of Moses was thirty-one days after the birth of the child. A second provision called for the rite of purification of the mother after childbirth, but this could not be carried out until after the full course of forty-one days following the birth of a son, eighty-one days after the birth of a daughter.

When the required days of Mary's purification according to the Law had passed, Joseph took her and the child to Jerusalem to celebrate in the temple the twofold rite, redemption of the child and a sacrifice of purification for the mother. Both ceremonies could have been performed before the chazan or leader of the congregation, at the Bethlehem synagogue, but since they were only a short distance away and were both of the royal line, and devout besides, they naturally went to the fountainhead of their faith, the great temple recently built by Herod the king.

Approaching Jerusalem by the Hebron road which just outside the city joined that from the seaport of Joppa, they passed almost under the walls of the citadel of Herod looming as a grim and forbidding reminder that Rome ruled here. Its three towers, called Hippicus, Phasael, and Mariamne, the last after Herod's beautiful wife whom he had murdered in a fit of jealousy, enabled observers to watch practically all activities going on in the city.

Entering by the Gennath Gate, they found themselves in the Upper City. Here was the timber market where beams were sold for supporting the flat rooftops of houses, a market for wool and cloth, such as Elam and Jonas had brought to Jerusalem, and foundries for smelting and shaping implements and utensils of copper.

From the stronghold of Herod in the northeast corner of the wall, the northern limit of the Upper City, where many of the richer people of Jerusalem lived, was marked by a wall running eastward to the western boundary of the large sanctuary area. North of this a suburb had grown up, spilling outside the city wall and spreading across the hilltops and past the skull-like outcropping of rock called Golgotha to the four-square tower of Antonia built by Herod at the very corner of the sanctuary.

Whatever evil Herod had done—and his faults were many—he had at least in its temple, under construction now for many years and still not complete, given Israel one of the most beautiful structures in the entire world. Space for it in the midst of the broad area of the sanctuary, encompassing some twenty-six acres, had been gained by excavating and flattening the hilltop and erecting a broad undergirding of solid masonry walls.

The outer part of the temple area formed the Court of the Gentiles. Beyond this, graven tablets in Greek, the most widely understood and spoken language in the Roman Empire, gave a grim warning:

Let no Gentile enter the limit and enclosure of the sanctuary. He who is caught will carry the guilt on himself, because death will follow.

The two sides of the Court of the Gentiles marked the boundaries of the Royal Porch. Its four rows of marble columns had been polished until they shone like gold. Roofed over with timbers hewn from cedar, they turned the area into a shady cloister where the teachers, called rabbis, held forth daily to any who would listen.

Next to the Court of the Gentiles was a section set off by a balustrade of stone, and beyond this a high wall by which the holy area itself could be turned into a fortress, as had been done on more than one occasion. Nine gates broke the solid line of the wall. One led to the Court of Women, beyond which was the Court of Israel, and still farther the Court of Priests. In the center of this latter court was the altar of burnt offering.

Strictly speaking, the various courts were outside the temple itself, which stood behind the altar. In the temple proper was first a vestibule, next the Holy Place, and finally the Holy of Holies, which only the high priest could enter, and then only on special occasions. The structure was built of white marble and its roof, towering to a height of nearly a hundred and fifty feet, was covered over with gold. True indeed was the saying, "He that has not seen the temple of Herod has never known what beauty is."

To a person visiting the temple for the first time, the outer court resembled a marketplace with its constant din of voices filling the air as animals were sold for the sacrifices, which were practically continuous from morning to night. Once the day's sacrifices had begun, the altar quickly took on much the appearance of a slaughterhouse and the priests that of butchers. Nor was this surprising, considering the fact that during one Passover period more than ten thousand lambs might be killed there.

The regular daily sacrifices in the temple included the burnt offering, for Israel celebrated both morning and evening, and the daily offering of meat and drink, as well as private devotions of thanksgiving, expiation by individuals for trespass and sin, and removal of the many ceremonial impurities which a person could easily incur by breaking one of the thousandfold prohibitions of the Law.

Support for the priests who carried out the temple worship came not only from their portion of the money offerings, which had to be in the Tyrian shekel, but also from taxes upon the crops, the tithe, the *hallah* levied upon dough for making bread, and many others. The temple itself required a tribute of half a shekel from every male Jew above twenty. When coupled with the levies put upon the people by Rome, these taxes for the support of the temple and the priestly hierarchy constituted a burden under which the population constantly groaned. Small wonder then that the tax collectors, Jews called publicans who worked for the Roman masters, were the most hated people in Israel.

Since the redemption of the firstborn child could be carried out before any priest, Joseph and Mary sought out one who stood at the entrance to the Court of Priests in a booth devoted to this purpose. First came the formal presentation of the babe, kicking naked upon the swaddling cloth of fine wool so that the priest could see if it were free of all blemishes. Next two short benedictions were pronounced, one for the Law of Redemption and the other for the gift of a firstborn son, in itself a sign of favor from the Most High. The redemption money, of the "Tyrian weight" required for all financial transactions in the temple area, was then paid.

As Mary wrapped the infant Jesus once again in the swaddling cloth, her happiness was very great, for He had now been offered ceremonially to the Lord, as Abraham had offered Isaac even to the point of preparing to slay him with his own hands, and had been ritually redeemed. Leaving the baby with Joseph, she now went to the Court of Women. There she deposited in the third of the thirteen chests, or "trumpets," set along one wall, the price of a pair of turtledoves as stated by a priest standing nearby. When the blast of a silver trumpet announced the kindling on the golden altar of the incense offering for which she had helped to pay, Mary presented herself with a number of other women who were then directed to stand on either side of the Nicanor Gate, at the top of the fifteen steps leading from the Court of Women to the Court of Israel where the men gathered. Here, without actually being in the Court of Israel where her presence was forbidden, Mary could witness the sacrifice. This was quickly performed, the prayers of purification intoned, and the ceremony completed.

On returning to the outer court, Mary saw an old man coming to where Joseph stood waiting for her with Jesus in his arms, a blanket around the swaddling cloth. She hurried to them for she did not know what such attention from a stranger might mean, and arrived, a little breathless, just as the old man spoke.

"Shalom," he said courteously to both. "My name is Simeon."

They returned the greeting politely for they could see that he was quite at home in the temple and judged him to be a priest.

"I shall not see death before I have seen the Lord Christ," Simeon explained, and held out his arms to take the child.

Mary had supposed that only she, Joseph, Elisabeth, and Zacharias knew the circumstances surrounding Jesus' conception and birth. But now, it seemed, Simeon too had somehow learned that the child sleeping peacefully within the blanket was more than just another baby. Eager to learn everything she could about her child, Mary nodded to Joseph to let Simeon take Jesus in his arms.

Raptly the old man looked down at the face of the sleeping infant, then lifting his eyes upward, he spoke in prayer: "Lord, now You are letting Your servant depart in peace, according to Your word; for my eyes have seen Your salvation, which You have prepared before the face of all peoples, a light to bring revelation to the Gentiles, and the glory of Your people Israel."

Joseph looked at the old man in astonishment, as it was strictly forbidden a pious Jew to reveal anything of his faith to a Gentile or have any near contact with the heathen. Yet be was familiar enough with the sacred writings of the prophets which were read each Sabbath in the synagogue to know that Simeon was referring to the words of Isaiah concerning the Expected One.

"Behold, this Child is destined for the fall and rising of many in Israel, and for a sign which will be spoken against," Simeon went on, handing the baby to Mary. Then his face grew grave as he concluded, "Yes, a sword will pierce through your own soul also, that the thoughts of many hearts may be revealed."

Suddenly afraid, Mary pressed Jesus so tightly against her breast that He woke and began to cry.

"Come, Joseph," she said quickly. "Our business here is finished. Let us go back to Bethlehem."

As they were leaving the outer court, an old woman stopped them. They recognized her from previous visits to Jerusalem as a prophetess named Anna who spent most of her waking hours in the temple serving God. And since there could be no possible harm in this pious woman of great age, they stopped courteously to answer her greeting.

"Blessed are you," Anna said to Mary as she looked at the child. For your Son shall bring redemption to all who shall look upon Him."

Mary and Joseph left as quickly as they could without being rude to the old priestess. They had been forewarned by the angel that the child Mary was to bear would be different from others, but so long as only a few people had known of it, they had not been afraid. Now it had begun to seem that many shared the knowledge, and if this were so, word of it might easily come to Herod, who had already ruthlessly exterminated everyone with any claim to the throne of Israel, however remote, even to the point of executing his own sons.

Now after Jesus was born in Bethlehem of Judea in the days of Herod the king, behold, wise men from the East came to Jerusalem.

Matthew 2:1

The king of Israel was afraid.

A determined man, utterly without scruple where he considered his own welfare to be involved, Herod had never been sure of his throne though he had reigned longer in Israel as king under Rome than had any other for a long while. One reason for his fear was the fact that he was not even a Jew by heritage or a member of any royal house in Israel or Syria.

Oppressed by both Herod, an alien king, and Augustus, an alien emperor, the Jews looked back longingly over almost exactly a thousand years to the glorious days of David and Solomon. David, the shepherd boy who became king, had united the loose confederation of families and tribes, descendants of those who had come storming across the Jordan behind Joshua to unlock the rich treasure chests of Canaan when God had sent the walls of fortress Jericho tumbling to the plain. For a brief period Israel had known a golden age, but the division of the kingdom following Solomon's death had made the nation the victim of a series of conquerors.

Israel as a nation and Judaism as a religion might actually have been destroyed during these trying years but for the Persian insult in deporting a large portion of the Jewish people to Babylon. There in servitude, as during the stay in Egypt a thousand years before, their unity of spirit and purpose through worship of the single God who had selected them as his own, was crystallized into the driving force that was to animate the Jews ever after, no matter how far they might be scattered abroad.

The prophet Ezekiel had fanned the flame in Babylon. When the Jews had finally been allowed to return to the homeland through the generosity of Cyrus of Persia, their poverty in numbers had been more than compensated for by their fervor of spirit and their confidence that God would once again raise up His kingdom for them with a glory exceeding even that of the days of David and Solomon. Peopled by only a few thousand of the fiercely devout who had returned from captivity in

Babylon and governed by a high priest and a *gerousia*, or senate, Judea was at first only a city-state under the domination of nearby Syria.

The conquering tide of Alexander the Great had swirled about the walls of Jerusalem when he laid siege to Tyre on the seacoast to the north, but he had graciously spared the city, even, it was said, making a sacrifice in the temple. Greek tolerance proved in many ways a greater enemy of Judaism than Alexander's armies, however, for it introduced the pagan philosophy of life called Hellenism. Greek cities sprang up all over the neighboring area, Greek influences penetrated Jerusalem and soon infiltrated into the very worship of the temple. Nor did Alexander's untimely death change this situation, for the rulers who succeeded him were Greek as well.

Hellenistic influences, and the inevitable reaction against them by the inspired core of Judaism in Jerusalem, soon altered the character of the worship in the temple. Opposed to this change, a group of pious men known as the Sopherim sought to keep intact the inheritance of Judaism from Abraham, Isaac, and Jacob. Organized as the Great Synagogue, they concentrated on the Torah, a history of God's dealings with His own people, and the Law handed down from Moses. From them came the most influential and most determinedly religious group in all of Israel, the Pharisees.

For a brief period under Syrian rule, however, Hellenism triumphed in Israel, and the high priest became hardly more than a Greek puppet, even participating in the worship of Greek gods. Antiochus IV entered the city and desecrated the temple in a vain attempt to destroy Judaism's remaining opposition to the Greek philosophies. The result was a period of national scourging for Israel from which a hard core of resistance emerged, strengthened in its determination to lead the people back to the old faith. Calling themselves the Chassidim, these "pious ones" chose death rather than allow the few copies of the Torah they possessed to be destroyed.

In the midst of this period of national chastening, a new hope arose, manifested in a mixture of poetry, song, and prophecy known as the apocalyptic writings. God, the pious Chassidim believed, would soon send them a deliverer, the "Anointed One," "Messiah," or "Son of Man" to set up the kingdom of the Most High on earth. Thus, in degradation and despair as once before in servitude in far-off Babylon, the Jews were buoyed up and given courage to resist paganism by the promise of delivery from oppression. As it happened, they were delivered, for the time being, by a group of their own leaders, sons of a priest called Mattathias.

When Appeles, an agent of Antiochus, ordered a heathen sacrifice at the town of Modin in the hills of Judea, an old priest named Mattathias killed the Jewish priest who was carrying out the insult to their God. The five sons of Mattathias—John, Simon, Judas, Eleazar, and Jonathan—killed Appeles and led with their father to the mountains, where they quickly gathered a small band of the Chassidim who had been driven out of Jerusalem by the forces of Antiochus, as well as by others who hated Syrian rule.

Under the leadership of the Maccabees, a name given the sons of Mattathias from the nickname "hammerer" of Judas, the great military leader of the group, what was actually a holy war began. Pitted in the struggle were the Hellenized chief priests in Jerusalem and the Syrian forces of Antiochus on one side, against the Maccabees, who came to be known also as the Hasmoneans, with their followers on the other.

A series of almost incredible victories followed for Judas Maccabaeus. One year later, he and his forces entered Jerusalem victorious, and three years from the day the first desecration of the holy altar had occurred, a sacrifice to the Most High God was offered upon it.

The military success of Judas Maccabaeus led him and his brothers, who successively ruled as priest-kings of Israel, to embark upon a program of conquest and expansion which almost restored the glories of David and Solomon to the land. Practically all the territory from the hills north of Galilee to the border of Egypt on the south and from the deserts of Arabia on the east to the seacoast on the west came under control of Israel, although its grip upon this broad area was never complete and constant fighting was required to maintain it.

During the rule of John Hyrcanus, many of the Chassidim began to have reservations about high priests who spent more time wielding the sword than worshiping God. Particularly hated was the Idumaean, Antipater, who had become the chief adviser of the Hasmonean house.

About this time a new group among the Pharisees, the scribes, arose. Highly versed in the Torah and in interpreting the Law, they began to assume an important place as teachers or rabbis and the true religious leaders of Israel. Meanwhile the wily Antipater was steadily conniving in the background, playing off various members of the royal Hasmonean house against each other.

When Rome, during the period of expansion spearheaded by Julius Caesar, conquered the old Seleucid kingdom, Syria was made a province, and Pompey moved south to seize Palestine, ending the brief period of the Jews' independence. The Greek cities of the Decapolis across the Jordan and beyond the Sea of Galilee were cut off from Judea. Samaria and Galilee were put under the rule of Syria and the thriving Greek cities along the Mediterranean coast were made independent. Hyrcanus II, a Hasmonean, served as the tetrarch of Jerusalem but Antipater was now the real power behind the considerably diminished throne of Judea.

Herod, the son of Antipater, served the Romans as well as had his father. Appointed first as governor of Galilee, he shortly came into virtual control of Judea and eventually was designated by the Emperor Augustus as "King of the Jews,"

Doubly hated, both by the Hasmoneans and their supporters because he had attained the throne for himself, and by the Jewish nationalists because of his service to Rome, Herod set about to endear himself to his subjects by building the great new temple which quickly began drawing Jews from all over the world to reconsecrate themselves to the worship of their God. It also brought money to Jerusalem, both in tribute and in business, and the whole area entered upon a season of unparalleled prosperity.

Prosperity for the Jews, as for many another people in history, had the effect of lessening nationalistic fervor. Weakening the opposition to Rome and Herod, it at the same time encouraged religious conservatism. A few zealots, often called *sicarii* because they carried daggers and occasionally used them, sporadically demonstrated against the foreign rulers with short-lived uprisings, but were put down ruthlessly.

Evidence of Herod's greatness as a temporal king, if not of his subservience to the Jewish God whom he at least pretended to worship, was everywhere: in the glorious beauty of the temple, the great arenas and amphitheaters that dotted the land, beautiful cities like Sepphoris, Sebaste, and of course the new city of Caesarea, erected upon the site of what had been called Strato's Tower, with a fine harbor formed by extending a great stone mole into the sea. But though honored by Rome and valued as one of the most dependable of the secondary rulers by Augustus Caesar, Herod found no peace in his latter days. His body wracked by illness, he was forced even on his sickbed to keep a constant watch for those who plotted against him, including his own sons.

Small wonder was it then that Herod felt the cold hand of fear gripping his heart when word was brought to him one day that three wise men from Arabia sought audience inquiring, "Where is He who has been born King of the Jews?"

II

Herod's pale, almost colorless eyes were unmoved as he heard his chamberlain repeat the question of the wise men. He had killed thousands in order to erase all who might have a claim to the throne he occupied, at one time destroying forty-five members of the highest court, the Sanhedrin, including many prominent members of the Hasmonean dynasty which had furnished kings to Israel. With this record of treachery and murder behind him, he would have no hesitation in putting to death, if he could locate Him, any newborn king.

For many hundreds of years the Jews had longed for the coming of the one they called the Messiah, or the Lord's Anointed, but no two of them seemed to have the same opinion concerning this Expected One. That He would be among the descendants of David was generally accepted, since the bloodline of the first really great king of Israel was the noblest and most honored among the Jews.

"Before the first oppressor was born," the ancient writings said of the Messiah, "the final Deliverer was already born." This could only mean that the leader would be a true "Son of the Living God," another Moses sent to free Israel from the present oppression as truly as it had been delivered from slavery under Pharaoh and led out of Egypt. News of the birth of a new king indicated to Herod that this might possibly be the expected Messiah; hence his fear.

"Shall I send the wise men on their way, noble Herod?" asked the chamberlain who had brought word of them.

The king shook his head. "Bring them in. I will question them myself."

Tall and dark-skinned, richly dressed and assured in manner, the men were far different from the rascally soothsayers of Arabia and the countries east of the Jordan who thronged to Jerusalem to prey upon travelers. They bowed courteously before Herod, showing the homage due him as king of Israel.

"What question would you ask me?" Herod inquired.

The tallest and eldest of the ambassadors answered for the group. "We would know where is He that is born King of the Jews."

"I am King of the Jews."

The soothsayer shrugged. "It is written, 'No man shall live forever.'"

"My sons shall rule in my stead," Herod insisted.

The question might well have been asked whether Herod would have any sons when the time came for the scepter of kingship to pass on to another. He had married many women and had many offspring by them, yet his constant fear that one of them would assassinate him and seize the throne led him to destroy many of his own offspring, while sending others into virtual banishment.

The tall Magus did not belabor the point. "We have seen His star in the East," he said quietly, "and have come to worship Him."

Herod shuddered and his body seemed to shrivel beneath the mantle of Tyrian purple about his shoulders. The seers of the East knew the stars like the streets of their own cities. If a new one had appeared and guided these men across the desert from the land of Yemen, whose kings also professed the Jewish faith, it could mean that the birth of the king they had announced was indeed no ordinary event but a sign auguring the coming of the Anointed One.

"What of this star?" Herod demanded.

"We are not of one opinion concerning its nature, noble king," another of the Magi admitted. "Some of us believe several bright stars are lying close together at this particular time. Others think it is a new star of unusual brightness."

"When did you first see it?"

"More than a year ago."

Herod frowned. If the men spoke truth, and he had no reason to believe they did not, valuable time had been lost and he must waste no more in finding out where this King of the Jews had been born.

"Rest here a while," he told the Magi. "I will see that you are given refreshment and we will speak again soon about where this babe may be found. It may be that someone among the priests and scholars will know from the ancient writings the location of His birth."

As soon as the visitors were out of the room Herod summoned the high priest and others among the priestly hierarchy who worked closely with him in Jerusalem. Belonging to the party known popularly as the Sadducees, the chief priests had perhaps known more prosperity and favor during the reign of Herod than in any previous period since the kingdom of Solomon, and were heavily obligated to him. To them Herod put the question, "Where shall the Christ be born?"

The least learned among the priests knew the answer, for the prophet Micah had written long ago: "But you, Bethlehem Ephrathah, though you are little among the thousands of Judah, yet out of you shall come forth to Me the One to be Ruler in Israel, whose goings forth are from of old, from everlasting."

Even Herod understood that this prophecy referred to no ordinary king. The phrase "whose goings forth are from of old, from everlasting," must mean that the ruler who would one day come out of Bethlehem had been eternal with God from the beginning. And that description fit only the Messiah.

Herod knew now that he must take immediate steps to destroy this newborn child who threatened everything for which he had worked. After sending the priests and scribes away, he called the wise men from Arabia to him again.

"Go and search carefully for the young Child," he told them. "When you have found Him, bring back word to me, that I may come and worship Him also."

The Magi left Jerusalem at once. Hardly were they outside the city when the star, which they had not been able to see for several nights and whose absence had led them to go to Jerusalem and ask Herod where the newborn king might be found, shone bright and clear before them. Nor did it falter in its brilliance all the way to Bethlehem and the home of Joseph the carpenter.

*When he arose, he took the young Child and His mother
by night and departed for Egypt.*

Matthew 2:14

Joseph and Mary had been disturbed by the coming of the shepherds to the inn on the night Jesus was born and the strange story they told of a voice from heaven announcing the birth of the Christ. In spite of the visits of the angel to Mary before her conception and to Joseph in the dream, they did not yet really understand the true identity of the child they had been instructed to call Jesus. But as the days passed uneventfully in Bethlehem and Joseph began to establish himself there as a carpenter and builder, the memory of those events had begun to grow faint. After Mary had accomplished the rite of purification in the temple and the child had been redeemed, their lives had once again taken up the even tenor to which they were accustomed. Bethlehem was a larger city than Nazareth and its proximity to Jerusalem, in addition to the fact that he had kinsfolk there, made it a more profitable place for Joseph to work, so he and Mary were soon busy in the quiet and pleasant life both preferred.

The coming of the dark-skinned Magi from Arabia had sharply interrupted the routine of their lives, and the stories the men told of being guided by a star to the birthplace of the King of the Jews had been disturbing. Even the precious gifts of gold, frankincense, and myrrh showered upon the baby by the visitors were out of place in the humble home of Joseph and Mary, and they were afraid that once the wise men were gone, an envious neighbor might report them to Herod's police on a charge of having stolen the treasures which were so obviously beyond their meager means.

Nor did their conversation with the Magi ease the minds of Joseph and Mary. The visitors from Arabia had not been deceived by Herod's pretext of wanting to locate the baby in order to worship Him. They strongly warned Joseph against the king and even left for their own country by a route which did not take them back to Jerusalem.

Thus, at a time when they were just becoming pleasantly situated in

Bethlehem, Joseph and Mary faced the urgent necessity of fleeing in order to save Jesus from Herod. The strange visit of the Magi and the lavish gifts the men from the East had brought, to say nothing of the story of how they had been guided on the long journey westward from Arabia, had caused considerable talk in Bethlehem. And with the town almost in the shadow of the grim castle called the Herodeion, word might spread to Herod almost any day.

Joseph's first impulse was to return to Nazareth, but Herod ruled there too, and if any more events like those which had taken place since the birth of Jesus occurred, the king's attention must certainly be drawn to them, even in Galilee. The Samaritan country north of Jerusalem was likewise in Herod's territory; besides, they could hope for no refuge among the Samaritans, who hated the Jews as intensely as the Jews hated them. Only one route of flight seemed at all safe, that southward by way of Hebron into Egypt, the route Abraham had taken more than two thousand years before when famine had driven him from Canaan. But that meant going into an alien land with all the hardships and uncertainty such a journey entailed.

Joseph tried to hide his troubled thoughts from Mary as he finished his chores and lay down to sleep. Busy caring for the child and still excited over the homage of the Magi and the precious gifts brought to Jesus, Mary did not fully realize the extent of the danger that faced them. Besides, women were accustomed to leaving such questions and decisions to the men of the family.

For a while Joseph could not sleep. His mind surveyed again and again the possibilities that lay before them, but could find nothing reassuring in any course they might follow. Finally he slept from sheer weariness and almost immediately began to dream. In his dream he heard once again the voice of the angel who had spoken to him at the time when he was considering putting Mary away with a letter of divorcement after learning that she was already with child. And as on that other occasion, the angelic voice resolved his uncertainty.

"Arise, take the young Child and His mother, flee to Egypt," the angel directed. "And stay there until I bring you word; for Herod will seek the young Child to destroy Him."

Awakening, Joseph did not hesitate to obey. Rousing Mary, he began making preparations for the journey. Flight into Egypt meant leaving everything they had gained in Bethlehem—a home, Joseph's business as a carpenter, the kinsmen and friends who had welcomed them. But when Joseph repeated the words of the angel to Mary, she did not hesitate. While she gathered their clothing together, Joseph went to arouse a kinsman and purchase a second mule to carry their possessions and the gifts of the Magi. He could not risk waiting for the regular markets to open in the morning, for there had been an urgency to the voice in the dream that warned him no time was to be lost.

The kinsman who was routed from his bed asked questions, but Joseph put him off as best he could while they bargained for the mule. Because of the urgency, he paid a higher price than he would have had to pay in the regular market, and most of his supply of coins was used up in buying the animal. He did not worry about that, however. The gold given them by the Magi as a present for the child, as well as the valuable gifts of frankincense and myrrh, could be readily exchanged in Egypt for lodging and the necessities of life, but he did not dare display them there in Bethlehem lest word reach the authorities and he be held on suspicion of theft before they could escape from the country.

Mary was saddened at having to leave Bethlehem, but the danger to Jesus put all other considerations from her mind. While Joseph was buying the mule, she busied herself binding up their meager possessions into packs which could be strapped on the backs of the animals. The gifts of the Magi she carefully secreted in the middle of a roll containing extra clothing and their sleeping pallets. What food was in the house was wrapped in a cloth so it could be lashed to the back of one of the mules along with the waterskin and their few cooking utensils.

Joseph's tools formed an important part of their belongings and these were carefully placed in a goatskin bag. With them he would need only a few moments' work in their new home to prove his skill as a carpenter. Artisans such as he moved about frequently, and the tools, plus proof of his ability to use them, were the only passport they needed in a world where the famous *Pax Romana* had opened the borders of all countries, except the few areas on the fringes of the empire where fighting was still going on.

It was almost dawn before they finished loading their belongings on the backs of the two animals. Jesus had been sleeping in the cradle Joseph had made for Him, and their last act before leaving Bethlehem was to lash this on top of one of the packs. Mary would walk and carry the baby in her arms much of the time, but for the rest of it He could lie in the cradle while she walked beside the animal. With her hand to steady the cradle, the rocking gait of the mule would lull the child to sleep. Whatever discomfort Joseph and Mary were to experience in this abrupt flight from their homeland, they were determined that Jesus should know as little of it as possible.

II

As they left Bethlehem dawn was breaking over the range of hills to the east that hid the leaden surface of the Sea of Judgment and the sulfurous mists, relics of the brimstone which had destroyed Sodom and Gomorrah, rising from it. The town still slept and Joseph led the pack animals carefully lest their footfalls arouse the soldiers of the small garrison assigned there to keep order and remind the people not to cheat the tax gatherers. They would have had trouble enough explaining why they were moving southward at such an hour, and if the treasures hidden deep inside the roll of sleeping pallets were discovered, could hope for nothing less severe than being hailed before a magistrate to explain whence such valuable things came.

As they took the road to Hebron, the castle of Herodeion was a grim reminder to them of the reason for their flight, but they did not yet feel the wrench of parting that would be their experience when they left Israel itself. Hebron, seventeen miles away, was the home of Elisabeth and Zacharias to whom Mary had gone after the angel's announcement of Jesus' conception. To anyone who questioned them, they planned to answer merely that they were going to visit this well-known priest and his family.

The road to Hebron led through a region rich in the history of Israel. When God had promised this land to the seed of Abraham, Hebron was already a chief city of the great Hittite Empire. Rameses II, the Pharaoh from whose grip Moses had delivered the Children of Israel, had broken the back of the Hittite confederation, but the promise of God to Abraham had not been completely fulfilled until Joshua had given Hebron and the surrounding territory to Caleb, his faithful lieutenant and the only other man of the generation that left Egypt to enter the Promised Land. In the cave of Machpelah near Hebron, Abraham had buried his beloved wife

Sarah. There, too, his own body lay with that of Jacob, brought up out of Egypt by his son Joseph in a magnificent funeral procession.

Altogether this was hallowed ground through which Joseph and Mary passed as they fled toward Egypt with Jesus. Long a heritage of the priests of Israel, Hebron was also a city of refuge, but Joseph knew the reputation of Herod and dared not rely upon his respecting that ancient tradition. They paused there only long enough to spend the night with Zacharias and Elisabeth, and to see the son born to them after the vision of Zacharias in the temple and dedicated by the Most High as a prophet. Some six months older than Jesus, John was a fine, strapping boy and a joy to his parents in these their later years.

Early the next morning the travelers set out again along the road leading to the border of Egypt at Beersheba, only a day's travel southward. The roadsides around Hebron were lined with grape arbors, the vines now bare of leaves. For over two thousand years much of the wine of Hebron had been boiled down to about one-third of its bulk to form a syrup called *dibash* or honey, some of which Jacob had sent to Egypt as a present to his son Joseph, long since given up for dead after being sold into slavery by his brothers.

On some other occasion Joseph and Mary might have enjoyed traveling through this region, so sacred to the history of Israel, but they could not help feeling sad now at leaving the land they loved. At Beersheba they crossed over the border into Egypt and, continuing two more days through the Wilderness of Shur, came to the "River of Egypt" which Moses had been instructed by God to use as a part of the borders of the Promised Land of Canaan. At Migdol, the frontier fortress of Egypt, they passed through the customs and at last were safe from Herod.

To a Jew, Egypt was a land of opportunity second only to his homeland. Greatly favored by Alexander when he had conquered Egypt, large numbers of Jews had migrated into the country. Here they had prospered and in some places, notably Alexandria, formed a large and racially distinct group with their own ethnarch as governor. As a skilled worker in wood, Joseph had little trouble in gaining membership in the guild of carpenters when he arrived at Tanis, the first large city south of the border. Here, in a friendly and warm land at the mouth of the Nile, he settled his family and began to work.

Even though far from his home in Israel, Joseph was not handling alien timber. Almost thirteen hundred years earlier, Israelite slaves had labored in this very city, building for their Egyptian masters. Jewish hands had helped care for the forests which now provided timbers for Joseph's saw, adze, chisels, and drills.

More recently Cleopatra had conspired with Mark Antony to deprive Herod for a while of most of the marvelously valuable seacoast cities of Palestine, as well as the lovely city of Jericho with its surrounding fields and gardens. There grew the balsam bush said to have come first from seeds brought as a gift to King Solomon by the Queen of Sheba. Cuttings of balsam, along with many other plants that flourished in warm and sunny Jericho, long favored as a winter resort by Romans and rich Jews, had been transferred at Cleopatra's order to the banks of the Nile where they grew and thrived as an herbal garden in the nearby city called On by the Jews. Although both Joseph and Mary yearned for beautiful Galilee, for all that was so particularly lacking in the flat Nile delta—the hills, valleys, and rushing streams of that mountainous land—yet they could hardly help being happy in Egypt. Jesus, too, thrived and was soon toddling about, exploring the exciting world of early childhood.

III

As he waited for the Magi to return and betray the whereabouts of the infant Messiah, Herod had grown more and more impatient, finally sending an envoy to Bethlehem in search of them. When the envoy came back with news that the wise men had departed for Arabia by the southern route, the king realized that they had fully understood the nature of his interest in the child whose star had led them from the east and had taken the alternate route homeward to avoid revealing His whereabouts.

Enraged at being thwarted in his intention to kill this child whose birth the star had announced, Herod next did a thing which for sheer horror eclipsed any of his previous crimes. An order was issued that all children under the age of two in Bethlehem and its immediate environs should be killed. The star had been seen by the Magi only a little more than a year before, and Herod thought by this brutal slaughter of innocent babes to be certain of destroying the child who was the Messiah. Hebron was not included in the sweeping edict, and the son of Zacharias and Elisabeth was spared. But there was weeping and wailing in Bethlehem as had been foretold by the prophet Jeremiah who said long ago, "A voice was heard in Ramah, lamentation, weeping, and great mourning, Rachel weeping for her children, refusing to be comforted, because they are no more."

Time was running out for Herod, too. Seventy years old and afflicted with a terrible disease that eroded his body with the same implacability he had displayed in destroying even those he loved most, he sought desperately for some way to defeat death. Borne to the baths of Callirrhoe beyond the Jordan, he found no relief even in these highly prized medicinal waters. Finally he was carried to the place he loved most, his palace at Jericho, where he prepared to die.

Even before death claimed Herod, the people had begun to rebel against his needless cruelties and his contempt for the one thing they revered most of all, the inviolability of their God. Although he had rebuilt the temple to please the priests and the people and to entrench himself as their king, he had also erected the forbidding fortress of Antonia at one corner of the sanctuary area so that his troops and the Roman cohorts which helped him keep Israel in subjection could be constantly alert for any sign of disturbance in Jerusalem. Above the entrance to the fortress he had placed a great golden eagle, the emblem of Rome, insulting the devout Jews of Jerusalem who had never forgiven him this indignity. Now that Herod was on the point of death they rose in revolt. Two rabbis, Judas and Matthias, led a party against the fortress and tore down the golden emblem.

Captured by the guards, the leaders of the revolt were brought to trial before the dying king. From his couch Herod judged and pronounced sentence; the prisoners were to be burned alive. When this only stirred the passion for freedom in thousands of others who wished to free their land from all foreign domination and set up a king from the line of David, Herod had ordered many of the noblest men of Israel shut up in the great hippodrome which he had erected in Jerusalem for the games, aping his masters in Rome whom he had always sought to please.

Convinced that his own son, Antipater, was conspiring against him, Herod seemed to linger on only to receive the permission he had requested of the Emperor Augustus to execute his own son. This given and the sentence promptly carried out, the king lived only five days more. Buried in splendor in the castle of Herodeion, whose grim bulwarks Joseph had seen on the day when he and Mary had hurried to Bethlehem and again on their flight into Egypt, Herod ended a reign of thirty-seven of the bloodiest, yet, strangely enough, the most prosperous, years Israel had ever experienced.

By Herod's will, Archelaus, son of Malthace, a Samaritan woman, was made ruler of Judea. Antipas, a younger brother to Archelaus and also called Herod, was given the governorship of Galilee and Peraea with the title of tetrarch, a sort of lesser king. Philip, son of Cleopatra of Jerusalem, was made tetrarch of that part of Herod's kingdom lying northeast of the River Jordan. Not one of Herod's sons inherited the title, King of the Jews.

Archelaus quickly proved himself another Herod in cruelty. Embarking upon a reign of terror, he sold the office of high priest to the highest bidder and sought to destroy all who dared resist him. His reign, though short, was turbulent and violent, ending finally in removal from office, trial before the emperor in Rome, and banishment to Vienne in Gaul. Judea was never again to know a king, for Rome now appointed procurators, civil servants who were responsible directly to the emperor.

IV

To Joseph, living quietly with Mary and Jesus on the banks of the Nile in Egypt, the angel of the Lord came once again in a dream with the command that he should return now to Israel. Echoes of the turbulence which had kept the district of Judea a virtual battleground since their escape had come even to Egypt, so Joseph chose to return to Nazareth rather than go to the City of David. And since he desired no contact with the reign of terror Archelaus was carrying out in Judea, he kept to the westward and came into Galilee from that direction.

Traveling as did thousands of wayfarers each year along the Way of the Sea, the great caravan route between Damascus and the cities of Egypt and one of the oldest thoroughfares in the world, Joseph and his family journeyed by way of Gaza, Ascalon, Jamnia, and Lydda, leaving Jerusalem well to the east. From Lydda, they went by way of Antipatris, keeping largely to the border between the Plain of Sharon and hilly Samaria, which was under the dominion of Archelaus. Following the eastern border of the Plain of Sharon and leaving the Roman capital of Caesarea on the seacoast to the west, they turned northeastward then toward Nazareth in the hills of southern Galilee.

6

And Jesus increased in wisdom and stature,
and in favor with God and men.

Luke 2:52

Upper Galilee, a land of mountains, caves, and passes, was a region of vast panoramas, crisp air, and rugged people. This same ruggedness produced many who fought against authority under the leadership of men who rose now and then to rebel against the yoke of Rome and the Herods. Judas the Gaulonite had come from this region and because of him many hundreds of Jews had been crucified before the government center of Sepphoris when he led a rebellion against Roman rule. Thus the dwellers in southern Galilee, the most populous and orderly portion of the land, distrusted northerners and gave them a wide berth whenever possible.

South of Lake Huleh the Way of the Sea crossed the turbulent Jordan by way of the *Jisr Benat Yakub*, the "bridge of Jacob's daughters." Icy cold and bluish green in color, the river hurried on to plunge into the Sea of Galilee. Along the river banks grew oleanders with beautiful white and pink blossoms and the tall, fanlike papyrus from which for thousands of years Egyptians had made long rolls for writing upon. Also growing there was the balsam whose nutlike fruit contained an oil much prized for making the famous "Balm of Gilead." This was the same balm the Ishmaelites had been taking to Egypt to sell when they had found the sons of Jacob in the act of conspiring to slay their brother Joseph.

The region just west of the Sea of Galilee was a land of broad fields and gently rolling hills. Here Asher had "dipped his foot in oil"—the oil that flowed like a river from the olive presses at harvest time—and had been blessed. Truly was it said, "It is easier to raise a legion of olives in Galilee than one child in the land of Judea."

In the lovely sunny land, away from the teeming cities of the lake, grapevines hung heavy with fruit and the wine was generous and rich. Grain sowed in the fall grew during the mild winters to a harvest of bounteous proportions. When wheat fields were ready for harvest, the heavy heads of grain bowed down in waves with a hissing noise as they rubbed together. Then the farmer would know the time had come to put in his sickle and reap the grain.

Living was not hard in Galilee as it was in Judea, where prices were often five times as high. In fact, so plump and tasty were the fruits of this region, particularly the Plain of Gennesaret lying on the northwestern shore of the lake, that the priests at Jerusalem would not allow them to be sold there at festival time, lest people from less favored sections come only to taste the fruits and forget their duties at the temple.

Life was busy and active in Galilee. In the towns many artisans labored, while shepherds, farmers, and the keepers of vineyards worked busily in the surrounding countryside. From the higher hills the eye could look westward to the Great Sea with its busy harbors and watch the many-oared vessels plying between them. Smoke rose from dozens of potteries and from furnaces where sand was melted into glass which Phoenician blowers expanded into delicate vases and other articles to be sold in the markets of the world. Weavers, dyers, and workers in wood and metal were always busy, for the excellence of their craftsmanship was widely known and the caravans moving westward to the market at Ptolemais on the seacoast were eager to purchase their products.

Jesus was a little over two years old when Joseph brought his family back to Nazareth. He was a sturdy boy toddling about, eager to explore the wonders of a small child's world when His father set up his carpenter shop once again. Since Joseph worked for the most part in the open court adjoining the house, that part of the home was naturally taboo for the boy, but in sleepy, quiet Nazareth there was still much to attract His eager curiosity.

Jewish home life was a warm and pleasant thing, the ties that bound parents and children very strong. Having been weaned at the age of two, as was customary, Jesus was no longer known by the diminutive of *jonek*, meaning "sucker," but was now *gamul*, the "weaned one." The weaning and their arrival from Egypt were celebrated with a feast, to which the many relatives of Mary and Joseph in this region were invited, some coming from as far away as Capernaum and Bethsaida on the shores of the beautiful lake, where several cousins near Jesus' own age lived.

The early years passed quickly and almost before Mary realized it, her son was no longer *gamul*, but *taph*, an active growing boy able to run and play with the other children. Early in boyhood the children of the village were sent out to watch the flocks by day. It was easy work, most of it play as they raced about the hillsides or swam in the brooks in summer, for all Jewish families were strictly enjoined to teach their children to swim. In the evening they would drive the flocks back to the safety of the fenced area just outside the town, and afterwards there would be exciting games in the streets and along the steep hillside overlooking the city.

At the age of five, Jewish children were expected, according to an ancient tradition, to begin reading the scrolls of the Torah in Hebrew, but this was generally done with only those who showed considerable precocity. Jesus belonged to this latter class, but His instruction was carried out first in the home, since He was too small as yet to be sent to the town school which was held in the synagogue. Everything about His everyday life and education was intended to inculcate in Him a love for God and God's Law, the dominant force in all Jewish life.

An ever-present reminder of every Jew's obligation to his God was the mezuzah attached to the doorpost of each dwelling. A small square of parchment, folded lengthwise, it contained exactly twenty-two lines from the words of God to Moses beginning:

> *Hear, O Israel! The Lord our God, the Lord is one!*
> *You shall love the Lord your God with all your heart,*
> *with all your soul, and with all your strength.*

The quotation from the ancient writings ended with the admonition which was the fountainhead of all teaching among, the Jews:

> *These words which I command you today shall be in*
> *   your heart.*
> *You shall write them on the doorposts of your house and*
> *   on your gates,*
> *that your days and the days of your children may be*
> *   multiplied*
> *in the land of which the Lord swore to your fathers to*
> *   give them,*
> *like the days of the heavens above the earth.*

Placed in a metal case and affixed to the doorpost, the mezuzah was touched by everyone entering the house. Afterwards each who touched it would kiss the finger and speak a prayer that, as promised by the psalmist,

"The Lord shall preserve your going out and your coming in, from this time forth and even forevermore." Even though carried in His mother's arms, Jesus could still reach out chubby fingers to touch the mezuzah, and it was a proud day when He could stand on tiptoes and reach the sacred metal box as He entered the house.

From the time He was able to speak, Jesus took part like all Jewish children in the daily prayers of the family and the enjoyment of the Sabbath, which was a time of rejoicing and praising the Lord. The passing of the seasons also brought the religious holidays or feasts.

Particularly enchanting for a child was the Chanukah, or Feast of Dedication, celebrated at the beginning of the winter season. Then in each house on the first day of the festival, one candle would be lighted for every member of the household, increasing by one each day until on the eighth and last evening the number was eight times that of the first. Then Nazareth blazed with light and the children moved through the streets or across the rooftops with hushed steps and eyes filled with awe to watch and pick out the houses of friends and relatives.

The Feast of Purim in the spring and the Festival of Booths or Tabernacles near the beginning of autumn were times of merrymaking and boisterous good cheer which particularly appealed to the boys. Most solemn of all was the Passover, held on the fourteenth day of Nisan, the first month of the religious year. Occurring in spring, it was a time of thanksgiving for the mercy of God in passing over the firstborn of the Children of Israel in Egypt, when the angel of death had warned Pharaoh to let the people go. At this feast the youngest in the family traditionally asked why it was celebrated and, while the family gathered around to listen, the father told once again the thrilling story of how the Children of Israel had been selected by God as His very own, how the land had been promised to Abraham, and how David the king had welded the tribes into a great and prosperous nation. Religion in a Jewish home was a thing of joy, the guiding spirit of every activity.

Because the works of the heathen in any form were considered outside the Jew's sphere of study, education was almost entirely religious in character. Almost from His first words, Jesus began to learn verses from the sacred writings, wise sayings, blessings, and benedictions used every day, and other bits of religious lore. Being a precocious child He read the Scriptures early and eagerly. Indeed, His mind could be said to resemble that of the ideal scholar described in the ancient writings, a well-plastered cistern from which not a drop of water could escape.

School met daily both morning and afternoon with a long midday recess in summer. The synagogue was used as the schoolhouse in most cases, but in larger towns there was sometimes a special building for this purpose. Presided over by the chazan, the leader of the congregation, the school was a place of strictest discipline. Children of five or six began their studies by reading the Book of Leviticus in Hebrew, first learning the letters from a board, and then learning how to form them into words. Leviticus contained the provisions of the Law which every Jew must know, hence its use as the first text. As the student grew older he learned to read from the writings of the prophets, the Torah, and the apocalyptic books, which were the most recent in origin of all the holy writings.

Not all students were taught to write but being an apt pupil, Jesus was. Ink was made from lampblack, although colored ink was sometimes used by the ostentatious. Reed quills were trimmed with a knife and used for pens. Writing could be on parchment rolls but in Israel was usually on very thin, dried skins, often split into an outer layer for rough work and an inner for more precious writings such as the mezuzah. Occasionally tablets of baked clay were used, as had been the custom in very ancient times.

II

As the years passed and Jesus grew in stature and knowledge like any other intelligent boy, the memory of the strange events which had accompanied His birth grew fainter in the minds of Mary and Joseph. They had recognized early that He was not exactly like the other boys of their household or of the village, being more studious in nature, more religious by inclination, and more tolerant and warmhearted in His love for others and His interest in them. These were qualities which all parents hoped to see in their children, however, and Mary and Joseph thanked God that Jesus showed every indication of growing up into a man who would be respected by His fellows for His piety, His kindness, and His intelligence, worthy of being a leader in the synagogue and in the community.

Jesus had long since outgrown the loving designation of *taph* and had become *elem*, meaning firm and strong. At the age of twelve He was approaching the state of *naar*, or youth, and in another year would take the ritual step from boyhood to young manhood by becoming bar mitzvah, literally the "Son of the Commandment." In keeping with rabbinical law, it was customary for a boy of this age to go up with his parents to Jerusalem for the first time to attend the services in the temple, in preparation for the impressive rite of putting away his boyhood. This Mary and Joseph arranged at the season of the Passover when Jesus was twelve years of age.

Traveling to Jerusalem was a thrilling event for a boy at any time, but on the occasion of the religious festivals many others of his own age, including friends and relatives, were also going to the temple, so it was naturally an occasion of considerable excitement. The party from Nazareth left a week before the beginning of the Passover, in order not to be forced to hurry over the distance of about a hundred miles. Actually, it was as much a social occasion as a journey, with the children running ahead to see every new sight, playing games and leaving the road to explore whatever struck their fancies.

From Nazareth they skirted the Sea of Galilee and came to Tarichaea near its southern end. A much straighter route led directly southward through Samaria, but Jews and Samaritans hated each other and travel through that land made a pious Jew unclean and entailed considerable personal risk as well. From Tarichaea the road descended rapidly as it wound along the west bank of the Jordan and they soon came to Scythopolis, a Greek city about the size of Jerusalem, where they crossed over to the east side of the river. Great fields of flax grew all around the city, watered by irrigation ditches from the Jordan.

Coursing like a giant snake in its narrow valley, the Jordan dropped steadily and the climate grew hotter, the strain on the travelers greater as they moved southward. The children stayed close to the others now and made frequent visits to the waterskins. No rain ordinarily fell at this season, so the travelers were quite comfortable sleeping in the open. All along the river were fig trees and date palms and broad fields of wheat and flax, flourishing in spite of the heat because of the plentitude of water from the Jordan. At the fords opposite Jericho, the travelers recrossed the river and set out on the last stage of the journey to the Holy City.

The climb from the deep rift in which the Jordan flowed to the high elevation of the hilly country around Jerusalem was laborious and the whole group traveled close together with grim-faced men bearing clubs guarding the flanks, since this area was heavily infested with robbers

The Crown and the Cross

who preyed on travelers going to and from the Holy City. It was worth the discomfort, the thirst, and the aching feet bruised by the rocky road, however, when finally they climbed the steep incline of the Mount of Olives and saw Jerusalem lying across the Kedron Valley, with the roof of the temple shining in the sunlight like purest gold and the black smoke from the altars of sacrifice curling upward into the afternoon sky. No Jew could fail to be moved by this sight, for here was the center of his faith, a golden monument to the glory of his God.

The pilgrims from Galilee did not go into Jerusalem on the day of their arrival but busied themselves selecting a campsite and setting up their tents on the western slope of the Mount of Olives. The Passover was the most sacred of all the Jewish religious festivals and more people came to it than to any other, so that space for camping was at a premium. In fact they had left early partly to find a place near enough to the city so they could come and go daily.

Jesus helped set up the camp but His eyes were constantly drawn to the beautiful city and particularly toward the temple, the place holiest in all the world to the worship of the Most High. As darkness began to fall and lights winked into flame across the narrow Kedron Valley to the west, while hundreds of campfires began to glow on the hillsides surrounding Him, Jesus' heart was filled with thanksgiving to the God to whose commandments and service He would soon be dedicated in the ceremony of bar mitzvah.

Seeing the glow of wonder and adoration in Jesus' eyes, Mary was happy, too. But as she looked across to where the massive stadium built by Herod the Great loomed, she could not help being reminded of another occasion when the angel had appeared to Joseph in a dream with the warning: "Arise, take the young Child and His mother, flee to Egypt, and stay there until I bring you word; for Herod will seek the young Child to destroy Him." Remembering the desperate flight southward from Bethlehem, she could not repress a shiver of fear.

III

By rising before dawn, the visitors from Nazareth were able to squeeze themselves into a synagogue inside the city. When the service there was ended, Joseph took Jesus into the temple with him, while Mary went

49

on to the Court of Women where she could see without encroaching upon the area from which women were barred.

The men of Nazareth had joined together, as was allowed by the Law, to purchase a lamb for the sacrifice. When the blast of a trumpet and the singing of the Levites, who were the lay assistants to the priests, announced the beginning of the sacrifices for the day, one of them hurried to the Gate of the Sheepfold at the northern sector of the terrace to claim his purchase.

The lamb obtained, the leader of the Nazareth delegation pushed through the Gate of the Sheepfold into the Court of Israel and the Place of Slaughter. Each placing his hands upon a lamb, thereby laying his sins upon it, the twenty men allowed to sacrifice at one time threw the animals to the floor and quickly cut their throats while the priests gathered the blood in bowls of gold and silver and dashed it against the base of the altar from which it drained away through openings in the floor. The dead lambs were quickly dressed and the fat removed and burned on the altar of sacrifice. As the Levites sang the hallel, the hymn of praise and thanksgiving, the carcasses of the animals were carried off by their buyers to be cooked and eaten at the paschal feast that evening.

All this Jesus watched with wide-eyed interest, but when it was over He did not go with the other boys to the booths where the animals for sacrifice were sold with much excited haggling over prices, or to the tables where the money-changers argued over the value of foreign coins. Instead, He hurried to the Porch of Solomon where the teachers sat, each with his back against a column, in the midst of a small circle of his disciples and students. Around them the crowds came and went, pausing to listen or ask a question before going on to hear what subjects were being discussed by other teachers who held forth here, especially during the festival season, interpreting the Law, in which they claimed to be expert. To a studious boy, this was the most exciting of the temple activities, and Jesus reluctantly left the Porch of Solomon when Joseph called to Him that they must return to the Mount of Olives so that the lamb could be prepared for the Passover feast.

At the camp on the hillside there was much bustling back and forth. While Joseph and several of the men from Nazareth dug a pit and built a fire to obtain a hot bed of coals, others prepared the lamb which had been slaughtered in the sacrifice. Early in the afternoon it was spitted upon a wooden stake, care being taken not to break any bones, and placed over the coals. The children took turns in rotating the spit so that the lamb would cook evenly, while the women prepared the unleavened cakes and dates and raisins mixed in vinegar which were an important part of the paschal meal. Meanwhile the children were rounded up and dressed in their best clothes, as were the adults, in preparation for the feast.

As darkness fell, the gleam of hundreds of cooking fires shone on the hillsides where paschal offerings were being prepared and the aroma of roasting flesh pervaded the entire area. When it was time for the ceremony to begin, each family gathered in its own tent, while the men distributed the meat of the lamb according to the number who would eat and the women arranged the children in a group around the improvised table upon which the food was placed.

In the tent of Jesus' family the ceremony was opened by sipping a cup of wine which Joseph blessed, followed by a ceremonial washing of the hands as all spoke a prayer together. Next each ate a small amount of the bitter herbs and vinegar mixed with raisins and dates, symbolic of the clay from which Israelites had been forced to make bricks while slaves in Egypt. Now, according to custom, the youngest child asked the reason for the feast and Joseph answered with the well-known story of how the Israelites had been spared while the firstborn of Egypt were struck down. Only when this traditional tale had been told did they turn to roasted flesh of the lamb and the unleavened cakes that were the main courses of the feast.

Many of the children were asleep in the tents before the ceremony ended, just before midnight, with the singing of the beautiful hallel:

> *Praise the Lord! Praise, O servants of the Lord, praise the*
> *name of the Lord!*
> *Blessed be the name of the Lord from this time forth and*
> *forevermore!*

As He stood alone to one side of the group, Jesus' heart swelled with pride and His eyes shone when He looked out across the glowing campfires to the great shadow of the temple.

IV

While they were camped on the Mount of Olives, Jesus visited the temple every day, spending most of the time listening to the rabbis who taught there. Knowing His studious nature and His deep-seated love of God and religious worship, Joseph and Mary had not been surprised. But when they left Jerusalem early one morning in the group returning to Nazareth and other cities of Galilee, it did not occur to them that He was not among the boys who raced ahead, eager to be on the way.

The end of the first day's journey brought them almost to Jericho, but Joseph and Mary did not begin to worry until Jesus failed to appear for the evening meal, which He would hardly have missed without obtaining their permission. They started looking for Him then but the camp was large; the Galileans were devout people and many came each year to Jerusalem for the Passover. It was late that evening before Joseph and Mary could be sure Jesus was not with them.

Knowing how heavily infested the area was with brigands, they were much disturbed by His absence, but reason told them robbers would hardly take a boy of twelve, especially one whose parents were not wealthy enough to pay a ransom of any size. A more likely presumption was that He had somehow failed to leave Jerusalem with them; acting upon it, they returned to the city the next day and began to search for Him.

Jerusalem was a large city in which to find a boy of twelve, and at first their efforts were fruitless. Mary could not see how the threat of Herod, which had sent them into Egypt, could hang over Jesus now, for Herod was dead and none of his offspring ruled here. Yet she could not help feeling that the two happenings were somehow closely allied. The strange events which had accompanied Jesus' birth came back to her now with renewed force and, as she and Joseph continued their efforts without avail, she was seized with more and more dread.

Distraught and almost convinced that Jesus had been destroyed for reasons which they could not at the moment understand, Joseph and Mary came finally to the temple on the afternoon of the third day of their search. And there they found Him where, had fear not distorted their thinking, they would have known He would be—listening to the doctors of Law.

Members of the Great Sanhedrin sat ordinarily as a court of law from the close of the morning sacrifice until the beginning of the evening ceremony. At this time they heard cases and pronounced sentence or settled civil disputes. On the Sabbath and on feast days, however, it was their custom to appear upon the terrace of the temple to teach and expound the Law to any who listened. Since this was not done on the first and holiest days of the Passover ceremony, but only on the *moed katon*, the minor festive days between the second and final days of the paschal season, they had not been teaching during the first days of Jesus' stay but only on the day before Joseph and Mary had departed with the Galilean group for the homeward journey. Crowds always thronged the terrace to hear them then, for complete liberty of questioning was allowed, even from boys of Jesus' age. It was this magnet, irresistible to a boy of His interest and concern with religious affairs that had drawn Jesus back to hear those considered to be among the finest minds in all of Israel.

"Son, why have you dealt with us thus?" Mary asked reproachfully when they found Him.

Jesus had been listening to a teacher, one of the principal followers of the great Shammai. When He turned to look at her, it was for a moment as if she were a stranger and He were seeing her for the first time.

"Why did you seek Me?" He asked, as if genuinely surprised that they should do so. "Did you not know that I must be about My Father's business?"

Neither Joseph nor Mary understood what He meant but they did not question Him concerning it; their relief at finding Him was too great for further reproof. As soon as they told Him how they had searched in the camp and had returned to Jerusalem, Jesus went with them willingly.

Mary, who was closer to Him than any others of the family, recognized that Jesus was changed after the visit to Jerusalem. There seemed to be a new purpose in His studies, an eagerness for knowledge that could hardly be satiated. But since sons almost always took up the occupation of their father, Jesus now began to work in the carpenter shop more actively, under Joseph's quiet direction. There was much to learn here too, and He devoted Himself to it with all the intensity that He put into everything He did.

Although Joseph fully realized that Jesus was not His son, He had always treated Him as His own flesh and blood, taking as much pride in the signs of His becoming a scholar as in His undoubted skill in working with tools on wood and stone. Between the two, the youth and the now elderly man, there was a warm relationship of mutual respect and love that grew as Jesus increased in stature and wisdom with the passing of the years. And when finally seized by a grave illness, Joseph went to join his God secure in the knowledge that in the capacity of eldest son, Jesus would care for the family as lovingly and as capably as he himself had always done.

*In those days John the Baptist came preaching
in the wilderness of Judea.*

Matthew 3:1

During the period when the Hasmonean king-priests were destroying themselves, with considerable assistance from Antipater and his son Herod, the Pharisees, successors of the early "pious ones," the Chassidim, had turned away from material considerations and moved closer in their own way to God. The Pharisees saw much of Israel's troubles as a punishment for the sins of its leaders and those who followed them; the only approach to God and eternal life, they felt, was through close attendance to the laws of God. Logically then, a man became increasingly righteous to the extent that he knew and obeyed the Law.

Laws, even those of God, required interpretation, however, and so there grew up a large group of pious men within the Pharisees called scribes whose concern for the details of the Law of Moses and for seeing that it was obeyed, steadily narrowed their concept of the eternal wisdom and understanding which characterized the God of Abraham and of Moses. Despondent over the human frailties of the Hasmoneans which had kept them from bringing about in Israel anything resembling the kingdom of God on earth for which pious Jews longed, the Pharisees and scribes turned more and more to the hope of a Messiah.

The Sadducees, on the other hand, numbering many of the noblest families in Israel and often highly placed in the priestly hierarchy, had regarded the collapse of the Hasmoneans and the final subjection of the nation under Rome as a purely political outcome of the world events taking place around them. Liberal in their approach to God and utterly realistic, they often played lackey to Rome for the obvious material benefits such a policy brought. In addition, they denied the resurrection of the body upon which the Pharisees based their hope of taking part in the glorious kingdom of God on earth that they confidently expected one day to take place.

Between these two points of view were the great mass of the people, the *am ha-arets*, who obeyed the Law when they could and who were the butt of contempt from the Pharisees when they did not. They admired and envied the splendor and the high places of the priests and other Sadducees. They listened with awe to the learned debates between various groups of Pharisees and scribes as these indulged in endless hairsplitting on technical points of the Law. Meanwhile they went their way, living each according to his own concept of his purpose and duty in life.

In Judea after the banishment of Archelaus, the rule of the procurators was not a heavy burden and most of the actual political control of the country was vested in the Sanhedrin. Composed of seventy members— sometimes more, sometimes less—it was largely a gathering of nobles and therefore controlled by the Sadducees, although containing a substantial representation from among the Pharisees and some artisans. Limited only by the necessity to gain the approval of the Roman governor for the sentence of death, the Sanhedrin was supreme in the administration of justice, whether religious or temporal. Actually there was no difference, for the Law of Moses was the law of the land and no other was needed or desired.

Being Roman and alien, the procurators made mistakes. The fifth in the series, Pontius Pilate, almost precipitated a rebellion when he brought the imperial standards of Rome into Jerusalem where no graven image could enter. He had withdrawn that order only when thousands of Jews plodded over the mountain roads to Caesarea and bared their necks to the sword in protest. Pilate's action somewhat later in using temple money to build a great aqueduct into Jerusalem created another stir, but the abundance of good water was tangible evidence of its benefit to the people in general, and the priests were known to be rich, so their protests were largely disregarded.

Thus there grew up in Judea the sort of complacency that comes with peace and prosperity. The Pharisees concerned themselves with the Law of Moses and the promise of the Messiah in the Psalms and other prophetic writings. The Sadducees administered the temple functions and grew rich. The common people groaned under the burden of taxes and hated the publicans, or tax gatherers, to whom the task of collecting the various tributes was farmed out. Nobody in a position of authority looked with any degree of longing toward the old bloody, if sometimes glorious, days of the Hasmonean dynasty, and no one wished to bring down the wrath of Rome by allowing anything to occur that might appear to be a rebellion. Thus Sadducees and Pharisees alike sought to prevent any disturbance among the vast crowds which thronged the Holy City for the daily sacrifices and the religious festivals.

In Galilee things were somewhat different. Dwelling in villages and smaller cities, the Galileans were a strong and turbulent people having for the most part only a few generations of identification as Jews behind them. While Judea had been freed from the rule of the hated Herods, Galilee had not, and soon a group of men came into being who hated both Rome and Herod, and were already beginning to call themselves Zealots.

The Zealots believed the expected kingdom of God in Israel could be established only by the sword. During Jesus' boyhood, they went to war behind one Judas, the Gaulonite, confident that God would give their tiny forces victory as He had given it to Judas Maccabaeus centuries before. Long experienced in such affairs, however, Rome had moved rapidly. The revolt was put down and hundreds of Galileans were crucified. Since then the activities of the Zealots had been sporadic, but the threat of an outbreak was always present and both Herod in Galilee and Pontius Pilate in Judea watched carefully for any sign of recurring strength among this faction.

One large group of pious men in Israel chose to retire from the world and live strictly within the original statements of the Law given to Moses, making no concession to any interpretations or adaptations to present situations. These were the Essenes, a band of ascetics whose interpretation and concepts of the Torah grew narrower while they preached that if the rest of Israel did not follow their ways, it was doomed to destruction.

Although small groups of Essenes were to be found throughout Israel, the greatest center for them was in the desert wilderness along the northwest shore of the Sea of Judgment where they had first dwelt m caves. Far enough removed from the priestly centers of Jerusalem and Jericho to afford them the feeling of withdrawal they so fervently desired, the thriving community was at the same time near enough for the voices of Essenes to be heard often in the Holy City and their teachings to be listened to by the crowds that thronged there.

Deeply committed to the essence of the Torah, these intensely dedicated men regarded themselves as having inherited the promises of God to Abraham, Isaac, Jacob, and the prophets of a great kingdom one day to be re-established on earth. To the pious Essene, man was in the midst of a constant struggle between good and evil, represented as Light and Darkness. Since the final days of the struggle, with the triumph of Light and the coming of the true kingdom of God on earth, was almost momentarily expected, their activities were accompanied by a deep sense of urgency and intensity of feeling.

In organization, an Essene community was very strict. A probationary period of two years was required of anyone wishing to become a member. During this time the applicant devoted himself to study, meditation, and the strictest of ascetic living. At the end of the period, if he were accepted, he turned all his property into the common fund and became a member of a group of ten, led by a priest. A council of twelve, with three priests among them, governed each Essene community, of which that on the shores of the Sea of Judgment was by far the largest unit. One among the group, descendant in authority from a martyred "Teacher of Righteousness" who had founded the order nearly two hundred years before, served as the leader.

The Essenes observed a ritual communal meal representing the great banquet of the righteous when at last God's task for men on earth was finished and His kingdom came in all its final glory. They were cleanly in their habit and used baptism with water as a sign that those baptized repented of their sins and sought ever afterwards to live according to the Law.

Like the Pharisees, the Essenes looked to the day when a new leader, perhaps a new "Teacher of Righteousness" like the martyred founder of their own order, would appear to usher in the kingdom of God on earth. Moses, they taught, had predicted this very thing when he said: "The Lord said to me, 'I will raise up for them a Prophet like you from among their brothers, and will put My words in His mouth, and He will speak to them all that I command Him.'"

For men to receive, understand, and obey the Torah, the Essenes believed they must receive a certain enlightenment. This state of enlightenment members of the various communities sought for themselves through meditation, study, withdrawal from the world, and self-denial. In this way they hoped to move upon higher planes of understanding and experience, secure in the knowledge that there was hope for even ordinary human beings to enjoy a communion with the Divine.

II

To the community of the Essenes near the Sea of Judgment came the youth named John, son of the priest Zacharias and Elisabeth who was the kinswoman of Mary, the mother of Jesus. Shortly after his thirteenth year, when he became a "Son of the Commandment" and took on the status of a young man, John had withdrawn into the desert and the community of the Essenes. There, while living the simple life of the community and denying himself the pleasures of ordinary men in order to make himself pure, he had studied the Law and the promises of God's kingdom to be brought about on earth.

Zacharias had told John about the strange circumstances surrounding both his birth and that of Jesus. In his quavering voice the old priest had described how he had been struck dumb when the angel of the Lord had revealed to him that Elisabeth, though well past the age of childbearing, would give him a son who would "be called the prophet of the Highest."

John had pondered upon these words while he went about the quiet life of the Essene community and sought the enlightenment which would prepare him for the coming kingdom of God. The intense, dedicated youth, convinced as he grew older that he had been singled out for a great purpose, became a fiery man whose spirit could not long be contained by the rigid rules and the intense preoccupation with the Torah characterizing the life of the Essenes. As time passed, John became more and more convinced that his mission was not, as the brethren of the Essene community held, to achieve his own salvation, but to bring to all men a warning of the impending coming of God's kingdom on earth and the necessity to repent of their sins in preparation for it.

Soon word began to spread that a prophet was teaching in the wilderness country at the northern end of the Sea of Judgment. A region of steep hills and black basalt boulders and caves, and of robbers who preyed on travelers, the region around what was called the "Fords of the Jordan" east of Jericho was admirably suited for the appearance of a prophet. Gaunt and fiery-eyed, John was like one of the volcanoes which had rumbled beneath this very area long ago; his turbulent spirit resembled the fires of God which had destroyed Sodom and Gomorrah when the whole vast rift in which the Sea of Judgment lay had rumbled and exploded as if in agony.

One of the most frequently traveled roads between Jerusalem and Galilee ran through this region. Near where it crossed the river, at a place called Bethabara, John began to preach from a natural pulpit among the rocks overlooking a grove of sycamores that sheltered his listeners from the burning sun of midday pouring down upon John's own unprotected head. Although still practicing the asceticism of the nearby Essene community where he had lived, John had put aside the white garments an Essene usually wore and, like Elijah of old, wrapped his body in a roughly-woven robe of camel hair with a leather girdle about his waist. Lodging in the villages when he did not sleep beneath the open sky, he ate the food of the poor, often locusts and wild honey.

Locusts were much liked by the villagers. Sometimes the insects, which swarmed everywhere, were simply roasted in an oven and eaten with salt. But often they were prepared more elaborately by first drying them in the sun, then grinding them into a slightly bitter powder which was mixed with honey and a little flour to make a highly prized cake.

As word of John's fiery preaching in the wilderness began to spread, more and more people stopped on the way to and from Jerusalem to hear him. There had not been a real prophet in Israel for hundreds of years, and word spread quickly concerning the angel who had appeared to his father at the very altar of the temple, announcing John as a prophet of God in the tradition of Elijah.

And John did not fail to live up to that tradition. From his rocky pulpit, he preached to ever larger crowds of people, thundering at them the necessity to repent and be forgiven of their sins through the symbolic Essene rite of baptism before it was too late. Nicknamed "the Baptist," John's desperate urgency communicated itself to those who heard him and soon many began to say that he was indeed the fulfillment of the prophecy of Isaiah: "The voice of one crying in the wilderness: 'Prepare the way of the Lord; make His paths straight. Every valley shall be exalted and every mountain and hill brought low. The crooked places shall be made straight and the rough places smooth. The glory of the Lord shall be revealed, and all flesh shall see it together.'"

Even the area where John preached seemed to fit in with the prophecy, for it was easy to see in the tumbled basalt boulders and the sulfurous fumes seeping through crevices in the rocks that God had indeed once filled valleys and brought mountains and hills low in this very region when He had destroyed Sodom and Gomorrah, at the southern end of the Dead Sea, because of their excessive sinfulness. This same sinfulness, John preached, would lead God to destroy the people once again unless they listened and repented.

Unable to comply fully with the complexities of the Law, the common people were always conscious of their sin. Even if they had not been, the Pharisees would not have left them unreminded of it, so John's thunderings concerning the imminent end of the present era and the coming of God's kingdom under an Anointed Messiah struck fear and trembling into nearly every heart. By thousands they came and camped along the banks of the Jordan and the several brooks that ran into it here. Campfires dotted the valley and extended into the hillsides, many of the campers sleeping in the caves that pocked the rocky slopes.

The Essene community nearby gave help to those who became ill or were too poor to buy their own food, but its resources were soon considerably overtaxed. Merchants from nearby Jericho and farther up the Jordan Valley brought food and supplies on mule trains to be sold at the usual high profit under such circumstances. The caravansary nearby, open to travelers as a shelter, was always filled to overflowing.

Every day after he preached, John led a procession of the repentant down into the shallows at the fords of the Jordan to be baptized in the Essene manner, but it was in the pulpit that he really became the prophet the people were already acclaiming him to be.

"Brood of vipers!" he flayed the religious leaders who came to listen. "Who warned you to flee from the wrath to come?" He went on to warn that no mere lip service would suffice to save them. "Bear fruits worthy of repentance, and do not think to say to yourselves, 'We have Abraham as our father,'" he shouted, referring to the tendency of Israelites to believe that as sons of Abraham they were favored of God and their sins would therefore be more easily forgiven. "For I say to you that God is able to raise up children to Abraham from these stones," he warned. "And even now the axe is laid to the root of the trees. Therefore every tree which does not bear good fruit is cut down and thrown into the fire."

With the odor of brimstone, which the ignorant people firmly believed came from the very fires of hell, still rising from crevices in the volcanic terrain nearby, this pertinent reminder had an immediate effect upon his listeners. Falling on the ground before him, repentant sinners cried, in an agony of fear and conviction of their own unworthiness, "What shall we do then?"

"He who has two tunics, let him give to him who has none," John answered. "And he who has food, let him do likewise." It was the simplest of God's commandments and, because of human greed, the one most frequently ignored.

"Teacher, what shall we do?" a tax gatherer asked.

"Collect no more than what is appointed for you," John advised sternly, referring to the publicans' habit of demanding from people greater taxes than they were legally required to pay—and pocketing the overage.

"What of me?" a soldier inquired. To him John said, "Do not intimidate anyone or accuse falsely, and be content with your wages."

John's teachings contained nothing that was really new; every Jew was required by the Law to practice these very things which John was advising. But when coupled with his dramatic appearance as a prophet who spoke the word of God directly to them, and his dire warnings that God's kingdom was soon to come and that those not worthy would be destroyed like the tree cast into the fire, they had a powerful effect upon his listeners.

So long as John did not claim Messiahship but identified himself merely as one warning of the coming kingdom of God, the authorities had been contemptuously tolerant of his simple doctrine. Only when he went further and attacked Herod Antipas, who, as a son of Herod the Great, ruled in the province of Peraea where the Baptist was preaching, did he bring down the fire of official displeasure on his head. Even then John could have avoided trouble by limiting his preaching to general terms, but, like the prophet he believed himself to be, he dared to attack even the ruler.

Herod Antipas had married the daughter of Aretas, king of the Nabataeans, a desert people dwelling to the east. It had been a good marriage for the wily Antipas, removing the threat of Nabatean attack from his eastern border, the only area from which he could expect trouble. Later, while on a visit to Rome, Herod had become violently enamored of Herodias, wife of his half-brother Philip, and shortly after he returned to Galilee, Herodias had followed him there with her adolescent daughter Salome. Soon Herod divorced his first wife and sent her back to King Aretas. But when he then married his sister-in-law, he committed a grave sin according to Mosaic Law and for this John forthrightly denounced him.

The tetrarch himself might not have paid much attention to John, for the outpourings of men styling themselves as prophets were not often heeded by the ruling class against whom they usually fulminated. But Herodias took offense at John's words, perhaps because they were spoken so close to Jericho, where Herod maintained a winter home, and entertained widely among the Romans and higher government officials. She began to seek a way to silence John the Baptist, as the ruling classes in Israel had more than once sought to silence prophets who accused them of betraying their obligations to God and the Law. And being a woman of little principle—a characteristic common to members of the Herodian house—it did not take her long to achieve her wish.

Now Jesus Himself began His ministry at about thirty years of age,
being (as was supposed) the son of Joseph.

Luke 3:23

The chill of an approaching winter night was already in the air but the children who were gathered in a half-circle around the slender man with a light brown beard and the fluent, expressive hands of a born teacher did not notice it. Every day on the way home from school they stopped in the open courtyard, where Jesus the carpenter worked with His tools, to hear the story He was always ready to tell them. Eyes eagerly uplifted to the Teacher, they dwelt on His every word as He told once again of the son who had traveled far away and spent his patrimony unwisely, returning to his father's house penniless. When He recounted how the father had gone out and clasped the prodigal and repentant son to his bosom, they voiced their approval with cries of pleasure.

From the door leading into the house, Mary watched the scene with a smile. She would always love her firstborn most of all the family, she knew, and not just because during His life He had given her little cause to worry. Since that one occasion when she and Joseph had returned to Jerusalem to look for Jesus and had found Him in the temple, He had been a model of obedience. As every boy was expected to do, He had begun to work in Joseph's shop as an apprentice shortly after His twelfth year.

Carpentry, as Joseph practiced it, was not an easy trade to learn. In Galilee most houses were made of stone or mud bricks or by plastering clay over a lathing of willow withes, but each required doors and window frames of wood and sturdy beams to support the roof upon which, except in the coldest season, the evening hours were spent. Furniture was also needed: stools, tables, shelves, boards for flattening out the cakes of bread, and chests for storing valuable belongings. These were simple articles any carpenter could make, but in Egypt Joseph had learned a considerably wider application of the woodworking trade.

Egyptian carpenters produced the large wooden cases in which the bodies of the rich were placed before being sealed in their tombs and also the small, richly carved boxes in which highly-pampered women kept their jewels. The irrigation pumps called *shadufs* which lifted water from the Nile were likewise made largely of wood, and considerable ability was needed to fashion them and set them in operation. Boats of all sizes and shapes had to be built, from shallow dug-out craft in which noblemen hunted birds with throwing sticks to large scows or barges for hauling stores up and down the river. Skilled hands were needed to carve plows and hoes from crooked limbs of trees and throwing sticks had to have the right curve and thinness if they were to return to the thrower in case of a miss.

All of these skills Joseph had taught Jesus patiently as they worked together in the shop. The boy learned that the short-handled adze of iron, carried always in the belt when at work so it could be easily reached, was His handiest tool, forming practically an extension of His own strong right arm. The skill required to gouge out a shallow wooden bowl or tray with a chisel was acquired only after long practice and many ruined pieces of wood.

Fortunately there was plenty of timber on the heavily forested slopes of the Galilean hills, but the trees had first to be felled and cut into proper lengths, then split into boards. A block of sandstone applied to the rough surface produced a smooth plank but only after long and laborious hours of rubbing. The saw was used carefully, for a carpenter could rarely afford more than one, considering the prices Phoenician smiths demanded for them. The teeth must be kept properly sharp and never allowed to touch metal or stone as the tool was pulled toward the user to cut the wood.

The carpenter's hammer was made of heavy stone with a hole drilled through the center for the handle. It was not used upon a table for the carpenters of Galilee sat on the floor of the open courts where they worked on all except the coldest days, dexterously fixing boards and timbers with their feet so that the hands were free to use the tools.

Since Joseph was also a builder, he had taught Jesus the importance of constructing upon solid foundations in this country where rain washing down the hillsides could easily undermine a poor foundation and let the house fall. The lad soon came to be handy with the stonecutter's hammer and trowel, whether in building a house or walls for sheepfolds and other enclosures. The first layer of stones had to be placed carefully upon the bedrock itself as a firm foundation and then set in place with mortar which was allowed to dry before the other layers were applied. Skilled masons had built the temple at Jerusalem, it was reported, without the sound of hammer or chisel being heard, the great blocks having been quarried and cut to pattern before they were set in place.

It was a busy life upon which Jesus had embarked when He first began to be *bachur*, a "ripened one," as He worked beside Joseph. After Joseph died, the burden of maintaining the household had fallen upon Jesus' teenage shoulders. By now there were others in the family: four boys, James, Joses, Simon, and Judas, and several sisters. Growing children needed much food and everyone worked, but Jesus, as head of the household, was the main breadwinner.

He had grown in stature and in wisdom as the years passed, a rock of strength to His family and a model to others in the community of what a true worshiper of the Most High should be. In the shop He always gave good measure and something extra. And in the synagogue on the Sabbath, He often rose to speak, impressing all with His quiet wisdom and His wide knowledge of the Scriptures.

A man was not expected to reach his full vigor of body and mind until he was thirty years old, and his opinions were not generally respected by his elders until that age, after which he took his place in the councils and discussions on an equal basis with others. In Jesus' case the people of

Nazareth came to respect His goodness and His wisdom well before He had reached that turning point, and very early He was given the respectful designation of "teacher," or rabbi.

Even with all His duties, Jesus had always found time to talk to the children who came by His shop after school and tell them the stories they wished to hear. Sometimes after they were gone there would be a short time of freedom before darkness and the evening meal.

There was one today. Calling to Mary that He would return soon, Jesus started up the winding path that led to the summit of the steep hill overlooking Nazareth at one point in the form of a craggy outcrop. From the doorway, Mary watched Him climb with steady, purposeful strides until He appeared upon the crest, an erect, vigorous figure, and turned to look about Him.

II

The hilltop above Nazareth was an ideal place for a seeker after solitude. The path leading upward was narrow and steep and since there was little grass on the rocky crag, the shepherds did not take their flocks up that high. From the steep cliff Jesus' eyes always turned first toward the western portion of the great plain called Esdraelon, or sometimes Jezreel, lying before Him. The most famous battleground in all of Israel, it was here that Deborah had called Barak to lead the armies in the thrilling battle which had destroyed the army of Sisera when the Lord had sent a great hail and rainstorm to bog down the iron chariots of the enemy.

On this same plain of Esdraelon, Gideon had attacked and defeated the Midianites with an effective force of only three hundred against an army of which the ancient writings said: "All the people of the East were lying in the valley as numerous as locusts; and their camels were without number, as the sand by the seashore in multitude."

To the east in the clear cool air just preceding sunset, the top of Mount Tabor was visible above the lower hills, and across the plain loomed the mountains of Samaria. The long range of Mount Carmel extended northwestward to the rocky promontory that jutted out into the Great Sea to form the southern tip of the Bay of Akka. Northeast of Nazareth the plains and rolling hills of upper Galilee ascended gradually toward snow-capped Mount Hermon with the beautiful city of Sepphoris among the foothills only a few miles away. To the east again, completing a full circle, lay the hills around the Sea of Galilee.

From the hilltop, Jesus could see almost the entire range of the land granted by God to the Children of Israel, from Dan in the northeast to Beersheba in the southwest. And simply by looking down He could easily sweep the entire town of Nazareth with a single glance. Many of the houses, with their flat rooftops sloped to let the rain run off, He Himself had helped build, being careful always to obey the mandate of the Law that: "When you build a new house, then you shall make a parapet for your roof, that you may not bring guilt of bloodshed on your household if anyone falls from it."

Reached by an outside stairway, the roof was the favorite gathering place for the family after the evening meal, a cool place to sleep during the hot summer nights, as well as a drying yard for grain, rushes, or wood by day. Sometimes the rooftops were covered by a shelter or second roof to form an upper chamber, usually incompletely walled. In fact, the first sign of increased prosperity came when a family could afford an upper chamber for their home.

Many of the houses in Nazareth were made of clay, kneaded and plastered over a wattle-covered framework and allowed to dry in the sun to the hardness of brick. On the inside, gray patches of saltpeter often exuded from the clay to cause the so-called "leprosy of the walls." Communication between houses was easy, being carried on across the rooftops where the people congregated in the evening, and a pleasant air of camaraderie pervaded these smaller towns.

Four things were always found in a well-kept house: a lamp with the stand for elevating it, a bushel for measuring grain (also used upended as a table or stool and as a stand for the lamp), skins of wine, and a small mill for grinding corn.

Wine bottles were made from the hides of goats with the hair inside, the openings tied off and the neck closed by spigots or stoppers. Hanging in the house, the skin dried gradually and the outside became cracked. Old wineskins had to be handled carefully for that reason and not filled with new wine, since fermentation would cause the fragile skin to explode and the wine to be lost.

The mill consisted of two round stones, the lower usually hollowed out slightly to receive the surface of the upper. A peg driven into a depression drilled in the center of the lower stone projected through a hole in the upper, and a handle set into one side of the upper stone allowed it to be turned, grinding the corn into flour.

Houses consisting of more than one room were arranged around an open court. Often a family of several generations would live in one of these groups of buildings with the workaday activities—if they were artisans, as so many were—being carried out in the central court. In such an establishment everyone had his task and each performed his share of the work.

As His gaze continued to sweep across the community He loved, Jesus could see a group of men gathered under the shade of a single large olive tree before the synagogue which fronted on the main square of the town. These, He knew, would be some of the older men, "elders of the congregation" who gathered there every afternoon when the weather allowed to engage in endless arguments about the Law and its interpretations. Unless, that is, a traveler happened to stop by; then they questioned him eagerly about what was happening in other parts of the land, in the populous and sinful cities around the lake that lay only a few miles to the east, or in Jerusalem. They were not much interested in what went on outside their own little world of Israel. So long as the Romans added no new taxes and did not hem them in with further restrictions, they were content to let things continue as they were.

In another part of the town Jesus could see the glow of forges and hear the clank of hammers on anvils as the coppersmiths fashioned utensils of that easily handled metal. From the area around the well came the soft murmur of women's voices as they drew up water for the night so that the earthenware crocks would not be dry when morning came and the men blame the women for not carrying out their duties.

Darkness was already beginning to fall as Jesus made His way down the hillside toward the town and His home. He did not want to be late tonight because He knew Mary had prepared a special feast in honor of His birthday, marking His thirtieth year, which was considered a turning point in a man's life; thereafter he was considered old enough by his fellows for his opinions to be generally respected.

He saw a stocky figure hurrying through the streets with a small bale upon his shoulder and surmised that James, next in age to Him in the family, was returning from the market at the southern edge of the town where the main road passed, having bartered some of the articles they made in the shop for cloth needed to make new robes for the family. James was clever at the give-and-take of barter in the marketplace so the task of selling the products was left to him. He was also the news gatherer of the family through his contact with the merchants who frequented the market to buy and sell.

The evening meal was ready when Jesus reached home and He paused only to wash His hands before sitting down to eat. Some people in Nazareth had adopted the Roman method of reclining around a table for their meal but since in this household they ate as the Jews had been eating since the earliest days, they now sat on the floor of well-swept earth around the large dish in which had been cooked the savory stew that Mary had prepared in honor of Jesus' birthday. The men ate first, as was the custom, while the girls and Mary waited just outside the doorway to hear the talk and be ready to supply more bread when needed, or to fill cups with the thin vinegar used instead of water on festive occasions such as this.

Like the others, Jesus dipped into the dish with a small piece of round flat cake and filled a bowl for Himself. When He finished, He carefully cleaned the bowl with a piece of bread which was called the sop. During a meal when a loved one was present who had been absent for a long time, it was the custom to pass the sop to him as a token of affection. Dates and preserved figs were enjoyed afterward when the men withdrew to the side of the room to talk while the women now ate from the big dish.

It had been evident throughout the meal that James had something of importance to say, but he kept silent until they finished eating. Now, after each member of the household had brought a small gift to Jesus in token of the occasion, James cleared his throat importantly.

"I talked to a traveler from Jerusalem today," he announced. "He told me something of our cousin John."

He had the attention of his audience at once. From time to time reports had come of the years John had spent with the Essene community at the northern end of the Sea of Judgment. The Essenes had increased in number steadily throughout the years and now were often seen in towns outside Jerusalem. Strange stories, too, were told about them; it was said that in the larger communities, like the one where John had lived, dozens of men worked constantly at copying the ancient writings of the Torah and the prophets upon scrolls of thin leather or engraving them upon sheets of copper. These were sealed in earthen jars and mysteriously carried away to some hiding place of which it was said only the leaders of the Essenes knew the location. In some towns there were Essene teachers, highly learned men who helped with the schools which every community was required by the law to maintain.

In becoming an Essene, John had set himself apart and the family was always eager to hear news of him.

"Where did the traveler see John?" one of the girls asked.

"By the fords of Jordan near Jericho," James said. "He is preaching there. They call him 'the Baptist' because he washes many with water from the river as the Essenes do."

"Do many people come to hear him preach?" Mary inquired.

"The traveler said their campfires line both banks of the river and the community of the Essenes near the fords can no longer give food and shelter to those who come to hear him."

For a kinsman to achieve so much fame that people would come from great distances to hear him—this was something exciting.

"What does he preach?" one of the boys asked.

"John claims to be the messenger sent to foretell the coming of the Anointed One," James said impressively.

'The Messiah who will lead Israel out of bondage?"

"John says even the valleys will be filled and the mountains and hills be brought low. Who could do such a thing except one who comes from the Most High to lead Israel in triumph over her enemies?"

No one argued the point, but there was no joy in their hearts at the thought. The bloody conflict over Judas the Gaulonite, who had claimed to be the Messiah, had swirled through these very hills around Nazareth. With no more effort than turning one's head, it was possible to see the white walls of Sepphoris to the north where thousands of Jews had been crucified by the Roman governor, Quirinius, when they had risen to support Judas. That had happened less than twenty years ago, within the memory of many in Jesus' own family. Galilee was peaceful now; the inhabitants wanted it to remain so.

"They say many Galileans have become disciples of John," James continued, "even our kinsmen, James and John, and Simon the fisherman, with his brother Andrew."

The sons of Zebedee were well known in Nazareth and so were Simon and Andrew who often visited there. Because of his great size and strength, Simon in particular was much admired by the younger men.

"There is always need of prophets, to remind the people of their duty toward the Most High," Mary said.

"But Nazareth wants no part of false Messiahs," James added. "We remember too well the other one."

"Is it true that John denounced Herod Antipas because of his marriage to Herodias?" one of the girls asked.

James nodded. "The merchant said Herodias has sworn to have John killed, but Herod believes him to be a prophet and will not harm him."

"Herod is wise," Mary agreed. "No one can be sure whether a man truly prophesies of God until his prophecies come true. It is a bad thing to kill any man, but particularly a prophet."

"Does John claim to know when the Anointed One will come?" one of the boys asked.

James shook his head. "The merchant didn't say, but from what John has been preaching, the people believe it will be soon. That is why so many are repenting so they will be ready for the kingdom of God."

There was silence in the room. Even to imagine the coming of God's kingdom on earth was an awesome thing, an event to bring both joy and fear. And the fact that no one knew the hour when it would come only made it more fearsome.

James broke the silence. "It is a good thing that everyone will know when the Messiah does come. The Prophets tell us there will be no mistaking Him."

Jesus had not spoken during the conversation. Instead He seemed to have withdrawn into Himself, as Mary and the others had noticed that He was doing more and more lately. Looking at Him now, Mary was startled by the light in His eyes and the look of decision upon His face.

The events of Jesus' birth and the time she and Joseph had found Him in the temple at Jerusalem when He was twelve were only memories now, things so long past that it could be doubted if they had ever occurred. Yet though Mary loved Jesus dearly and knew that He loved her, she had recognized long ago that there was a part of Him, a side to His nature, which she had never been able to share as she did with the others.

The rest of the family was busy discussing John the Baptist and his sudden rise to prominence. They did not notice when Jesus got to His feet and went out into the courtyard, but Mary followed as far as the doorway. She could see Jesus standing in the middle of the small court beside the house where He worked most of the time, His eyes lifted to the star-lit winter sky. His lips moved in prayer but she could not hear the words He spoke.

The family soon went to their sleeping pallets, but Mary's eyes did not close until long after when she heard Jesus come into the house and seek His own pallet beside the others. Somehow she knew without being told that He had come to a decision out there in the courtyard, a decision that must be related to what James had said about their cousin John. But she had no inkling of what the decision was until He came to her in the morning and told her He was going to the fords of Jericho where John was preaching and then on to Jerusalem for one of the feasts.

She did not argue. Yesterday had been Jesus' thirtieth birthday. From now on, He was entitled to make His own decisions.

9

Behold, the heavens were opened to Him,
and He saw the Spirit of God descending like a dove
and alighting upon Him.

Matthew 3:16

Following the winding course of the River Jordan southward on the east bank, the group of travelers Jesus had joined at Tarichaea came at last to the Plain of Jordan and Bethabara, which meant "House of the Ford." Here, at the southernmost spot above the Sea of Judgment where the Jordan could be forded, one of the busiest roads in the area crossed the river and led to Jericho and Jerusalem. Near this spot Joshua had led the Children of Israel across on dry land when earth cliffs on the west bank upstream near Adamah, undermined by the swift passage of the river as it plunged southward, had tumbled into the stream and blocked it, as had happened several times before. Of course, the miracle was that God had done it for His people at just the moment that they needed to cross.

The ford was not dry now, for the rains had been copious that year and the area along both banks of the river was green with vegetation. Hundreds of small thatched shelters woven from reeds growing within the small zone of amply watered ground along the river bank had been erected by those who had come to hear John. These same reeds were widely used in Jerusalem and elsewhere, not only as canes but for making furniture and mats and the screens which largely formed the partitions in the houses.

Bethabara could hardly be called a town. Actually it was little more than a customs station where the traveler from Jerusalem passed from the area ruled by the Roman procurator, Pontius Pilate, into the region presided over by Herod Antipas, tetrarch of Galilee and Peraea. A small post of frontier guards was stationed at the fords, more to keep order than to disturb the travelers, who could move freely from any part of the Roman Empire to another so long as they paid the necessary tolls. Near the fords was the usual temporary shelter for wayfarers called a caravansary or *khan*.

A little east of the river, near a grove of white poplars and close to a spring that burst from the side of a small hill, John had found among the tumbled black basalt boulders a natural pulpit from which to preach to the crowds. Looking southward from Bethabara, his listeners could see the forbidding mountains of Moab. From a peak in this range, Moses had looked across Jordan into the Promised Land of Canaan which his people were to enjoy as their home: "All the land of Gilead as far as Dan, all Naphtali and the land of Ephraim and Manasseh, all the land of Judah as far as the Western Sea, the South, and the plain of the Valley of Jericho, the city of palm trees, as far as Zoar." In these mountains also was the palace-fortress of Machaerus, frontier stronghold of Herod Antipas, where he often went for feasts and wild celebrations with his Roman friends.

II

Jesus did not speak to John until they faced each other as He stood in the shallows of the Jordan to be baptized. The two were not, however, entirely strangers. Elisabeth had told her son of Mary's coming to Hebron during the time that Elisabeth was carrying John within her body. She had repeated the story Mary had told her of having been visited by an angel, and how again when, with Jesus, Joseph, and Mary had stopped at Hebron during their flight into Egypt, they had told Elisabeth and Zacharias about the angel warning them in a dream to leave Bethlehem.

That was years ago, and the memory had grown dim with the passing of the years. But when he saw Jesus standing before him now, John remembered these things Elisabeth had told him about his cousin. The slender man waiting before him to be baptized, however, seemed more like a carpenter of Nazareth than the Messiah sent from God whose coming

John had been foretelling. Uncertain just what course he should follow, he hesitated. Then as Jesus did not help him, he said quietly, "I need to be baptized by You, and are You coming to me?"

It was a dramatic moment. If Jesus accepted the designation of Messiah which John was prepared to give Him, it could be announced to the crowd who were already beginning to wonder why the prophet and the slender man confronting each other in the water did not proceed with the rite of baptism. And certainly nothing could have provided a greater fulfillment of John's preaching than his identification of the Son of God then and there.

Jesus made no move to utilize the situation for any dramatic effect, however. Instead, He spoke in a low voice which only John could hear. "Permit it to be so now," He said, "for thus it is fitting for us to fulfill all righteousness."

Because the two men were deeply imbued with the same purpose, there was between them from the first moment of meeting a communion which removed the need for words. It was a disappointment to John not to be able to identify the Divine One whose advent he had been predicting, but he recognized that Jesus' will took precedence over his own. He might have asked why Jesus should seek baptism, since the Son of God was without sin and therefore had no need to repent. And he had every right to question why he, who had announced himself as a messenger, should not be allowed the honor of recognizing the Man whose coming he had been prophesying.

These things were in John's mind as he stood facing Jesus with the water swirling about their feet, but he recognized Jesus' words, however softly spoken, as a command from God. John understood too that baptism was not, in Jesus' case, an act of repentance, an acknowledgment of sin and a washing away of all uncleanness, as it had been with the others he had baptized. Instead, this was Jesus' way of publicly announcing His subservience to the will of His Father and His willingness from thenceforward to do only God's purpose. More than that, though neither John nor the onlookers could have been expected to understand, the rite of baptism was an act of abasement for Jesus. By being washed in the water with the multitude who sought to fit themselves for the kingdom of God, He was placing Himself on their level and renouncing divinity in order to reach men's hearts, not through fear or subservience to divine will, but by means of His own humanity.

John made no further objection. As Jesus had requested, he baptized Him.

III

Until James had brought the merchant's account of John's preaching at Bethabara, Jesus had been content with His lot in Nazareth. He loved the beautiful countryside of Galilee, the mountains and plains, the fields rich with grain, the "Ho-ho-ho" of the shepherds as they called across the hilltops to each other while watching the flocks, and the fruit hanging heavy on the trees and vines. He had enjoyed the sense of comradeship with friends and neighbors as He read from the sacred scrolls in the synagogue on the Sabbath, worshiping His Father in heaven as the others did. And He particularly loved the times when the children gathered at His shop and He put aside His tools to tell them stories they so loved.

Jesus had not been wondering just when it would be that His Father would call Him to a greater sphere of activity and the beginning of His real ministry. He had not reached thirty; the people of Nazareth respected Him because of His wisdom and listened when He spoke in the synagogue, but He could not expect other people to do so. He had been content to fill His own small place in the world represented by Nazareth and its immediate surroundings, certain that God would reveal His duty to Him in good time.

Whatever sensation Jesus had expected from the simple rite of baptism, the intensity of the experience that claimed Him now came as a surprise. As He came out of the water, He stood for a moment with His eyes closed, conscious of a presence and a deeply felt communion unlike anything He had ever experienced. He opened His eyes, lifting them to heaven, and for a moment was blinded by a great light, a glory and a warmth stronger than He had ever known, even in His deepest moment of religious exaltation.

It lasted only an instant as He stood in the shallows, but in the midst of it He saw what seemed to be a vision, yet clear and distinct, the shape of a white dove descending to light upon His shoulder like the Spirit of God coming to rest upon Him. And His whole being was seized with a great and moving joy and dedication while the warmth of divine love surrounded Him.

The voice that spoke to Him then was for His ears alone. "This is My beloved Son," it said, "in whom I am well pleased."

Jesus had found the answer for which He had come to Bethabara. From thenceforward He was in God's hands, committed to obey divine will as Moses and the Children of Israel had been instructed in Egypt with God's own words:

"Now therefore, if you will indeed obey My voice and keep My covenant, then you shall be a special treasure to Me above all people."

IV

Jesus' experience during the baptism possessed His mind as He crossed the river and started toward Jerusalem for the ritual visit to the temple that He had planned before going back to Galilee. A few hours' walk brought Him to Jericho.

In one of His few praiseworthy acts, the ill-starred Archelaus had conducted aqueducts from the village of Neaera to furnish water for irrigation, and the region around Jericho now bloomed like a lush garden. Its broad streets heavily shaded by palms and towering sycamore trees against the warmth of the sun which shone intensely here, even in winter, Jericho was now one of the most important cities of Israel.

The voice which had spoken to Jesus as He came from the waters of baptism had named Him the Son of God, but being human He could still feel doubt concerning His own worthiness. And as He walked along the road, He was conscious of the need to withdraw from the world, to remove Himself like the Essenes from the temptations of the flesh in order to achieve through prayer, fasting, and contemplation a fuller understanding of the purpose of God than He had received that morning.

Behind the great spring at the edge of Jericho, said by some to be the "Fountain of Elisha" whose waters the prophet had healed of their bitterness, rose a rugged, naked, and arid height. When Jesus reached the foot of the mountain, He turned aside and began the laborious climb up the precipitous slope. The wilderness of underbrush, crags, and steep-sided gullies was a world apart from the pleasure-loving city lying below. Here, sheltered in one of the many caves that pocked the surface near the summit, Jesus drew away from the world for a period of fasting and self-discipline while He sought to find within Himself, or through revelation from His Father, the assurance of His own strength for whatever lay ahead.

He was no stranger to fasting; pious Jewish families such as that of Mary and Joseph often fasted, so it was natural for Jesus to think of abstention from food as a means of putting aside the appetites of the flesh in self-discipline. Thus had the prophets of old sought divine revelation and received it.

As the days passed and Jesus continued to fast upon the mountaintop, the insistent demands of His body, which was entirely human, tempted Him more and more to succumb. Buffeted by storms and the heat of the sun, torn by hunger and thirst, no miracle was required for Him to hear the voice of evil say, "If You are the Son of God, command that these stones become bread."

The Son of God could easily have turned stones to bread, but the act would have meant nothing, except that He could use divine power for His own satisfaction—in itself an admission of weakness. And so Jesus answered the voice sternly: "Man shall not live by bread alone, but by every word that proceeds from the mouth of God."

The voice of evil would not be silenced, however. Next the devil took Him as in a vision into Jerusalem and set Him on the pinnacle of the temple from which He could look down upon the priests as they performed the sacrifices and the Levites as they marched in the morning ritual. This time the voice of evil demanded that He perform a miracle which would announce His identity to the chief priests and to the people thronging the temple. "If You are the Son of God," the voice said, "throw Yourself down. For it is written: 'He shall give His angels charge over you,' and 'in their hands they shall bear you up, lest You dash Your foot against a stone.'" It was a passage Jesus Himself had read many times before the congregation at Nazareth, but something deep inside Him, part of the communion He had experienced during His baptism, now told Him it was His Father's will that the kingdom of God should be established first in the hearts of men.

"It is written again," He answered this new temptation, "'You shall not tempt the Lord your God.'"

Next the devil took Him in another vision to a high mountain from which He could see many of the cities of Israel and, visualized in the blue haze beyond His range of vision, the great centers of the world. And the voice of evil He had heard twice before spoke once more, daring Him to seize all He saw for Himself.

That He possessed the power to make everything in sight His own, Jesus did not for a moment doubt. So great was His faith in the Father who had spoken to Him on the banks of the Jordan that He was convinced He had only to speak and immediately, through the power of God, He would become the highest of all, Ruler even of the emperor at Rome. But He understood now that this was no more God's purpose for Him than the other temptations had been.

For the third time, Jesus answered the mocking, deriding, ever-tempting voice of evil. To use God's power for His own glorification, He knew now, would be to worship evil. There could be only one answer; the words had been spoken long ago by God Himself to Moses and came easily to Jesus' tongue. "You shall worship the Lord your God, and Him only you shall serve."

With the act of speaking the words aloud, Jesus felt His indecision and the tempting voice vanish. The will of God, He understood now, would be revealed to Him in good time.

This beginning of signs Jesus did in Cana of Galilee, and manifested His glory.

John 2:11

The success of John the Baptist in an area less than twenty miles from Jerusalem, beside one of the busiest thoroughfares for people going and coming from the Holy City, had inevitable repercussions there. The priestly group headed by the high priest Caiaphas had never allowed themselves to be disturbed by the appearance of religious fanatics who claimed to be prophets and, occasionally, the Messiah. But when an Essene, whose teachings fitted neither the liberal beliefs of the Sadducees nor the strict attendance to the Torah and its interpretation practiced by the Pharisees, gained such a large following and at the same time denounced the legal tetrarch of a province, there was grave danger that he might stir up the common people to acts of violence which conceivably could bring down the wrath of Rome upon Israel as a whole.

On the day of His return journey to Galilee that Jesus reached Bethabara, sometimes called Bethany-beyond-Jordan to distinguish it from the other Bethany that was actually a suburb of Jerusalem, a delegation of priests, Pharisees, and Levites from Jerusalem arrived there. The delegation found John near the spring just outside Bethabara, preaching in the grove of white poplars that formed his favorite amphitheater. When John had finished speaking and had baptized those who requested it, the delegation approached the lean Essene in his rough robe and leather girdle as he sat on a rock with his immediate followers surrounding him. Jesus remained in the background but John had seen Him and knew He was there.

The Jerusalem delegation was at first inclined to be contemptuous of John, but they were not fools and could see that he exerted a tremendous hold upon those who came to hear him and upon the group of men, largely Galileans and therefore doubly to be watched, who made up his immediate disciples.

"Who are you?" the chief of the delegation asked.

John realized what was behind the question and made no attempt to dissemble. "I am not the Christ," he said positively.

"Are you Elijah?" the priest insisted. The return to earth of the prophet Elijah, who according to the sacred writings had been taken bodily up into heaven, had been predicted by other prophets. It was generally believed that his coming would herald the Messiah.

"I am not," John repeated.

Are you the Prophet?"

"No."

"We must give an answer to the authorities at Jerusalem who sent us," the priest said impatiently. "What do you say of yourself?"

John turned his eyes southward to the wild country around the Sea of Judgment where he had dwelt so long in preparation for his ministry.

Large crowds had listened eagerly to John's voice every day and because of his message thousands had repented of their sins and been baptized. He experienced a natural desire to impress these haughty men too. The mere act of publicly identifying the Son of God whose coming he had announced would cause a sensation, particularly with the representatives of the temple here at Bethabara, and his own role as discoverer of the Messiah would undoubtedly be great. But John did not yield to the temptation to glorify himself.

"I am the voice of one crying in the wilderness: 'Make straight the way of the Lord,' he answered, "as the prophet Isaiah said."

The Sadducees had the answer they sought. John had admitted he was not the Messiah or even a prophet but only an itinerant preacher warning people to be conscious of their sins. There was no reason for them to take any action against him.

The Pharisees among the deputation were not content to leave matters as they were, however. Minute points of the Torah, as interpreted by the rabbis, were involved here and they never overlooked an opportunity to argue on such questions.

"Why then do you baptize if you are not the Christ, nor Elijah, nor the Prophet?" the leader asked.

John knew many of his disciples considered him to be the Messiah or at least one of the great prophets of old returned to earth. To answer truthfully the question put to him by the Pharisee, he must destroy that belief and perhaps with it their faith in him, yet he did not hesitate.

"I baptize with water," he said, "but there stands One among you whom you do not know. It is He who, coming after me, is preferred before me, whose sandal strap I am not worthy to loose."

No clearer statement of the difference in station between John and the Messiah could have been made. When guests arrived at a Jewish home, it was a mark of greatest respect on the part of the host to kneel and loosen their shoes so they could be removed and the dirt of travel washed from their feet. A murmur of disappointment went up from John's disciples at his admission that he was neither the Messiah nor even an important prophet. Some of the Galileans who had become his disciples in the belief that the Baptist was the Messiah now turned away in disappointment and began to prepare for the return home.

As Jesus' ministry expanded, John realized that his own role must grow smaller and smaller, and by the shrunken number of his disciples when he began to teach the next morning. But John was a servant of God, and, as an Essene, accustomed to denying himself in order to further divine purpose. He did not rebel against the fact of his own abasement but, as always, taught and baptized and afterwards gathered his disciples around him for a more intimate communion.

He was thus engaged on the following day when he saw Jesus standing at the edge of the group listening but doing nothing to attract attention to Himself. Forthright and honest, John could not remain silent; he could not permit himself to benefit from a refusal to call his disciples' attention to one immeasurably greater than he. "Behold! The Lamb of God who takes away the sin of the world!" he said, looking across the heads of the disciples to where Jesus stood.

Some of the Galileans among the disciples of John knew Him, and two of these, John, one of the sons of Zebedee, and Andrew, got up and left the group to follow Him as He moved away from the crowd.

"What do you seek?" He asked the two men gravely.

"Rabbi, where are You staying?" Andrew asked, using the title to which, having heard Jesus preach in the synagogue at Nazareth, he knew He was entitled.

"Come and see," Jesus told them simply and began to walk along the path leading from the grove to the caravansary nearby. The two remained with Him most of the day there and, long before it was over, they were ready to leave John—as indeed they had already decided to do—and follow Jesus. When night began to fall, Andrew went to fetch his brother Simon, John his brother James.

Simon of Bethsaida was a big man with enormous strength to haul in the nets. He was known up and down the length of the Sea of Galilee and well into the area around it as the best fisherman in the entire region. But more than for his physical prowess, he was admired because of his greatness of heart, his impetuous generosity, and his deep-seated love of God.

Like many another devout Jew, and with the natural fervor of a Galilean, Simon yearned for the kingdom of God, when the Anointed Messiah would lead Israel to its manifest destiny. Being a man of action rather than a thinker, he had never troubled himself about just how or when this would happen. When John first began to preach, though, Simon had wondered if here was not the way to gain the freedom from foreign oppression which all desired—through the Messiah whose coming the Baptist announced daily. Caught up by John's fiery spirit, Simon had dared to hope that John himself was to be that mighty leader. That is, he had been hoping it until yesterday. But now Simon was a disillusioned man, ready to go back to Galilee and his nets, to the realities that had never betrayed him as had his attempt to understand the will of God.

Andrew was in many ways more serious than Simon, for the tall fisherman, when he felt something deeply, was likely to be impetuous in both action and speech. When Andrew came to him now as he was preparing the evening meal over a small fire near the poplar grove, Simon was impressed by his brother's glowing eyes and his obvious conviction—impressed until he learned the cause.

"We have found the Messiah, Simon!" Andrew announced.

Simon looked up morosely from the fire. He had been disappointed in one possible Messiah and was not ready to run after another. Work and the satisfactions it brought were things he could understand and appreciate; these he could return to on the morrow.

"Leave the Messiahs to the priests," he growled. "Your food is ready."

"But I have found Him," Andrew insisted. "The true Messiah!"

"Who is He?"

"Jesus, the Teacher of Nazareth."

Simon already knew Jesus as an eloquent teacher in the synagogue and a carpenter of rare skill, but not as a Messiah. He and Jesus were probably even distantly related, as were so many families in Galilee—another reason why he could not consider Him divine. "Come and eat," he said. "It will calm you."

"Will you go and talk to Him?"

"Why should I?"

"John and I have been with Jesus since morning," Andrew said. "He has gone to get James."

"Does John think the Nazarene is the Messiah?" Simon asked.

"We both do."

Simon looked thoughtfully at the bed of glowing coals. John and James, the fishing partners of Simon and Andrew, worked for their father Zebedee, who operated near the city of Capernaum, one of the largest fishing establishments on the shores of the Sea of Galilee. The four were very close, with the deep, enduring friendship of men who faced danger together in the storms that often lashed the waters of this inland sea into a maelstrom. If John were so impressed by the Teacher of Nazareth, Simon told himself, there must be something more to Him than at first thought had seemed likely.

"Eat your supper," he said to Andrew. "Then we will go to see the Nazarene."

James and John were already sitting with Jesus around a small fire when Simon and Andrew approached the caravansary. When the tall fisherman loomed out of the shadows, dwarfing them all by his size, Jesus looked up and smiled. "You are Simon the son of Jonah," He said. "From now on you shall be called Cephas." The word Cephas, or Peter, meant a stone, a tribute to Simon's size and his solid strength.

A feeling warm and pleasant passed between the two men, a forerunner of the great love that was to bind Simon Peter, along with James and John, as part of Jesus' inner circle, for these three would become closest to Him. And Simon, who was here now only to please his brother Andrew and because his two friends, the sons of Zebedee, had been listening to the Nazarene Teacher, found himself sitting at the feet of Jesus, listening eagerly with the others.

The five men spent the night there together and early the next morning began preparations for the return journey to Galilee. While they were making ready, another Galilean from Bethsaida joined them. His name was Philip and when he heard them talking about Jesus and His teachings, he went in search of his brother Nathanael so that they might all journey northward together.

Nathanael was standing in the shade of a fig tree, listening to John the Baptist, when Philip approached. He was a rather deliberate man, less impetuous than most Galileans and somewhat older than Philip. Like them, he had been disappointed when John had been forced to admit yesterday that he was no more than a forerunner of the Messiah who was yet to come. But he had not let disappointment blind him to John's obvious virtues or to the truth of the message that the gaunt Essene brought in his daily sermons.

"We have found Him!" Philip cried, obviously much excited.

Nathanael regarded his brother with a tolerant smile. "Who is it this time?" he asked. Philip had been fully as enthusiastic when they had first come to John here at Bethabara.

"The One whom Moses and the prophets wrote of, Jesus of Nazareth, the son of Joseph!"

Nathanael knew Nazareth well for he lived not far away. In his estimation not even a prophet could be expected to come from so mean a place, much less the Expected One. "Can anything good come out of Nazareth?" he asked amiably.

"Come and see!" Philip urged him.

It would be simpler to let Philip have his way, Nathanael decided; the younger brother would be disillusioned soon enough. He said no more but left the shade of the fig tree and went with Philip.

Jesus and the others were standing near the caravansary, waiting for Philip to rejoin them before taking the road northward. When the two men approached, Jesus said, "Behold, an Israelite indeed, in whom is no deceit!"

Nathanael was startled. "How do You know me?" he asked. "Before Philip called you, when you were under the fig tree, I saw you," Jesus told him.

Nathanael turned to look in the direction from whence he had come. The fig tree was invisible from this point and Philip had brought him directly here, so there was no possibility that Jesus could have seen him except by some miraculous power.

Moved by an impulse he had never felt before, Nathanael said earnestly, "Rabbi, You are the Son of God!"

Jesus looked at him intently for a moment, as if He were probing Nathanael's soul. "Because I said to you, 'I saw you under the fig tree,' do you believe?" He asked. "You will see greater things than these."

Only much later did the six understand Jesus' next words: "Most assuredly, I say to you, hereafter you shall see heaven open, and the angels of God ascending and descending upon the Son of Man."

Jesus turned and started along the road that led to Galilee, none of them questioning Him further. There had been something in His face when He spoke, a glory and yet a sadness coming from depths within this man to whom they had been so powerfully drawn, depths which they sensed they could not fathom.

As John the Baptist watched Jesus depart with the six Galileans who had been among his staunchest followers, he could not help feeling lonely. His own place upon the stage of events had now been taken by another and his star was on the wane.

II

About seven and a half miles north of Nazareth near a fine spring giving an ample supply of water lay the village of Cana. Nathanael, also called Bartholomew, lived there. Since Cana was on a fairly well-traveled road between Magdala, which lay south of Capernaum on the western shore of the Sea of Galilee, and Ptolemais, or Akka, on the coast of the Great Sea, Jesus and His friends had turned westward at Magdala, leaving the lake to the east. Nazareth lay nearby but when He reached home, Jesus found that His family was at Cana helping celebrate the wedding feast of a kinsman.

Since the sons of Zebedee also were kin to the bridegroom, they all went on to Cana from which it was only a short day's walk to Capernaum where Simon Peter lived, and the fishermen could go on there tomorrow.

Mary had been busy all day at the home of their kinsman preparing for the festivities. When Jesus arrived, she welcomed Him warmly and was pleased to see Him in the company of friends and kinsmen. She had been worried when He had left so abruptly for Bethabara and Jerusalem, but now He was back and, as far as she could see at the moment, no different from what He had been before. It was true, she thought, that the men who accompanied Him were oddly deferential to Him, but for a long time now in Nazareth Jesus had been known by the title of Teacher or Rabbi, and that no doubt explained it.

Marriage was both an occasion of joy and gravity with the Galileans. Since ancient times the same ritual had been rigidly followed in the small villages and towns. First came negotiations between the families of the bride and groom during which the various details were agreed upon, including the amount of the "bride price" or *mohar* to be paid to the father of the bride. According to custom, most of the *mohar* was given to the bride by her father, to serve as her dowry and be put away in case she became a widow.

On the day of the wedding the bridegroom, wearing a crown of bright-colored flowers, marched through the town with a procession of friends who were also garlanded. The young people sang and danced and clashed cymbals along the way to drive away evil spirits by letting them know this was a wedding procession and not a funeral. After the groom had taken his bride to his home, the wedding feast was celebrated, usually until late at night. At the conclusion of the feast, the groom would carry his bride over the doorsill of the bedchamber and the ceremony would be ended.

Cana was a small village and the arrival of Jesus and those who had come with Him filled almost to overflowing the house where the feast was being held. Before long the skins of wine—always well diluted with water at such festivities—which the bridegroom had considered adequate for the feast were empty. When such a thing happened at a marriage feast, it not only brought disgrace upon the groom for being unable to provide for his guests but also was considered an ill omen with which to start married life.

Concern over the shame that would come upon their kinsman brought Mary to Jesus when the wine was used up.

"They have no wine," she said. As the head of their household, it was Jesus' duty to do whatever He could to insure that no shame came to the family. Besides, His own arrival with the six Galileans had been largely responsible for the shortage. On the other hand, He could hardly travel to Nazareth and bring wine for a feast that was already well in progress, and it was much too late to buy more now.

Jesus was fully conscious of His own responsibility as a kinsman, yet He knew that once the only step open to Him was taken, there could be no going back for long to the quiet of the house in Nazareth and the music of children's laughter as they listened to the stories He told.

Mary had instructed the servants to do whatever Jesus bade and He saw that they were waiting now for His bidding. There was plenty of water; thick stone waterpots stood ready, each partly filled as was required for the ritual purification by devout Jews before eating, and other containers had also been filled by the women in anticipation of the feast.

"Fill the waterpots with water," Jesus told the servants.

They were quickly filled but it was still water, having been poured from the very jars in which the women had brought it from the spring.

"Draw some out now, and take it to the master of the feast," He directed them.

The servants obeyed Him, wondering what strange game this was where a man pretended that water was wine. He might convince Himself that it was wine, but the thirsty Galileans would raise an outcry the moment they tasted it and found only water. Customarily the first bowl of any new mixture was brought to the master in charge of the feast so that he could taste it and be sure it was of a quality to be served at so important a function. The master of the feast took the cup from his lips and nodded to the servants to go ahead and serve the wine.

But there was a frown on his face as he went to find the bridegroom. "Every man at the beginning sets out the good wine," he said severely, for it was bad to break a precedent. "When the guests have well drunk, then the inferior wine is served. But you have kept the good wine until now!"

The bridegroom could not explain what had happened, but the servants knew and were not long in making the story known. Word quickly spread that He who had been known as a carpenter of Nazareth had accomplished the miracle of turning water into wine. The gaiety of the feast now was quickly replaced by fear, and being afraid, the people resented Him who was responsible for their uncertainty. By the time the feast ended, Jesus, who had sought only to keep shame from His kinsman, was being shunned by the crowd.

What had been done at Cana that night, however, was soon noised abroad. There could be no going back now to the quiet life in Nazareth that Jesus had loved so much. From henceforth His sphere of activity was to be an ever-widening one, like the circular ripples that spread from the dropping of a stone into the center of a pool.

And rose up and thrust Him out of the city; and they led Him to the brow of the hill on which their city was built, that they might throw Him down over the cliff.

Luke 4:29

Unlike John the Baptist, who had preached in a natural amphitheater under the trees at Bethabara, Jesus taught at first in the synagogues where the people gathered to worship God on the Sabbath and during the weekday services. In every town where any large number of Jews lived, some building or portion of it was set apart as a place of worship. Where a village was small and contained only a few devout Jews, worship services were held in a house. Everywhere, the internal arrangements were generally the same.

The men sat on benches occupying the main floor of the building, while the women were restricted to a gallery protected by a wooden lattice. In the center of the main floor was a small elevated platform called the *bima* and upon it the desk or *luach*, from which the Law was read.

Praying toward the east was forbidden by the Law, so the entrance to a synagogue was usually on the eastern side with the congregation facing away from this direction. The ark, a cabinet in which the scrolls of the Torah were kept, was usually against the south wall with the seats for the elders before it. Generally the gallery for the women was at the north end. Over the lintel of the door a carving usually ornamented the wood or stone of which the structure was built. Sometimes this was the traditional seven-branched candlestick, but an open flower set between two lambs of the Passover, bunches of grapes, vines, leaves, or occasionally a pot of manna such as the Children of Israel had fed upon in the wilderness could serve instead.

According to the Law, no synagogue could be erected in a village unless there were ten batlanim, men who could spare the time to oversee the worship and administration. In practice there was usually no difficulty here, for attendance at worship was a privilege highly regarded by the Jews.

On the evening before the Sabbath, each household prepared for the coming day of worship. The Sabbath lamp was lit and the best raiment put out to be worn on the morrow. The table was set with the best meal of the week and the *qiddush* or benediction spoken over a cup of wine liberally diluted with water, which was then drunk. On the Sabbath morning the devout hastened with quick steps to the house of worship, showing their eagerness to serve the Lord; by ancient usage the returning gait was always slow and lagging, expressing regret at leaving.

Although the chazan was officially the leader of the congregation, the elders or rulers, called the *zeqenim*, were the most honored members. They also formed the local court or Sanhedrin, and were responsible to the Great Sanhedrin at Jerusalem in both religious and civil disputes.

The Sabbath devotions were opened by chanting a series of prayers which began: "Blessed are You, O Lord, King of the world, who forms the light and creates the darkness, who makes peace and creates everything." They ended with: "Blessed be the Lord who in love chose His people Israel."

Following this, the *Shema*, or creed, was recited. In it the worshiper willingly took upon himself the yoke of the kingdom of heaven and the yoke of the commandments. Other eulogies and benedictions followed with such special prayers as the season or occasion dictated.

The liturgy finished, the chazan removed the roll of the Law from the ark where it was kept, and various persons chosen for the day read portions of it. Selections from the scroll of the prophets were also read, usually by the teacher who was to deliver the main address or sermon during the remainder of the worship period.

Most of the congregation, especially in Galilee, neither spoke nor understood Hebrew well, so an interpreter known as the methurgeman, or more colloquially a dragoman, translated the words into the Aramaic language. He was not allowed to use a written translation, lest it become regarded as authoritative, but rendered the Hebrew into the common tongue at each service. Actually the members of the congregation were usually quite familiar with the passage being read, and the methurgeman gave the translations in a brief and almost synoptic form.

When a popular rabbi was preaching, the synagogue was usually filled to overflowing. And since teachers customarily went from place to place for the purpose of giving the sermon, or *derashah*, the presence of a visiting rabbi was not at all uncommon. The rare simplicity of Jesus' sermons had a wide appeal, and even before the miracle at Cana He was already well known as a teacher in Nazareth and the surrounding area. Neither interlarding His discourse with complicated references to details of the Law nor speaking condescendingly as did the Pharisees, He taught simply but clearly the lessons of man's duty to God and how that duty should be discharged. Referring often to the ancient writings of the Jews, He drew new interpretations from them which were easily understood by everyone.

In less than a day's journey from His regular dwelling place in Nazareth, Jesus could easily reach most of the centers around Galilee where He spoke on the Sabbath. The six Galileans who had left John the Baptist to follow Him had gone back to their homes and their daily tasks after the wedding feast at Cana, so He was usually alone as He moved about. He had not performed any further miracles but His forthright preaching that "the time is fulfilled and the kingdom of God is at hand. Repent, and believe in the gospel" found eager ears here just as when

John had spoken much the same words in the wilderness at the fords of the Jordan.

For a brief period after the miracle at Cana, there was no marked change in Jesus' life or work. Then two things happened which considerably affected both. The first also occurred at Cana.

II

Herod Antipas was a rich man. Having inherited great wealth from his father, he had shrewdly invested much of it in lush vineyards and fields around the Sea of Galilee and among the rich valley lands beside the Jordan. He was fortunate in being served by many honest and capable men, not the least of whom was Chuza, his steward in the region around Capernaum. Conscientious, capable, and pious, Chuza managed to serve his master well and at the same time earn the respect of his fellows for his honesty and business acumen.

Chuza had prospered, too. He had a comfortable home overlooking the lake, wore fine clothes, and was respected as a nobleman in both the marketplace and the synagogue. His wife had servants to run the house; his young son was his favorite child. By all ordinary standards, Chuza was well favored, but when his son became ill, even Herod's own physician was not able to help him. Soon it was apparent that the child would die unless a marked improvement in his condition quickly took place.

Distraught, for he loved the boy dearly, Chuza did not know where to turn until an old serving woman came to him. "Master," she said, "I have heard the fishermen talking of a Nazarene who performs miracles. If you went to Him, He might help the boy."

On any other occasion, Chuza would have scoffed at the rumor, for tales of miraculous cures were common in this region where so many of the afflicted flocked to the healing springs along the lake shore.

"Was it a miracle of healing?" he asked.

"He turned water to wine—at a wedding feast. The fisherman drank some himself and said it was better wine even than that purchased here in Galilee."

Chuza hesitated to dismiss the story. He had seen the trick performed by traveling magicians but he had never known them to offer others the wine they claimed to have produced. "Who was the fisherman?" he asked.

"James, one of the sons of Zebedee."

Zebedee was a highly respected elder in the synagogue at Capernaum, and his sons were well known to Chuza. They would not be deceived by a magician's trick or tell an idle story just for effect.

"Where was this done?" he inquired.

"In Cana. But the Teacher called Jesus is of Nazareth."

Chuza knew the town and, like Nathanael, he thought, "Can any good thing come out of Nazareth?" But he was also desperate and since it was not far, he determined to seek out this man called Jesus. Ordering a horse made ready he started at once but learned when he reached Nazareth that Jesus was at Cana. Hurrying on he inquired in the village and was directed to the home where Jesus was visiting.

Chuza was disappointed by his first sight of the Nazarene. To him, Jesus looked no different from hundreds of men he saw every day in his travels about Galilee. His robe was of common cloth and the sandals on His feet had obviously been made in a village shop. Nevertheless, the nobleman had come this far and nothing was to be gained by not asking for help, even from such an unlikely source.

"Come to Capernaum with me, Master, and heal my son," he begged. "He lies at the point of death."

Jesus knew Chuza by reputation as a good man, in spite of the fact that he served an evil master. He was sure the reason the steward had come to Him for help was that he had heard of the miracle at the wedding feast. Yet compassionate as He always was for the sorrows of others, He could understand the concern of a father for his child.

"Except you see signs and wonders you will not believe," Jesus said quietly.

In his anguish, Chuza did not understand. "Sir," he begged again. "Come down to Capernaum before my child dies."

"Go your way," Jesus told him then. "Your son lives."

Chuza could not believe the child had been healed by the simple words. His coming to Jesus had been an act of desperation, and he had really not expected anything from it. Sorrowfully, he mounted his horse and started on the return journey to Capernaum.

He was hardly halfway home when he saw men riding toward him. As they came closer, he recognized two of his servants. Strangely enough their faces were joyful.

"Your son lives!" one of them called out to him while still some distance away.

The servants could tell the happy father only that the child had suddenly improved and his wife had sent them posthaste to find him, knowing he would want the news as quickly as possible. In his joy at learning that his son was safe, Chuza quite forgot his interview with Jesus until he was entering the outskirts of Capernaum. Then a thought came to him and he turned to the servants who rode behind him.

"What hour was it when the boy began to improve?" he asked.

"The seventh hour, master," he was told. "The fever left him suddenly. Why do you ask?"

Chuza did not answer. How could he explain to them that at just the seventh hour, the carpenter of Nazareth had said to him in Cana, "Go your way. Your son lives"?

III

With His fame as a teacher and a worker of miracles growing daily now, the time had come for Jesus to reveal His identity and the mission for which He had been sent to earth. Naturally He chose for this important announcement the synagogue at Nazareth. On the Sabbath following the healing of Chuza's son, He entered the place of worship as usual and, when the time came for reading a passage from the writings of the prophets, He took up the scroll. Unrolling it, He began to read from the writings of Isaiah:

"The Spirit of the Lord is upon Me, because He has anointed Me to preach the gospel to the poor; He has sent Me to heal the brokenhearted, to proclaim liberty to the captives and recovery of sight to the blind, to set at liberty those who are oppressed; to proclaim the acceptable year of the Lord."

The reading finished, He calmly rolled up the scroll again and put it down. The listeners had heard the passage read many times before because scholars considered that it referred to the Messiah, whose coming Isaiah had so fervently predicted. And yet when Jesus spoke again, His words struck them like a bolt of lightning.

"Today this Scripture is fulfilled in your hearing," He said loudly enough for His voice to be heard by those who were listening outside.

The people of Nazareth had known Jesus as a good neighbor and a kind, patient, and deeply religious man who had taught their children, built their homes, carved plows for the farmers, and made furniture in His shop. A few had recognized a change in Him when He returned from Bethabara, but many others baptized by John had also changed, so this was in itself nothing unusual. There had been murmurings of amazement at the story of His turning water to wine at Cana and also when He had cured the son of Chuza in Capernaum. But when He did no miraculous things in Nazareth itself, the memory of those miracles was quickly forgotten.

Because of Jesus' eloquence and the simplicity of His teaching, the synagogue was filled every Sabbath that it was known He would speak, and today the congregation had spilled over into the yard. Some in Galilee had already named Him a prophet, but no one had been prepared for His dramatic announcement that He was the Anointed One whose coming Isaiah had predicted in the eloquent passage read to them that morning. If this were true, it was indeed a wondrous thing; but how could they be expected to believe it of one they had known first as a boy here in Nazareth and later as a skilled carpenter, the son of a carpenter, and the breadwinner for His family after His father's death?

Understandably, most of those who heard Jesus in Nazareth that morning found it impossible to believe He was the Messiah. And if He were not, then He was guilty in their eyes of blasphemy for naming Himself the Anointed One. Blasphemy was the one crime that could stir any devout Jew to anger, for the very act of blasphemy was a mortal affront to the Most High God. In the Books of the Law the penalty for the crime was death by stoning, the traditional method of execution for those guilty of the worst of crimes.

Murmurs of anger were already beginning to rise when Jesus spoke again, but the very boldness of His address and His militant bearing kept even the hardiest among them from crying out the dread charge against Him inside the synagogue.

"You will tell the physician to go heal himself," He said to them. "You will ask why he does not do here in his own city what you hear he has done in Capernaum. Truly, I say to you, no prophet is accepted in his own country."

On these last words, Jesus' voice had grown sad. But now it rang out challengingly. "But I tell you truly, many widows were in Israel in the days of Elijah, when the heaven was shut up three years and six months, and there was a great famine throughout all the land; but to none of them was Elijah sent except to Zarephath, in the region of Sidon, to a woman who was a widow. And many lepers were in Israel in the time of Elisha the prophet, and none of them was cleansed except Naaman the Syrian."

Familiar as the congregation was with the ancient stories from the history of Israel, this was more of an insult than they could stand. Naaman was not a Jew nor was the woman of Zarephath, yet because both of them had obeyed the commands of God as spoken through the prophets, they had received God's favor. At the same time, as Jesus reminded the congregation, Jews had been denied that favor for themselves because they had not deserved it.

The anger of the listeners had been welling up while Jesus talked. At the end of the service they surrounded Him as He left the building, shouting and gesticulating in a frenzy of indignation. When He made no move to justify Himself or retract anything He had said, He was seized and hustled from the yard of the synagogue by a mob of angry men.

Up the winding pathway leading to the summit of the rocky crag jutting out above it the crowd dragged Jesus, pummeling and cursing Him all the way. People who had been His friends and neighbors yesterday spat upon Him now and called Him a blasphemer as He was dragged to the very brow of the crest. Nor was there any doubt about their intention to kill Him; the body of a man pushed or thrown from the crag would be broken and crushed on the rocks below.

At the brow of the hill, however, even the angriest drew back, waiting for someone else to make the first move to shove Jesus over the brink. Bleeding from the many times He had been knocked to the ground, His robe torn and soiled, He faced His executioners calmly. Had He chosen to speak then, Jesus could have convinced them that He was innocent of blasphemy. The miracles at Cana and Capernaum, the fact that John the Baptist had publicly designated Him the Lamb of God, the circumstances surrounding His birth and flight into Egypt—all these would have supported His claim to be the Son of God.

Jesus spoke of none of these things, however, but faced the crowd with His back to the edge of the cliff. Any one of them could have thrust Him over it, but no man moved as He started walking toward the now silent mob. Asked what it was in His manner that cowed them, no one of those facing Him could have said. But as He moved toward them, they drew back and, like guilty children caught in an act of mischief, made a clear way for

Him through their midst. Nor did any man so much as reach out to touch Him when He walked past them and started down the path leading to the town and His own house. Only when He had disappeared, did they slink away, silent, to their homes.

Jesus left the next day for Capernaum. Almost as if the rejection by His fellow townsmen were a pattern for the future, He was never again to know any place as a real home.

Follow Me, and I will make you become fishers of men.

Mark 1:17

But fruitful vines and the fat olives' freight,
And harvests heavy with their fruitful weight,
Adorn our fields: And on the cheerful green,
The grazing flocks and lowing herds are seen. . . .
Perpetual spring our happy climate sees,
Twice breed the cattle and twice bear the trees.

So wrote a Roman poet in praise of his beloved homeland, but almost he might have been writing of the lovely region around the Sea of Galilee, and especially of the Plain of Gennesaret near where the Jordan, icy cold and bluish in color, plunged into the harp-shaped surface of the lake.

Capernaum lay almost at the edge of the plain, and here Jesus began a new phase of the mission He had been allowed to glimpse on the high peak in Judea, where He had been tempted to proclaim Himself king over all the world. In Nazareth a few days before, He had announced Himself as the Messiah and had been rejected. Here in the teeming cities of the lake region He could hope to be better received, but for a while He made no further claims to divinity.

The Galileans were a many-sided people composed of diverse types and nationalities. In the cities of the lake one might meet in the short space of an hour representatives from at least half the countries of the empire. Jews from the strong peasant stock of the region, almost militantly devout, yielded to no one. Pharisees and scribes from Judea walked the streets, their heads held high in contempt for the often defiled *am ha-arets* or common people, their tasseled robes much in evidence and phylacteries, small boxes containing portions of the holy writings, prominently worn upon their foreheads and wrists. Romans in togas and military trappings rubbed elbows with tall Nabateans from the east in flowing robes, hooded men with dark skins who kept proudly aloof. Swarthy Syrians from Antioch and the cities to the north argued with fat merchants from Damascus. Lean Phoenician sailors from the seacoast discussed the prices of precious stones and spices with Persians from the lands to the east. A giant Nubian, the slave of a Roman officer, stood head and shoulders above the crowd, his ebony-black skin shining in the always bright sunlight. Merchants, artisans, caravan drivers, traders—men of every occupation and ancestry rubbed elbows with beggars and with women whose bright garments and jingling ornaments proclaimed their profession. In fact, the small arc where the Way of the Sea, the Via Maris of the Romans, followed the northern shore of the Sea of Galilee before bearing westward again, was truly a crossroads of the world, joining the ancient east of the Persians to the brawling west of the Romans, the sophistication of Egypt in the south to the peasant simplicity of the Jews from the Galilean villages among the hills to the north.

Near the eastern boundary of Galilee, separating it from the domain ruled over by the tetrarch Philip, the mountainous backbone of land that rose steadily as one traveled eastward from the Great Sea, dropped suddenly in the form of a great divide at the bottom of which flowed the River Jordan. Arising on the western side of Mount Hermon, the Jordan flowed for only a short distance at a level above that of the Great Sea to the west. Dropping steadily in the deep rift at Lake Huleh, sometimes called Lake Semechonitis, where it first spread out for a short distance, the river was only about the height of a tall man above the level of the Mare Nostrum, as the Romans called the Great Sea. South of Lake Huleh the river again descended to plunge into the Sea of Galilee, more recently renamed by Herod Antipas the Lake of Tiberias in honor both of his new city located upon its western shore and the Emperor Tiberius in Rome. Here the lake bed was more than six hundred feet beneath sea level.

On the eastern side of the lake the hills rose to a high plateau upon which stood several Greek cities belonging to the Decapolis. Roman villas lined a part of this eastern shore, with terraced gardens descending the hillsides and marble stairways leading down to the water where sumptuous pleasure barges awaited their owners. Because of the hills surrounding the lake, the winds often spilled down upon it suddenly, setting up storms which made the trade of the fisherman a hazardous one.

A number of cities surrounded the Sea of Galilee. Located at its extreme northern tip was Bethsaida, often called "Fish Town." Built by the tetrarch Philip and also named Julias to curry favor with the Romans, it was located a short distance from where the Jordan entered the lake. A populous center, Bethsaida was the seat of Philip's court during most of the year. A group of springs in the hills behind it poured their water through a Roman aqueduct to supply the city, the overflow cascading into the lake. Striking the cold stream of the Jordan from the north as it plunged into the lake, this current set up a swirling motion and, perhaps because of the sharp change in water temperature at this point, fish in huge numbers frequented the area. A traveler on the Via Maris could easily see them leaping in great shoals and often the water seemed almost alive.

A short distance westward from Bethsaida was the customs house marking the boundary between the domain of Philip and Herod Antipas. Beyond this lay the beautiful and lush Plain of Gennesaret and the bustling city of Capernaum, where the great caravan road from Damascus bore westward away from the lake to the seacoast.

Southward from Capernaum along the shore lay Magdala and a little beyond it Herod's magnificent new city of Tiberias. Shunned at first by devout Jews because it had reputedly been built on the site of an old cemetery, Tiberias was now a busy government center. A few miles south of it another group of springs, hot and heavily mineraled, burst from the rocky hillside. Here the sick, particularly those with inflamed or stiffened joints, came to bathe.

All along the western shore of the lake the pungent odor of drying fish rose from sheds built at the water's edge. Many women worked in the sheds, splitting, cleaning, and drying fish caught by the men who plied the boats on the lake or fished along the shore. The greatest single business in all the lake region, the drying of fish gave Galilee a product highly prized as far away even as Jerusalem.

It was in this busy, often turbulent region that Jesus began to preach.

II

Accustomed to the hills of southern Galilee from whose peaks He could watch the sun dip into the Great Sea beyond Mount Carmel, Jesus found the depression between the hills where the lovely, harp-shaped Sea of Galilee lay an entirely different world. Alternately storm-tossed and glassy smooth, the lake dominated the scene as it dominated the lives of the people around it. Pelicans dropped like plummets from clear skies to seize unwary fish. Graceful black cormorants stalked in the shadows, now and then stabbing their beaks into the water to seize their prey. Boats of every size with sails of every color floated on the water, while the occupants busied themselves fishing.

Jesus could not help missing the olive groves of the Nazareth region, the locust-bean trees, and the beauty of the iris. But here among the jagged piles of black volcanic rocks that sequestered small grassy areas, thistle, wild fennel, and yellow chrysanthemums grew. And beside the brooks that came tumbling down from the rocky hillsides stood heavy thickets of oleander and chaste trees.

On the Plain of Gennesaret, however, palms, figs, walnuts, olives, vines heavy with grapes, citrons, and all manner of delicate fruits and vegetables flourished. Grain, stalks were bowed almost to the ground at harvest time, and even during winter the shores were green and in spring roses could be picked on every hillside. For three of the four seasons the climate was pleasant and mild, never cold as in the higher elevations of northern Galilee. Only in summer, when the rays of the sun poured down into the cup in which the lake lay and no breeze swept the area, was the climate in the least oppressive. Then all who could retired to the hillsides for a season.

One of the busiest centers along the lakeshore, Capernaum possessed the largest synagogue in that region, built for the people by a respected Roman centurion named Paulos who lived there. It was here that Jesus began to teach on the Sabbath, and, because the people were more tolerant in their thinking than the villagers of Nazareth, He immediately began to excite comment.

Isaiah had foretold the coming of the Messiah to this land in one of the most beautiful passages among his often lyrical writings:

> The land of Zebulun and the land of Naphtali . . .
> By the way of the sea, beyond the Jordan,
> In Galilee of the Gentiles.
> The people who walked in darkness
> Have seen a great light;
> Those who dwelt in the land of the shadow of death,
> Upon them a light has shined.

Jesus' coming to Galilee was in every sense a fulfillment of this prophecy, especially during the first months of His ministry. When not teaching during the Sabbath and weekday services in the synagogue, He went about the city and along the surrounding shoreline, speaking to any who would listen. His favorite spot soon came to be a small cove along the shore north of Capernaum, beside the road leading to Bethsaida-Julias. Here He could be heard, not only by the crowds who followed Him but by the fishermen who waded in the shallows near the shore with their robes tucked up while with skillful movements they threw out the broad circular nets used for shallow-water fishing.

A larger net was used by the boats which usually fished in pairs at night. Ordinarily one or more nets were spread out by two boats and then dragged together so that the trapped fish could be hauled into the boats along with the nets. Still other fishermen worked along the shore using hooks of iron fastened to long cords which they tossed out into deeper water. The catch was either put into a pouch hanging from the waist, or strung on a cord attached to the fisherman's foot.

One day when Jesus walked along the shore as was His custom, an unusually large group of people followed Him. In their eagerness to hear, they spilled over the confines of the small natural amphitheater and threatened to push Him into the shallows of the lake. Simon Peter and Andrew, with James and John, the sons of Zebedee who were their fishing companions, had been fishing all night but had caught nothing. Now they had brought their boats into the shallows and were standing in the water washing out the nets before spreading them on the shore to dry. While they worked, they listened to Jesus, as the fishermen often did when He taught on the shore of the lake.

The press of the crowd becoming too great, Jesus stepped into Simon's boat and asked him to pull out a little way from the shore. From this vantage point He could still be heard, for the walls of the cove were almost like an amphitheater. Sitting there in the gently rolling boat, He spoke to the crowd, teaching them the same lessons of tolerance, understanding, and love for each other that He had taught the children of Nazareth. To these He added the stirring message He had brought to the synagogue in His home city, that the kingdom of heaven was at hand and that in order to prepare themselves for a place in it, people should repent of their sins. But He did not stress here, as He had in Nazareth, His own identity as the Messiah.

When Jesus had finished teaching, He turned to thank Simon Peter who had been holding the boat motionless with an oar pressed against the bottom. Peter was tired; all night long he had cast out and drawn in the heavy nets, weighted at the edges to make them sink and trap the fish, with but little result. His discouragement at having worked fruitlessly through the night showed in his face, and Jesus was moved by it.

"Launch out into deep water," He said, "and let down your nets for a catch."

Peter hesitated. "Master," he protested, "we have toiled all night and caught nothing."

Jesus did not answer but continued to look at him levelly, almost as if He were testing him. The two had not been together much since they had journeyed back to Galilee from Bethabara and had attended the wedding feast at Cana. Some of Peter's enthusiasm for following Jesus may even have waned, especially after Cana, for nothing else of a startling nature had happened and he had heard how Jesus' own people at Nazareth had rejected Him.

Whatever doubts Simon Peter felt, however, they evaporated now before the quiet look in Jesus' eyes. "Nevertheless at Your word," he said, "I will let down the net."

Andrew brought the nets, which had been drying in the sun, and the two brothers began to row the boat out upon the lake. Fishing with boats was almost always carried on at night, and since it was already well into the day, they could not have much hope of a catch. Notwithstanding, they let their nets down into the water as Jesus directed, paying them out in the circular pattern used to trap the fish.

Though to a master fisherman like Simon Peter, it might have seemed a foolish waste of time, it did not take long for him to realize that something unusual was happening. The circle of water encompassed within the confines of the net suddenly began to boil with fish, and when the two men tried to draw in the net, the fibers of the cords started to part under the weight of their catch.

James and John, with their father Zebedee, were still in the shallows with the other boat. When Peter signaled them to come and help pull the net, they got into the boat and rowed hurriedly out to where the two fishermen were struggling desperately to save both the net and their tremendous catch.

Even with five men working and two boats, the catch was so large that both boats were soon in danger of sinking. Very much afraid now, Peter prostrated himself in the boat at Jesus' feet.

"Depart from me, O Lord," he begged, "for I am a sinful man!"

Jesus merely smiled and with a gesture that took in not only Simon and Andrew in the boat with Him but James and John in the other boat, said quietly, "Come after Me, and I will make you fishers of men."

Their apprehension calmed, the men worked together to bring in the catch. Along the shore the strange phenomenon of a net filled in the daytime to bursting had already begun to attract attention. When the boats finally reached the shore and the fishing establishment of Zebedee, a great crowd had gathered, but the two pairs of brothers paused only to help deliver the catch to the fishhouse.

This done, they left boats and nets and followed Jesus.

III

Although Capernaum had never been known for the piety of its inhabitants, being second only perhaps to Magdala in wickedness, the manner of Jesus' teaching in the synagogue there, as well as His doctrine that the kingdom of heaven was at hand, drew considerable attention. He preached now with an almost militant authority, as if He were giving the Law Himself rather than merely interpreting it as the scribes did.

The Sabbath after the four fishermen gave up their work to become His disciples, Jesus entered the synagogue with them. When the time came to speak, He rose and began to teach once again. This time, however, there was an interruption. Among those in the synagogue was a man so afflicted in mind it appeared that two people inhabited his body, one good and one evil. This type of illness was not at all uncommon, and its victims were generally believed to be possessed by a devil or an evil spirit.

While Jesus was speaking, the sick man stood up and cried out loudly, "What have we to do with You, Jesus of Nazareth? Did You come to destroy us? I know who You are—the Holy One of God!" A sudden silence fell upon the congregation, but before any further commotion could arise, Jesus said quietly, "Be quiet, and come out of him!"

Immediately the sick man fell down upon the floor in a convulsion, a not unusual thing in such cases. This time, however, there was a difference; when the man's spasm was over, he seemed to have lost his illness entirely, and went out of the synagogue praising God for the miracle that had made him whole.

Jesus and His disciples left for Peter's house as soon as the Sabbath service was ended, but word of the miraculous cure of the demoniac was already racing through the city. Soon the sick and afflicted began to converge upon Peter's house from all parts of Capernaum, stumbling or crawling through the streets, while those unable to walk implored friends and relatives to bear them to the healer.

Before nightfall a large crowd had gathered around the small house, filling the courtyard where Jesus was performing His miracles of healing. To all who sought Him, including Peter's mother-in-law, whose fever He healed, Jesus gave Himself unstintingly. But when some of the sick insisted on naming Him the Christ, He rebuked them gently and told them not to speak.

I have not come to call the righteous, but sinners, to repentance.

Luke 5:32

The household of Simon Peter was still asleep when Jesus rose before dawn and left the house. Threading His way along deserted streets, He came to the outskirts of the city and began to climb the rocky hillside, following a path that terminated in a small isolated plateau. On the hilltop the air was fresh and clean as it had been among the hills of Nazareth, and filled with the fragrance of flowers blooming in the meadow. As dawn began to dispel the mists shrouding the narrow lowland along both sides of the Jordan, He knelt to pray.

Gradually the rays of the rising sun revealed details of the countryside among the mountains to the east. Across the lake it bathed with a warm glow the marble columns of Hippos, known as "the city on a hill which cannot be hidden" because it was visible at almost any point around the lake. As the sun rose higher, the white buildings of Bethsaida-Julias, the tetrarch Philip's capital at the northern end of the lake, took form and the voices of the fishermen, still invisible in their boats because of the veil of mist that shrouded the lake at night, could be heard across the water as they returned home with their catch.

Slowly the lovely new city of Tiberias materialized on the western shore. Symbol of heathen rule, it was nevertheless beautiful in its pristine whiteness against the background of the jagged black basalt cliffs overlooking the lake. Nearby was smaller Magdala, looking almost innocent in the morning light in spite of its brazen sinfulness. From His lofty perch Jesus could look down upon the whole lake region, asleep now and for a brief period untroubled by human complaints and misery.

In Simon Peter's home, almost directly below where Jesus was still in prayer, the household began to stir. When Peter discovered that Jesus had left during the night, he went to confer with the sons of Zebedee but no one knew where He had gone. With the people already beginning to gather in the street before the house, demanding the attention of the Nazarene healer, the three were at a loss to know what to do.

The dilemma was partly resolved when a shepherd who had been tending his flock on one of the small meadows behind the city reported seeing Jesus following a cliffside path some time before dawn. The people outside were growing restless, so the disciples decided to go into the hills and seek the Master, as they often called Him now. Those of the crowd who were able to walk followed, and a considerable procession, growing all the while, fell in behind Peter's tall figure as he climbed the narrow path.

Jesus heard the clamor of the crowd when they were still some distance below Him, but He made no move to go and meet them. Peter was the first to reach His side, puffing a little and red-faced from the climb.

"All are seeking you, Master," he said with a note of reproof in his voice.

Because of his size, his wide acquaintance in the region of the lake, and because it had been in his house that miracles of healing had been performed, the people naturally looked upon Simon Peter as the leader of those who were following Jesus. So he could hardly be blamed for feeling hurt that the man he served had left that morning without telling him where He was going.

Jesus did not explain His action, perhaps sensing that it would be difficult for Peter and the others to understand that His mission was not simply to restore broken and diseased bodies but to heal the souls of men with a new medicine of infinite power. Instead He said simply, "I must preach the kingdom of God to the other cities also, because for this purpose I have been sent."

Seeking new listeners now, Jesus began going from city to city while the crowds grew larger and the fame of His healing, if not of His teaching, spread abroad. People thronged to Him from all of Galilee and the cities of the Decapolis across the lake, even from as far away as Judea and Jerusalem and the other side of the lower Jordan. Soon the synagogues could no longer hold those who came, and Jesus was forced to teach as had John, using any open space large enough to accommodate the crowd.

II

Of all the diseases to which man became victim, none was so dreaded as leprosy. No remedy for this malady had been included in the ancient writings of the Torah and a sufferer from leprosy was treated literally as if he were already dead. He at all times had to have the appearance of a mourner, his clothes rent, his hair and beard unkempt. The lower part of his face had to be almost continually covered, a precaution probably taken originally to hide the thickening of the tissues about the nose and below the eyes that was one of the earliest signs of the disease.

Wherever he went the leper was required to announce his presence with the mournful cry of "Unclean! Unclean!" a signal for all to draw away lest they be contaminated by the dread scourge. Lepers could mingle only with their own kind and could not enter the temple at Jerusalem nor any walled city on pain of being lashed with not less than forty lashes. Since all religious authorities admitted to being utterly without power to cure the leper, what help he obtained could come only from God.

On one of the rare occasions when Jesus happened to be alone, He was walking by the lake and a leper approached Him. Jesus could have drawn Himself away without incurring any onus, for the leper was forbidden to come nearer than four cubits. Instead, however, Jesus waited until the man approached, crawling upon the ground and voicing his cry of "Unclean!" as was required. The odor of his uncleanness went with him, for lepers avoided bathing lest they defile any source of water.

When the desperately sick man was the required four cubits away, he looked up at Jesus and said piteously, "Lord, if You are willing, You can make me clean!"

Jesus recognized more in the sick man than simply the desire to be healed. The words, "Lord, if You are willing, You can make me clean," were in themselves a statement of complete faith and trust, such as one gives only to God. And being who He was, Jesus could not repudiate the faith of the sick man. Stooping, He did what no Pharisee, no rabbi, and not even any devout Jew would have done; He touched the leper and said, "I am willing; be cleansed."

At the touch of Jesus' hand, the disease vanished and the man stood up and groveled no more. He sought words to express his gratitude but Jesus forestalled him. "See that you tell no one," He directed, "but go your way, show yourself to the priest, and offer the gift that Moses commanded."

The man understood His instructions for it was expressly stated in the Torah: "This shall be the law of the leper for the day of his cleansing: He shall be brought to the priest," and numerous ritual acts were listed which had to be carried out to complete the cleansing. So great was this leper's joy at being healed that on the way he forgot the command of Jesus and told everyone he met what had happened. Thus news of this greatest of all Jesus' miracles spread rapidly, and soon He could no longer enter a city openly because of the crowds, and hundreds followed Him even into the desert country away from the lake.

The long days of teaching and healing were exhausting and when Jesus voiced a wish to return to Capernaum and rest awhile, Simon Peter attempted to protect Him. The journey was made by boat and the arrival timed for early morning, when few people would be about to spread word of His coming. Unfortunately, Simon's boat fell in with the fishing fleet which was returning from the teeming waters where the Jordan plunged into the lake. And, since the fishermen knew Jesus by sight, word spread quickly that He had returned to Capernaum. As always, the sick and the afflicted stormed Simon's house and the streets around it, but the tall fisherman took strenuous action to keep them away so that Jesus could have a period of companionship and discussion with the men who were closest to Him. He shut the gate to the courtyard and posted strong guards so none could enter.

III

Arza, the coppersmith, had been ill and now lay paralyzed. One side of his body was useless, and even if he lived, he knew he would never wield the hammer or pump the bellows again. He had been unconscious when Jesus had performed the miracles in Capernaum several months before, and having heard people say that the press of the crowds following the miracle-worker was now so great that He did not enter cities, Arza had almost given up hope of ever reaching the Nazarene. When he was told on the morning of Jesus' visit to Capernaum that the prophet of Nazareth was at the home of Simon Peter, Arza sent his son posthaste to beg that Jesus visit him.

When the boy returned, Arza saw in his face that he had failed. "Simon has shut up the courtyard," his son reported. "But even if he had not, you could not reach the Teacher. The streets are packed all around the house and they say Jesus is only resting and teaching there and will not heal any more while He is in Capernaum."

Arza could not accept failure. If the Nazarene did not heal him, he might as well be dead.

"Go hire four strong men," he told the boy. "Have them come here at once."

"But why, father?"

"To carry me to the Nazarene."

"The streets are packed. You could not get through."

"Is the road of the roof blocked?" Since many of the buildings in Capernaum had common walls, as in most cities, it was possible to travel from one rooftop to the other. People frequently used this route when visiting in the cool of the evening, hence the reference to the "road of the roof."

"No," the boy said, "most of the people are in the street." Then his face fell. "But it will take all you have saved to hire the men. And if they fail—"

"They will not fail," Arza said. "They must not. Hurry now before Jesus leaves Simon's house."

With so many people thronging the streets, it was no problem to hire four strong men for an easy task like carrying a man on his pallet. Bearing Arza, they approached Peter's house. When the press of the crowd increased to where further progress was blocked, the coppersmith directed the bearers to enter the house of his friend Henadad, the seller of doves.

Henadad welcomed Arza and courteously granted the strange request that the bearers be allowed to carry him to the rooftop of the house. Moving from roof to roof, Arza and his bearers finally reached Simon Peter's house. There was no guard on the roof, but Arza could see that the house and courtyard were packed with the disciples and members of their families, listening to Jesus as He stood under a covered gallery between the house and the court. Nor was there a chance of getting the pallet down the stairway outside the building, for the press of people at the foot of the stairs was much too great.

Arza had not come this far only to experience failure. When the men carrying him stumbled over one of the loose tiles forming the roof of the gallery, he had the solution to his problem. Quickly he directed them to lay him down and remove the tile above the place where Jesus stood, being careful to cause as little noise as possible. Since the tiles were laid side by side and were not bound down, an opening was quickly made. Before Peter realized Arza's strategy, the bearers were lowering him and his pallet through the opening.

When those around Jesus saw what was happening, willing hands reached up to support the pallet from below and lower Arza to the ground at Jesus' feet. And seeing to what lengths the sick man had gone in order to get help, Jesus said quietly, "Son, be of good cheer; your sins are forgiven you."

The coppersmith felt strength flowing into his wasted limbs like the current of the Jordan pouring into the lake. He moved the arm and leg that had been paralyzed for so long, and a great joy filled him at being whole again. In his happiness at his own healing, he did not notice two Pharisees standing nearby, until one of them spoke.

"Blasphemy!" the Pharisee shouted. "The Nazarene claims to forgive sin, which only the Most High can do."

Jesus seemed unconcerned by the charge. "Why do you think evil in your hearts?" He demanded of the Pharisee sternly. "Is it easier to say, 'Your sins are forgiven you'? Or to say, 'Arise and walk'?"

The Pharisees had no answer. "But that you may know that the Son of Man has power on earth to forgive sins," Jesus said, turning to Arza, "I say to you: Arise, take up your bed, and go home."

Arza obeyed immediately. Getting to his knees, he rolled up the pallet on which he had been carried into the presence of Jesus, put it upon his shoulder, and stood erect. As proud and straight as he had ever been, he walked through the crowd which, stricken with amazement that a man known to be dying of the palsy should in an instant be whole again, opened a way for him to pass.

14

For God so loved the world that He gave His only begotten Son, that whoever believes in Him should not perish but have everlasting life.

John 3:16

Jesus and His Galilean followers were busy that winter moving about Galilee while He taught and healed the sick. Simon Peter and Andrew, James and John, with Matthew the tax gatherer who had been called as he sat in his booth at the customs station on the Way of the Sea, were with

Him always. As time went on, others became members of this inner circle which accompanied Him wherever He went.

When spring came, Jesus journeyed to Jerusalem with His small group of intimate followers to celebrate the Passover at the fountainhead of the Jewish faith, the Holy City with its gleaming golden temple. As He went about Jerusalem, a crowd soon began to follow, for word of the wonderful things He had been accomplishing in Galilee had gone before Him. At the same time He was closely watched by the scribes and Pharisees because neither He nor His teachings, they felt, gave proper respect to the Law.

Among the many lapses of which they accused Him was failure to observe the ritual of handwashing. The true Pharisee kept a jug of water standing never more than three paces from his bed, since the Law let him go no farther without washing his hands upon arising. In addition he washed before entering the synagogue, when he returned home from any public place, and both before and after eating. Some of the strictest Pharisees even washed between the courses of a meal.

Nor was the washing merely a perfunctory dipping of the hands into a basin of water. First the hands were carefully washed to remove any dirt, whether visible or not. Because they became defiled by the dirty water after washing, they were next rinsed with clear water, the hands being held up so the water would run down the arms and drop off the elbows. If it did not reach as far as the wrist during this rinsing, the hands were not considered clean and had to be washed again. By insisting upon such strictness, the Pharisees made it impossible for the ordinary working Jew to maintain complete purity under the Law, as they interpreted it.

Jewish custom demanded that when praying, the pious should wear, attached to a band around the forehead and the wrist, a small leather box called a phylactery containing pieces of parchment upon which were written portions of the Law. The boxes grew larger and more noticeable as time passed, and many Pharisees had come to wear them continually except when asleep, so that the over-large phylactery had become a badge of the self-righteous Pharisee.

An ancient custom also dictated that Jews should wear blue fringes or tassels at the four corners of the robe or mantle. Again the Pharisees, believing that their piety increased with the width of the fringes, wore broad and heavily ornamented ones which could be seen by the world.

They made themselves conspicuous, too, by stopping to pray in public places where they would be seen by men and admired for their great piety.

Nowhere was the absurdity of Pharisaic custom more evident than in the observance of the Sabbath. A wedding could not be celebrated on the Sabbath or on the days preceding and following it lest the feast extend over into the holy day. No removable teeth could be worn on the Sabbath because that would constitute carrying a burden, nor could more than two letters of the alphabet be written. A gray hair could not be plucked from the head, or a husk of wheat shelled. One who had a sore throat could not gargle on the Sabbath because he would be practicing medicine and therefore doing work. If a man suffered an aching tooth, he must find a Gentle to extract it. And nothing heavier than a scroll of the holy writings could be carried; even in the case of fire, a really pious Pharisee could flee his house on the Sabbath with only the clothing he wore, lest again he be accused of carrying a burden. Thus the Pharisees had reduced almost to an absurdity what was originally a day of rest and thanksgiving to God, and had made it practically impossible for one who did not concern himself every moment with the Law to avoid breaking some portion of it.

Jesus ignored these minute and literal interpretations which perverted the spirit of the Law, and the Pharisees were angered because He did not encourage the people to follow these strict precepts. Knowing that the easiest way to discredit Jesus would be to catch Him in the act of breaking the Law, the group who sought to destroy Him trailed Him everywhere He went in Jerusalem and watched His every act.

North of the temple where the road entered from the Mount of Olives and the suburb of Bethany was the Sheep Gate, so named because it was near the sheep market. Near this gate was a pool fed by an underground spring. Known as the Pool of Bezatha, or more popularly Bethesda, it was surrounded by five terraces, sometimes called porches, one of which projected into the pool and almost separated it into two parts.

Intermittently the rush of water from a subterranean spring feeding one section of the Pool of Bezatha caused the water to boil up. Pious Jews believed an angel roiled the waters of the pool at these times, and tradition said that the first sick or afflicted person who stepped into the water after it was disturbed would be healed. As a result, there was always a group of the afflicted lining the terraces at the Pool of Bezatha, and there was a great scramble to be first into the water when it boiled up.

On a Sabbath day during this visit to Jerusalem, Jesus came to the Pool of Bezatha and stood looking down at the poor unfortunates gathered there. Every eye except His was on the water, eager to detect the periodic roiling and be the first into the pool.

Jesus noticed one man whom He had seen in this same spot on several previous journeys to Jerusalem. In fact, it was said that this man had been afflicted for thirty-eight years with a paralysis, never once having been able to enter the pool at the moment when it boiled.

"Do you want to be made well?" Jesus asked the afflicted man.

The paralytic took his eyes off the pool with some reluctance, lest he miss the next stirring up of the waters. "Sir," he said, "I have no man to put me into the pool when the water is stirred up; but while I am coming, another always steps down before me."

He was not complaining nor had he lost his faith that God would heal him when he was the first to enter the pool. The fault, in his opinion, was not God's but his own.

"Rise, take up your bed and walk," Jesus told him. Immediately the man got to his feet, rolled up the scrap of quilt upon which he had been lying, and walked away from the terraces of the pool.

He had not gone far when a scribe stopped him. "It is the Sabbath," the scribe said severely. "And it is not lawful for you to carry your bed."

"He who made me well said to me, 'Take up your bed and walk,'" the healed man replied.

"Who told you this?" the scribe demanded.

But Jesus was by now lost in the crowd that came and went around the pool, and the healed man could not point Him out. So the scribes were deprived of an opportunity to accuse Him of breaking the Law both in healing the man and in directing Him to carry a burden upon the Sabbath.

The next day Jesus saw in the temple the man who had been paralyzed. "See, you have been made well," He told him. "Sin no more, lest a worse thing come upon you."

Recognizing his benefactor, the man went to the scribes and pointed out Jesus as the one who had healed him and directed him to do work on the Sabbath. The scribes were naturally overjoyed. At last, it seemed, they had an opportunity to convict Jesus of a crime. And in Jerusalem they could be sure that the court which would hear the charges would be of their way of thinking.

When they began to accuse Jesus, He stopped them with the stern warning, "My Father works even now, so I work."

At that His accusers set up a mighty clamor, accusing Him not only of having broken the Sabbath but of blasphemy in saying that God was His Father, for that would have made Him the equal of God, which in their sight, no man could be.

"The Son can do nothing of Himself, but what He sees the Father do," Jesus told them, "for whatever He does, the Son also does in like manner. For the Father loves the Son, and shows Him all things that He Himself does; and He will show Him greater works than these, that you may marvel."

The scribes were taken aback by His words, for He spoke as He had in the synagogues of Galilee, with authority, not as one who was simply interpreting the Law. He had not named Himself the Son of whom He was speaking and, if He were the prophet many believed Him to be, the terms He used were lawful, for mystics were not expected to be bound by ordinary rules. "He who hears My word and believes in Him who sent Me has everlasting life," Jesus told them. "He shall not come into judgment, but has passed from death into life. For as the Father has life in Himself, so He has granted the Son to have life in Himself, and has given Him authority to execute judgment also, because He is the Son of Man."

He looked pityingly at those who sought to condemn Him for healing a man who had been paralyzed for thirty-eight years. And unable to meet His gaze, they could only look away.

"You search the Scriptures," He told them, "for in them you think you have eternal life; and they testify of Me. I do not receive honor from men. But I know you, that you do not have the love of God in you. I have come in My Father's name, and you do not receive Me. How can you believe," He added scathingly, "when you receive honor from one another, and do not seek the honor that comes from the only God?"

By now the scribes, who had been sure they had Him trapped, were embarrassed and humiliated under the lash of His words as He denounced them for their excessive searching for honor from each other, rather than seeking to deserve the blessings of God for what they were within themselves.

"Do not think that I shall accuse you to the Father," Jesus added. "There is one who accuses you—Moses, in whom you trust. For if you believed

Moses, you would believe Me; for he wrote about Me. But if you do not believe his writings, how will you believe My words?"

II

The Great Sanhedrin was largely dominated by the Sadducees, and the more intolerant Pharisees who, with the high priest Caiaphas as their leader, made up the majority of its members. The membership did include a small number of Pharisees who, in both religious and political life, were more tolerant than those who sought to punish severely every infraction of the Law, but who were stricter than the worldly Sadducees. One of the most prominent among these conservatives was a lawyer named Nicodemus. When he heard how Jesus had parried the attack of the scribes, he determined to find out for himself just what it was that distinguished the Nazarene from the self-styled prophets who were constantly turning up at the temple during the religious festivals.

Jesus was resting at the camp His disciples had made on the slope of the Mount of Olives overlooking Jerusalem when Nicodemus came to Him. "Rabbi," the Pharisee said respectfully, "we know that You are a teacher come from God; for no one can do the miracles that You do unless God is with Him."

Recognizing the sincerity of the visitor and his real desire to know the truth, Jesus wasted no words but went to the very heart of His own doctrine.

"Most assuredly, I say to you," He told Nicodemus, "unless one is born again, he cannot see the kingdom of God."

"How can a man be born when he is old?" Nicodemus asked. "Can he enter his mother's womb a second time?"

"Unless one is born of water and the Spirit of God," Jesus explained, "he cannot enter the kingdom of God. That which is born of the flesh is flesh, and that which is born of the Spirit is spirit."

Nicodemus could see the difference now, the fact that a man could change in his soul with no actual change in his body.

"Do not marvel that I said to you, 'You must be born again,'" Jesus told him. "The wind blows where it wishes, and you hear the sound of it, but cannot tell where it comes from and where it goes. So is everyone who is born of the Spirit."

"How can these things be?" Nicodemus protested, for it went against all his training and previous belief to say that a man could enter the kingdom of God merely by a spiritual regeneration without rigidly following the Law which every pious Jew believed to be the only route to eternal life.

"Are you a teacher of Israel, and do not know these things?" Jesus reproved him gently. "We speak what We know and testify what We have seen, and you do not receive Our witness. If I have told you earthly things and you do not believe, how will you believe if I tell you heavenly things?"

Jesus knew Nicodemus had come to Him in a sincere desire to understand what His teachings were and what power He possessed, not, as had the scribes, with any desire to trap Him. So when He saw that the lawyer still did not understand, He used an example from the history of the Children of Israel. As they had journeyed from Egypt toward the Promised Land of Canaan, the Israelites had become discouraged and their faith had wavered, especially when they were troubled by a plague of venomous snakes. God had instructed Moses to place a serpent of brass on a pole in the center of the camp and to announce that if any who were bitten looked at the serpent they would be saved. The serpent of brass was not a cure in itself, but the act of looking was a test of faith in God's willingness to help those who trusted Him.

"As Moses lifted up the serpent in the wilderness," Jesus said, "even so must the Son of Man be lifted up. For God so loved the world, that He gave His only begotten Son, that whoever believes in Him should not perish but have everlasting life. For God did not send His Son into the world to condemn the world, but that the world through Him might be saved."

To a Pharisee, whose testimony could destroy Him, Jesus had revealed the eternal truth of His mission on earth and His divine nature in a way which could not be misunderstood. If Nicodemus returned to the Great Sanhedrin and testified that Jesus had named Himself the Son of God, Caiaphas and his followers would then have all they needed to destroy Him, for few who had authority in Israel would believe that the Son of God could be a despised Galilean or, even worse, a Nazarene.

As He saw the light of comprehension dawning in the eyes of the lawyer, Jesus added these clarifying words: "He who believes in Him is not condemned; but he who does not believe is condemned already, because he has not believed in the name of the only begotten Son of God. And this is the condemnation, that the light has come into the world, and men loved darkness rather than light, because their deeds were evil. For everyone practicing evil hates the light and does not come to the light, lest his deeds should be exposed. But he who does truth comes to the light, that his deeds may be clearly seen, that they have been done in God."

Jesus' faith in Nicodemus was not misplaced; ever afterwards this high-ranking official was His devoted follower and friend.

III

It was Jesus' custom to teach in the synagogue of Capernaum whenever He was in that city. Upon His return from Jerusalem He entered the building on the Sabbath to enjoy the service of worship He loved, and to teach here where He had so many friends and devoted followers. The critics who had followed Him from Jerusalem were also there, hoping to convict Him of a frank violation of the Law of Moses inside the synagogue where it might be possible to arouse the emotions of the worshipers to the point where they would immediately condemn Him. These men watched closely as the people entered the synagogue, and when a man with a withered hand appeared, they felt they had the pretext they needed.

As was the custom when there was a visiting rabbi, members of the congregation were allowed to ask questions concerning the Law after the sermon was finished. A lawyer from Jerusalem rose and asked, "Is it lawful to heal on the Sabbath day?"

Knowing this to be a trap, Jesus swept the congregation with His eyes and noted the man with the withered hand sitting near the front. The afflicted man had no part in the scheme himself, and when Jesus asked him to stand up, he rose to his feet rather reluctantly.

Everyone could see the withered hand and Jesus turned to the lawyer who had asked the question. "I ask you," He said, "is it lawful on the Sabbath to do good or to do evil, to save life or to kill?" Turning to the listeners, Jesus added, "What man is there among you who has one sheep, and if it falls into a pit on the Sabbath, will not lay hold of it and lift it out? Of how much more value then is a man than a sheep?"

The lawyer could not refute Him, and Jesus spoke to the afflicted man. "Stretch out your hand," He commanded.

A murmur of awe rose from the people when they saw that the palsied hand was now completely whole although Jesus had not touched him. No one could doubt that He had actually healed the afflicted man, yet He could not be accused of breaking the Sabbath for He had performed no work.

The rising favor with which the great mass of the people in Galilee regarded Jesus, in addition to their growing conviction that He was at the very least a prophet sent from God and perhaps actually the Messiah, inevitably brought Him to the attention of the agents of Herod Antipas. Jesus had not attacked the tetrarch, as had John the Baptist, so they limited their activities to following Him and listening for any utterances which might be treasonable to Herod or to Rome.

As for John, he had continued to denounce Herod, and when Herodias increased her nagging, the harried tetrarch finally ordered the arrest of the Baptist, using the excuse that the crowds who listened to him might be excited to revolt.

Shut up in Herod's border castle of Machaerus among the hills overlooking the Sea of Judgment, John was quickly forgotten by many who had listened to him and deserted by most of his disciples. Word of his arrest came to Jesus following His return from Jerusalem. With the messenger who had cried in the wilderness, "Make straight the way of the Lord," now silenced, Jesus began with increasing boldness to preach to a sinful people the message, "The time is fulfilled, and the kingdom of God is at hand. Repent, and believe in the gospel."

15

And seeing the multitudes, He went up on a mountain.

Matthew 5:1

There was a new urgency to Jesus' mission. John the Baptist had been arrested. Herod Antipas, through his agents in Galilee, had joined forces with the scribes and the chief priests in Jerusalem to oppose Him. He was in constant danger now of being imprisoned and silenced as John had been, and He could no longer act alone as teacher and healer. The time had come to send out disciples to preach His doctrine and heal the sick in His name.

From those who were closest to Him Jesus chose twelve men. They were no longer to be simply followers and listeners; now He gave them a part of His own authority as the Son of God.

For the ordination of the Twelve Jesus chose a mountain known as the Horns of Hattin, near a road leading from Tiberias to Akka on the seacoast. Here ancient volcanoes had long since cooled but the black basalt blocks and boulders characteristic of the area were everywhere. The mountaintop had once been the site of a city said to have been Madon, but it was now a ruin. Its vantage point afforded a sweeping view of the lake to the east and the countryside extending northwestward toward Nazareth. From a small flat area at the summit, the ground sloped gradually to the south, so that there was space enough for the people to gather, which they did as soon as the sun rose across the lake.

There were Simon, James, and John, the three who had followed Jesus almost from the beginning. To them and to Andrew, Simon's brother, also chosen as one of the Twelve, He had spoken earlier on the shore of the lake, telling them He would make them fishers of men.

Levi (or Matthew) had been chosen as he sat at the customhouse and had followed Jesus ever since. In time, others had gradually entered the circle. There were Philip and Bartholomew (also called Nathanael) who had come to Jesus at Bethabara after His baptism by John. A close friend of Matthew's named Thomas, sometimes called Didymus because he was one of a pair of twins, had also joined the group.

The sons of Zebedee were Jesus' cousins, their mother Salome being a sister to Mary, and three of the others were relatives of His family through Joseph. These included James (often called the son of Alphaeus to distinguish him from James, the son of Zebedee), Judas (usually called Lebbaeus from his hearty nature, but sometimes Thaddeus), and another Simon who, since he had belonged to the Zealot party, was called Zelotes to distinguish him from the tall fisherman of Galilee who was already a close intimate of Jesus.

All these men were Galileans, most of them almost members of Jesus' own household, since they were either related to His family or were friends of long standing. The only member of the Twelve not a Galilean was Judas, a native of Kerioth, a town of Judea. To Judas of Kerioth (referred to sometimes as Judas Iscariot from the words *Ish Kerioth*, a man of Kerioth), was given the thankless task of handling the common purse and making provision for the material needs of Jesus and His disciples.

When, on the morning after a night of prayer, the disciples came to Jesus on the site of ancient Madon, followed by a great number of people, He called those He had chosen to sit in a half-circle at His feet. Speaking directly to them but heard also by the people on the slope, He charged the Twelve with the doctrine which they would manifest abroad as His representatives.

II

Jesus opened this most important discourse with a set of simple precepts which put into words the way men everywhere could live in peace, respect, and love for each other:

> *Blessed are the poor in spirit, for theirs is the kingdom of heaven.*
> *Blessed are those who mourn, for they shall be comforted.*
> *Blessed are the meek, for they shall inherit the earth.*
> *Blessed are those who hunger and thirst for righteousness, for they shall be filled.*
> *Blessed are the merciful, for they shall obtain mercy.*
> *Blessed are the pure in heart, for they shall see God.*
> *Blessed are the peacemakers, for they shall be called the sons of God.*
> *Blessed are those who are persecuted for righteousness' sake, for theirs is the kingdom of heaven.*
> *Blessed are you when they revile and persecute you, and say all kinds of evil against you falsely for My sake.*
> *Rejoice and be exceedingly glad, for great is your reward in heaven, for so they persecuted the prophets who were before you.*

Now He turned His eyes upon a group of scribes and Pharisees who sat just below the disciples, waiting to twist His words into false meanings. He regarded them broodingly for a moment before He turned again to the Twelve.

"You are the salt of the earth," He said, His voice now warm and tender. "But if the salt loses its flavor, how shall it be seasoned? It is then good for nothing but to be thrown out and trampled underfoot by men. You are the light of the world. A city that is set on a hill cannot be hidden."

From the Horns of Hattin everyone could see the Decapolis city of Hippos, its white Grecian columns shining upon a hilltop across the lake to the east. They were all familiar with His reference, for there was a saying in the lake region that Hippos could not be hidden.

"Nor do they light a lamp and put it under a basket, but on a lampstand, and it gives light to all who are in the house. Let your light so shine before men, that they may see your good works and glorify your Father in heaven."

His voice was like a sensitive musical instrument, swelling to full timbre when He wished to drive home a point and dropping to a normal tone when He spoke for only a few to hear.

"Do not think that I came to destroy the Law or the Prophets," He assured His listeners. "I did not come to destroy but to fulfill. For assuredly, I say to you, till heaven and earth pass away, one jot or one tittle will by no means pass from the law till all is fulfilled."

A murmur arose from the crowd at this assurance of His own devotion to the Law of Moses, for His enemies claimed that Jesus sought to destroy that Law, a crime for which He could be punished by death. Now He was admitting the primacy of the Law of Moses, as it had first been handed down, but not the mass of interpretations by the scribes and Pharisees which had put an unbearable burden upon the people.

"For I say to you"—Jesus' voice rose now so that His detractors could not fail to hear— "that unless your righteousness exceeds the righteousness of the scribes and Pharisees, you will by no means enter the kingdom of heaven."

He paused and looked around Him at the faces of the Twelve sitting at His feet amid the ruins of the city which had once occupied this commanding hilltop. No one listening could fail to understand that He was denouncing the false righteousness of the Pharisees.

"You have heard that it was said to those of old, 'You shall not murder, and whosoever murders will be in danger of the judgment,'" He said, pursuing a new line of thought. "But I say to you that whoever is angry with his brother without a cause shall be in danger of the judgment. And whoever shall say, 'You fool!' will be in danger of hell-fire. Therefore, if you bring your gift to the altar, and there remember that your brother has something against you, leave your gift there before the altar, and go your way. First be reconciled to your brother, and then come and offer your gift.

"You have heard that it was said to those of old, 'You shall not commit adultery.' But I say to you that whoever looks at a woman to lust for her has already committed adultery with her in his heart. If your right eye causes you to sin, pluck it out and cast it from you; for it is more profitable for you that one of your members perish, than for your whole body to be cast into hell. And if your right hand causes you to sin, cut it off and cast it from you; for it is more profitable for you that one of your members should perish, than for your whole body to be cast into hell."

The crowd was hushed under the hypnotic spell of His voice as He continued to speak.

"You have heard that it was said, 'An eye for an eye and a tooth for a tooth.' But I tell you not to resist an evil person. But whoever slaps you on your right cheek, turn the other to him als0. If anyone wants to sue you and take away your tunic, let him have your cloak also. And whoever compels you to go one mile, go with him two."

The reference was to a Roman law which required civilians to carry baggage and supplies whenever the legions were on the march, but no man could be forced to carry this burden more than a mile. This law had always been a source of resentment to the Jews who prided themselves on being slaves to no man. Now Jesus was telling them to humble themselves and go another mile, a truly astonishing thing for a Jew and a command any man would find it hard to obey without resentment.

"You have heard that it was said, 'You shall love your neighbor and hate your enemy,'" Jesus continued, taking no notice of the murmur of anger that came from the crowd. "But I say to you, love your enemies, bless those who curse you, do good to those who hate you, and pray for those who despitefully use you and persecute you, that you may be sons of your Father in heaven; for He makes His sun rise on the evil and on the good, and sends rain on the just and on the unjust. For if you love those who love you, what reward have you? Do not even the tax collectors do the same? And if you greet your brethren only, what do you do more than others? Do not even the tax collectors do so? Love your enemies and do good to them and lend, hoping for nothing again. Your reward shall then be great and you shall be sons of the Most High, for He is kind toward the unthankful and evil. Be merciful, even as your Father is merciful."

On the slope below, people were beginning to grumble. As they saw it, the doctrine Jesus was now teaching laid upon them a burden fully as heavy as the Pharisees' interpretations of the Law. But Jesus continued.

"Be perfect therefore as your Father in heaven is perfect. Take heed that you do not your righteousness before men to be seen by them. Else you will have no reward from your Father who is in heaven. And when you do your alms, do not sound a trumpet before you as the hypocrites do in the synagogue and in the streets that they may have glory of men. But when you do alms, let not your left hand know what your right hand does, so your alms will be in secret and your Father who sees in secret Himself, will reward you openly.

"And when you pray, be not as the hypocrites are, for they love to pray standing in the synagogues and on the corners of the streets, that they may be seen by men. When you pray, enter into your closet and when you have shut the door, pray to your Father who is in secret. And your Father who sees in secret will reward you openly.

"When you pray do not use vain repetitions, as the heathen do, for they think they shall be heard for their much speaking. Do not be like them, for your Father knows what things you need before you ask Him. Pray therefore after this manner:

> *"Our Father who is in heaven,*
> *Hallowed be Your name,*
> *Your Kingdom come,*
> *Your will be done,*
> *In earth as it is in heaven.*
> *Give us this day our daily bread,*
> *And forgive us our trespasses, as we forgive those who*
> *   trespass against us.*
> *And lead us not into temptation, but deliver us from evil,*
> *For Yours is the kingdom, and the power, and the glory*
> *   forever. Amen."*

His voice softened as He explained the prayer. "If you forgive men their trespasses, your heavenly Father will forgive your trespasses. Judge not and you shall not be judged. Condemn not and you shall not be condemned.

Forgive and you shall be forgiven. Give and it shall be given unto you, good measure, pressed down and running over shall men give. For with the same measure that you mete, it shall be measured to you again."

Once more He had laid a heavy burden upon those who would obey Him. They must be the first to forgive, but in the nature of man that was hard to do. Jesus understood this because He was a man like them and tempted as they were, so He now spoke a parable to make His meaning clear.

"As you would that men should do to you, do you also to them likewise," He said, putting man's whole duty to God into one simple precept. "Can the blind lead the blind? Shall they not both fall into the same ditch? The disciple is not above his master, but everyone that is perfect shall be as his master. Why do you see the speck in your brother's eye but do not consider the beam in your own eye? Cast the beam first out of your own eye and then you will see clearly how to pull out the mote that is in your brother's eye."

He paused, then continued with another parable. "A good tree does not bring forth corrupt fruit, neither does a corrupt tree bring forth good fruit. Every tree is known by its own fruit for men do not gather figs from thorns nor grapes from a bramble. A good man out of the good treasures of his heart brings forth that which is good. And an evil man out of the evil treasures of his heart brings forth that which is evil."

He turned somber eyes then upon His disciples. "Whoever comes to Me and hears My sayings and does them is like a man who built a house and dug deep and laid the foundation on a rock. When the flood rose, the stream beat vehemently upon that house but could not shake it for it was founded upon a rock. But he that hears and does not is like a man that built a house on the surface without a foundation; the stream beat vehemently against it and immediately it fell and the ruin of that house was great."

When He had finished this simplest and most concise of all His sermons, Jesus left the mountaintop followed by His disciples and went down to Capernaum again. At the edge of the city He was met by the Roman centurion named Paulos who had charge of the soldiers policing this area. The officer had earned the respect and affection of the leading Jews in Capernaum, not only by his upright conduct but because he had been instrumental in building their synagogue. The leaders of the congregation were with him now to second the request he had come to make of Jesus.

"Lord," the centurion said humbly, "my servant lies at home sick and grievously tormented."

"I will come and heal him," Jesus said at once, for the soldier and his reputation were well known to Him.

"Lord, I am not worthy that you should come under my roof," the Roman protested. "Only say the word and my servant will be healed. For I also am a man under authority having under myself soldiers. I say to this one 'Go' and he goes, and to another 'Come' and he comes. And to my servant 'Do this' and he does it."

Jesus' eyes warmed at the understanding the officer showed of his position of authority under God. "Truly with no man in Israel have I found so great faith," He said. "Go your way; as you have believed, so be it to you."

Without hesitation the centurion turned back to his house, knowing he would find his servant healed as Jesus had promised. Jesus watched him go, a somber look on his face. This man who possessed such faith was not a Jew but a citizen of Rome.

III

Before Herod Antipas built Tiberias, his lavish capital overlooking the Sea of Galilee from the west, Magdala had been the most important city on the western shore. A center for the dried-fish industry, it was said to pay each year a wagonload of taxes to the tax collectors, and its fleet of fishing boats, as well as its piers and drying sheds, were the largest on the lake. The dried fish of Magdala were sold as far north as Antioch and as far south as the cities of the Nile delta. Even its Greek name, Tarichaea, was derived from the salting and drying of fish in which its inhabitants excelled.

Near Magdala, the Way of the Sea left the lake region and ascended the heights to the east; with several other important routes joining the shore road at this point, Magdala was a prosperous and cosmopolitan city. Its population was about equally Jewish and heathen, the latter making up such a great number that they had built a hippodrome for the better enjoyment of such Greek pastimes as sports and gladiatorial games. In ancient times the priestly order of Ezekiel had been centered in Magdala, but lately any priestly qualities the city might once have possessed had been lost and it was shunned by devout Jews as a city of harlots.

Surely the most beautiful woman in Magdala was the woman called Mary, usually with the surname Magdalene, since there was a Mary in nearly every Jewish household. For many years, she had been a dancer, well known in Alexandria, until she was brought back to Israel with a man named Gaius Flaccus, a Roman soldier and nephew of Pontius Pilate. Few understood the story of this relationship. Fewer still understood the strange illness characterized by seizures which would often rack her body and throw her to the ground unconscious. Because of her malady, Mary rarely traveled any great distance from her home. If the illness came upon her while she had guests, she excused herself and withdrew. Her malady could be controlled—provided she did not become emotionally disturbed—with a special medicine prepared for her by one of the most famous physicians of Alexandria. For that reason, the sickness did not keep her from entertaining widely, and her household was a favorite meeting place for many prominent people of the region, including Romans and Greeks as well as the wealthier Jews and officers of Herod's court at nearby Tiberias. Though her relationship with Gaius Flaccus was whispered about among the Jews, it was not an issue among these who enjoyed currying favors. Although a Jewess by birth, Mary of Magdala lived in the Roman manner as befitted a consort of a Roman soldier, employed many servants, and entertained widely.

A group of friends had gathered at the home of Gaius Flaccus home one evening. From the cool atrium where a fountain played continuously, the guests had been conducted by a servant to the triclinium. Here each reclined according to the Roman custom upon a low couch, with platters of viands, fruit, and sweet cakes before them upon a low table, and silver cups of wine which a servant was always ready to refill.

Mary herself drank little. Her eyes glittered, but with the restlessness that always drove her. And her hand, when she lifted a bunch of the rich grapes that came from the fertile vineyards of Gennesaret was steady.

One of the guests was a Roman officer, Phaedas, a centurion on the staff of Pontius Pilate who was occupying a villa belonging to Herod Antipas at nearby Tiberias.

"Why has the procurator come to Galilee?" Mary asked him jokingly. "Doesn't he trust Herod?"

"Pontius Pilate doesn't trust his own wife." The officer was already drunk or he would not have spoken so freely. "They say the Lady Procula's been listening to the teachings of a Nazarene."

Mary leaned forward. "Who is He?"

"I can't remember His name," the Roman admitted. "But word came to Jerusalem of some miracles He has performed, healing lepers and such. The Lady Claudia Procula was curious and went to listen to the fellow. Her servants say she has not been the same since."

"It is true about the miracles," a Jew named Hosea said. "So many people are following the Nazarene that even Herod is beginning to be disturbed."

"Did you hear about the servant of the centurion Paulos?" one of the women asked.

The Roman officer nodded. "Paulos was once a friend of mine, but lately he has become too sanctimonious for my liking."

"Is that the same Paulos who built the synagogue in Capernaum?" Mary asked.

"The same," Phaedas said.

"What about the servant?"

"To hear Paulos tell it, the man was dying and the Nazarene restored him to life without even touching him. But Paulos is no physician and I understand that nobody saw the servant."

"They say in Capernaum that the Nazarene casts out dev—" Hosea stopped suddenly and an awkward silence filled the room. No one present had ever seen Mary in a seizure but her condition was well known in Magdala and Tiberias. Her servants had reported her to be possessed by "seven devils," no doubt because they had now and then been lashed by her temper.

Mary's hand tightened suddenly on the edge of the table. "Go on, Hosea," she said, her voice suddenly hard. "Why do you hesitate?"

"It is probably only idle gossip," Hosea mumbled, "not worth repeating."

"You were saying this man casts out devils," Mary insisted. "Is that right?"

"The people who follow Him say He has healed many who were possessed," Hosea said. "They claim that all evil spirits are subject to Him."

One of the women giggled. "The priests claim He casts out devils in the name of Beelzebub, Mary. Go to see Him and you might acquire more. Then no one could best you in business."

Mary smiled without amusement. "My wits are enough to keep me ahead, my dear Herra," she said smoothly. "Why should I need help from Beelzebub?"

There was a round of laughter at that and the party soon broke up. When the guests had departed, Mary paced the atrium for a while, then sent a slave for her steward, Hadja. Although she gave only lip service now to her upbringing as a Jewess, having adopted the Greek point of view toward religion while at Alexandria, Hadja was pious and attended the synagogue regularly. He had been with Mary's family since childhood and between the two there was a deep bond of affection. She could be sure the old steward would tell her the truth about the Nazarene.

"I am sorry to disturb your rest, old one," she said, using the name by which she had called him since she was a child. "Can you tell me anything about a Nazarene healer?"

"Do you mean Jesus?"

"I suppose so. I didn't hear His name."

He is a good man," Hadja said, "a teacher or perhaps a prophet."

"Does He really heal the sick?"

"The son of Herod's steward, Chuza, was saved from death."

"Do you know this is true?"

"I had it from Chuza's own lips."

"Chuza is a man of truth," Mary said thoughtfully. "He would have no reason to lie."

"Jesus also healed a leper and a man suffering from a palsy."

"What of the rumor that evil spirits are subject to Him?" she asked.

It is no rumor," Hadja assured her. "Jesus cast devils out of a man in the synagogue at Capernaum on the Sabbath day. I know men who were there and saw it done. They heard the evil ones name Him a Holy One of God."

"Some say He uses the power of Beelzebub."

"The Nazarene's followers believe He is the Son of God," Hadja said.

"Then He could heal me?"

"If He would."

Mary's quick temper flared. "Why not me, if He heals others?"

"They were Jews who believe in God. Once you were one of us, but now—"

Mary tossed her head angrily. "Must I grovel in the dirt and beg this Nazarene to heal me?"

Hadja looked at her for a long moment before he spoke. "You might save yourself if you did," he said. "It is written, 'Pride goeth before destruction and a haughty spirit before a fall.'"

"Why should I humble myself?" Mary demanded, her eyes blazing. "Go find this Nazarene. Tell Him I have been treated by the finest physicians at the museum in Alexandria and have paid them well though they did not help me. Bring Him here and I will pay Him what He asks to cure me. But don't expect me to grovel."

Hadja had withstood the brunt of his mistress's anger more than once. He knew her good qualities and loved her for them, but he also knew her weaknesses. "The Nazarene seeks out no one," he said. "Those who wish help must come to Him and request it. He asks no recompense."

Mary looked at him suspiciously. "Do you follow this—this devil-exorciser?"

"I believe the way to eternal life lies through Him," Hadja said quietly. "One day I hope to be worthy of it."

"Well, I will not seek Him out," Mary said with a toss of her head. "You may go. And see that you don't waste your time listening to false prophets."

Hadja withdrew and Mary called for her maid to prepare her for bed. She knew that anger and emotional disturbance tended to bring on the seizures, so with an effort she controlled herself and put all thought of the conversation with Hadja from her mind. Almost as soon as she lay down, she was asleep.

IV

A few days later Mary of Magdala was walking by the lake with Hadja when she noticed a small group of boats approaching the shore just north of Magdala. The main fishing fleet had already put ashore and the fishermen were unloading their catches, but these boats were not loaded and did not contain nets. Instead they seemed to be almost packed with men.

Mary shaded her eyes with her hand and watched the boats. "Those are not fishermen," she said to Hadja.

"They seem to be coming from Bethsaida," the old steward said.

"Can you tell who they are?"

"The tall man in the lead boat looks like Simon of Bethsaida," Hadja said. "He is the leader of those who follow Jesus of Nazareth, so I imagine the Nazarene and His disciples are in the boats."

Mary stiffened. "They will touch shore a little way from here. I will wait while you bring the Nazarene to me."

"Jesus is at no one's beck and call," Hadja said. "If you want His help, you must go to Him yourself and ask it."

"Who is He that I should beg Him for favors?" she said.

"Many believe He is the Son of God," Hadja said simply.

With an effort Mary gained control of herself. She had no desire to bring on a seizure here in public; it would only confirm the rumor that she was possessed.

"We will go back to the house," she said and set off at a rapid walk along the shore toward her home which was some distance up the steep slope overlooking the lake. Before she had gone far, Mary realized with rising panic that her senseless anger at a man she had never seen had already betrayed her. She could feel the familiar premonitory tenseness of her muscles, the flashes of light bursting like stars before her eyes even when she closed them in desperation. She held out her hand to Hadja, wordlessly begging him to guide her so she would not fall. She knew that if she fell the seizure would be upon her before she could rise and she would be unconscious almost immediately.

Hadja had been with his mistress through many of the attacks. He took her hand and guided her along the road as she stumbled blindly beside him, but while they were still following the shore, the boats in which Jesus and His disciples had crossed from Bethsaida grounded on the beach a little beyond them. A number of people had seen the boats approaching and as Simon Peter helped Jesus from the lead boat they crowded around Him and for the moment blocked any passage.

There was no pride in Mary now, only a desperate need to pass through and get home before the seizure reached its climax. Half-blinded by the light that blazed before her eyes even when they were closed, she clung to Hadja as he tried to lead her through the crowd. The people were thronging around Jesus, waiting to listen to His words.

"We cannot get through," Hadja told Mary. "We must wait for the crowd to part."

"I can't wait!" she cried. "Get me home, Hadja!"

"Perhaps if you asked the Nazarene for help—"

"Do anything!" Mary, half-conscious, was beyond caring now, her face already drawn by the beginning of a seizure. "Only get me home."

Half-carrying his mistress, Hadja cried out, "Make way for one possessed by seven demons!"

As the old steward had shrewdly surmised, his cry was the only one that would have opened the way. Frantically trying to get away from one who was possessed, the crowd opened a wide path for them as if they were lepers. No one wanted to be near any demons the Nazarene might exorcise from this beautiful woman in the rich silken robe who was being supported by the old man. Some recognized Mary and, having heard the rumors of her malady, scrambled away all the more desperately.

Mary did not know where she was being guided, nor did she care. Already her mouth was so drawn by the seizure that she could only moan, "Help me! Help me!" Her body was beginning to jerk in the familiar spasms.

Hadja tried to support her but he was old and not strong. She sank to her knees as they came toward Jesus, who stood on the shore listening to a question being propounded to Him by a group of men who had come to meet Him.

"Help me! Help me!" Mary sobbed blindly in her agony and her shame.

Suddenly the contractions of her muscles ceased and her mouth relaxed. Wonderingly, she opened her eyes and found that she was no longer half blind. Never before had a seizure ended so abruptly; they had always run their course and afterwards she had slept, sometimes for a whole day and a night, awaking with a feeling of exhaustion, both mental and physical.

Now it was as if nothing had happened, and strangest of all, she felt no loss of pride at finding herself on her knees before this man whose robe was of rough homespun and whose sandals were worn and patched. Slowly she raised her head until she could see His face. The eyes that looked down at her were filled with warmth and suddenly Mary felt such peace as she had never known flowing through her.

She knew that when she had cried out for help, this man had healed her of her infirmity. But He had done more than that; He had given her something else, perhaps an understanding of herself which she had never before possessed. No word passed between them and Jesus did not touch her, but Mary knew instinctively that He understood the gratitude that flooded her heart. Bowing her head, she bent forward and kissed Jesus' feet, feeling the taste of the dust upon her lips while the tears of gratitude she had found at last poured down to wash the dust away.

An excited hum rose from the crowd as they realized that they had witnessed another miracle by the Nazarene. Mary did not resist when gentle hands raised her to her feet, or when Hadja, with his arm about her shoulders, guided her through the crowd.

Behind her she could hear one of the group around Jesus ask for a sign from heaven and His voice replying sternly, "When it is evening you say, 'It will be fair weather for the sky is red.' And in the morning, 'It will be foul weather today, for the sky is red and lowering.' O you hypocrites! You can discern the face of the sky, but can you not discern the signs of the times? A wicked and adulterous generation seeks a sign and no sign shall be given it but the sign of the prophet Jonah."

Some childhood memory kindled a spark in Mary. The story of Jonah and his strange adventure with the whale was a favorite of Jewish children and she had loved it as a girl. But she was sure that Jesus was referring to something else now, something she could not remember.

"What does He mean by the sign of the prophet Jonah, Hadja?" she asked.

"Jonah was sent by God into the city of Nineveh because of its great sinfulness," he told her. "He cried out, 'Yet forty days and Nineveh shall be destroyed.' But the people humbled themselves and asked God to forgive them and were spared."

"Was that why the Nazarene healed me?" Mary asked. "Because I humbled myself and begged for help?"

"He turns no one away who seeks Him," the old man said. "In humbling yourself you repented of your greatest sin, the sin of pride."

Mary nodded slowly, her eyes shining. "And I am not ashamed, Hadja."

"That may be an even greater miracle than His healing you," the old steward said. "Jesus once told His disciples, 'He that is least among you all, the same shall be great.' Others in high places have not been ashamed to serve Him. Why should you?"

16

Are You the Coming One, or do we look for another?

Matthew 11:3

South of the Sea of Galilee, the Jordan wound a serpentine course toward the Sea of Judgment, sometimes called the Salt Sea, through a green and fertile valley that extended at no point more than ten miles from the river itself. Heavily laden with mud and silt, which in times of flood was deposited upon the land, the Jordan annually replenished the fertile soil along its banks very much as did the Nile its valley in Egypt. Since ancient times the deep rifts that split the country in two here, between the Great Sea and the vast deserts of Arabia to the west, had been cultivated intensively. Irrigation canals brought water from the Jordan, and many rivers and brooks poured into it along its course, offering additional sources of life-giving water.

From the narrow strip of the Jordan Valley, the mountains rose steeply, on the east to a hilly plateau divided by four rivers. From north to south, beginning almost at the level of the southern end of the Sea of Galilee, these were the Yarmuk, the Jabbok, the Amon, and the Zered near the southern tip of the Salt. Sea.

Extending from the River Jabbok, the center of the area known since ancient times as Gilead, to the Arnon, which poured into the Sea of Judgment, was the province of Peraea, ruled over by Herod Antipas. Eastward the district bordered upon the domain of King Aretas, a frontier that had been in a state of battle almost constantly since Herod had divorced the Nabatean princess. Generally the region of Peraea was referred to by its inhabitants simply as "beyond Jordan." At the northern end of the Salt Sea, the Jordan Valley rapidly narrowed and the mountains belonging to the ancient kingdoms of Ammon and Moab rose directly from the water. Near the River Arnon in a grim and rugged region overlooking the metallic surface of the Sea of Judgment was the lofty mountain upon which stood Herod's palace-fortress of Machaerus. Fortified first by the ill-starred Alexander Janaaeus of the Hasmonean line, it had been greatly reinforced and enlarged by Herod the Great as a buttress against the Nabateans of the desert to the east, and had later been turned into a luxurious palace by Herod Antipas, who inherited it from his father.

Just below the summit of the mountaintop upon which the fortress stood, passages had been hewn from the solid rock leading to a number of dungeon chambers. In these it had been the custom of the Herods, both father and son, to imprison those whom they wished to remove from the face of the earth. It was here that John the Baptist was imprisoned when Herod, on the urging of Herodias, arrested him.

John's imprisonment, though galling, could have been more unpleasant than it actually was. When he was taken from his dungeon for a daily period of fresh air in the courtyard, he could see from the mountaintop the lush area of the Jordan Valley around the fords at Bethabara where he had preached. From time to time his disciples were allowed to visit him, bringing news of the outside world. In this way, John had learned of the miracles his kinsman had been performing in Galilee and in Jerusalem.

When Jesus did not announce His identity as the Messiah, whose advent the Baptist had so confidently preached, John began to doubt. If Jesus really were the Anointed One, He would possess the power to free John himself from imprisonment. Yet he had not done so. Out of the depths of his doubt and his increasing despondence at being confined, John sent two of his disciples to Galilee to see Jesus.

"Are you He that is to come?" they asked as they had been instructed. "Or do we look for another?"

"Go and show John again those things which you hear and see," Jesus answered. "The blind receive their sight and the lame walk. The lepers are cleansed and the deaf hear. The dead are raised up and the poor have the gospel preached to them."

Jesus knew John would understand this reference to the words of Isaiah concerning the coming of the Messiah:

> *Then the eyes of the blind shall be opened, and the ears of the deaf shall be unstopped.*
> *Then shall the lame man leap as an hart, and the tongue of the dumb sing.*

By answering John's questions with the prophecies of Isaiah, Jesus avoided the public announcement of His identity for which the agents of Herod and the representatives of the high priest could have condemned Him. He understood John's doubt and was trying to make the Baptist understand that he would not free him from imprisonment by Herod, even though He possessed the power. For if Jesus defied Herod—and Rome—by freeing John through a miracle, He would be pitting Himself publicly against political authority; He would be choosing an earthly kingdom in which He would be in immediate conflict with Rome, rather than the spiritual kingdom He hoped to bring about in the hearts of men.

To soften this blow to John's hopes, Jesus added to the message these words, "Blessed is he who is not offended in Me." Knowing John would understand that the kingdom of God was more important than either of them, Jesus was strengthening him in whatever trials were to come.

His eyes still filled with sorrow because He had not been able to save one He loved from further imprisonment, Jesus spoke again to the people He had been teaching when John's disciples questioned Him. "Come unto Me all you that labor and are heavy laden, and I will give you rest," He told them. "Take My yoke upon you and learn of Me." The taking on of the symbolic yoke of obedience to God's will was a part of the regular liturgy of the Sabbath service. "I am meek and lowly and you shall find rest unto your souls, for My yoke is easy and My burden is light."

II

One of Jesus' most conspicuous miracles had been the healing of the demoniac—the popular term used to describe those suffering from mental disease—in the synagogue at Capernaum when His ministry in the lake region was just beginning. Later He had healed many others with similar symptoms and hearing of this, the authorities in Jerusalem sought a way to condemn even His success in curing mental disorders.

A new group of tormentors was sent from Jerusalem to Galilee with instructions to spread a rumor devised in the fertile minds of the chief priests. Not being known to the people who followed Jesus from day to day, they were able to mingle with the crowds and continue to instill the subtle poison that Jesus must be possessed by the very king of devils himself, Beelzebub, and was therefore able to cast out demons through this evil power.

It was not long before the vicious rumor came to Jesus. When it did, He took forthright action by attacking the source. Calling before Him the men who had come from Jerusalem for this special purpose, He demanded, "How can Satan cast out Satan?"

The scribes were dumfounded at having their argument turned so neatly against them.

"If a kingdom be divided against itself, that kingdom cannot stand," Jesus continued with irrefutable logic. "If a house be divided against itself, that house cannot stand. And if Satan rise up against himself and be divided, he cannot stand but is at an end."

Although the scribes were silenced by His logic, their libel had already spread widely and continued to damage Jesus' cause. The accusation of being in league with the devil had been a shrewd move on the part of His enemies, typical of the objections that the Pharisees, with their endless hairsplitting on religious questions, would devise.

As the fires of controversy over Jesus and His teachings became hotter, and the enmity of the religious authorities in Jerusalem more evident, Jesus' own family pleaded with Him to keep silent on controversial questions. They came one day where He was teaching beside the Sea of Galilee, a great crowd gathered around Him as usual. They were unable to get through, but word of their presence was passed from one listener to another until it came to those nearest Jesus.

"Your mother and brethren are yonder seeking you," He was told.

Jesus slowly surveyed the crowd. His gaze did not pause when He saw Mary of Nazareth and the other members of His family standing at the edge of the crowd; nor did He give any sign of recognition.

"My mother and My brethren are those who hear the word of God and do it," He said quietly after a moment and went on with His teaching.

Whenever Jesus taught the crowds, a number of devout women who followed Him to minister to His comfort remained at the edge of the gathering. Today Mary Magdalene, Joanna the wife of Chuza whose son had been healed by Jesus early in His ministry, and another woman named Susanna, together with several others, were waiting there. They had seen Jesus' family at the edge of the crowd but had not recognized them until their presence was pointed out to Jesus. When He spoke the words meant to show that His concern must now be always for the large family of sinners whom He sought to bring into His kingdom, Mary

Magdalene sensed that they did not understand and were hurt by what He had said.

A few months ago she would, in their place, have felt the same hurt, for she had been proud then and unsure of herself, but everything had changed since the morning on the shore just outside of Magdala. Her talent for leadership and the greatness of her heart had made her the leader of the women who served Him. Seeing His mother and the others moving away now from the crowd, she hurried to catch up with them and touched Mary of Nazareth on the shoulder.

"The mother and family of my Lord are always welcome at my house," she said. "I am called Mary of Magdala."

Mary raised dull eyes to meet the younger woman's gaze. "You heard Him," she said. "He has rejected those who love Him."

"You must not feel that way," Mary protested.

"How else should we feel?" A stocky man who had been supporting Jesus' mother with his arm about her shoulder asked harshly. It was James, the next oldest brother.

"You should feel proud," Mary told him. "Proud that one with so much to give to the world lived in your house for thirty years."

James had never forgiven Jesus for leaving him to maintain the family. "What does He give but strife and discord?" he demanded. "Our neighbors shun us because they say one of us is now an agent of Beelzebub. The agents of Herod watch the house constantly, hoping Jesus will come home so that they can arrest Him. And now He has shamed us before the multitude."

Mary Magdalene turned to Jesus' mother. "You bore Him in your body," she said softly. "Surely you know who He is."

The older woman's eyes took on a faraway look. For a moment she was a young girl again, an affianced bride, happy and yet a little fearful. She heard again the voice of the angel and remembered the promise that had made her flee to Elisabeth at Hebron for confirmation of the unbelievable message the angel had brought. Once again she felt the jostling of the mule as she and Joseph rode into Bethlehem, the pain when her womb contracted in the early forewarnings of childbirth. The inn at Bethlehem came back to her now as clearly as on that day when she had sat upon a bale and waited while Joseph argued with the innkeeper. She felt the agony of Jesus' birth in the stable and the soft touch of the cloth which the servant had given her to wrap about Him.

She remembered the visit of the Magi and the flight into Egypt to escape from Herod. And as clearly as on the day a serious-faced boy of twelve had spoken to her and Joseph in the temple, she could hear His words now, "Know you not that I must be about My Father's business?"

Remembering things which she had not thought of for a long time, Mary of Nazareth began to comprehend. She had been honored above all women by being chosen as the vessel through which the Son of God might come into the world in human form. She had been granted the boon of loving and protecting Him through the years of His infancy and childhood and the even greater gift of her son's love. Now, she recognized at last, she could no longer claim Him as her own. Like any other child who grows up and seeks His own life away from home and family, Jesus was about His Father's business and she had no right to upbraid Him if His duty took Him away from her and the others.

Mary of Nazareth raised her eyes to meet the kind and understanding gaze of the beautiful woman who stood beside her. "When He was only twelve," she said, "He told me this would happen. But I didn't understand."

"And now you do?"

"Yes. But it is hard, especially when people revile Him."

"You must see that He had no choice."

"Yes, I see that now."

"We must help Him, all of us who love Him," the woman of Magdala said.

"He does not help us," James broke in angrily. "Though He has a disciple whose only task is to carry the purse!"

Mary Magdalene started to answer but Mary of Nazareth spoke first. "Let me explain to them later," she said. "We love Jesus. It was because they seek to kill Him that we came here to plead with Him to come home."

"He knows that," Mary Magdalene assured her. "I saw His eyes just now and they were sad when He spoke of you. But His mission must come first."

She turned to James and the others. "Try to understand that Jesus is not like the rest of you, or like any of us. He—he healed me of a grievous affliction because I begged Him for help. A great honor has been given you to be members of His family. I would give up everything I possess to have that honor for myself."

James was fair, if overly strict. He studied Mary Magdalene and saw that she spoke the truth. If she would gladly exchange places with Him, he thought, he might be wrong to be resentful toward Jesus.

James looked across the crowd to Jesus, who sat upon a rock that placed Him a little above the level of the crowd so He could be heard more easily. He saw that the months since Jesus had left Nazareth had taken their toll. The smile with which He had greeted the children in the courtyard each afternoon when they came to listen to His stories was rarely seen now. His body was leaner and deep lines of care and concern for those to whom He had been sent were etched into His face. In His eyes there was a deep sadness where before there had always been the ready flash of a quick and warm smile.

Now James realized something of how hard these months of travel across the face of Galilee, and the constant nagging of the Pharisees and scribes who had been sent to torment Jesus must have been. Compared to this, life in Nazareth had been easy and pleasant; except in pursuit of a higher duty, no man would have preferred to live Jesus' life.

Looking at Jesus, James was deeply ashamed. He could not yet comprehend the identity of Jesus; that would come later. But he could sympathize now, and the burning resentment which had been a painful wound inside him began to leave him.

"You must all be weary." The voice of Mary of Magdala soothed James' thoughts. "Come home with me and we will all rest a while and refresh ourselves together."

Mary of Nazareth hesitated only momentarily as she looked across the crowd to her Son who was still speaking to the people. Strangely, though He gave no sign that He saw her or knew that she was there, something passed between them, a deep communion of spirit which comes only to those whose bodies have originally been one. Mary saw that though Jesus must be about His Father's business to the exclusion of everything else, nothing had changed between them since that day when she had wrapped Him in the swaddling cloth and laid Him in the manger at Bethlehem.

III

As if the act of publicly ignoring His immediate family had made a change in His life, Jesus turned now to a different method of teaching. Where before He had taught almost exclusively about the kingdom of God, He now began to speak largely in parables, a method by which He could instruct without giving His enemies further grounds to attack Him.

"There went out a sower to sow," He said to the crowd that followed Him everywhere now. "As he sowed, some seed fell by the wayside and the birds of the air came and devoured it. Some seed fell on stony ground where it had not much earth. It sprang up immediately because it had no depth of earth over it, but when the sun was hot, it was scorched, and because it had no roots, it withered away. Some seed fell among thorns which grew up and choked it and it yielded no fruit."

This was a comparison they could all understand, for wherever a field was left unfilled for long, the burnet thorn that covered the rocky hillsides quickly engulfed it and nothing else would grow there until the thorn bushes were dug up and their roots removed.

"Other seed fell on good ground and yielded fruit that sprang up and increased and it brought forth, thirty, sixty, and even a hundredfold," He said, ending the parable.

When Jesus was alone with the Twelve and some others who stayed near Him, He was asked about the parable's meaning.

"To you it is given to know the mystery of the kingdom of God," He told them. "But to others all these things are done in parables. The sower sows the word and those by the wayside where the seed is sown are they who, when they have heard, Satan comes immediately and takes away the word that was sown in their hearts.

"Those which are sown on the stony ground are they who, when they hear the word receive it immediately with gladness, but they have no root in themselves and so endure only a little while. Afterward, when affliction or persecution arises for the word's sake, they are offended.

"Those which are sown among thorns are such as hear the word but the cares of the world, the deceitfulness of riches, and the lusts of other things enter in and choke the word so it becomes unfruitful. But they which are sown in good ground are such as hear the word and receive it and bring forth some thirtyfold, some sixty and some an hundred.

"Unto what shall we liken the kingdom of God?" He asked as He ended the discourse. "Or with what comparison shall we compare it? It is like a grain of mustard seed which, when it is sown in the earth, is less in size than all the seeds in the earth. But when it grows up, it becomes greater than all herbs, and shoots out great branches, so that the fowls of the air may lodge under its shadow."

Once again He had used an illustration which even the simplest farmer among His listeners could readily understand. Mustard grew wild in all parts of Israel, often reaching a size that permitted a man to stand beneath its spreading leaves. In the spring whole fields were golden with its blossoms, and the linnets and finches flocked to eat the seeds. It was a valuable plant, too, for not only were the leaves gathered and cooked as a green vegetable, but the powdered seeds were used both as a flavoring for food and as an application to the skin in treating disease. The listeners easily understood from the simile how Jesus' teachings, sown like mustard seed, would grow first within the heart of each hearer and then more widely to bring about a true flowering of God's kingdom on earth.

17

He who loses his life for My sake will find it.

Matthew 10:39

On the eastern side of the Sea of Galilee and the Jordan stood the Decapolis (after the Greek word for ten), a federation of ten heathen cities within the territory of Israel. Almost entirely Grecian in their architecture, language, and religion, they had their own government and were independent of Israel. Nevertheless, many Jews lived in the Decapolis cities, and when Jesus had finished teaching at Capernaum one evening, He boarded Simon Peter's boat with His disciples and was rowed across the lake to the shore near Gadara.

It was morning before the boat reached the other side and Jesus stepped from it to the shore. At once a shout arose from the rocky hillside, and a man came bounding down a path that wound through the tombs which the Greeks of Gadara had hewn there for burying their dead. His hair and his beard were long and matted with filth and his eyes burned with the glare of a maniac while he shouted unintelligible sounds and made threatening gestures at Jesus and His companions.

The disciples drew back fearfully at the sight of the demoniac, for he was larger even than Simon Peter and the muscles of his massive arms bulged with a strength that would have made it difficult to bind him with ordinary fetters. Jesus did not draw back, but took a step toward the sick man and held out His hand in His usual gesture of compassion for those who were ill. While the awed disciples watched, the huge man knelt before Jesus and intelligible words began to pour from his mouth as he thanked God for his cure. The demons within the man (indeed there were many, for their name was Legion) had requested permission to enter a herd of swine that grazed on the hillside. Jesus granted it. And, because demons always seek destruction, the herd promptly dashed down the hillside and into the lake where they drowned.

When the people of that region heard what had happened to the swine and saw this man they had known for years as a wild beast living among the tombs now clothed and in his right mind, they were very perturbed and begged Jesus to leave the country. This He did, but before He embarked He charged the man who had been healed to return to his home and tell of the great things God had done for him. In this way there was much talk about Jesus in the cities of the Decapolis, although He did not actually continue His intended mission there.

When Simon Peter's boat reached Capernaum on the return journey, a considerable crowd had gathered, having seen the boat when it was still some distance from the shore. With them was Jairus, one of the rulers of the synagogue at Capernaum. As Jesus stepped from the boat to the shore, Jairus prostrated himself before Him. "My little daughter lies at the point of death," he said. "I pray you come and lay hands on her, so she will be healed, and shall live."

Jesus knew Jairus was a good man and was moved by his faith. Lifting the anxious father to his feet, He started for the elder's home but as He was moving through the crowd, a woman suffering from a blood disturbance touched His robe. She was instantly healed by the mere contact with His garment, but Jesus had felt her touch and turned to ask, "Who touched My clothes?"

Simon Peter by virtue of his size was leading the way through the crowd. "The multitude presses all around you, Master," he said. "How can you ask who touched you?"

Just then the woman came forward and threw herself at Jesus' feet, explaining how she had touched Him and had been healed. He did not upbraid her but said, "Daughter, your faith has made you whole. Go in peace and be well of your plague."

The interruption by the woman had delayed Jesus. Now as He moved on, a man pushed his way through the crowd and spoke to Jairus. "Your daughter is dead," he reported. "Why trouble the Master any further?"

Jesus heard the words. "Be not afraid; only believe," He counseled the grief-stricken father.

When Jesus, Simon, James, and John arrived with Jairus at his house, they found the family already mourning for the girl. "Why do you make this ado and weep?" Jesus reproved them. "The girl is not dead but asleep."

The family had all seen the girl lying upon the bed and were quite sure she was dead. Several men laughed scornfully at Jesus' words, but He ignored them and ordered everyone from the chamber except the three disciples, Jairus, and his wife. With them He went to the girl, lying still and white upon a couch, her face covered with a sheet.

"*Talitha cumi*," He said, taking her hand and speaking in the Aramaic tongue used by the Galileans. The words meant, "Damsel, I say to you, arise."

Immediately the girl rose and walked. Jesus charged those who were with Him to say nothing of the miracle, but others had seen the child lying upon the couch, apparently dead. When they now saw her walk from the bedchamber as if she had never been ill, they were astonished and word spread through Capernaum that the Teacher from Nazareth had raised the daughter of Jairus from the dead.

II

Herod Antipas was celebrating his birthday with a lavish banquet at the castle of Machaerus. The great chamber was filled with nobles of the court, his captains, the richer landowners of Galilee who paid tribute to him, and a number of high Roman officials. The tetrarch was a generous host; wine had flowed freely and by midnight everyone was drunk—except Herodias.

Herod's consort was Jewish but no more pious than he. She was a proud woman. She knew that Herod's action in putting away his former wife had angered King Aretas and that now the Nabatean armies were poised on the eastern border, watching for a chance to attack. The public denunciation by John the Baptist of the circumstances surrounding Herod's latest marriage, in addition to his naming her an adulteress, had made her husband less acceptable to the religious authorities at Jerusalem where the wily tetrarch of Galilee hoped one day to be crowned king of the Jews.

With John the Baptist in prison, Herodias had felt safer, but lately Herod had been visiting the Essene prophet. Though Herodias did not know the subject of their conversations, she was certain that John had continued to denounce her. She was therefore more than ever determined to destroy the Baptist before Herod realized how much this marriage to her had cost him. As the gaiety of Herod's birthday feast reached its climax, Herodias acted.

She had brought with her from Rome her daughter Salome, a lovely girl about seventeen years of age, already fully mature. When the feast was at its height, Herodias slyly suggested to her husband that Salome dance for the guests, dancing being an art in which the princess was well trained. To this the drunken tetrarch gave enthusiastic assent.

Herod was highly pleased with Salome's performance. "Ask of me whatever you will," he drunkenly assured the flushed and happy dancer, "even though it be half my kingdom."

When Salome ran eagerly to her mother inquiring what favor she should ask of her stepfather, Herodias knew that her scheme had succeeded. "Ask him for the head of John the Baptist."

Salome would have preferred a gift of jewelry but she did not argue. To a princess of the Herodian house, a prisoner beheaded was no more important than a bird killed with a throwing stick during the hunt. Herod the Great had killed thousands upon considerably less provocation than John had given to Antipas and Herodias, and Archelaus had without justification murdered almost as many. Returning to Herod and the other guests, Salome said, "I will that you give me the head of John the Baptist on a charger."

The request sobered Herod. While the ascetic Essene had been in prison, Herod had come almost to admire him, and occasionally he had listened to John's teaching about the coming kingdom of God. In Israel prophets had always been allowed considerable latitude in speaking against the rulers and the priestly regime. As Isaiah, Jeremiah, and other prophetic figures had denounced the kings of Israel for their iniquity, so had John denounced Herod Antipas and Herodias. There was no real precedent for executing him. But Herod had sworn an oath and if he broke it now, he would be shamed before his guests to whom the beheading of a Jewish rabble-rouser was nothing.

The order for the prisoner's death was issued and the captain of the castle guards sent to carry it out. In a little while the head of John the Baptist, still dripping blood, was brought into the banquet hall upon a charger and presented to Salome, who immediately gave it to her mother.

The sight had a chilling effect upon the drunken guests. They could not fail to see that Herod now was stricken with fear for having killed a prophet of Israel. Herodias, however, was happy. The voice which had branded her an adulteress had been silenced.

John's few remaining disciples who had stayed nearby laid his body in a tomb where it could not be further desecrated. This done, some returned to the nearby Essene community, the others started for Galilee to tell Jesus what had happened.

III

As He moved from city to city and village to village in Galilee, Jesus came once again to Nazareth with His disciples.

As usual He entered the synagogue on the Sabbath day humbly like any other worshiper, accompanied only by the disciples who were closest to Him. When it was time for visitors to speak, He rose and addressed the congregation eloquently, teaching the gospel which He had already preached to thousands on the shores of the lake and throughout the land of Galilee.

Many of the Nazarenes marveled at Jesus' teachings. "Whence has this man this wisdom and these mighty works?" they asked each other. But the majority remembered only that Jesus had once lived in their own city and began to question each other about Him.

"Is not this the carpenter's son?" one demanded.

"Is not His mother called Mary?" another asked. "And His brothers James and Joses and Simon and Judas?"

"And His sisters," the women whispered to each other. "Are they not all with us? Whence then has this man all these things?"

Unable—and unwilling—to accept the truth that the Anointed One of God had been born of woman and lived as one of them in order that He might know the temptations and weaknesses of the flesh as they did, the people of Jesus' own city rejected Him once again and began to murmur against Him.

Jesus stopped the murmuring and ended His discourse with a bitter statement. "A prophet is not without honor," He told them, "save in his own country and in his own house."

He did remain to heal the sick and perform a few miracles as was His custom. Rebuffed by the hostility of His former neighbors, He avoided them and left the city to return there no more. So in Nazareth the prophecy of Isaiah concerning the Messiah was fulfilled not once but twice: "He is despised and rejected of men, a man of sorrows and acquainted with grief. And we hid as it were our faces from Him; He was despised and we esteemed Him not."

The somber mood with which Jesus withdrew from Nazareth was not lightened when He received the news brought by John's disciples that His kinsman had been beheaded.

IV

Soon after leaving Nazareth, Jesus called together the Twelve whom He had singled out as His most trusted disciples. The time had come for them, like children leaving home to make lives for themselves, to take up their own ministry in order that word of the kingdom of God might be spread abroad.

"The harvest is truly plenteous," He told them, "but the laborers are few. Pray the Lord of the harvest therefore that He will send forth laborers unto His harvest."

When they had finished a prayer, He charged the disciples before sending them out two by two. "Go to the lost sheep of Israel and as you go, preach, saying, 'The kingdom of heaven is at hand.' Heal the sick, cleanse the lepers, raise the dead, cast out devils." The disciples were given the same miraculous powers which He Himself possessed.

"Freely you have received, freely give," He continued. "Provide neither gold, nor silver, nor brass in your purses, nor scrip for your journey. Neither two coats, neither shoes nor yet staves, for the workman is worthy of his meat. Into whatever city or town you shall enter, inquire who in it is worthy and there abide until you go thence."

Next He gave them a warning out of His own bitter experience as well as a foretaste of the future. "Behold, I send you forth as sheep in the midst of wolves. You shall be brought before governors and kings for My sake, for a testimony against them and the Gentiles. You shall be hated by all men for My sake, but he that endures to the end shall be saved."

Now His voice rose in a paean of hope and inspiration for all who would serve Him and suffer for their loyalty. "Are not two sparrows sold for a farthing? Yet not one of them shall fall to the ground without your Father's knowledge. The very hairs of your head are all numbered. Fear not, therefore; you are of more value than many sparrows. Whoever shall confess Me before men, him will I confess before My Father which is in heaven. But whoever shall deny Me before men, him will I also deny before My Father which is in heaven. He that does not take his cross and follow after Me is not worthy of Me. And he that loses his life for My sake shall find it."

18

Lord, to whom shall we go? You have the words of eternal life.

John 6:68

Until now opposition to Jesus had come mainly from the Pharisees and scribes who saw in His liberal interpretation of Mosaic Law a threat to what they considered the welfare of Israel. The concept of the Anointed One, the Messiah who was to come, had been formed in a period of national trial and travail, when Judaism as a religion and the Jews as a people had been fighting for their very existence.

The Pharisees had visualized the Messiah as a great national deliverer, or perhaps as two persons, an earthly leader to bring political freedom and a spiritual leader, probably a high priest, who would be the very epitome of the orthodoxy which the Pharisees revered. They were very strict in this provision, and much of their enmity toward Jesus arose because He threatened their rigid concepts of Judaism.

At first the Pharisees at Jerusalem had considered Jesus an impostor worthy only of contempt. But when His following increased so rapidly, and particularly when the sending out of the Twelve marked a widening phase of His ministry, their efforts to thwart Him intensified. In addition, because Jesus was a Galilean, His growing popularity, with so many openly naming Him the Messiah, now became a source of concern to Herod who ruled here for Rome.

When the belief began to spread in Galilee that Jesus was the Messiah, He also became a threat to the priestly class at Jerusalem, largely composed of the Sadducees. If He succeeded in convincing the masses that He was the Anointed One, they would be forced to yield the temple and its worship to Him as the direct representative of the Most High, giving up the enormously profitable revenues that poured in daily.

As the time approached for the Twelve to return and give an account of their stewardship, Jesus faced steadily increasing tension and difficulty. Opposed bitterly by the Pharisees and scribes on one side and by the Sadducees and Herodians on the other, He had to curb at the same time the eagerness of the crowds who would make Him king in the hope that He would free them from the burdens of taxation and Roman oppression. All these secular conflicts inevitably hindered His mission to preach the kingdom of God.

II

Spring was far advanced and the dry season approaching when the Twelve returned. Jesus greeted them warmly. "Come apart into a desert place and rest a while," He told them and led the way to a large fishing boat drawn up on the shore at the establishment of Zebedee.

East of Bethsaida near the region of Hippos in the Decapolis there was a lonely, uninhabited area lying between two brooks which, though dry during the summer, were now turbulent from the spring rains. Here the heights of the tableland north of the lake closely approached the shore, leaving only a narrow strand of flat land, heavily carpeted with green grass. The crowd following Jesus around the northern arc of the lakeshore as He and the disciples crossed in the boat had not reached this area when He and His companions debarked and climbed into the hills to a secluded spot. The Twelve told glowingly of healing the sick, curing mental diseases, and performing miracles in Jesus' name which had attracted the attention of the crowds and made them marvel.

By now a crowd had gathered on the narrow strip of lakeshore at the foot of the hill where Jesus had retreated with His disciples. Most of them had walked, but many crippled had been brought by boat. When He saw the effort the people had made to follow Him, Jesus could not refuse them His miracle-working power; leaving His disciples, He descended to the grassy shore and began to heal.

The afternoon passed in this way and the crowd was still there when the sun began to sink toward the mountains of Galilee. Since the evening meal was the only large one eaten during the day, the approach of night found most of the listeners without food and with no way to procure it.

Judas of Kerioth carried the money pouch, and it was therefore his task to provide for the material needs of Jesus and the disciples. Some loaves and fish had been hurriedly procured before they left Capernaum, but these were barely enough for their own needs. When Jesus showed no sign of dismissing the crowd and sending them home for the night, Judas sought out Simon Peter and the two approached the Master.

"This is a desert place and it grows late," Simon reminded Him. "Send the people away so they can go into the villages and buy bread."

"Give them food to eat," Jesus directed and turned back to His teaching.

"We have only about two hundred denarii," Judas said indignantly to Peter. The disciples had obeyed Jesus literally when He had told them to carry neither silver nor gold nor brass coins. "That would not even begin to feed five thousand people."

The two approached Jesus again. "Shall we go and buy two hundred pennyworth of bread and give it to them to eat?" Judas asked a little sarcastically.

"How many loaves have you?" Jesus asked.

"Five loaves and two fish," Simon reported.

Jesus got to His feet. "Bring them to Me," He directed.

While Simon and Judas went to get the loaves and the fish, Jesus directed the crowd to divide themselves into groups of about fifty each.

When traveling any distance, most Galileans carried a small basket into which they put fruit left on the trees by the pickers, fish too small to be dried, and anything else of value they found on the way. Jesus now blessed the loaves and the fish and directed representatives from each of the groups of fifty to pass before Him with their baskets as He divided the food.

As the line of men carrying baskets approached Jesus, a murmur of jeering laughter began to rise from some parts of the crowd. He ignored it, however, and began to break the bread and fish into pieces and drop them into the baskets that were held out to Him. As He did so, the laughter faltered and then vanished. Beneath Jesus' swiftly moving hands, the fish and the bread seemed to multiply again and again. Each basket that passed before Him was filled and yet there was no sign of an end to the plenitude of food He had produced from one small basketful.

The people looked warily at the baskets carried out to them, uncertain whether they were not being tricked. A few reached in and took the food, carrying it gingerly to their mouths and tasting it carefully, as if afraid it was unreal. But when Jesus Himself began to eat and after Him the disciples, the people followed their lead. Soon the whole five thousand were eating joyously, for there was such a supply that no one needed to eat sparingly.

Judas had been astounded when Jesus produced such a vast quantity of food from almost nothing, but he did not let his astonishment overcome his frugal nature. Under his direction, twelve baskets of fragments were gathered for the morning meal and, as he supervised their collection, his mind worked busily. Before he had joined the Twelve, Judas had been sure that Jesus' miracles could be turned to profit. Now the feeding of the five thousand showed him how they could. In following Jesus he had made a wise choice indeed!

III

The other disciples too were excited by the implications of the miracle they had witnessed. Jesus, however, did not allow them to question Him or discuss it with the crowd. Instead He sent them away secretly by boat that same evening, promising to follow later.

Excited as they were and engrossed with their own plans for the future, none of them noticed that a storm was building up until it descended upon them near the center of the lake with all the sudden fury of which storms were capable in this deep, hill-lined cup. Before they could even lower the sail, the boat was half-filled with water.

Gone now was their jubilation at the prospect of seeing Jesus at last assume His rightful place as King and Messiah in Israel. As the waterlogged boat was tossed about by the winds and their situation grew worse by the moment, they began to cry out from fear, certain that they were to be drowned.

With the keen eyes of a fisherman, John was the first to see what appeared to be a man walking on the water toward them. As the figure approached, they saw that it was Jesus but the sight only increased their fear, for they were sure now that the Master had been killed and they were seeing His spirit.

"It is I," Jesus called out to them from some distance away. "Be not afraid."

The disciples could hardly believe it was really Jesus in the flesh, although that very afternoon they had seen Him perform a miracle fully as great as that of walking on the water. Simon Peter was the first to find courage to speak.

"If it is you, Lord," he called to Jesus, "bid me come to You on the water."

"Come," Jesus said at once.

Hesitantly, Simon rolled up the hem of his robe and stepped out of the boat. The water supported him and he took a few tentative steps toward Jesus. Then the faith that had led him to leave the boat began to desert him in the face of the waves that bore down upon him. And being afraid, he at once began to sink.

"Lord, save me!" Peter cried desperately, reaching out imploring hands to Jesus as he sank into the water.

Without trying Peter further, Jesus stretched out His hand and lifted Him to the surface again. "O you of little faith!" He said reprovingly. "Why did you doubt?"

Together Jesus and Peter, who was greatly ashamed at having failed in the test of faith, boarded the boat. The storm subsided shortly and they were able to continue back to Capernaum.

IV

Arza, the coppersmith, had prospered since the day when he had been let down through the roof of Simon Peter's house. Many who had witnessed the miracle were curious to see if it were permanent and came to visit Arza in his shop, sometimes bringing him business. Soon he had been forced to employ additional smiths and was able to wear a fine robe on the Sabbath. Since he was industrious, aggressive, and pious, there had been talk lately of making him one of the rulers of the congregation, an important position in a synagogue as large as that of Capernaum.

Arza had not seen Jesus since the day he had been healed, but he had heard of the further miracles the Nazarene was performing and knew that many people now believed Him to be the Messiah. When word spread through Capernaum that Jesus and His disciples were at the fishing sheds of Zebedee, Arza assigned enough work to his smiths to keep them busy for the rest of the day and hurried off to the shore. He was curious to hear the teachings of one who might be the Messiah and besides, he might even have a chance to speak to Jesus and call the crowd's attention to himself and his new-found prosperity.

Arza had arrived only in time to see Jesus and the disciples embarking to cross the lake, but when the crowd began to follow around the northern shore, he had joined it. There he had listened as Jesus taught through the afternoon and healed the sick. And as he watched, a growing conviction had developed in the coppersmith's mind that he was witnessing the manifestation of a power which could come only from God and might also be used for material benefits.

Then had come the astounding miracle of feeding the five thousand with the loaves and fishes. Arza had eaten heartily himself and knew that this was no trick, and as he considered the implications of a power that could create food where there had been nothing, a deep excitement began to rise within him, the nucleus of a plan which, could he but put it into effect, might easily mean a rich future for Arza himself, considerably greater than that of a successful coppersmith, or even of a ruler in the synagogue.

When the meal was finished and the fragments gathered up, Arza began to visit the groups of fifty who gathered around the campfires they had built along the shore to discuss the astounding miracle they had just witnessed. Wherever Arza went among them he stayed only long enough to start one topic of conversation and implant the idea that a man who could feed five thousand people from a few loaves and fish must possess also the power to become king in Israel, destroying the Romans and the hated son of Herod the Great with the thunderbolts of God which He no doubt also commanded.

Fresh from experiencing the miraculous power of Jesus, many of the crowd eagerly took up the suggestion, but Arza delayed his approach to Jesus or the disciples. And when he saw Jesus send the disciples back to Capernaum by boat shortly after nightfall he was pleased. He would go to Jesus in the morning with a fully formed plan, and to this end he enlisted the help of several others in the crowd whom he knew. One was a fellow smith named Ahab, another a merchant of Tiberias named Shobeal. They listened and eagerly agreed to stir up enthusiasm for Arza's scheme among the crowd.

Arza intended to remind Jesus that he had been among the first to be healed by His miraculous power. Then, as planned, he would announce the crowd's decision to acclaim Jesus as king and usher Him in triumph to Tiberias where He could assume the throne of Herod in Galilee before going on to Jerusalem for the final act of naming Himself King of the Jews. According to the plan, Ahab and Shobeal would lead the people in a surge of triumphant acclamation which must surely eliminate any reservations Jesus might have. To the coppersmith it was unbelievable that Jesus could have any objection to his plan or that a man who possessed the power to be king would refuse to exercise it.

He slept little that night, excited by the possibilities of his scheme. He did not doubt that Jesus would make Arza himself anything less than a chief minister in His court. But when the sun rose, Arza and his fellow plotters were dumfounded to learn that Jesus had disappeared in the night.

The coppersmith was not one to give up easily, however. The same persistence which had made him hire men to carry him across the housetops and let him down on his pallet through the roof made him refuse to admit defeat now. He recovered himself quickly and, at the head of the crowd, started back to Capernaum, sure that Jesus must have walked there during the night and that they would find Him in the city.

But once again, Arza found himself blocked. The Master had not gone to Capernaum but had withdrawn to teach His disciples after their arrival following the storm. All that day Arza fumed angrily at the miscarriage of his scheme to make Jesus a king, and himself chief minister. Even in his annoyance, however, he did not fail to attend the Sabbath service the next day, since his absence might have prejudiced those who were considering him as a future ruler of the congregation. To his surprise, he found Jesus in the synagogue, teaching as usual.

Arza waited impatiently for the service to end, then with Ahab and Shobeal he accosted Jesus in the yard outside as the people were leaving. In his eagerness to carry through his project while the news of the miraculous feeding of the five thousand was still fresh in people's minds, he was almost brusque in his approach.

"Master," he demanded, "when did you come here?"

Jesus studied the coppersmith and his companions for a moment, reading what was in their hearts. "You do not seek Me because you saw the miracles, but because you ate of the loaves and were filled," He said severely. "Do not labor for the meat that perisheth, but for that meat which endures unto everlasting life."

"What shall we do that we might work the works of God?" Shobeal asked eagerly.

"This is the work of God, that you believe in Him He has sent."

Arza was not satisfied. Something spectacular was needed, something that would arouse the people of Capernaum as the feeding of the five thousand had stirred the crowd who had eaten the loaves and the fish. "What signs will you show that we may see and believe?" he demanded.

If Jesus had not experienced and put away this form of temptation long ago when He had wrestled with the voice of evil on the mountain after His baptism by John, He might have been tempted now to give the people the sign they wished. But He had no desire to achieve earthly glory or to attain high position in the eyes of men.

When Jesus did not answer Arza's question, the merchant Shobeal spoke again. "Our fathers ate manna in the desert," he said. "And it is written, 'He gave them bread from heaven to eat.'"

The merchant was challenging Jesus to produce bread here in Capernaum out of nothing, an act which must surely have made a tremendous impression upon the crowd, many of whom were always hungry. But again Jesus did not rise to the challenge.

"Moses did not give you that bread from heaven, but My Father gave you the true bread from heaven," He replied. "The bread of God is He that comes down from heaven and gives life to the world."

They still did not understand, thinking He meant bread in the same sense as that of the loaves and fish He had provided. "Lord, evermore give us this bread," Ahab begged, thinking to impress those of the people who had not eaten with the five thousand.

"I am the living bread which came down from heaven," Jesus said. "If any man eat of this bread he shall live forever."

In the silence someone in the crowd called out in a loud and contemptuous voice. "How can He say, 'I come down from heaven' when we know He comes from Nazareth?" he demanded.

At that the people began to laugh. Arza realized now that Jesus would not let Himself be made king in Galilee. To save face, he turned and began to move away. All of them had heard Arza and the others ask Jesus for a sign to prove He was the expected Messiah and had heard Him refuse. To them this could only mean that He had no divine power; it was unthinkable that a man should possess such power and refuse to reply to a demand that He prove it.

When Jesus saw that many of those who had listened to His teachings were now leaving Him, He turned to the Twelve. "Will you also go away?" He asked.

For a moment no one answered. Many of them, too, had been shaken by His failure to announce Himself as the Anointed One of God. It was Simon Peter, who put into words the very essence of his faith.

"Lord, to whom shall we go?" the tall fisherman asked. "You have the words of eternal life."

No one, having put his hand to the plow,
and looking back, is fit for the kingdom of God.

Luke 9:62

During the spring Jesus moved about northern Galilee and the border region of Syro-Phoenicia, taking His message to the smaller villages and towns. The approach of summer had already begun to bathe the Sea of

Galilee with an intense heat which would grow steadily more enervating as the season advanced. Herod's hostility had steadily increased when spies had brought the tetrarch word of the abortive attempt to make Him king after the feeding of the five thousand. For these reasons Jesus decided to leave Galilee and spend some time in the mountainous region to the north where the climate would be more pleasant. In addition, He could be sure of less political opposition in this region, for Philip, the tetrarch who ruled there, had shown no animosity toward Him.

Leaving Bethsaida-Julias on the Sea of Galilee, Jesus and the disciples traveled northward on the east bank of the Jordan toward Caesarea-Philippi. The river in this area was about twenty-five paces wide, a swift-rushing stream filled with fish and fringed by a belt of oleanders, zakkum, tall fan-like papyrus, and giant reeds which made penetration for any distance from the road almost impossible. Along the river were many towns and villages where Jesus paused to teach, for although this was predominantly a Gentile region, many Jews lived here.

Almost halfway from Bethsaida to Caesarea the Jordan widened out to form a small body of water called Lake Huleh by the Jews and Lake Semechonitis by the Gentiles. At its southern end, the lake was an impenetrable canebrake or morass with a very large growth of papyrus. Wild mustard grew to a great height with giant lilies whose petals met overhead like a canopy. The jungle-like swamp abounded with. animals, birds in great numbers nested here, and the hum of bees was a constant obbligato to the rush of water.

A broad, fertile plain extended north of Lake Huleh for some eight or ten miles. To the east were the foothills of Mount Hermon and in the midst of a fertile plain the ancient city of Dan or Laish, "a place where there is no lack of anything that is in the earth," according to the ancient writings. On the west side of the city, at the foot of the slope upon which it lay, a great stream burst forth from the earth to form one of the sources of the Jordan, joining another which arose some distance away. The northernmost town in ancient Israel, when its limits extended from "Dan to Beersheba," the city had always been a polyglot one.

From Laish to Caesarea-Philippi was a two hours' walk along a road winding upward from the lower slopes of Mount Hermon. With the coming of summer the snow had begun to melt, but the crest of the mountain was still a glossy white and there were streaks in the bottoms of the ravines. From the mountain's lofty crest, visible upon a clear day from almost every point in Israel, the Great Sea could be seen and, looking southward, the jewel-like outlines of Lake Huleh and the Sea of Galilee with the Jordan connecting them like a silver band. To the east the white roofs of Damascus might also be visible.

At the foot of the slope upon which Caesarea stood, the chief source of the Jordan burst from beneath a high wall of rock in what had been called since ancient times the Cave of Pan. Here in the beautiful region around Caesarea where the air was fragrant with flowers and cool even in summer, Jesus and His disciples withdrew together from the press of the crowds which had followed them for so many months.

II

From the slopes of Mount Hermon where He had gone alone to pray, Jesus could look down upon the whole broad panorama of the Jewish homeland and the people to whom He had been sent. When finally He returned to where the disciples waited, they could see that whatever it was that His prayers had revealed, it had brought Him no joy. There was a look of gravity and sadness in His eyes.

The Twelve gathering around Him again, He propounded to them the simple question, "Who do men say that I am?"

"Some say John the Baptist," He was told, "and others Elijah."

Another of the disciples added, "One of the prophets."

"And who do you say that I am?"

Simon, the tall, impetuous fisherman answered, "You are the Christ," he said simply. "The Son of the living God."

Jesus smiled and His great love for the big man with the simple faith and love was declared by the glow in His eyes. "Blessed are you, Simon, son of Jonas," Jesus said. "For flesh and blood did not reveal it to you but My Father which is in heaven. I say to you that you are Peter and upon this rock I will build My church, and the gates of hell shall not prevail against it."

Here was more than a play on the words *Petros* meaning Peter and *petra* which meant rock. Jesus here announced publicly what had been apparent to the disciples for a long time; Simon Peter was close to the Master and, after Him, their rightful leader. At the same time, Jesus had not denied Peter's identification of Him as the Christ, a fact which they interpreted to mean that He had at last announced Himself as the Messiah.

Some of the disciples had joined the group because they believed Jesus to be the Messiah who would soon assume temporal power in Israel and the religious leadership of the people. His refusal to seize that power when it had been offered Him in Galilee had strongly shaken their faith. Now they were overjoyed to hear Him admit His identity as the Christ, a term with the same meaning as Messiah, even though the identification had been made indirectly by Peter. Then hopes rose that when they returned to Galilee, He would assume political power.

Jesus' next words dashed their hopes, for He charged them not to tell anyone the true nature of His divine calling. "The Son of Man must suffer many things," He explained, "and be rejected of the elders and the chief priests and scribes, and be slain, and be raised up on the third day."

Simon Peter rebuked Him. "Be it far from you, Lord," he protested. "This shall not happen to you."

"Get thee behind Me, Satan," Jesus said sharply to Peter, "for you mind not the things of God but the things of men!" Then He turned to the others, "If any man will come after Me, let him deny himself and take up his cross and follow Me. For whoever will save his life shall lose it, and whoever shall lose his life for My sake shall find it. What does a man profit if he gain the whole world and lose his own soul?"

III

For six days Jesus and the disciples moved through the towns and villages in the prosperous region around Caesarea-Philippi. At the end of that period, He took with Him the three whom He had first called on the shores of Galilee and climbed part of the way up the slopes of Mount Hermon. There He drew aside and began to pray.

It had been a tiring climb and as the three waited, their eyes grew heavy. Describing long afterward what then had proceeded to happen, none of them could be sure whether it was that they had seen a vision there on Mount Hermon or had only experienced an extraordinarily vivid dream.

Jesus had gone a short distance away from them into a wooded glen on the mountainside. For a moment they had lost sight of Him, then, as a brilliant white light began to fill the glen, they saw Him reappear. The blinding glory flooded the whole area with a light such as none of them had ever witnessed before and Jesus stood in the very midst of it. Now His rough garments were white and glistening, as were those of the two men who stood at His side talking with Him. The lines of care that had been in His face of late were erased and His countenance was as that of a King—or God.

The two men who shared with Jesus the center of the unearthly brilliance were much older than He, yet they seemed to speak to Him with deference. The disciples could not hear the words, but Simon Peter, impetuous as ever, called out to Jesus, "Lord, it is good for us to be here. Let us make three tabernacles, one for you and one for Moses and one for Elijah."

Ever since the Children of Israel had come up out of Egypt, the building of the small booths of interlaced branches called tabernacles had been customary with them when they worshiped God in a place where there was no synagogue. During the Feast of Tabernacles, every pious Jew built such a structure in his yard and lived there for the period of the feast, thus symbolically putting aside the temptations and the sins of everyday life and dwelling intimately in the presence of God.

It was this custom that now moved Peter to suggest building the tabernacles. He could not have said why he spoke the names of the prophets, except that he, as James and John, was now conscious of the identity of the two men there with Jesus. Strangely, the three of them had felt no fear in the presence of these men who had been dead for hundreds of years.

Jesus did not answer Peter's suggestion that they build tabernacles for Him and Moses and Elijah. But a thick white cloud now rolled across the face of the mountain, shutting from their view the glen and the scene they had been witnessing and blotting out the brilliant white light. From the midst of the cloud, they heard a voice, like none they had ever heard before.

"This is My beloved Son, in whom I am well pleased," the voice said. "Hear Him."

Slowly the cloud drifted away. When it was gone, the three now saw Jesus standing in the glen clothed in His usual homespun. But when they told Him excitedly what they had seen, He instructed them not to reveal it to anyone. Only long afterward, when the nature of the vision had at last become clear to them, did any of the three reveal what happened that afternoon on Mount Hermon.

At the foot of the mountain a crowd had gathered, among them some scribes who had been questioning the rest of the Twelve.

"What do you question them?" Jesus asked, and a man stepped from the crowd leading a boy.

"Master, I have brought you my son who has a dumb spirit," he said. "When the demon seizes him, he tears him and the boy foams and gnashes with his teeth and pines away. I asked Your disciples to cast the demon out and they could not."

Jesus' eyes went from one to another of the nine who had remained behind when He went up on the mountain with Peter, James, and John. One by one they looked away, unable to meet His eyes.

"O faithless generation," He said. "How long shall I be with you? How long shall I suffer you?" Then He turned back to the father of the boy. "Bring him to Me," He directed.

As the father led him forward, the boy was seized with a fit and fell to the ground, thrashing about and foaming at the mouth in a severe epileptic convulsion.

"How long has he had this?" Jesus asked.

"Since he was a child," the father said. "Sometimes it has thrown him into the fire or the water to destroy him. If you can do anything, have compassion on us and help us."

"If you can believe," Jesus told him, "all things are possible."

The father of the afflicted boy dropped to his knees, with tears running down his cheeks. "Lord, I believe," he said, "help my unbelief!"

When He saw the man's faith, Jesus spoke and the boy was cured. Later the discomfited nine came to Him and asked, "Why could not we cast out the demon?"

"Because of your unbelief," He told them. "Truly I say to you, if you have faith the size of a grain of mustard seed, you shall say to this mountain, 'Remove hence to yonder place,' and it shall remove, and nothing shall be impossible to you."

After healing the epileptic child, Jesus and the disciples turned westward from the district of Caesarea-Philippi and entered northern Galilee, moving down on the west side of the Jordan toward the lake once more. On the way He tried to tell them what had been revealed to Him on the mountain. "The Son of Man is delivered into the hands of men," He said, "and they shall kill Him. And after He is killed, He shall rise on the third day."

But they thought He was speaking in a parable and did not understand.

IV

In the Law of Moses it was written: "They shall give, every one that passeth among them that are numbered, half a shekel after the shekel of the sanctuary. A half-shekel shall be the offering unto the Lord. Every one that passeth among them that are numbered, from twenty years old and above, shall give an offering to the Lord."

In accordance with this law, a half-shekel tribute was exacted annually from each adult Jew for the support of the temple and the regular religious services there.

As soon as Jesus and the disciples returned to Capernaum from the region around Caesarea-Philippi, those concerned with collecting the half-shekel tribute came to Peter, knowing him to be close to Jesus. "Does not your Master pay the tribute?" they asked.

Remembering how often Jesus had denounced the temple authorities at Jerusalem as charlatans in the house of the Most High, Peter should have immediately recognized the reason for the question. If Jesus failed to pay the half-shekel, He would be transgressing a strict Mosaic Law and could be brought to trial and severely punished. On the other hand, if He paid the shekel, the act would be cited as evidence that He supported the priestly hierarchy.

Peter, however, did not stop to consider the deeper implications of the seemingly innocent question. The Law said the tribute was to be paid, everyone knowing that much of the money went into the already heavy purses of the chief priests n Jerusalem. Peter did not consult Jesus but went into the house to get money for the tribute.

Jesus had heard and seen all this, and when Peter came for the money, He stopped him. "What do you think, Simon?" He asked. "Of whom do the kings of earth take custom or tribute? Of their own children or of strangers?"

Peter could give only one answer. "Of strangers."

"Then the children are free," Jesus pointed out to him. Peter was greatly troubled by Jesus' words. He had told the tax gatherer Jesus would pay the tribute. Not only would he lose face if now he had to admit that he had spoken untruly, but to announce Jesus' refusal to obey such an important provision of the Law could cause further serious conflict with the religious authorities.

Jesus understood Peter's concern and its source. "Notwithstanding, lest we should offend them," He said quietly, "go to the sea and cast a hook and take the first fish that comes up. When you open its mouth you will find a piece of money. Take that and give it to them for us."

It was a strange task Jesus had set Peter, more strange even than His instructions long ago near this very spot to let down the net into the deep waters of the lake in the daytime when no one could expect to catch fish. On that occasion the catch of fish had almost sunk both Peter's boat and that of the sons of Zebedee—it was a thing that a fisherman could be counted on not to forget.

Peter did not quibble but went immediately as Jesus had instructed him. And when he drew up a fish and looked into its mouth, there he found a shekel which he gave to the tax gatherer.

The wily tax collector could neither say that Jesus had paid the tribute nor that He had not.

V

Position meant a great deal among the Jews. Even at the simplest dinners, guests were seated strictly according to their importance in the community, and the greatest honor was to occupy the place at a feast next to him who gave it. Being only human, some of the disciples began speculating who would occupy the most important positions after that of Jesus Himself in the kingdom which He had assured them was to come.

As always, Jesus understood what was in the hearts of those He loved. He had labored to teach these men the great truths which should guide them in even the smallest activities of their daily lives; He found no pleasure now in realizing how little had actually taken root even in the minds of these men who were His constant companions. As soon as they came into the house of Simon Peter at Capernaum, after a trying day in which arguments among the Twelve had been particularly heated, Jesus called them together and began to explain how the kingdom of heaven would be ordered. "If any desires to be first," He told them, "the same shall be least of all and the servant of all."

Peter's little son had been standing nearby listening. Jesus drew the boy to His side and put His arm about him. "Except you be converted and become as a little child," He told the disciples, "you shall not enter into the kingdom of heaven. Who therefore shall humble himself as this little child, the same is greatest in the kingdom of heaven. And whoever receives one such little child in My name, receives Me."

Then His voice grew stern. "But if anyone shall offend one of these little children which believes in Me, it will be better for him that a millstone be hung around his neck and that he were drowned in the depths of the sea."

Now He turned to a parable, the method of teaching He loved best. "If a man has a hundred sheep and one of them has gone astray, does he not leave the ninety-nine and go into the mountain to search for the one that has gone astray?"

The boy's eyes were bright as He watched Jesus' face and listened, for children always loved the simple stories.

"And if he finds it," Jesus continued, "he rejoices more for that sheep than over the ninety-nine which did not go astray. Even so it is not the will of your Father in heaven that one of these little ones shall perish."

The rabbinical schools argued endlessly concerning how far a man should tolerate others who attacked him before he rose up and smote his enemies. Some of the rabbis said a trespass should be forgiven three times, others seven. Jesus had just told the disciples that a man who desired to be first in His kingdom must be the servant of all, but Peter still asked, "Lord, how often shall my brother sin against me and I forgive him? Till seven times?"

Jesus looked at the tall disciple soberly, for Peter should have known the answer. "I do not say seven times, but seventy times seven," He answered. Then so there could be no question in their minds, He gave them another parable. "The kingdom of heaven is like a certain king who decided to take account of his servants. When he had begun to reckon, one was brought to him who owed him ten thousand talents. And since he could not pay, his lord ordered that the servant be sold with his wife and his children and all he possessed, and payment made.

"The servant therefore fell down and worshiped him saying, 'Lord, have patience with me and I will pay you all.' Then the lord of that servant was moved with compassion and freed him and forgave him the debt. But the same servant went out and found one of his fellow servants who owed him a hundred pence. He laid hands on him and took him by the throat saying, 'Pay me what you owe.'

"Then his fellow servant fell down at his feet and besought him saying,

'Have patience with me and I will pay you all I owe.' But he would not and cast him into prison until he paid the debt.

"When his fellow servants saw what was done, they were very sorry and came and told their lord. Then his lord called him and said, 'O wicked servant! I forgave you all that debt because you asked me. Should you also not have had compassion on your fellow servant, even as I had compassion on you?' Then the lord was wroth and delivered him to the tormentors till he should pay all that was due."

Jesus looked soberly at the group sitting around Him for He was troubled by their lack of faith and understanding. "So likewise shall My heavenly Father do to you, if from your hearts you do not forgive your brothers their trespasses," He told them.

The conditions under which men could come to Him and share what He had to give, including the gift of eternal life, He had now made clear, but He added a final admonition: "No man, having put his hand to the plow and looking back, is fit for the kingdom of God."

But many outside the Twelve lacked faith and forsook Him.

Mary has chosen that good part,
which will not be taken away from her.

Luke 10:42

Early autumn brought the Feast of Tabernacles and Jesus made plans to go quietly up to Jerusalem with His disciples to attend it. First, however, He wished to widen the sphere of His ministry by sending out a new group of followers to teach and heal in His name. For this purpose He chose from outside the Twelve, who now went with Him everywhere, seventy men who believed implicitly in His teachings and had given themselves up unreservedly to furthering His kingdom. As with the Twelve when He first sent them out, He instructed the seventy.

"Go your ways," He told them. "Behold I send you forth as lambs among wolves. Carry neither purse nor scrip nor shoes, and salute no man by the way."

Custom ordinarily required an elaborate routine of salutations when a devout Jew came into the home of another. But time was short and so much had to be accomplished before the final events Jesus had revealed to His disciples would take place, that He instructed the seventy to waste none of it in the elaborate exchange of these salutations that the Pharisees doted upon, but to be about His work while there was yet time for Him to witness the results of their labors.

"Into whatsoever house you enter," He told them further, "first say 'Peace be unto this house.' And if the Son of Peace be there, your peace shall be upon it. If not, it shall return to you again. Remain in the same house, eating and drinking such things as they give, for the laborer is worthy of his hire. Go not from house to house.

"Into whatsoever city you enter and they receive you, eat such things as they set before you. Heal the sick and say to them, 'The kingdom of God has come near to you,' but into whatever city you enter and they do not receive you, go your way out into the streets and say, 'Even the dust of your city which cleaves upon us, we wipe off against you. Notwithstanding, know this, that the kingdom of God has come near to you.' I say to you that it shall be more tolerable in that day for Sodom than for that city."

Having sent the seventy to teach and heal in His name, Jesus now started for Jerusalem by the direct route through Samaria. On Mount Gerizim, the Samaritans had built their own temple which they considered holier than the one built by Herod at Jerusalem. In the first village in which Jesus planned to stop, the messengers sent ahead to find lodgings were told that the people would not receive Him because He was going to Jerusalem and they refused to associate with Jews who worshiped at the temple there.

Not without good reason had the sons of Zebedee, James and John, been nicknamed "Sons of Thunder" by Jesus' company. They were easily stirred by anger and now, fired by the insolence of the Samaritans in spurning the Son of God, John begged, "Lord, let us bid fire come down from heaven and consume them!"

Jesus rebuked him and turned away from the country of the Samaritans. He had sought to bring the good tidings to Samaria, but being rejected there He did as He had counseled the seventy and shook the very dust from His feet, taking the longer route by way of Peraea and Jericho which the pilgrims from Galilee ordinarily followed.

II

The hilly country of Judea and Galilee was especially suitable for growing grapes for wine. Situated mainly on the slopes of the hills where drainage was adequate and the vines would not rot from dampness during rainy periods, the vineyards occupied broad terraces with retaining walls of stone. Some were hundreds of years old, having been handed down through many generations. Each year the vines were individually trained and pruned back to the original stem. Nothing else was planted in the vineyards, which were surrounded by hedges of thorn bushes to keep out thieves and animals which might nibble at the vines and damage the valuable parent stem. Larger vineyards usually had a tower from which a lookout kept watch during the harvest season.

In the soft limestone of each hill crowned with vineyards a cave had been hollowed out to contain the winepress. Here the rich purple grapes picked from the vines at harvest were trampled with bare feet to press out the juice which was collected in large vats at a lower level. The coming of autumn brought the annual season of the harvest to the vineyards, an occasion of much merrymaking in connection with the gathering of the grapes.

Because the making of wine played so important a part in the life of the Jews and their economy, it had very early in their history come to have a religious significance, the harvest period being celebrated with rejoicing and thanksgiving to God in what was called the Festival of Booths or Tabernacles. Everyone who could went up to the temple to make a sacrifice of penance and expiation for his sins, but the real celebration took place at home where merrymaking was not only allowed but expected, since this was truly an occasion for joyful thanks to the Lord for the bounteous harvest.

According to custom the Jews lived during the Feast of Tabernacles in the open booths which they constructed with boughs of green trees woven together to produce a cool, leafy arbor. Sometimes these booths were upon the roofs of the houses, but usually they were in the yards. All the ordinary activities—playing, eating, sleeping, and the like—were conducted in the booths, the house becoming for that period only a secondary dwelling. The cool autumn days were ideal for enjoying this brief period of freedom from encompassing walls before being shut into the houses for the winter season.

The most heavily traveled road from Jericho approached Jerusalem across the summit of the Mount of Olives which was separated from the city itself by the Kedron Valley, through which flowed the brook of the same name. Just east of the Mount of Olives was the small but lovely village of Bethany. Here dwelt a family consisting of two sisters, Martha and Mary, and a younger brother, Lazarus.

When the family had been orphaned by one of the plagues which periodically swept the countryside, it had fallen upon the older sister, Martha, to take on the role of parent for the other two. She was not unfitted for the role, being vigorous, thrifty, and conscientious. Under her guidance, and a certain amount of prodding, Lazarus had managed the estate well and it had continued to prosper.

Mary was gentle and gave Martha no trouble. She was kept busy and happy with her flower gardens and the welfare of the people who worked on the estate, supervising the weaving and sewing of cloth for their garments, teaching the children, and keeping strictly the religious observances of the family, for which Martha's duties in supervising the manifold activities of the household did not leave much time.

Now Mary was especially busy with preparations for the Feast of Tabernacles. Since Martha, Mary, and Lazarus were not poor, their booth was large. Mary was busy directing the servants in weaving the last of the green branches from which it was made and moving into it the sleeping pallets and the utensils for the festive meals which were to be served there during the period of the feast. She was happy at her task for not only was she creating something of beauty, but she was also taking part in the worship of the Most High.

The booth was almost completed when Mary, looking up, saw two men entering the yard. They appeared tired and their robes were dusty, so she judged them to be pilgrims on the way to Jerusalem for the Festival. One was tall and broad-shouldered with a naturally commanding presence, the other slender and dark-eyed, with quick, almost nervous movements.

"Shalom, my daughter," the tall man said. "Could we drink from your well before going on?"

"Of course," Mary said warmly. "I will draw water for you myself."

Moving to the well, she drew water in a jar and, taking a cup from beside it, filled it first for the tall man and then for the slighter one.

"Are you on the way to Jerusalem?" Mary asked. She was of a friendly nature and could see that these men were not like the rabble that often clogged the roads on their way to beg in Jerusalem during the feast periods.

"My name is Simon," the big man said. "And this is John, the son of Zebedee. We have walked ahead to seek a lodging place near Jerusalem for the Master."

"But you are not sla—" Mary bit her tongue.

The man called John smiled. "No, daughter, we are not slaves," he said. "We are disciples of Jesus of Nazareth. He and the others are on the road a little way behind us."

Mary's eyes brightened. "Nicodemus, a friend of ours from Jerusalem, has spoken of Jesus." Then a thought occurred to her. "You say you are seeking a place for Him to stay?"

"Yes," Simon told her. "'It must be outside the city, but close enough for Him to reach Jerusalem easily."

"Wait here," Mary told them. "I will be gone only a little while."

While the men rested in the cool shade beside the well, Mary ran into the house where Martha was working over the oven, baking bread. The older sister's face was red from the heat and damp with sweat.

"Martha!" Mary cried. "Jesus of Nazareth is coming. Can't we let Him stay here?"

Martha straightened up and wiped sweat from her face with her sleeve. Lazarus had gone into Jerusalem for the first day of the Feast, but he would no doubt return soon bringing guests. And already she had more than she could do at this holiday season.

"But we don't—" she started to say.

"You remember Nicodemus spoke of Jesus," Mary cried.

"He says the Nazarene is gentle and kind and many in Galilee believe He is the Messiah! Besides," she added, perhaps not quite truthfully, "He has nowhere to stay."

For all her thrift, Martha was fundamentally generous and kind. The thought of anyone without a place to stay during the Feast of Tabernacles was something she could not ignore.

"Perhaps He wouldn't like it here," she demurred, but Mary, in her happiness at the thought of having a famous Teacher in her own home, where she could listen to Him as long as she wished, was already tugging her sister through the door into the yard.

"My sister will welcome your Master to our house," she told Simon Peter and John breathlessly. "If He would care to stay here," she added.

The disciples had already noted the large and comfortable house and the spacious booth being erected in the yard for the Feast. Only on rare occasions, they knew, was Jesus welcomed into such a home as this at Bethany. It would be an ideal place for Him to stay, far better than the camps the pilgrims usually made on the slope of the Mount of Olives overlooking Jerusalem, and the distance to the city was only a little greater around the mountain.

"I am sure Jesus will be happy to stay here," Simon told her. "If you are sure He is welcome." The last was addressed to Martha who had now had time to catch her breath during Mary's impetuous dash from the house. But she could see, as Mary had, that these men belonged to no rabble. Their friend Nicodemus had indeed spoken glowingly of Jesus and had even gone to Galilee to listen to His teachings.

"We will be honored to have Jesus of Nazareth in our house," Martha said. "I will go and ready a chamber for Him."

The preparations necessary to entertaining an unexpected guest kept Martha busy, even after Jesus arrived. With such an important visitor, she wanted to be sure everything was exactly right, and bustled about the kitchen, preparing food and directing the servants in making ready a chamber for Him, the guest of honor, and space in the other chambers and surrounding buildings for the members of His party to sleep. As soon as Jesus had washed the dust from His hands and face and made Himself comfortable, however, Mary took a place at His feet, eagerly absorbing every word He spoke.

When Mary did not come to help her, Martha's irritation at what she considered her sister's neglect increased until she dared to speak to the guest about it.

"Lord," she said in protest, adopting the term of address used by the disciples. "Do you not care that my sister has left me to serve alone? Bid her help me."

Jesus looked at Martha and a warm smile came over His face. He saw that she was troubled and understood the reason, for many people to whom He wished to bring the great truths of God's kingdom were too busy with mundane affairs to listen and comprehend.

"Martha, Martha," Jesus said gently. "You are careful and troubled about many things, but one thing is needful, and Mary has chosen that good part which shall not be taken away from her."

In her concern with the material side of entertaining her guest, Martha had thought of the things of the moment only—the food, its serving, Jesus' comfort and accommodations. But Mary, perhaps because she was the younger and more sensitive of the two, had preferred to listen and to pay the respectful homage that was Jesus' due. There was a place for what both women had to offer, but neither could be expected exactly to understand the other's point of view.

Jesus' words also had a deeper meaning which neither woman understood. His stay on earth was limited and there was all too little time in which to give His great spirit to any who would receive it and understand.

Having arrived during the first days of the Feast, Jesus did not go into Jerusalem until, as custom dictated, these were past. Even though He stayed in Bethany outside the city, His presence could not be kept secret from the authorities at the temple, nor did He wish it so. As had been the case with the Galileans and the Samaritans, the people of Jerusalem had to be given an opportunity to hear His message and accept or reject it.

While the temple authorities and the leaders of the Pharisees waited and watched to see what He would do, Jesus remained at the cool and pleasant home of Mary and Martha in Bethany, delaying the time when He would go into the temple and begin to teach, as was His right, from the Porch of Solomon where the other teachers of Israel sat and gave their opinions concerning the relationship between man and God. When Lazarus returned in a few days, he quickly gave himself up to the teachings of Jesus, as his sisters had already done.

This brief period of peace and happiness was precious to Jesus. The household at Bethany grew very dear to Him, and from that time became His home when He was in the vicinity of Jerusalem.

III

E lam, the Pharisee, had done much since that evening, a little over thirty years ago, when he had taken the last couch in the inn at Bethlehem and forced a mother to bear her child in the manger. Already well-to-do, he had prospered even more during the intervening years and had soon moved from Hebron to Jerusalem, where he acted as agent for the weavers of Hebron, selling their cloth in the markets of the Roman Empire at a far greater profit than could have been made in Jerusalem itself.

As Elam grew in wealth, his soul had shriveled. He maintained an outward piety, keeping the Law so strictly—and so publicly—that he impressed people everywhere with his righteousness. But as the years passed he had gradually become a Pharisee of the Pharisees, the leader of the most intolerant and bigoted faction in the sect whose intolerance and bigotry were their greatest pride.

Elam had brought Jonas to Jerusalem with him, but the climate, with its cold winters and raw winds, had worsened the little hunchback's infirmity. With Elam, whatever was unproductive, whether a growing vine, or a sick human being, was cut off and thrown away with no qualms and no regrets. He had finally freed Jonas from his service, casting the little hunchback out to fend for himself, as he had the right to do under the Law. Jonas had been forced to take any job he could find and then, when there was no other employment, the lowliest task remaining to one who would not beg, that of the woodsellers who gathered wood outside the city and carried it in on their backs, selling it from house to house.

Because he liked to be seen at the temple, Elam went every day to voice his opinions authoritatively to any one who would listen. His richly fringed robe and the over-large phylacteries he wore attached to his forehead and about his wrists marked him as a rich and important man, and many stopped to listen and to admire his piety.

Solomon's Porch was a busy place on the morning Jesus came into the temple during the middle days of the Feast of Tabernacles. Word of His coming had been spread abroad by His disciples and a crowd was waiting for Him to appear on the cool porch. While they waited, the people were discussing Him among themselves and, seeing a knot of them talking together, Elam joined the group.

"Jesus is a good man," a herder from Galilee was saying. "I have seen Him heal the sick many times and He even raised the daughter of Jairus, one of the rulers of the synagogue at Capernaum, from the dead."

This was too much for Elam. "The cursed Nazarene leads the multitude astray," he said sharply, daring the Galilean to take issue with a person of his importance. "What He does is by the power of demons."

Accustomed to accept the statements of Pharisees, particularly an important one like Elam, as the final authority on religious matters, none of the Jerusalem Jews in the immediate circle disagreed with him. The Galilean, however, was not so easily silenced.

"Many in Galilee believe the Nazarene is the Messiah," he insisted. "They say even John the Baptist named Him such."

"Where is the Baptist now?" the Pharisee sneered.

"Dead," the Galilean admitted. "At the hand of Herod Antipas."

"Even as the Nazarene will be put to death for stirring up the people," Elam said. "When the Messiah comes we will know Him. David said of Him in the psalm:

> *"You shall bruise them with an iron rod!*
> *You shall crush them like a potter's vessel!"*

The Galilean had begun to realize that he was no match in an argument over religion with a Pharisee but was unwilling to give up.

"What of the words of Isaiah?" he demanded.

Elam shrugged contemptuously. "Isaiah said much, and not always what people such as you could understand."

"I mean where he said:

> *"Behold My servant whom I uphold,*
> *Mine elect in whom my soul delights.*
> *A bruised reed shall He not break,*
> *And the smoking flax shall He not quench."*

"The rabbis do not believe that passage refers to the Messiah," Elam said. "But answer me a question about this man called Jesus. Of what town is He?"

"Nazareth."

"In what region?"

The Galilean saw what was coming but could not go back now. "Galilee," he admitted.

Elam turned to the Jerusalem Jews and spread his hands in a gesture of derision. "I leave it to you," he said. "Can anything good come out of Nazareth? Or a king of Israel out of Galilee?"

The laughing crowd shouted, "No!" to the considerable discomfort of the Galilean, and the argument ended when a commotion broke out at the end of the portico where the stairway led from the temple court to the streets of the city below. Jesus had appeared there, surrounded by His disciples, the tall form of Simon Peter close beside Him. Without pausing, He moved through the crowd to an empty space before one of the tall shining columns. There, with no ostentation or any claim to be more than the other teachers, He turned to face the crowd that quickly left the other rabbis to throng about Him.

When Jesus started to speak, a tense silence fell, for even His first words were different from those of the other teachers. Where these others buttressed their pronouncements with the authority of this or that of the great rabbis—here Shammai and there Hillel, the two greatest rabbinical schools of Judaism—Jesus spoke with only an occasional reference to the Law and the prophets and quoted no rabbinical authority at all. Yet His words had such a ring of authority that the people were impressed.

At the fringe of the crowd, some of the teachers who had lost their audiences spoke disparagingly of Him, seeking to draw the attention of the people away from Him.

"How does this man know these things when He is unlearned?" one of them demanded, for it was unbelievable to them that a rabbi could be educated anywhere except at the fountainhead of Judaism in Jerusalem.

Jesus heard the question, even though it had been spoken on the outskirts of the group. "My doctrine is not Mine," He said speaking directly to the rabbis, "but His that sent Me. If any man will do His will, He shall know of the doctrine whether it be from God or whether I speak of Myself. He that speaks of himself seeks his own glory, but He that seeks the glory of the One who sent Him, is true and no unrighteousness is within Him."

And then, knowing how they sought to discredit Him by emphasizing His lack of rabbinical authority, He said more severely, "Did not Moses give you the Law, and yet none of you keep the Law? Why do you go about to kill Me?"

"You have a devil that goes about to kill you!" Elam shouted indignantly, referring to the rumor which had been spread in Galilee and which Jesus had refuted long ago.

"Moses gave you circumcision and on the Sabbath you circumcise a man," Jesus answered. "If a man receives circumcision on the Sabbath day, that the Law of Moses should not be broken, why are you angry at Me because I have made a man completely whole on the Sabbath day? Judge not according to appearance but judge righteous judgment."

The listeners were amazed at His logic and the truth He spoke. "Is not this He that the leaders seek to kill?" one man asked of another. "Yet see how boldly He speaks and they say nothing to Him! Do the rulers know indeed that this is not the very Christ?"

Elam heard him and his face purpled with anger. "We know from whence this man comes!" he shouted. "The Galilean there admitted He was from Nazareth. But when the Christ comes, no man will know from whence He comes."

Jesus heard Him and answered. "I did not come of Myself but He that sent Me is true whom you know not," He said. "I know Him, for I am from Him and He has sent Me."

Here, for the first time in Jerusalem, Jesus had announced that He had come from God Himself, the nearest in this area that He had yet approached to proclaiming Himself the Messiah. Hearing Him now, the temple authorities wished to arrest Him for blasphemy at once, but were afraid of the crowd who clamored to hear more. Jesus had said all that He wished on this first day, however. "Yet a little while am I with you," He said as He prepared to leave, "then I shall go to Him that sent Me. You shall seek Me and cannot find Me, for where I am you cannot come."

IV

A grim-faced group of men gathered in the private chambers of Caiaphas, high priest of Israel, on the morning of the last day of the Feast of Tabernacles. The seat of honor at the long table where this Priestly Council, a division of the Great Sanhedrin, met from time to time to set the policies of the temple and the religious worship, was given to Annas, the former high priest and father-in-law of Caiaphas, but there was no doubting who dominated the meeting.

At Annas's right as he doddered in his chair, sat Caiaphas, lean-faced, sharp-eyed, a Sadducee of the Sadducees, and as much Roman as Jew. Caiaphas was an opportunist of great shrewdness who through marriage had established a place in the upper ranks of the priesthood for himself and had quickly worked his way to the position of high priest. Next to Caiaphas was Elam, fiercely proud of his own righteousness and hating

Jesus because he had spoken against him in the temple. At the other side of Annas was a rabbi named Jochai who sought to please everybody by straddling the doctrinal chasm between the schools of Shammai and Hillel, which divided practically all the learned men of Israel.

A few members of a more moderate faction among the Pharisees were present. One of these was Nicodemus, who was resented by both Caiaphas and Elam because of his tolerance and because he had consistently opposed their attempts to trap Jesus and condemn Him to death. Of somewhat the same mind as Nicodemus was Joseph of Arimathea, a wealthy merchant who was respected because of his business position. The last in the group and not actually a member was Abiathar, burly captain of the temple police and Caiaphas's agent in much of the double-dealing and thievery which had enabled him to maintain his high office.

"What shall we do about the man called Jesus of Nazareth?" Caiaphas said when the meeting was joined.

Nicodemus spoke at once. "Why do anything about Him? He has the same right to teach from Solomon's Porch that Jochai here does."

"But not to teach blasphemy!" the rabbi sputtered. "The man openly proclaims Hiimself to be the Son of God!"

Nicodemus spoke softly. "Have you forgotten that Nebuchadnezzar, when he had cast Shadrach, Meshach, and Abednego into the fiery furnace, looked within the flames and said, 'Lo, I see four men loose, walking in the midst of the fire, and they have no hurt. And the form of the fourth is like the Son of God.'"

"What has this to do with the Galilean?" Elam demanded.

"If the Son of God took the form of man once, He could do it again."

The thought brought them up short, but not for long. Jochai was the first to find an answer. "The man in the furnace was not born of woman," he said triumphantly, "I have it upon the authority of a rabbi in Nazareth that this Jesus is the son of a carpenter who lived there, a man named Joseph."

"We cannot let Him preach blasphemy in Jerusalem," Caiaphas cut short the argument impatiently. "People of Galilee were ready to name Him the Christ not long ago."

"Jesus would not let them do it," Nicodemus reminded him. "That alone should prove His innocence."

"Let Him go back to Galilee," Annas said. "Then Herod will have to cope with Him."

"Herod is afraid of the Nazarene," Elam said contemptuously. "Ever since he executed John, he has quaked for fear the Baptist will rise from the dead and haunt him."

"They say in Galilee that Jesus spends most of the time in the district of the tetrarch Philip now," Jochai added. "We can expect no help from him."

"The Nazarene must be taken here in Jerusalem," Caiaphas said positively. "We cannot wait for Him to stir up the Galileans to revolt as did Judas the Gaulonite."

"There must be no revolt," old Annas echoed. "Even if it succeeded, we might be saddled with another line like the Hasmoneans."

"I have heard Jesus teach," Nicodemus interposed. "And I would wager my hope of eternal life that He has no desire to be king in Israel."

"Why does He stir up the people then?" Caiaphas demanded hotly.

"If He is loyal to us, He would not criticize the Pharisees," Elam added.

"There is much to criticize," Nicodemus retorted.

"By those who are not willing to obey the Law," Elam said. There was no love between him and the lawyer.

"This is no place for a battle among ourselves," Caiaphas interposed to calm the troubled waters. "We must decide on some way to stop this Nazarene before He causes trouble with the Romans."

Just then a soldier entered and spoke briefly to Abiathar, who turned to Caiaphas. "The Galilean has entered the temple again, noble Caiaphas," he announced.

"Take some men and arrest Him then," Caiaphas ordered. "We will question Him here and then bring Him before the Sanhedrin."

"On what charge?" Nicodemus asked.

"Many have heard the Nazarene blaspheme here in Jerusalem. We will have no trouble finding three men to testify against Him."

The implication was obvious. Under Mosaic Law, the testimony of three or more witnesses could condemn a man to death. Caiaphas would provide the men needed to swear to any charge of blasphemy. Such things had happened before in respect to people who made nuisances of themselves. They could, without doubt, happen again.

21

He who is without sin among you,
let him throw a stone at her first.

John 8:7

A great crowd had gathered when it was announced that Jesus had come into Jerusalem again on this final day of the Feast of Tabernacles and would speak from the Porch of Solomon. Just as Abiathar arrived with the guards at the edge of the crowd, Jesus began to speak in ringing tones, voicing a credo which all could follow if they would: "If any man thirst, let him come to Me and drink. He that believes on Me, as the Scripture has said, out of his belly shall flow rivers of living water."

Once again He was speaking in the form of a parable, characterizing as a river of living water the Holy Spirit, which they who believed on Him would receive after He returned to His Father. Familiar with the writings of the prophets which were read each Sabbath in the synagogue, it seemed to many who heard that He was referring to the words of Isaiah who had said of the Messiah:

> *Behold a king shall reign in righteousness and princes shall*
> *rule in judgment*
> *And a man shall be as a hiding place from the wind and a*
> *cover from the tempest,*
> *As rivers of water in a dry place, as the shadows of a great*
> *rock in a weary land.*

Thinking that Jesus had actually proclaimed Himself the Messiah, the crowd set up a shout.

"Of a truth this is a prophet!" some cried.

"Nay, He is the Christ of God!" another echoed.

Abiathar had good reason to know the temper of Caiaphas, but he also valued his own life. With the people in such a ferment, any attempt to arrest Jesus could easily cause him and his men to be torn to pieces. Around him people were shouting for Jesus to name Himself the Christ and take His rightful place at the head of the temple and the nation of

Israel. With only the slightest encouragement, they would no doubt, in their enthusiasm for the Messiah sent from God to liberate Israel, have risen up to thrust the Roman garrison from the city.

Jesus made no such move, however. Gathering His disciples around Him for protection, He left the temple as He had done before under somewhat similar circumstances. Descending the stairway to the streets, through which He quickly made His way, He returned to Bethany. Abiathar could not have reached Him if he had even tried, but the captain of the temple guards was too prudent to inflame the crowd any further. He knew how much the common people hated Caiaphas and the priestly group for their corruption and venality; he had no desire to turn that hatred upon himself and his men.

By Jesus' sudden departure, the crowd was left without a focus. Taking advantage of their uncertainty, some of the scribes who had hoped to seize upon Jesus' words as blasphemy, now sought to create a diversion and take the minds of the people off the man they had been ready to acclaim as Messiah and King. Cleverly, they used the traditional contempt of the Judeans for the Galileans.

"Shall the Christ come out of Galilee?" one of them shouted.

Immediately one of the rabbis who had lost his audience when Jesus came into the temple took up the controversy. "The Scriptures say the Christ must come of the seed of David and out of the town of Bethlehem where David was," he announced.

As the scribes intended, the people began to argue among themselves in small groups about the Messiah and how He would come. The immediate danger was abated. Leaving several guards to take care of any trouble that might arise, Abiathar returned to the chamber of the high priest.

When Caiaphas saw that the captain was empty-handed, his sallow face stiffened with anger. "Why did you not bring the Galilean?" he demanded.

Abiathar reddened at his master's tone. "No man ever spoke as this one," he grumbled. "The people would have torn us to pieces if we had harmed Him."

"Are you also led astray?" Elam demanded contemptuously. "Have any of the rulers believed in this Galilean? Or any of the Pharisees?"

Abiathar shook his head. "I heard none," he admitted.

"Then it was only this accursed multitude, who do not know the Law."

"Does our Law judge any man before it hears him and knows what he does?" Nicodemus asked.

Elam turned his anger upon the lawyer. "Are you of Galilee?" he demanded. "Search and look, for no prophet shall rise in Galilee."

The argument raged bitterly back and forth until Caiaphas, realizing it would achieve no unity of purpose, stopped urging the Council to try to bring Jesus to trial. There were other ways of getting rid of troublemakers, ways he knew well. If they could not catch the Nazarene breaking the Law where He could be arrested privately, an incident must be created to turn the people against Him. If the crowd then stoned the man to death for breaking Mosaic Law, as had happened many, many times in the history of Israel, even the Romans could not hold Caiaphas responsible.

II

No crime except blasphemy deserved more immediate and drastic punishment than adultery. "You shall not commit adultery," the injunction read. "The man that commits adultery, both the adulteress and the adulterer shall surely be put to death." Hardly a city existed in all Israel whose walls were not stained by the blood of those executed by stoning for breaking the seventh of the great commandments.

Knowing that the time when He must be put to death and rise from the dead had not yet come, Jesus had deliberately left the temple to avoid stirring up the people, and had withdrawn to a garden called Gethsemane on the Mount of Olives where He often went for prayer and meditation.

After the night of prayer and fasting, He came to the temple early and took His place once again with the other teachers on Solomon's Porch. And as always, the crowd soon deserted the others and gathered around Him.

Caiaphas had not been idle. Together, he and Abiathar had devised a plan which seemed certain to accomplish their aims. As soon as it was known that Jesus was returning to the temple, guards had been sent to arrest a woman on a charge of adultery. They came now dragging the sobbing victim before Jesus.

"Master," a Pharisee who had been selected by Caiaphas and Elam to serve as one of the accusing witnesses addressed Him with a great show of humility. "This woman was taken in adultery, in the very act. Now in the Law, Moses commands us to stone such. What do you say about her?"

Jesus knew quite well why the woman had been arrested and brought before Him. In His teaching He had stressed the willingness of God to forgive sins and His own promise to do so, precepts which had found immediate favor among the common people upon whom the harsh judgment of the Law placed a heavy burden. But the word of the Law was also quite clear and, whatever His answer, the Pharisees obviously intended to make trouble for Him. If He said the woman's sin could be forgiven and her life thereby saved, they could accuse Him of blasphemy for not obeying the Law of Moses. On the other hand, if He condemned the woman to death forthwith, the people to whom He had promised forgiveness could rightly cry that He did not practice what He preached.

Jesus did not answer at once but did a strange thing. Stooping He began to write in the dust of the floor with His finger, as if He were debating what to do with the woman. When the puzzled Pharisees and scribes pushed closer to see what He had written, He merely went on making these seemingly meaningless marks in the dust. Finally, when all were filled with suspense, He raised His head and said quietly, "He that is without sin among you, let him first cast a stone at her."

The agents of Caiaphas, who had been confident that the hated Nazarene could not escape from this trap, were thunderstruck by His answer. The Law of Moses required that the woman be stoned to death if judged guilty. There could be no doubt about her guilt, for the guards had stated that they had taken her in the very act of adultery. Yet no man among them could say he was without sin, for only God could make that claim. He who announced himself free from sin and gained the right to cast the first stone would, out of his own mouth, condemn himself for blasphemy.

Jesus did not look at His critics again but, stooping once more, began to trace the same idle pattern of marks in the dust. He felt rather than saw the discomfiture of those who had been certain they had finally trapped Him. Only when they had slunk away, did He raise His head again to look at the lovely copper-haired woman who remained kneeling before Him.

"Where are your accusers?" He asked her. "Has no man condemned you?"

"No man, lord."

"Neither do I condemn you. Go and sin no more."

Jesus watched the woman leave, then turned to face the people who still remained before Him. "I am the light of the world," He told them. "He that follows Me shall not walk in darkness, but shall have the light of life."

Elam had been watching at the back of the crowd; now he pushed his way through. "You bear witness of Yourself," he accused. "And Your witness is not true."

"I bear witness of Myself and the Father that sent Me bears witness of Me," Jesus corrected him.

"Where is Your Father?"

"You know neither Me nor My Father," Jesus told the Pharisee sternly. "If you had known Me you would have known the Father also."

Once again He had foiled them in their desire to find reason to seize Him, but He did not stop there. "I go My way and you shall seek Me," He said. "And whither I go you cannot come."

"Will He kill Himself?" one listener asked another. "For He said, 'Whither I go you cannot come.'"

Jesus heard the question and explained His meaning. "You are from beneath and I am from above," He said. "You are of this world and I am not of this world. I said therefore to you that you shall die in your sins if you do not believe that I am He." He meant that He was the Messiah and that they could save themselves from death by believing on Him.

But Elam did not choose to understand. "Who are you?" he demanded.

"Even the same that I said to you in the beginning," Jesus told him. "When you have lifted up the Son of Man, then you shall know that I am He, and that I do nothing of Myself. But as My Father has taught Me, I speak these things. He that sent Me is with Me; the Father has not left Me alone, for I do always those things that please Him."

Perhaps more clearly than at any other time in His ministry Jesus had described the relationship between Himself and His Father in heaven. He spoke so convincingly that even many in the temple believed in Him.

Jesus now turned to these who had accepted Him here where so many sought to destroy Him. "If you continue in My word," He told them, "you are My disciples indeed. You shall know the truth and the truth shall make you free."

III

Joachim, the beggar, had never seen light, for he had been blind from the day of his birth. To him the world existed only in terms of what he could touch, hear, or smell. The passing of the seasons revealed to him little of their beauty but only the sensation of warmth and cold upon his skin as he plodded about the city with the other beggars, pleading for alms. He had heard talk of the Nazarene healer and had even thought of trying to reach Him, but the press of the crowd whenever Jesus taught in the temple was so great that he could find no one to lead him there. Some said Jesus had actually given sight to the blind. Joachim could hardly believe this, for such a power could come only from the Most High Himself and unless this Nazarene were really the Messiah, such a thing was impossible. And yet he dared to hope that someday God might give him his sight, for help could come from no other source.

Joachim heard the people shouting Jesus' name as He left the temple. Stumbling along, tapping with a stick on the stone paving of the street to guide himself, he moved nearer. The sound of voices and particularly the rough tones of the fishermen of Galilee who, he had heard, made up most of the Nazarene's disciples, told him he was approaching the party, but he did not dare call to the Teacher Himself lest he be pushed aside by the crowd and passed by. The only thing he could do was to give his customary warning.

"From the day of my birth I am blind," he intoned as he tapped along. "Have mercy and give me alms for the love of God."

Jesus heard the cry, as He always heard the pleas of the afflicted, and stopped beside Joachim. Before He could speak to the blind man, however, one of the disciples asked a question.

"Master," he said, "who sinned that this man was born blind? He or his parents?"

This was no idle question, for it was written that the Lord said to Moses, "Who hath made man's own mouth? Or who makes the dumb or deaf or the seeing or the blind? Have not I the Lord?" Obviously then God would not so punish anyone except for sinning.

"Neither this man nor his parents have sinned," Jesus explained. "He is blind that the works of God may be made manifest in him. I must work the works of Him that sent Me while it is day, for the night comes when no man can work. As long as I am in the world, I am the light of the world."

While the disciples pondered what He had said, Jesus knelt beside Joachim. Spitting into the dust, He quickly made a ball of moist clay with His fingers. As He rubbed the clay on the blind man's eyelids, He told him, "Go wash in the pool of Siloam." And without saying more, He passed on toward Bethany, leaving Joachim with the clay still sticking to his eyes.

Part of the crowd that had been following Jesus remained behind, expecting a miracle. But when nothing happened, some small boys in the group began to jeer at the blind man because of the dirt on his face.

Something, perhaps the quiet confidence in the voice of the Nazarene Teacher, gave Joachim the courage to start across the city to the pool of Siloam. Descending from the elevated area of the temple where the beggars congregated because worshipers there might be generous with their alms, Joachim made his way across the Lower City toward the pool of Siloam which lay near the Water Gate.

The pool had been built by King Hezekiah at the terminus of a tunnel dug beneath the city to bring the waters of the spring called Gihon in the Kedron Valley to this section so that women could more easily carry water for their families. More recently, Herod the Great had erected a colonnaded building in the form of a hollow square around the pool, so that it was always cool and shady there.

At the edge of the pool, Joachim knelt and washed his eyes with the cool water, as Jesus had instructed him. When he saw the water of the pool, and the faces of the women who were filling their jars reflected in it, he cried out in wonder and got to his feet, stumbling about like a drunken man in the ecstasy of seeing—the beauty of the colonnade, the bright-colored robes of the women, the green of the trees—Joachim was like a man dying of thirst who suddenly finds a pool in the desert. "I see! I see!" he cried, and throwing away his stick, he started running through the streets to go tell his family, shouting as he ran to everyone he passed about the miracle which had given him his vision.

"How were your eyes opened?" one of the neighbors asked.

"A man called Jesus made clay and anointed them!" Joachim explained. "Then He said, 'Go to the pool of Siloam and wash.' I washed as He said and immediately I received my sight!"

Some of the neighbors had been in the temple that morning and had heard the Pharisees arguing with Jesus. They now persuaded Joachim to go with them to Elam with the story of how he had regained his sight.

The Pharisee questioned the beggar closely but he told the same story about what had happened and would not change it. He realized that Elam was particularly eager to establish the fact that the healing had taken place on the Sabbath, but he did not understand the reasons for his concern until Elam and another Pharisee began to argue between themselves.

"This man is not of God because He does not keep the Sabbath day," Elam said.

"But how could a sinner perform such things?" the other asked.

Elam turned back to Joachim. "What do you say of Him that opened your eyes?" he asked.

"He is a prophet," Joachim said confidently.

Elam did not question Joachim further but turned to the beggar's father and mother who had come with him. "Is this your son who you say was born blind?" he demanded. "How then does he now see?"

Joachim's parents were reluctant to antagonize the Pharisee, for it was rumored in the city that anyone who acknowledged the Nazarene as the Christ would be thrust from the synagogue.

"We know this is our son and that he was born blind," the father said respectfully. "But we do not know by what means he now sees, or who opened his eyes. He is of age. Ask him and he shall speak for himself."

"Give God the praise," Elam commanded Joachim. "We know that the man is a sinner."

"Whether He is a sinner or not I do not know," Joachim said quietly. "One thing I do know, that whereas I was blind, I now see."

"What did He do?" the Pharisee demanded, hoping to make Joachim give a different story from the one he had first told and thereby discredit him before the people.

"I have told you already and you did not listen," Joachim answered. "Why would you hear it again? Will you also be His disciple?"

Elam drew himself up angrily at the effrontery of this beggar. "We know God spoke to Moses," he said. "As for this Nazarene, we do not know from whence He comes."

"Herein is a marvelous thing," Joachim scoffed. "You do not know from whence He came and yet He opened my eyes. We know that God does not hear sinners, but if any man be a worshiper of God and does His will, he shall be heard. Since the world began, has it been heard that any man opened the eyes of one born blind? If the Nazarene were not of God, then He could do nothing."

IV

Angry at Joachim for arguing that Jesus was divine and refusing to believe his testimony or that of the people who had known Joachim when he was blind, Elam took steps to have him driven from the city in disgrace as a perjurer.

When Jesus heard how Joachim had been exiled from Jerusalem, He sought him out. "Do you believe on the Son of God?" He asked.

Joachim had never seen Jesus and so did not recognize Him. "Who is He, lord," he asked, "that I might believe in Him?"

"You have seen Him. It is He who talks with you."

Then the eyes of Joachim's soul were opened also and he fell to his knees crying, "Lord, I believe!"

Jesus put His hand on Joachim's shoulder and lifted him to his feet. "For judgment I come into this world," He said gently, "that they who see not might see, and that they who see might be made blind."

Some of those who had followed Joachim now came up to Jesus. "Are we blind also?" they asked.

"If you were blind you should have no sin," Jesus told them, meaning that if they had not possessed sight, they could be forgiven for not recognizing and acclaiming Him. "But now you say, 'We see'; therefore, your sin remains."

Turning to those who stood nearby, Jesus spoke to them, using a parable. "Truly I say to you, he that enters not by the door into the sheepfold, but climbs up some other way, the same is a thief and a robber. But he that enters in by the door is the shepherd of the sheep. To him the porter opens and the sheep hear his voice and he calls his own sheep by name and leads them out. And when he puts forth his own sheep, he goes before them and the sheep follow him for they know his voice. A stranger they will not follow, but will flee from him, for they know not the voice of strangers."

When He saw that they did not understand His meaning, He went on to explain: "The thief comes only to steal and to kill and to destroy, but I am come that they might have life and have it more abundantly. The good shepherd gives his life for the sheep. But he who is a hireling and not the shepherd, and who does not own the sheep, sees the wolf coming and leaves the sheep and flees. Then the wolf catches them and scatters the sheep. The hireling flees because he is a hireling and does not care for the sheep, but I am the good shepherd and know My sheep and am known by them. As the Father knows Me, even so know I the Father, and I lay down My life for the sheep."

V

While Jesus was at Bethany, teaching and healing in the towns of Judea around Jerusalem, the seventy whom He had sent out returned to Him and reported joyfully, "Lord, even the devils are subject unto us in Your name."

"Behold I give you power to tread on serpents and scorpions and over all the power of the enemy, and nothing shall by any means hurt you," Jesus told them. "Notwithstanding, do not rejoice that the spirits are subject to you, but rather rejoice because your names are written in heaven."

A lawyer had listened closely while Jesus was talking. "Master," he asked now. "What shall I do to inherit eternal life?"

"What is written in the Law?" Jesus asked him. "How do you read it?"

"You shall love the Lord your God with all your heart, and with all your soul and with all your strength and with all your mind; and your neighbor as yourself."

"You have answered right," Jesus told him. "This do and you shall live."

"Who is my neighbor?" the lawyer persisted.

Jesus answered him with a parable: "A certain man went down from Jerusalem to Jericho and fell among thieves, which stripped him of his raiment, and wounded him and departed, leaving him half dead. By chance there came down a certain priest that way and when he saw him he passed by on the other side. Likewise a Levite, when he was at the place, came and looked on the man and passed by on the other side. But a certain Samaritan, as he journeyed, came where he was, and when he saw him had compassion on him. He went to him and bound up his wounds, pouring in oil and wine, and set him on his own beast and brought him to an inn and took care of him. And on the morrow when he departed, the Samaritan took out two pence and gave them to the host and said, 'Take care of him; and whatever you spend in addition I will repay you when I come again.'"

Speaking directly to the lawyer, Jesus asked, "Which now of these three do you think was neighbor to him that fell among the thieves?"

The man could give only one answer, but even then he quibbled at the hated word, Samaritan. "He that showed mercy on him," he admitted reluctantly.

"Go and do likewise," Jesus counseled.

The lawyer departed sorely troubled, for he recognized the truth of what Jesus had told him but did not wish to carry it out.

VI

Knowing that the temple authorities were still plotting to kill Him, Jesus did not return to Jerusalem for several months but continued to travel through Judea with His disciples, maintaining His headquarters at the home of Martha and Mary and their brother Lazarus at Bethany. As always, He spoke in the synagogues on the Sabbath. And when people begged Him to heal the sick and afflicted, He did not withhold His miracle-working power from them, although the Pharisees continued to upbraid Him for healing on the Sabbath day. As He went about He tried wherever possible to teach His disciples privately, using the parables which explained to them, perhaps more clearly than actual preaching, the great truths which He had come to earth to make known to man.

"Are not five sparrows sold for two farthings, and not one of them is forgotten before God?" He assured them. "Even the very hairs of your head are numbered. Fear not therefore; you are of more value than many sparrows. Also, I say unto you, whoever shall confess Me before men, him shall the Son of Man also confess before the angels of God. But he that denies Me before men shall be denied before the angels of God. And whoever shall speak a word against the Son of Man, it shall be forgiven him, but to him that blasphemes against the Holy Ghost it shall not be forgiven.

"And when they bring you to the synagogues and to the magistrates," He advised them, "take no thought how or what you shall answer or what you shall say, for the Holy Spirit shall teach you in the same hour what you ought to say."

During the cool and sometimes frosty months of autumn, Jesus moved about in the hill country of Judea but did not come nearer to Jerusalem than Bethany. Only upon the occasion of the Feast of Dedication at the beginning of the winter did He return to Jerusalem in order to preach to the crowds which gathered there for the religious holiday.

The occasion celebrated by this festival was the dedication of the temple after Judas Maccabaeus had taken Jerusalem from the Seleucid emperors of Syria, almost exactly two hundred years before. The festival lasted for eight days and because it was usual for the weather to be pleasantly cool at this time, large crowds came to Jerusalem.

As was His custom, Jesus entered the temple and began to preach from Solomon's Porch. This time one of the listeners put the question of His mission on earth directly to Him. "How long will you make us doubt?" he demanded. "If you are the Christ, tell us plainly."

"I told you and you did not believe," Jesus answered a little sadly. "The works that I do in My Father's name bear witness of Me, but you do not believe because you are not of My sheep. As I said to you, My sheep hear My voice and I know them and they follow Me and I give them eternal life. They shall never perish, neither shall any man pluck them out of My hand. My Father who gave them to Me is greater than all, and no man is able to pluck them out of My Father's hand. I and My Father are one."

This bold claim of direct kinship with God was more than some of the questioners could accept. Indignant at what they considered blasphemy, they took up stones to kill Him.

Jesus stopped them with the power of His voice. "Many good works I showed you from My Father," He said sternly. "For which of these works would you stone Me?"

"For a good work we would not stone You," His critics answered. "But for blasphemy and because You, being a man, make Yourself God."

"Is it not written in your Law," He demanded, said, "You are gods"? If He calls them gods to whom the word of God came and the Scripture cannot be broken, would you say of Him whom the Father sanctified and sent into the world, 'You blaspheme,' because I said that I am the Son of

God? If I do not do the works of My Father, do not believe Me. But if I do, though you do not believe Me, believe the works, so that you may know and believe that the Father is in Me and I am in Him."

They would not listen, however, having been stirred up by the Pharisees and the chief priests to stone Him then and there for blasphemy. But as had happened on another occasion, the crowd protected Jesus. Surrounded by His disciples He moved out of the temple. This time He did as He had advised His disciples to do when a city would not receive them; He shook the dust of Jerusalem from His feet and departed toward the east, going beyond the Jordan to the town of Bethabara where John had first baptized Him.

His mission had now come a complete circle, for here it had begun.

22

Rejoice with me, for I have found my sheep which was lost.

Luke 15:6

The district called Peraea or sometimes simply "beyond Jordan," was populated with Jews, but because the Greek cities of the Decapolis were also within the area, it was not so traditionally Pharisaic in its religious worship as was Judea. Jesus chose this region because from there He could readily return to teach during the religious festivals when the city teemed with people from all parts of Israel as well as with the Jews of the Dispersion. Samaria was largely forbidden by the intense enmity between Jews and Samaritans, so that Peraea was a natural choice.

Only a day's journey from Jerusalem for a vigorous man, the Jordan Valley was warm and pleasant during the months when the hill country around Jerusalem was chill and bleak. Although the largest cities were mostly Greek, there were in the "wilderness" across Jordan many villages and towns where Jesus found large audiences and little of the opposition which had made His mission in Jerusalem and other large cities so difficult.

For Jesus, Bethabara had nostalgic associations. Here He had been baptized by John and had experienced the vision from heaven and heard the voice of His Father. Here, too, on His return from the temptations, His first disciples had followed Him. Now He came to dwell in this pleasant place and to teach in the villages and in the sycamore grove that had been John's pulpit.

The river was not yet swollen by the melting snows of Mount Hermon as it would be later in the spring. In the thick groves along its banks the leopard still stalked his prey and the thickets teemed with smaller animals and birds. The slopes of the mountains were covered with sycamore, beech, terebinth, ilex, and great fig trees. Altogether it was a hospitable place in which to spend the winter months.

Jesus had always received all who came to Him, and He stayed in any house where He was sincerely invited to rest. Often this meant consorting with tax collectors and with the common people shunned by Pharisees as "the accursed multitude who know not the Law." When He was upbraided by the self-righteous for associating with sinners, Jesus answered with a series of parables which were among the most beautiful and expressive in all His teachings.

"What man of you, having an hundred sheep, if he lose one of them, does not leave the ninety and nine in the wilderness and go after that which is lost until he finds it?" He asked. "When he has found it, he lays it on his shoulders, rejoicing. And when he comes home, he calls together his friends and neighbors, saying to them, 'Rejoice with me; for I have found my sheep which was lost.' I say unto you, there shall be more joy in heaven over one sinner that repents than over ninety and nine just persons who need no repentance."

Then to drive home the truth that God was ready to receive with joy any who sincerely repented of their sins, even the common people who found it impossible to obey strict Mosaic Law, Jesus told another story.

"A certain man had two sons," He said. "And the younger of them said, 'Father, give me the portion of goods that falls to me.' And he divided to them his living. Not many days after, the younger son gathered everything together and took a journey into a far country and there wasted his substance with riotous living. When he had spent all, there was a mighty famine in that land and he began to be in want. Then he went and joined himself to a citizen of that country who sent him into the fields to feed the swine, and he would have filled his belly with the husks, but no man gave to him."

For a Jew, to whom even to touch a pig was defilement, eating the husks of grain thrown to the swine was the worst possible humiliation.

"When he came to himself," Jesus continued, "he said, 'How many of my father's hired servants have bread enough and to spare while I perish with hunger! I will arise and go to my father and will say to him, "Father, I have sinned against heaven and before you and am no more worthy to be called your son. Make me as one of your hired servants.""

"Then he arose and came to his father. But when he was yet a great way off, his father saw him and had compassion and ran and fell on his neck and kissed him, and the son said to him, 'Father I have sinned against heaven, and in your sight and am no more worthy to be called your son.'

"But the father said to his servants, 'Bring forth the best robe, and put it on him. Put a ring on his hand, and shoes on his feet, and bring the fatted calf and kill it. Let us eat and be merry, for this my son was dead, and is alive again; he was lost, and is found.' And they began to be merry.

"Now his elder son was in the field," Jesus continued. "As he came and drew nigh to the house he heard music and dancing, so he called one of the servants and asked what these things meant. The servant said, 'Your brother has come and your father has killed the fatted calf, because he received him safe and sound.'

"Then the brother was angry and would not go in, but the father came out and begged him. 'Lo, these many years have I served you,' he answered his father. 'Neither have I transgressed your will at any time. Yet you never gave me a kid that I might make merry with my friends. But as soon as your son came back who had devoured your living with harlots, you have killed the fatted calf for him.'

"Then the father said to him, 'Son, you are ever with me and all that I have is yours. It was fitting that we should make merry and be glad, for this your brother was dead and is alive again; he was lost and is found.'"

With His divine genius for understanding and reaching the hearts of men, Jesus had made clear through this beautiful story how boundless was the love of God for those who sought to serve Him. The elder son represented those who were sincere in their concern for obeying the Law of Moses but not puffed up with pride because of their own righteousness. They, in the words of the parable, were "ever with me and all that I have is yours." But like the single sheep who was lost from the ninety and nine, there was also a place in the boundless realm of God's love for those who, having sinned and wasted the endless riches of life He had given them, still repented and came asking forgiveness and a place in His kingdom.

As Jesus Himself had said on another occasion in Capernaum, "I am come not to call the righteous but sinners to repentance."

II

It was raining as Lazarus rode home late one afternoon, a chilly drizzle that promised a beginning soon of the *moreh* or spring rain. In the valleys the harbingers of spring could be seen. Sprigs of green were appearing upon the carefully pruned grape vines, small clusters of tender violets grew among the rocks, and here and there the broad leaves of wild daffodils, sea leeks, and mandrake were beginning to unfold, while the tiny yellow and mauve blossoms of the crocus peeped forth. Only in the Judean highlands was winter still in undisputed possession.

Lazarus's spirits were always a little dampened during the often grim Judean winter but his depression quickly evaporated once the green began to show upon the vines. He had been on a tour of the family holdings that day, receiving the report of the herdsmen and seeing that the keepers of the vineyards were busy repairing the fences of sharp thorns. These were tasks Lazarus loved for he was at heart a husbandman, as concerned with his task of overseeing the not inconsiderable family holdings as Martha was with their spotlessly clean house on the eastern side of the Mount of Olives.

Mary was the dreamer of the three, he thought fondly. Noticing an especially fine clump of violets peeping up beside the road, he stopped his mule and got down to pick them for her, even though the rain was falling and his clothing was already soaked. He and Mary were much alike in their love of beauty, he thought, as he mounted the mule again. Perhaps it was as well that they had had practical, and sometimes stern, Martha to hold them to their tasks after their parents had died some years before. If she had not kept him busy while a youth, Lazarus knew, he might have spent the time roistering as so many young men in Jerusalem did, indulging in the Greek love of luxurious living instead of being industrious and keeping the Law. It was from Martha he had learned the rewards of industry and under his management the inheritance had grown like the story Jesus loved to tell about the mustard seed falling upon fallow ground and multiplying sometimes thirty-, sometimes sixty-, and sometimes a hundredfold.

Yes, it was good to be alive in this Promised Land at this season. Even the tough parasitic burnet thorn that covered the rocky hillsides was fully alive with the promise of spring. The leaves were already a blanket of rich green and in barely another month the tiny red blossoms, whose scarlet tint was the hue of blood, would suddenly turn the slopes into a riot of color.

As he rode by, Lazarus called a courteous greeting to Jonas, the hunchbacked old woodseller who was gathering dried thornbushes on the hillsides and pulling up green ones to put away to dry. The burnet thorn made an intensely hot flame that left little ash and was much prized by lime burners and by the potters of Jerusalem who made fine ware to sell to visitors.

As his mule wound its way along the path, Lazarus could see the road from Jericho to Jerusalem twisting across the hilltops and the summit of the Mount of Olives. Many of his friends left the Holy City at this time of year, preferring the warm sun of Jericho and the luxury of the hot mineral baths there. Once Lazarus, too, would have sought his pleasure among the Romans and the members of Herod's court, but that had been before Jesus had begun to stay at their house in Bethany during His visits to Jerusalem for the religious festivals. Hearing the Master teach the duty of men to love one another and to love God rather than rigid adherence to the details of the Law that a young man of spirit instinctively resented, Lazarus had gained a new view of life and work.

"The laborer is worthy of his hire," Jesus had said in His gentle voice, describing the dignity of work and its rewards in personal satisfaction through accomplishment. Lazarus had always looked upon the task of overseeing the vineyards and the olive groves as something Martha had devised to keep him from more pleasurable pursuits. But when Jesus spoke of how the shepherd went into the hills, perhaps on just such a cold and damp day as this, seeking a lost sheep, he had gained a new respect for the dignity of even the simplest occupation.

Lazarus had wanted to follow Jesus as one of His disciples, but when he heard the Master say, "Let your light so shine before men that they may see your good works and glorify your Father who is in heaven," he had understood that he could serve God as effectively here in Bethany as traveling the mountain paths of Peraea with Jesus.

In his heart, Lazarus knew that the satisfactions of following Jesus were deeper than any others could be. Nicodemus, the lawyer and an old friend of the family, had spoken of his talk with the Master one night at the camp of the Galileans on the slope of the mountain overlooking Jerusalem. "For God so loved the world that He gave His only begotten Son, that whoever believes in Him should not perish but have everlasting life," Jesus had told Nicodemus. And Lazarus had realized that this was the secret which bound all who loved the Master, the trust that death would be merely a journey to another country in His company, there to dwell with Him forever.

A shoulder of the Mount of Olives hid Jerusalem from Bethany, but as Lazarus rode down a winding path along the hillside, he could see the cloud of black smoke from the fires of the afternoon sacrifices drifting down the Kedron Valley. In another month, Jesus would be returning to Jerusalem for the Passover and there was sure to be trouble again between Him and the authorities.

It was no secret that some of the more revolutionary-minded Galileans had wished to proclaim Jesus Messiah during the Feast of Dedication. At least two of His own disciples, Judas of Kerioth and Simon called Zelotes, belonged to that group, Lazarus was certain, while James and John, the "Sons of Thunder" were of much the same mind. The truth, Lazarus himself knew, was that Jesus had no political ambitions. Had He possessed them, His enthusiastic following among the common people and their readiness to name Him the Messiah on more than one occasion would already have enabled Him to accomplish that purpose.

Not that all the trouble had been centered on Jesus in recent months. The group who sought to free Israel from the domination of Rome had been growing more brazen lately, and the daggers of the sicarii had found a mark among the Sadducees and the Herodians who worked hand in glove with the procurator, Pontius Pilate, to keep control of the people and of the vast revenue from the tribute that flowed into their coffers. Only this winter there had been a brief but bloody flare-up when a group of Galilean Zealots had killed a prominent Sadducee within the confines of the sanctuary.

A sharp battle had followed. Outnumbered by the Galilean Zealots and their followers, Abiathar, the captain of the temple guards, had been forced to call the Roman soldiers from the nearby fortress of Antonia. The Romans had ruthlessly cut down the rioters and blood had been spilled upon the floor of the temple itself. A wave of indignation against Pontius Pilate for this desecration had swept the city, for many were in sympathy with the Galilean Zealots, if not willing to support them actively. In the end it had amounted to nothing, except a pertinent reminder that the strength of the Romans was great and that the Sadducees, though Jews, would not hesitate to levy upon it to maintain their control.

III

M ary ran to meet Lazarus when he rode into the courtyard. The rain had stopped, but his robe and cloak were soaked and his body already so chilled that his teeth chattered as he gave the mule to a servant and started for the house.

"Why didn't you find shelter until the rain stopped?" Mary scolded him as she half-pushed him through the door into the house. Inside it was warm and the fragrance of the savory stew Martha was preparing met his nostrils.

"And be late for such a feast?" Lazarus asked banteringly, removing his cloak and handing it to Mary so she could hang it up to dry. "I am only a little wet; the heat will soon drive it away."

Mary was bustling about bringing towels and a fresh robe. "Dry yourself and put this on," she directed. "I will be in the kitchen if you need me."

"Bring me a hot drink," Lazarus called after her. "It will warm me more than anything else." He removed his tunic of linen, made from flax grown in the rich farming area around Jericho where the delicate pink flowers of the plants were already beginning to color the fields. Drying himself vigorously with a cloth, he put on the robe of light wool Mary had laid out.

Mary came in as he finished dressing, carrying a posset of hot spiced milk sweetened with honey. Martha, her broad homely face shining with the heat from the kitchen, also came to the door to greet him.

"We had word today of Jesus from a traveler who stopped here," she said. "He says the people beyond Jordan are flocking to hear the Master and many have already believed."

Lazarus's eyes brightened; the fire, the dry clothing, and the hot drink were already dispelling the chill from his body.

"Is He coming back soon?" he asked.

"Peter sent word that they will return for the Passover," Mary said, "and stay here."

"Of course He will stay here," Lazarus said proudly. "This is the Master's home in Judea and always will be."

"He does seem to like it here," Martha agreed.

Lazarus put his arm around his older sister's shoulder. "Why not, with such a good housekeeper," he said warmly.

Martha smiled. "Your supper is almost ready, if you have finished warming yourself."

"The smell of that stew drove the cold from my bones." Lazarus followed his sisters into the other room and went to sit cross-legged before the dish Martha lifted from the fire. Even in this relatively well-to-do household, the ancient customs of Israel were rigidly observed at mealtime. They bowed their heads while Lazarus spoke a prayer of thanksgiving for the food and then the women served him. Only when he had finished did they eat.

The wind still howled outside and the rain drummed occasionally against the shuttered windows, but inside there was warmth and the happiness of mutual love. Even the wealthy retired shortly after the coming of darkness and, tired from the day's work, Lazarus soon went to the heavily quilted sleeping pallet which Martha unrolled for him. The three slept in the main room of the house, as did all but the very wealthiest among the Israelites. Soon there was no sound save the rhythmic breathing of the sleepers and an occasional rustle when one of them turned in sleep. Like all Israelites, they slept fully clothed.

It was Mary who first realized something was wrong when Lazarus's teeth suddenly began to chatter in a severe chill. By the time she had lit a candle from the coals of the cooking fire and set it beside her brother's pallet, the rigor was so severe that his whole body was shaking.

Thoroughly alarmed, the sisters busied themselves putting more covers upon Lazarus and building up the fire to warm the room. In the full grip of the chill his face had turned almost blue and they cried out for fear that he would die then and there. But with the covers holding in his body warmth and the brightly burning fire heating the room, the chill gradually subsided. He still breathed in quick gasps, however, and sweat had broken out on his forehead from the agonizing pain in his chest every time he tried to breathe deeply.

Martha had seen this sickness before and her heart was heavy. Striking suddenly, usually during the winter months when the weather was frequently chill and damp, it often felled its victims in a few days while even the most skilled physician stood by helpless. She sent Mary to grind up mustard seeds and steep them in water for a poultice to apply to Lazarus's chest on the right side where the pain seemed to be most intense when he breathed.

The poultice and hot stones finally eased the pain somewhat and Lazarus was able to breathe without gasping. Martha could see how shallow his respirations were, however, and toward morning he began to cough up a small amount of dark, rusty-colored matter, sure sign of the swift destroying fever that so often attacked even the young in just this fashion.

When the dawn began to break, a servant was dispatched to Jerusalem to seek out Joseph of Galilee, the leading physician of the city who served as *medicus viscerus* of the temple in addition to having a busy practice among the well-to-do. Joseph was an old friend and, like Nicodemus, was also a believer in Jesus of Nazareth. If any man could help Lazarus, she knew, it was he.

By the time Joseph came from Jerusalem, Lazarus's face was flushed with fever and he was muttering with delirium and picking at the bed clothes. His breathing grew steadily more rapid in rate and shallower in depth. The physician was a tall, vigorous man, far more learned in his profession than the ordinary physicians in Israel, having studied at the great museum of Alexandria, a center of knowledge more renowned than Rome itself. In the temple he cared for the ills of the priests, but he was not in sympathy with the autocratic practices of Caiaphas and kept his position only because his skill exceeded that of any physician in Jerusalem.

Joseph examined Lazarus carefully, even as did the Greek physicians, putting his ear to the young man's chest and listening to the sounds of his breathing. By the time he completed the examination, his face was grave and he nodded to Mary and Martha to come into the adjoining room.

"Lazarus is seriously ill," he told them. "You must already have realized that."

Mary's eyes filled with tears, for she and her brother, the youngest of the three, were very close. Martha's heart was heavy, too, for she loved Lazarus as she would have loved the son she never had. But she was also the strongest and could not give way when the others needed her.

"The fever grows worse then?" she asked.

Joseph nodded. "I see many such at this season of the year."

"But he will recover?" Mary asked. "Say he will recover, Joseph!"

The physician did not give her the answer she wished to hear. "I do not know," he said. "Lazarus is young and strong, but often those are the ones who go the quickest."

"Is there nothing you can do?" Martha asked.

"Poppy leaves and wine will quiet him and let him rest," said the physician. "Cases such as this either get well suddenly in a few days or—" he did not complete the sentence, but opened the bag he carried to get the powdered leaves of the poppy plant which possessed an almost magical power to relieve pain and bring sleep. This, and the root of the mandrake, were the most valuable weapons in the armamentarium of the physician.

Martha brought wine and Joseph stirred up the powdered leaves to make a concoction which they gave Lazarus to drink. Although his eyes still burned with the fever of delirium, he took the medicine submissively. Later Joseph knew he would resist violently, but Martha and Mary would have trials enough to face in the next few days—if Lazarus lived and there was nothing to be gained by warning them now.

Joseph had left Jerusalem before the morning meal and Martha would not hear of his returning without at least some dates, a cake of bread, and fresh goat's milk to drink. While she bustled about the kitchen preparing the food, an idea began to take shape in her mind. When Joseph had eaten she gathered courage to speak to him about it.

"You believe Lazarus will die, don't you, Joseph?" she asked.

"I have seen few develop fever as quickly as he did and live." He looked at her keenly. "What is in your heart, Martha?"

"Jesus is our friend. If He were here He could save him."

Joseph did not question the statement. All too many of the conditions he was called upon to treat were beyond any help he could give, yet more than once he had seen them cured by the miraculous powers Jesus possessed. And if any man ever had need of these powers, it was Lazarus.

"Do you know where Jesus is?" Since the last attempt by the temple authorities to stone Him, those who loved Jesus had tried to keep His whereabouts as secret as possible.

"We had word yesterday. From a traveler. He is in Peraea, beyond Jordan."

"How far beyond the river?"

"About a day's journey, from what the traveler said."

Joseph knew the crisis would come before a messenger could find Jesus and return to Bethany with Him, but he hesitated to point this out to Martha and destroy her hope.

"Send word to Jesus, certainly," he said. "I can do nothing that you are not already doing. Only the will of God can save Lazarus now."

Quickly Martha sent for a trusted servant. "Find the Teacher of Nazareth," she directed, "and tell Him Martha sends this message: 'Lord, behold, he whom You love is sick.'"

Mary did not leave the bedside of her brother for her presence there seemed to have a quieting effect upon him. Martha, while equally concerned, was grateful for the household chores that kept her busy—keeping stones heated to maintain the warmth in Lazarus's body and subdue the racking chills that sapped his strength, or making rich broths which Mary could feed him in sips when he woke.

As the hours passed, Martha saw that her brother's breathing grew steadily more shallow as the mounting fever burned brighter in his eyes and in his cheeks. As she moved about the house, she would pause to pray that the messenger would find Jesus in time. She had given up hope that the Master could arrive in Bethany before Lazarus died, but she remembered how He had healed the son of Chuza in Capernaum though the boy was in Cana, several hours' journey away. She had also heard Peter describe how He had healed the servant of the Roman centurion and the daughter of a Syro-Phoenician woman without being in the actual presence of either. With nothing else to cling to, she dared to hope Jesus could accomplish the same thing for Lazarus even at the greater distance of two days' journey.

Mary never lost confidence that Jesus would save Lazarus and Martha did not mention her own misgivings to her young sister. Through the long day and the even longer night, the women watched, but when Joseph came the next morning, it was clear that death could not be many hours away. Already Lazarus's ear lobes were dusky in color and his lips were almost blue, while the skin of his body, except the almost blistered area where the application of ground mustard had irritated the skin, showed the same dark blue tint of approaching death. Friends and relatives had already gathered to help and comfort the two sisters while Lazarus lay dying, for it was futile now to hope that Jesus could reach Bethany in time, even had the messenger found Him.

Mary had remained at Lazarus's side, serenely confident that Jesus would save him. Only when, before midday, her brother ceased to breathe did they finally lead her from his pallet, so stunned by his death that she sat, dry-eyed, staring at the wall.

IV

The common burying ground of a town could not be less than fifty cubits from the outermost house. Located in a dry and rocky place if possible, graves by custom had to be at least a half-pace apart, since it was considered a dishonor for any person to walk over a grave. Public cemeteries were used largely for the poor, even the only moderately well-to-do having their own private tombs, usually located near their houses.

The family tomb of Mary and Martha, in which rested the bones of their father and mother, was in the garden adjacent to the house, a cave hollowed out of the rocky hillside, as were most private burying places in Bethany. Five cubits in width and four cubits in height, sufficient for a man to stand erect, it was six cubits long and contained space for eight bodies, three on either side and two across the end. The *kukhin*, as the cave tombs were called, were usually closed with a large stone known as the *golel*.

Since burial was carried out on the day of death whenever possible, the women relatives, who had been called in by Martha, began to prepare Lazarus's body for burial as soon as Joseph pronounced him dead. First the corpse was washed and then anointed with many spices, including myrrh and aloes. Next it was dressed in a white garment of fine wool and the face covered with a handkerchief of finest linen, bound lightly in place so that it could not blow off as the body was carried to the tomb.

The funeral procession was large, for the three were well known in Bethany and, being well-to-do, were entitled to a last tribute from the neighbors and those who served them as shepherds, vineyard tenders, and tillers of the soil. In Galilee it was customary for the hired mourners, both men and women, to precede the body, but in Judea the custom was reversed and they followed after, wailing constantly with the peculiar high-pitched cry which was their specialty. After these mourners came the family with Mary, still stunned by what had happened, supported by Martha and their friend Nicodemus from Jerusalem.

An elder of the synagogue at Bethany delivered a brief eulogy. Then the bearers carried the body in and placed it upon one of the niches carved from the wall of the cave. One by one the mourners passed the mouth of the cave taking leave of their friend with the words, "Depart in peace." This done, the procession returned to the house where each mourner made an expression of sympathy to Mary and Martha, repeating it, according to custom, seven times.

At the end of the ceremonial burial, a mourning period of thirty days began. During this time relatives and friends would be going and coming constantly, and at all times a large number of people would be in the vicinity. Martha found some surcease from her own grief in greeting the visitors and providing for their comfort. Mary, however, went directly to the mourning chamber.

As she worked, Martha could not keep from her mind the thought that if Jesus had been there, Lazarus would not have died. In a way, she felt the Master had failed her.

23

He who believes in Me, though he may die, he shall live.

John 11:25

It was near the end of the second day after his departure from Bethany that Martha's servant found Jesus. The Master was preaching outside a village about a day's journey north of Bethabara on the east bank of the

Jordan. He gave Martha's words to Jesus as he had been instructed, and described the gravity of the disease and the rapidity with which it had developed.

Jesus heard him patiently, almost as if He had been expecting the message. "This sickness is not unto death," He said, "but to the glory of God, that the Son of God may be glorified thereby." Then He turned to Thomas who, with a few others of the disciples, was with Him, and ordered that word be sent to the rest to rejoin Him as quickly as they could from the outlying villages where they had been teaching.

The following day the other disciples arrived, tired and dusty from the journey. They had not had a successful mission and were depressed.

"Lord," said Simon Peter to Jesus, "increase our faith."

Jesus sat beside a black mulberry bush, called in this region a sycamine tree. "If you had faith the size of a grain of mustard seed," He said severely, "you might say to this sycamine tree, 'Be you plucked up by the root and planted in the sea,' and it should obey.

"But which of you having a servant plowing or feeding cattle, will say to him when he comes from the field, 'Go and sit down to eat'? And will not rather say to him, 'Make ready wherewith I may sup and gird yourself and serve me, till I have eaten and drunk, and afterward you shall eat and drink'?

"Does he thank that servant because he did the things that were commanded him? So likewise when you have done all those things that are commanded of you, say, 'We are unprofitable servants, for we have done only that which it was our duty to do.'"

The tired and depressed disciples were not particularly pleased by His words, which they took to mean that, had they exerted themselves more in His service, they would have achieved more lasting results. Jesus did not reprimand them further, but said, "Let us go into Judea again."

Judea was a good two days' journey away and their last visit to Jerusalem had almost ended in a riot from which they had been lucky to escape, so some of them were shocked by the idea of going back into the zone of danger.

"The Jews sought to stone you," one of them pointed out. "Why go there again?"

"Are there not twelve hours in the day?" Jesus asked sternly. "If any man walk in the day he does not stumble because he sees the light of this world. But if a man walk in the night, he stumbles because there is no light in him."

Again He was reproving them for their lack of faith. Whatever waited for them in Judea was God's will. If they walked as they should, in the light of their faith in Him and His Father, they could not stumble.

In a softer tone now, Jesus explained why they must go into Judea. "Our friend Lazarus sleeps," He said. "But I go that I may wake him out of sleep."

"Lord," said one of the disciples a little testily, for he was weary from the forced journey to rejoin Jesus. "If he sleeps he does well."

"Lazarus is dead," Jesus then explained. "I am glad for your sakes that I was not there, to the intent that you may believe. Nevertheless let us go to him."

"Let us also go that we may die with Him," said Thomas, and the rest of them were ashamed now at their reluctance to accompany Jesus when He was going into danger. They all set out together and after two days' journey came to Bethany.

When Jesus arrived, Lazarus had been dead and in the tomb for four days.

II

The room to which Mary went when she returned from the funeral had already been prepared as a chamber of mourning, a purpose it would serve for the next thirty days. As was the custom, the couches had been upturned and chairs tumbled over in token of sorrow. The women sought to comfort Mary but she went directly to a corner and knelt there, her eyes uplifted as she prayed to God. It was not for Lazarus that she prayed, but for herself, that she might have faith in what Jesus had taught of the truth of eternal life, faith to be certain that they would all be joined with Lazarus in heaven.

While Mary prayed, the lines of grief in her face were gradually relieved as the assurance she sought came flowing into her soul. Lazarus was gone; she would mourn him, for she loved him, but even in the depth of her sorrow, she was comforted by the knowledge that the separation from her brother would be only like the absence of a loved one who has gone on a long journey.

When Mary rose from her knees, her face was composed. The other women marveled at the deep and abiding faith that showed in her eyes and one of them spoke to Martha of it.

Martha still somewhat resented that Jesus had chosen this time to be absent from Bethany when He might have saved Lazarus, and it offended her that Mary seemed to have put away her grief so quickly.

"It is not seemly to give up mourning so soon," she said. "You look almost happy and not even a week of sorrow has passed." By custom a special week of sorrow began the mourning period. Traditionally the first three of the seven days, always excepting the Sabbath when all mourning was suspended, were the most intense.

"Have you forgotten the words of Jesus to Nicodemus?" Mary asked.

"What do you mean?"

"When Nicodemus first talked to Jesus, the Master told him God so loved the world He sent His Son so that whoever believes in Him shall not die but have everlasting life."

Martha was taken aback. Concerned with the present and with material things, she had lacked the inner faith and the peace it could bring.

"Lazarus is dead only for a little while," Mary said confidently. "He will rise again in heaven and we shall be with him."

"But he was so young to be stricken down," Martha protested, her eyes filling with tears again. "If Jesus had been here, Lazarus would not have died."

"But he will live again and we shall be with him." The promise was enough for Mary, but Martha could not yet find in her soul the fundamental faith she needed in order to be comforted.

The first days of deepest mourning were not yet finished when Jesus came to Bethany. As head of the household, Martha was busy with the needs of the friends, relatives, and retainers who had come to mourn with them. For her, physical action had always served to solve the emotional problems she was unable to cope with herself. She was in the kitchen directing the servants as they baked bread in the large ovens when word came that Jesus was approaching.

Leaving the house, she ran to meet Him and came upon Him and His party before they reached the yard surrounding the house. Dropping to her knees before Him, she said impetuously, "Lord, if You had been here, my brother would not have died."

Jesus sensed the reproof in her tone and, knowing how she had loved Lazarus, understood. As soon as she spoke, however, Martha realized her presumption and, overcome now with shame, she added quickly, "But I know that even now whatever You ask of God, God will give it to You."

Martha's expression of faith had come belatedly, but Jesus was compassionate for the frailties of human character. As on that other occasion when she had protested that Mary sat at His feet while she labored with the household duties, He understood Martha's good qualities as well as her weaknesses and was gentle with her. Taking her by the hand, He lifted her to her feet.

"Your brother shall rise again," He told her.

Martha had not yet been able to find in her own heart Mary's joyful confidence that they would be joined again with Lazarus in the resurrection. She thought mainly of the present and material, Mary of the spiritual and eternal, and it had been hard for her to find a meeting ground between the two.

"I know he shall rise again on the resurrection at the last day," she said, but still somewhat doubtfully.

When Martha had run to meet Jesus, most of those gathered in the courtyard outside the house had followed her. Some were followers of Jesus while others were merely curious to see what the prophet of Nazareth would do for these people who were among His closest friends. They had stood a small distance away and the disciples, too, had held back while Jesus was talking to Martha, hesitating to intrude upon the meeting between Him and the bereaved sister. Jesus lifted His voice now so all could hear.

"I am the resurrection and the life," He said. "He that believes in Me, though he were dead, yet shall he live. And whoever lives and believes in Me will never die."

Turning to Martha again, He asked in a lower tone, "Do you believe this?"

Martha could not yet understand what Jesus was promising her. She believed that He could have kept Lazarus from death if He had been at Bethany when her brother became ill. But Lazarus was dead now; four days ago she had seen his body washed and anointed and placed in the tomb. Her practical mind recoiled from a death that was not death.

"Lord, I believe You are the Christ," she said humbly. The Son of God, which should come into the world."

Belatedly Martha remembered that Mary sat with the mourners in the upstairs chamber and she went to tell her sister of Jesus' arrival. Mary left the mourning chamber and ran immediately to kneel before the Master.

"Lord," she said, "if You had been here my brother would not have died."

The words were those Martha had used, but there was an infinity of difference in the meaning. Where Martha had reproached Jesus for being absent and letting Lazarus die, Mary was stating a truth she had instinctively realized deep in her soul through that warm communion of spirit which existed between her and Jesus, the truth that those who stood beside Him could never die, even though they went through the tomb itself.

Tears filled Jesus' eyes and ran down His cheeks. For whom did He weep?

Certainly He wept for the "lost sheep of Israel" whose faith did not even equal that of Martha and could never equal that of Mary. And for that lack of faith, they must die, not like Lazarus, with the certainty of resurrection to life eternal, but condemned eternally for their refusal to see the light.

Once again Mary had "chosen that good part," the sublime conviction of faith in God and His Son "which shall not be taken away from her."

Jesus' travail lasted only a moment. The time left Him was growing short.

"Where have you laid him?" He asked.

Mary and Martha answered together. "Lord, come and see."

As Jesus and Mary and Martha now moved through the garden toward the tomb, one of the men watching said wonderingly, "Behold, how He loved him!"

But another, of the same practical turn of mind as Martha, said, "Could not this Man who opened the eyes of the blind have kept Lazarus from dying?"

At the end of the garden the three stopped before the tomb, with the *golel*, the great stone, guarding it.

"Take away the stone," Jesus directed.

Again Martha's sense of the practical overrode her faith.

"Lord, by this time he stinks!" she cried, horrified at the thought of exposing a rotting body, the ultimate of defilement under Jewish ritual beliefs. "He has been dead four days."

"Did I not say to you, if you believe, you would see the glory of God?" Jesus asked.

Ashamed, Martha made no more objections and some of the disciples joined the men who had come to mourn in pushing away the stone.

Standing before the cave, Jesus raised His eyes to heaven in prayer. 'Father, I thank You that You have heard Me," He said. "And I know that You hear Me always. But because of the people who stand by I spoke it, that they may believe You have sent Me."

Then He lowered His eyes and said in a loud voice, "Lazarus, come forth!"

Something stirred in the gloomy depths of the tomb, and then a white-robed figure slowly arose from the niche where the body of Lazarus had been placed. Stumbling a little, for the napkin was still bound across his face, Lazarus walked from the tomb.

"Loose him," Jesus directed, "and let him go."

In the garden and the courtyard outside the house, people were falling to their knees to worship Jesus and beg Him to teach them to believe. But a few slipped away to Jerusalem, eager to be the first to bring Caiaphas and Elam the news that the prophet of Nazareth had accomplished, almost on the doorstep of the temple, the ultimate miracle, that of raising a man dead four days and wrapped in his grave clothes.

In raising Lazarus, Jesus had now cast down the gage. The final phase of the conflict between Him and the authorities at Jerusalem had begun and its climax was inevitable.

III

News that Jesus had returned to Bethany and raised Lazarus from the dead struck Caiaphas with amazement. Previously Jesus had visited Jerusalem only at the time of the religious festivals, and Caiaphas had already begun to make plans which he expected to put into effect when the forthcoming Passover season began. Now Jesus was in Judea well before the Passover and, if the excited reports from Bethany were to be believed, making a startling impression upon the people who had seen Him raise Lazarus from the dead or heard the reports of it that were being circulated.

It was true that Jesus had seemed to overcome death on other occasions, notably when He had apparently restored the daughter of Jairus to life in Capernaum, but those happenings had been far from Jerusalem and there was reason to doubt that they were miracles at all. In the case of Jairus's daughter, Jesus Himself had said she was not dead but asleep.

Concerning Lazarus, however, no one could doubt. He had been pronounced dead by a physician; his body had been prepared for burial by people who could swear that he was indeed dead; and afterward he had lain in the tomb for four days. To Caiaphas, these facts could not be explained unless Jesus healed by the power of Beelzebub, the prince of devils, which the high priest devoutly believed to be the case.

For still another reason, Caiaphas and the Sanhedrin were particularly concerned by the reappearance of Jesus now in the suburbs of Jerusalem. Not long before, a brief outburst of violence had flared in the sanctuary area itself when a group of Galilean Zealots, headed by a bandit named Barabbas, had tried to stir up a rebellion, apparently more in the hope of committing a spectacular robbery during the following confusion, than with any expectation of overthrowing the temple hierarchy. Watchful for just such occurrences, the troops of Pilate had swarmed into the temple without stopping to consult the high priest and had cut down the Galileans, taking only their leader prisoner. In the words of the horrified priests, Pilate had "mingled the blood of the Galileans with their sacrifices," a reminder of another occasion when heathens had desecrated the great altar of the temple on the order of Antiochus IV.

A wave of indignation had swept Jerusalem at this new indignity by the Romans, and since he often cooperated with Pilate, Caiaphas had been heavily blamed by the Sanhedrin. He was determined to prevent another such incident, for the Sanhedrin could depose him if they wished and name another high priest in his stead, as could the procurator as well. Caiaphas knew, too, that Pilate was not pleased with him for having let the abortive attack occur at all.

The members of the Great Sanhedrin were equally concerned when they met on the morning after word came that Jesus had raised Lazarus from the dead. Following the recent disturbances when the Galileans had been executed in the temple, any commotion due to Jesus' presence in the area might be interpreted by Pontius Pilate as the beginning of another uprising. In such a case the procurator would move swiftly and this time considerably more people might be involved. Roman justice was thorough but sometimes, especially in the hands of an impulsive man like Pontius Pilate, completely ruthless. To the members of the Sanhedrin, the crisis posed by Jesus' presence could profoundly influence the future of Israel as a nation.

Nearly three hundred years before Jesus was born, Jews who sought to combat the Greek influences and maintain the traditions of a nation founded under God with a code of laws in the Torah had organized themselves in what came to be called the Great Synagogue. Even before the revolt led by Judas Maccabaeus, a senate or *gerousia*, also called the Sanhedrin, had existed in Jerusalem for the purpose of administering the affairs of state for the Jews as a whole. Religious in nature, it was also political, for the Law had come from God through Moses and the two were considered inseparable.

As the Pharisees, with their strict observance of the Torah and their antagonism to the liberal beliefs of the Sadducees, dominated the life of the people under Roman rule, they came to be more and more influential in the Sanhedrin. Under the Hasmoneans, the Sadducees gained power but when Herod the Great murdered forty-five members of the Council, the balance swung again to the Pharisees.

Under Herod, the Sanhedrin had become weak, only to regain its authority when Archelaus was deposed and Judea was made into a province of Rome under a procurator. It became the final supreme court for all cases involving breaches of Mosaic Law. In Galilee, where Herod Antipas ruled, the Sanhedrin at Jerusalem exercised little power except in strictly religious matters. But in Judea and Jerusalem the high court could order arrests and condemn criminals to any punishment short of death. Only capital offenses required the procurator's approval.

The high court met twice weekly in its own building on the west side of the temple elevation. Although composed of seventy-one members, twenty-three constituted the traditional quorum and the entire membership was rarely present. As a result, the small Priestly Council, largely dominated by Caiaphas, carried on most of the business of the court.

Generally Caiaphas did not convoke the larger group. On the present occasion he summoned it. The question to be discussed was a grave one.

The court sat in a great arc extending from one side of the meeting chamber to the other, a line of men of all ages and of diverse appearance. The priests were richly dressed, the wealthier Pharisees equally so. But there were also artisans and men of little wealth here, many of them teachers whose influence was great.

Annas, the former high priest, spoke first by custom. "We are gathered to decide what must be done with the Nazarene Jesus," he said in his quavering voice. "This man does many miracles and if we let Him alone, all men will believe Him. Then the Romans will come and take away both our city and nation."

The recent trouble with the Galileans was uppermost in the minds of all. Had that uprising spread into the city where hatred of the Romans was strong, the punitive actions of Pilate would not have mingled the blood of merely the offending Galileans with their sacrifices. Many of those present had witnessed the cruelties of Herod; some of this very group had been imprisoned by him in the Hippodrome and saved only by the king's death. They were determined now that trouble be kept from Jerusalem at all costs.

"There is no reason to connect Jesus of Nazareth with the revolt of the Galileans," Nicodemus said. "If He raises men from the dead, surely He must be the Messiah."

This was too much for Elam. "The Nazarene performs miracles through the power of Beelzebub!" he shouted angrily. "Would you turn over the temple of Israel to the devil himself?"

"Jesus refuted that argument," Nicodemus protested.

Elam only shrugged. "Would Satan admit his identity? Demons always answer with a lie."

A chorus of assent arose from the members.

"This man does good work," Joseph of Arimathea protested. "Who can accuse Him of any evil?"

"Is it not evil to teach people to break the Law?" a rabbi demanded hotly. "He ignores the Sabbath and uses it as if it were any other day."

"And He teaches people to eat without washing," another cried.

"Besides," Elam added, "there are known revolutionaries among His disciples."

"He eats with publicans and sinners," Joachai argued, "encouraging the evil to do more evil."

"But if He is the Messiah," Nicodemus managed to interpose, "He could do all those things and it would not be wrong."

"Would the Messiah break the Law?" Elam demanded incredulously.

"The Messiah will come from God," Nicodemus said. "The scribes have not hesitated to interpret the Law as they see fit. Why should the Son of God not interpret it as He sees fit?"

The argument was logical and made an impression upon some members. Nicodemus was gaining support for his proposal to leave Jesus, as a prophet, unmolested, but Elam broke in with a familiar argument.

"Will the Anointed of God be a Galilean? A Nazarene?" he demanded contemptuously. "Tell me whether any good can come out of Nazareth."

Even Nicodemus could not immediately answer this appeal to the deep-seated prejudice of the Jerusalem Jews against Galileans.

"Nothing but trouble comes out of Galilee," Jochai added. "Remember Barabbas."

Before the battle of words could start again, Caiaphas spoke. He had shrewdly waited, letting Annas make the first thrust against Jesus and allowing the others to fill the air with vehement oratory. Now he spoke as a conciliator, a peace-maker who would save them all from trouble.

"You know nothing at all that would name this man Jesus the Messiah save His own words," he said. "Nor do you take into account that it is better one man should die so that the whole nation should not perish."

Most of these men were sincere. For a few, the chief priests among them, Jesus meant a threat to their control of the vast temple revenue. But what the ordinary members of the Sanhedrin feared was that the Nazarene might stir up the populace and bring down upon the city the wrath of the impetuous Roman governor. They had not troubled themselves about Jesus when He was in Galilee; He had been Herod's problem then. But now that He was on the outskirts of Jerusalem, performing the miracles that had brought thousands of people flocking to Him in Galilee, even acclaiming Him the Messiah and seeking to make Him king, He threatened the stability of their own world.

Caiaphas had advanced a shrewd argument. Even if Jesus were a prophet, His destruction as an individual was preferable to the bloodbath Pontius Pilate would release if the people of Jerusalem showed signs of proclaiming the Nazarene king. Viewed in that light, one man's death was a low price to pay for the welfare of the many.

And so when Caiaphas introduced the question of how to combat the menace of Jesus' presence in Bethany, the vote went heavily for a sentence of death. The method the members gladly left to the high priest, a silent tribute to his skill in such matters. The small minority in the Sanhedrin who protested, particularly Nicodemus and Joseph of Arimathea, were shouted down and the decision was made. The Nazarene must die.

For indeed, the kingdom of God is within you.

Luke 17:21

Jesus and His disciples were resting at Bethany, rejoicing with Mary and Martha that Lazarus had returned to life. The action of the Sanhedrin, reported to them at once by Nicodemus, had taken place on the day preceding the Sabbath. The arguments had occupied most of the morning, so there was little reason to believe Caiaphas would move until after the day of rest. Jesus therefore stayed with His party at Bethany until the Sabbath had passed and then departed early on the following morning.

It was their custom to go to Peraea and Galilee by way of Jericho but now that Caiaphas was actively plotting His death, Jesus chose a less traveled route. Moving north toward Samaria He came into the hilly district lying between Jerusalem and the border and stopped at a small village called Ephraim.

Originally a town of Samaria, Ephraim had been added to Judea almost two hundred years before. Although little more than a day's journey from Jerusalem, it was still a frontier place where the authority of the Sanhedrin would not be strong. The town lay in the midst of a populous and highly cultivated area, but hardly a mile to the east a ridge of high land began and extended to the Jordan Valley, the hills being densely wooded and best described as a wilderness. From the nearby heights the whole of Judea could be seen, extending as far to the southeast as the Sea of Judgment. A deep valley on the south and a range of hills to the north helped to seclude the area, and the nearest road of any significance passed west of the town. This out-of-the-way location made it possible for Jesus and His party, now fugitives from authority, to reach Ephraim without using any well-traveled roads where agents of Caiaphas and the Sanhedrin might be waiting to seize Him, or the sicarii, whose knives were always for hire, to assassinate Him.

From Ephraim, if the occasion demanded, He could quickly move into Samaria and, by a rapid journey along roads that were not heavily traveled, into Galilee. Or should flight into Peraea be indicated, a quick journey would bring Him to the Jordan and the crossing just south of its confluence with the River Jabbok. Thus the area was especially suitable for Jesus and His companions to rest and teach for some weeks before undertaking the next journey to Jerusalem for the Passover.

II

On other occasions, Jesus had visited Jerusalem for the religious festivals without any fanfare. During the previous Feast of Tabernacles He had even waited in the home of Mary and Martha at Bethany until the first days of the week of celebration were past, entering the temple to teach only toward the end when many people had already left. But the action of the Sanhedrin now forced Him to choose between defying Caiaphas and the court or abandoning Jerusalem and Judea altogether. This latter choice would limit His activity to Peraea where the tetrarch Philip still tolerated Him, or would force Him to leave Israel and go to the Gentiles.

From the beginning Jesus had said He was sent to the "lost sheep of Israel." If He were ever to be recognized as the Messiah, no time would be more appropriate than the Passover, the most holy season, when the greatest crowds would visit the city. To approach Jerusalem unheralded would now be impossible, however. The only alternative was to enter the city with such a concourse of followers that even a desperate man like the high priest would hesitate to arrest Him.

These were the arguments Simon Peter and the leaders of the disciples used. Jesus agreed, though He was saddened by the failure of the disciples to understand the meaning of the events which were to follow. Since a great crowd was to accompany Him to Jerusalem for the coming Passover, He and His disciples soon left Ephraim and moved to the southern district of Galilee, passing through Samaria.

Ten lepers who had somehow learned that the Galilean healer was coming that way stood by the roadside as Jesus entered a small village near the border of Galilee. By the Law they could approach no nearer than seven cubits and as Jesus came near, they lifted their voices in a chorus of pleas, begging Him to have mercy upon them and cleanse them of their loathsome disease.

Jesus looked at the men, His eyes warm at their faith. "Go and show yourselves to the priest," He said, directing them to complete the customary ritual evidence of their cleansing required under Mosaic Law.

Overjoyed, nine of the men hurried on to obtain the coveted certificate of cleansing. The tenth, who was a Samaritan, turned back to fall on the ground before Jesus, glorifying God and giving thanks for the miracle that had made him whole.

"Were not ten cleansed, but where are the nine?" Jesus said sadly. "Were there none found who returned to give glory to God, save this stranger?"

The Jews who were listening dropped their eyes in shame and Jesus looked down at the prostrate man. "Arise and go your way," He told him. "Your faith has made you whole."

Jesus' steps were heavy as He continued on the road that would lead eventually to Jerusalem and the Passover. Of the ten who had been shown the way into the kingdom of God by faith, only one, and he a Samaritan, had chosen to follow Him.

III

Jemuel was a man of substance and proud of his accomplishments. Though barely thirty he was one of the rulers of the synagogue in his town, and was respected by the people for his industry in caring for his vineyards and his olive groves, his fairness to all who worked or traded with him, and his strict observance of the Law. Jemuel had every reason to believe the Most High approved of him, for did God not favor with earthly wealth those who obeyed His commandments? On the Sabbath he often read from the Law and the Prophets and he kept the festivals religiously, always going up to Jerusalem for the Passover and. sometimes attending the other feasts as well.

Word had come even to the small town that the Nazarene Teacher was a controversial figure and that it was said the Sanhedrin at Jerusalem had condemned Him to death. But certainly there had seemed nothing controversial about the slender man with the warm friendly eyes who had stopped to teach the children of the village and had blessed them so graciously. He had even healed several people who were known to Jemuel, so when this visiting rabbi was invited to speak, no one had objected—until they heard His words.

When He taught, the Teacher changed from the simple unassuming man in the homespun robe who had come walking into the village the day before at the head of a small procession of His followers. His voice was still soft and His manner still restrained, but He spoke words they had never heard before, prophesying the imminent coming of the kingdom of God, preaching the need to repent of their sins if they were to be saved from death and given eternal life, and stressing the need to reorder their lives. As He had stood upon the elevated platform for the reading of the Shema, both the Teacher and His words took on an authority and urgency that stirred and troubled the hearts of many of His listeners. Some had even come to Him after the Sabbath service asking to hear more; a few were reported to have put aside their work and followed Him.

Jemuel was not one of those to become followers; he had possessions he could not afford to leave and a position in the community he would not give up. Nevertheless his mind was uneasy as he walked home from the Sabbath service. His steps were lingering, as tradition required, but more than tradition made him delay. A deep uncertainty troubled his mind and neither the festive gaiety of the Sabbath meal nor his handsome wife, fine children, and beautiful home could elevate his spirits.

Jemuel could not understand what the Nazarene had meant by the coming of the kingdom of God. It was true that all Jews, except the Sadducees, who denied the reality of eternal life, looked forward to the creation of God's kingdom on earth and the coming forth from the grave of those who had kept the Law—as Jemuel did. But Jesus had obviously meant something else, a kingdom of God here and now in the everyday lives of men and their relationships one with another. And this Jemuel could not understand, for to him the present was already sufficient.

He had his possessions and his family. He had the satisfaction of one who keeps the Law. He was looked up to by his fellow men as a leader in religious worship. He had the joyful knowledge of all these things each day of his life. What should he do that he was not doing?

Friends came to visit that Sabbath afternoon and discussed the Nazarene Teacher. But none could say anything to ease Jemuel's mind, and his evening prayers, strictly observed as always in the presence of his family, brought no relief from the vague uneasiness that troubled his soul.

Jemuel's wife could not help him. She had talked with some women who had taken their children to the Nazarene to be blessed, but these women had been prompted only by the feeling that the touch of one reputed to be a holy man should bring health and good luck. One woman had heard the teacher reproving His disciples because they had tried to keep away the women and children, but the words the Nazarene had spoken made little sense to Jemuel.

"Whoever shall not receive the kingdom of God as a little child shall in no wise enter therein," the Teacher had said before blessing the children. But what could Jemuel's little son, playing on the floor of hard-packed earth, know about the kingdom of God when the scribes and learned rabbis argued endlessly about it? And how could a man become a child again so that he might enter that kingdom—if such a place existed?

Jemuel was a practical man, accustomed to resolving a question and making a final decision to which he then adhered without change. But tonight he failed. In his quandary, he visited his friend Zaccai, who was considered in the village something of a thinker and who had remained to listen to the Nazarene after the Sabbath service was over.

"I saw the Nazarene and His disciples eat without washing their hands," Zaccai reported with a note of disapproval in his voice. "And one of them said they often traveled on the Sabbath day."

"Many people do not obey all the Law," Jemuel said. "But not rabbis who must tell others what they should do."

"What if He is a prophet?" Jemuel asked.

Zaccai shrugged. "Some said John the Baptist was a prophet, but Herod beheaded him and the Most High has not punished Herod."

"Did the Nazarene tell you anything about this kingdom of God He speaks of so much?"

"I remember only one thing," Zaccai said, "but it makes no sense."

"What was it?"

"The Teacher said, 'The kingdom of God is within you.'"

"Do you suppose He meant that one who keeps the Law already dwells in the kingdom in his own heart?"

"You keep the Law," Zaccai reminded him. "Why are you so troubled then?"

Jemuel did not know the answer but he felt no better for Zaccai's observation. "Did He say anything else?"

"Something about light—yes, I remember. He said, 'I am the light of the world. He that follows Me shall not walk in darkness, but shall have the light of life.'"

"What does that mean?"

"I am not sure," Zaccai said. "Once, when John the Baptist was preaching at the fords of the Jordan, I went to hear him. The Essenes make much of what they call the light. Some of the same men who now follow the Nazarene were disciples of John."

Jemuel nodded. "Jesus and John were kinsmen."

"When I listened to John, I stayed for several days at the community of the Essenes near the fords," Zaccai said thoughtfully. "Some of what the Nazarene said sounds like their teachings."

"Is Jesus an Essene, then?"

"I think not, for the Essenes obey the Law in every respect, and He does not. They believe that the powers of good in the world representing the light are constantly battling the evil forces of darkness. And that when the light triumphs, a new kingdom of God will begin in our time. That might be what the Nazarene means."

"Prophets like Isaiah and Esdras used much the same words," Jemuel said.

"Yes. But there is something else about these Essenes. Their order was founded a long time ago by one they call the Teacher of Righteousness. They expect him to return to earth. Or expect at least another Teacher of Righteousness to come who will lead the forces of light to victory and bring the kingdom of God to pass on earth."

"Then when Jesus says, 'I am the light,' He may be announcing that He is the Teacher of Righteousness who is to come?" Jemuel said eagerly.

"I thought of that. But the Nazarene does not claim to be an Essene and does not follow their rules."

"The Essenes care for the sick as He does," Jemuel said.

"But they do not heal with miracles. Jesus raised Lazarus of Bethany from the dead only a few days ago and since then His disciples have been proclaiming openly that He is the Messiah."

"But that is impossible!" Jemuel cried. "Everyone knows the Messiah will come in glory, surrounded by the angels, to rule in Israel."

"I could not believe it either," Zaccai agreed. "That is why I did not stay with the Nazarene any longer."

IV

When Jemuel found the next morning that uncertainty still troubled him, he went to the caravansary where Jesus and His party were already astir, preparing to take the road. Going directly to where Jesus stood beside the road, Jemuel knelt at His feet. "Good Master," he said, "what shall I do to inherit eternal life?"

"Why do you call Me good?" Jesus asked. "None is good save one, God."

Being familiar with the Scriptures, Jemuel knew He was referring to the ancient writing which labeled the Most High, "The good one of the world."

"You know the commandments," Jesus continued. "Do not commit adultery. Do not kill. Do not steal. Do not bear false witness. Honor your father and mother."

"All these I have kept from my youth up," Jemuel protested.

Jesus looked into the young ruler's heart. He saw a man whose pride in his own accomplishments and his possessions threatened to destroy his soul, even though he was extremely pious by the traditional standards of his faith.

"Yet you lack one thing," Jesus told him gently. "Sell all you have and distribute to the poor and you shall have treasures in heaven. Then come and follow Me."

Jemuel understood at last the reason for the disturbance of his spirit. He was proud of his riches and of his position in the community. To obey

Jesus would mean giving up all he held dear and he slowly turned away, his head bowed; even with all his strength, he did not possess the courage to follow Jesus' advice.

With sadness in His eyes, Jesus watched him go. How near this young ruler of the congregation had been to the true kingdom of God and treasures greater than any on earth! And yet he could not give up what he thought were his possessions, the worldly goods that really possessed *him*.

"How hardly shall they who have riches enter into the kingdom of heaven!" Jesus said to the waiting disciples. "It is easier for a camel to go through the eye of a needle than for a rich man to enter into the kingdom of God."

"Who then can be saved?" one of the disciples asked.

"The things which are impossible with men are possible with God," Jesus reminded him cryptically.

"Lo, we have left all and followed You," Peter said to Jesus.

"Truly I say to you," Jesus said, "no man has left house or parents or brethren or wife or children for the kingdom of God's sake who shall not receive manifold more in this present time, and in the world to come life everlasting."

The others had already started along the road, but Jesus called them back so that He could answer more fully by means of a parable the question Jemuel had raised.

"The kingdom of heaven is like a man who was a householder and went out early in the morning to hire laborers for his vineyard," He told them. "When he had agreed with the laborers for a penny a day, he sent them into his vineyard. He went out about the third hour and saw others standing idle in the market place and said to them: 'Go also into the vineyard and whatsoever is right I will give you.' And they went their way.

"Again he went out about the sixth and ninth hour and did likewise. And about the eleventh hour he went out, and found others standing idle and said to them, 'Why do you stand here all day idle?'

"They said to him, 'Because no man has hired us,' and he said, 'Go also into the vineyard and whatever is right, that you will receive.'

"When evening was come, the lord of the vineyard said to his steward, 'Call the laborers and give them their hire, beginning from the last to the first.' When they came that were hired about the eleventh hour, they received every man a penny. But when the first came they supposed that they should have received more and they likewise received every man a penny. When they had received it, they murmured against the good man of the house saying, 'These last have worked but one hour and you have made them equal to us who have borne the burden and heat of the day.'

"But he answered one of them and said, 'Friend, I do you no wrong. Did you not agree with me for a penny? Take what is yours and go your way; I will give to the last even as unto you. Is it not lawful for me to do what I will with my own? Is your eye evil because I am good?'

"So the last shall be first and the first last," Jesus said as He ended the parable, "for many are called but few chosen."

The Son of Man did not come to be served,
but to serve, and to give His life a ransom for many.

Matthew 20:28

It had been a long time since Mary of Magdala had visited Jerusalem for the Passover. She vividly remembered journeying as a child with a festive party of Galileans through the valley of the Jordan and along the steep climb from Jericho to the Holy City. It had been exciting to run ahead with the other children, one of the few times when boys and girls were allowed to play together after they became old enough for school. But of the ceremony itself she remembered only the long lines of marching men who were blowing trumpets and clashing cymbals loudly in the warm spring sunshine.

She had buried her head in her mother's skirts when men in white robes already spattered with blood threw lambs to the floor and cut the animals' throats. She remembered crying out in protest and being reproved by her mother. She had a vague memory of a hillside afterwards dotted with the dying coals of many campfires, and of voices lifted in the beautiful melody of the hallel floating through the darkness.

Until that day in the temple when Jesus had protected her from the Pharisees and then had cast out demons from her. Since then Mary had spent much of her time helping the disciples look after the sick and afflicted—the lame, the halt, and the blind who flocked to Jesus to be healed. They had needed help afterward, too, for many of these unfortunates now had nothing at all; deserving no more alms now that they were well, they found it hard to keep alive. Some, when they discovered that it was easier to beg than to work for a living, had demanded that Jesus give back their afflictions to them.

What time Mary could spare, she had spent in reading the ancient writings again, the moving story of how a motley group of tribes had been welded into a nation under Moses and Joshua, of the judges and kings who had followed them, of how they had finally found a king in David who led them to success as a nation, and of the turbulent events which had followed his reign.

It was a warm spring afternoon when Simon Peter trudged into the shady courtyard of Mary's home. She had been planting flowers in a bed near the fountain when she heard the gate open and saw the tall familiar figure coming across the courtyard toward her.

"Simon!" she cried, running to embrace him. "Is the Master with you?" Peter shook his head and sank down on a bench while Mary went to bring a cup of cool water for him. The hem of his robe was caked with dust and so were his legs. He drank the water before he answered her question and wiped his face with the towel she hurried to bring him.

"I left the Master in Peraea," he said. "He will not come to this part of Galilee again before going to Jerusalem for the Passover."

"Is it true that He raised Lazarus from the dead in Bethany?"

"Yes. Four days after he died."

"How could anybody doubt Jesus after that? Now Jerusalem will surely acclaim Him as the Messiah."

"Only if we force them to do it. That is why I have come."

"But how? You know Jesus would not agree to violence of any sort."

"There will be none," Peter assured her. "At least not begun by us. Some would like it; Simon the Zealot, perhaps, and Judas, and one or two others. They believe once the sword is lifted the people will rise up and force the corrupt priests and the Romans out of Judea. Then Herod would be driven from Galilee and the land would be free."

"Jesus does not want that," Mary protested. "You are so close to Him, Simon. Surely you know that?"

"So I told them," the big man said. "But there is another way. If the Master enters the city at the head of a large enough procession, the authorities will have no choice except to acknowledge Him as the Messiah."

"Do you think such a crowd will escort Him?"

"If we work hard enough to bring together all those who have been healed by Him and love Him."

Mary shook her head doubtfully. "How many thanked Jesus for healing them? Do you remember His parable about those invited to the feast who all begged to be excused?"

"There are enough of us who know He is the Messiah," Simon said confidently. "And He is gaining hundreds of new followers in Peraea every day."

"I hope you are right. What can I do?"

"When the authorities see that we are accompanied by a large group of women, they cannot pretend that we intend to use violence. The women will be your responsibility."

"I will send word to all I know," Mary promised. "And I will bring Jesus' mother to Jerusalem, if she will come."

"Good!" said Simon, rising to his feet. "I will leave that task in your hands then."

"Rest a while. I can see that you are weary."

"I have many people to see before I go back to Peraea," Simon told her. "This will be a procession such as has never before been seen in Jerusalem, Mary. Caiaphas will tremble at the sight of it."

He was at the gate of the courtyard when Mary spoke again. "Simon," she called. "Does Jesus know about this plan of yours?"

"Not the details, but surely He would not mind those who love Him journeying together to Jerusalem for the Passover."

"I mean, will He let you proclaim Him the Messiah there?"

"He can hardly object to that either from so great a multitude."

"What of His prophecies that He will die in Jerusalem?"

"He was speaking in the form of a parable," Simon assured her. "I think He meant that He will put away His old self when He becomes the Messiah."

"But He has spoken of it several times lately," she insisted.

"So has He spoken of the mustard seed," Simon said, a little irritated by her persistence. "You know the Master often repeats parables to different groups. You will join us then in Peraea on the way to Jerusalem, with as many women as you can gather?"

"I will do my best," Mary promised. "And pray that nothing goes wrong."

"Nothing can go wrong," the tall fisherman assured her confidently. "Jesus will enter Jerusalem in triumph, surrounded by a multitude of people. The whole city will be His."

II

Joanna, the wife of Herod's steward Chuza, was a woman of great pride. She kept the Law with her household, but she also adhered strictly to the teachings of Jesus that the righteousness of those who were His followers must exceed even the righteousness of the Pharisees. She disliked dissembling, but tonight she did not tell her husband what was in her heart until he had finished his evening meal. Having servants, they ate together, not the men first as was customary in most Jewish households. When Chuza had finished the excellent meal and had washed his hands and dried them, Joanna spoke.

"I had a visitor today," she said casually. "Mary Magdalene."

"We do not see Mary often enough," Chuza said warmly. "I am glad you invited her to come."

"I didn't invite her. There is something she wants me to do."

"Mary would not ask you to do anything wrong. You can be sure of that."

"Then you will not mind if I go?" she asked.

"Go where?"

"Up to Jerusalem for the Passover. With Mary and the other women who follow Jesus."

"Was that why she came?"

"Yes."

Chuza rubbed his chin. "I had a visitor, too—Simon Peter. And he asked me to do the same thing."

"Did you agree?" Joanna asked eagerly. "We have not been to Jerusalem for the Passover in several years. It would be good if we could go together."

"Did Mary tell you why she wants the women to go just now?" he asked.

"So the chief priests will see how many people follow Jesus. Then they cannot deny any longer that He is the Messiah."

Chuza nodded. "That is only part of it. Simon wants to convince Caiaphas and the Romans that Jesus means no violent overturn of the government. The presence of one of Herod's chief stewards in the crowd following Him would go a long way to do that."

"Did you tell Simon you would go?"

Chuza shook his head. "This is an important decision, Joanna. One that may affect our whole lives."

"How can that be?"

"If Jesus is to be acclaimed the Messiah in Jerusalem, Herod must respect Him even more than he respects the high priest and the Sadducees. Herod is more Roman than Jew, but he is no fool. Jesus will wield great power over the people, and unless Herod at least pretends to respect and accept Him, there could be a rebellion here in Galilee."

"Then Herod should be glad that his steward from this part of Galilee is a follower of Jesus."

"I said *if* Jesus is acclaimed the Messiah, and without violence," Chuza reminded her. "Remember the way Pontius Pilate put down the Galileans led by Barabbas. We have to think what will happen if the plans of Simon and the others fail."

"How can they fail? Jesus possesses the power of God. We know that from the way He healed our son."

"Jesus does have the power," Chuza agreed. "But will He use it? He never has used it before for purposes like this. The crowds in the temple have almost proclaimed Him the Messiah several times, but He would not allow them to do it."

"Then I did wrong in telling Mary I would go?" Joanna said.

"No," Chuza told her. "I have been thinking about this ever since Simon came to me. Jesus gave us the life of our son; we can never repay Him for that. Whatever happens at the Passover, He will need in Jerusalem all His friends and those who love Him. We will go up to Jerusalem together in the company of Jesus."

"But suppose something goes wrong and Herod punishes you?"

"The Master has warned His disciples that all who follow Him will have to suffer for His sake. If it must come to us, too, then it must come."

III

Salome, the wife of Zebedee, was proud of her sons and rightly so. They were tall and strong, and from boyhood had hauled in the nets in company with their good friends Simon and Andrew, handling their own boat and holding their place with the other fishermen. No others on the lake pulled in such weighty catches and none loaded such heavy boatloads at Zebedee's piers. In marrying Zebedee, she had made a good marriage, Salome thought now. His fisheries were among the largest on the lake; he was a man of substance in the community, an elder and a ruler of the congregation respected both for his wealth and his piety.

Salome often told herself that she had done much better than her sister Mary. Mary's husband, Joseph, had never risen above operating his carpenter's shop in Nazareth. In fact, Mary had found it difficult at times to feed and clothe her family from what Joseph made, and Salome had occasionally helped her out. Of course, in a way it was Mary's fault for giving part of her own small stores to the wife of Joseph's brother Alpheus, particularly after Joseph's death, when Jesus became head of the family.

Salome was an aggressive woman and when Jesus lived in Nazareth He had seemed to her too quiet and unassuming to be a success in any trade. It was true that He worked hard and gave Mary no trouble. Sometimes Salome herself could have wished that her own sons resembled Him in that respect; not for nothing were James and John called "Sons of Thunder" by the other young men around the lake. They were inclined to be violent, particularly in their hatred of Herod Antipas and his Roman masters. More than once there had been sudden outbreaks of violence in Capernaum in which they had been the ringleaders, along with the tall Simon and his stockier brother Andrew. Salome knew little of the details concerning such events; only occasionally did her sons mention them. But she gathered that Simon with his great strength had more than once got them out of dangerous scrapes.

Salome had not been disturbed when James and John had become disciples of John the Baptist. Zebedee could spare them from the boats and the nets part of the time, and with John preaching to thousands at Bethabara, it was good for her sons to be known as leaders among the Baptist's followers. And if John were really the Messiah, as many claimed, her sons might occupy high places in the new kingdom when it was proclaimed.

When James and John had come back to Capernaum from Bethabara with the news that her own nephew, Jesus of Nazareth, was the Messiah, Salome had been thunderstruck. She had discussed it with Zebedee and decided that this could be only a passing fancy, perhaps born of their sons' disappointment when the Baptist had refused to let himself be named the Messiah.

The whole idea was absurd, Salome told herself. Jesus was the son of Joseph and her sister Mary. She did vaguely remember Mary's mention of some strange events connected with the child's birth, but then Mary had always been highly imaginative, and Salome had attributed all of it to a young girl's fancy.

When James and John, together with Simon and Andrew, had laid down their nets after the largest catch ever recorded in the region and set out to follow Jesus, it was a heavy blow to Salome's ambitions for them, as well as to Zebedee's hopes that his sons would eventually take over their father's prosperous fishing establishments. He and Salome argued and pleaded, but in vain; in the end they had to accept that James and John were now disciples of Mary's son. Eventually both had come home and returned to work, but it had been a bitter humiliation to their parents, and for long months Salome had nursed a deep feeling of resentment against her sister and Jesus.

John had recognized this grievance in his mother and had spoken to her about it, trying to explain to her what it was that he and his brother saw in Jesus. Gradually, she had come to understand and to lose her resentment, but a faint feeling of disappointment had always remained in her mind that her sons had failed to reach the high position which, like a mother, she had wanted for them.

Then had come the exciting time when the crowds had sought to name Jesus King and Messiah. It was true that He had eluded them then, but John and James had shown their mother that Jesus actually was the Messiah, and she looked forward now to the time when all power would be His, certain that James and John, by virtue of their close association with Him, would occupy a high place in His kingdom.

When the time of the Passover approached and word came from Simon Peter that a great crowd would travel up to Jerusalem with Jesus for the feast, Salome could not suppress a rising sense of excitement. Now at last the Lord would name Himself the Expected One and all Judea would flock to acclaim Him the Messiah. Now her sons would rank high in His kingdom, perhaps even occupy the places of honor on His right and left hand.

IV

Peter had done his work well in Galilee. When Jesus finally turned His steps southward in Peraea about a week before the Passover season, a great throng of followers from Galilee and the region beyond Jordan joined the party. Joanna and Chuza were there, and Salome, the mother of James and John. Mary of Magdala had brought Jesus' mother in her party, with James, the somewhat dour brother who was now head of the household in Nazareth. Present, too, was Mary Cleopas, Joseph's sister, who also lived in Nazareth.

The disciples had ignored Jesus' frequent warnings of the tragedy that would await Him in Jerusalem. Instead they were confident that at long last He would proclaim Himself the Messiah and use His miraculous powers to establish His own kingdom there. It was a festive group that took the road to Jericho and Jerusalem, for not only were they going up for the Passover, the most joyful as well as the most sacred of the religious festivals; they were also going to see Jesus assume His rightful position as the deliverer of the Jews.

Nor did Jesus' own demeanor do anything to dispel that impression— at first. He walked at the head of the procession and seemed eager to reach their destination. They traveled slowly, however, for as always a throng had gathered along the road, begging Jesus to heal the sick and have mercy upon the afflicted, and never having denied Himself before to those who needed Him, Jesus did not do so now.

They were almost to Jericho and the final stages of the journey when Jesus called the disciples aside one evening after He had finished teaching the remainder of the party. His face was grave as He looked at the twelve men with whom He had shared both hardship and triumph during the past several years.

"Behold, we go up to Jerusalem and all the things that are written by the prophets concerning the Son of Man shall be accomplished," He told them gravely.

The disciples did not ask themselves just what it was He meant by this. The prophets had often spoken strange words which each rabbi interpreted in his own fashion; two teachers might give contradictory judgments on the same passage from the sacred writings.

"He shall be delivered to the Gentiles," Jesus continued. "And shall be mocked and shamefully treated and spit upon. They shall scourge Him and put Him to death. And the third day He shall rise again."

When He said no more but sought His own sleeping pallet, the disciples began to disperse. Mary of Magdala had been sitting before her tent near Jesus as He spoke to the disciples and had heard what He said. When Simon Peter passed her on the way to his own sleeping place, she called out to him and he paused beside her.

"I heard the Master's words just now, Simon," she said. "What does He mean?"

The tall fisherman squatted beside the coals of the fire that Mary's servant had built and held out his hands to warm them, for the night was already cool. "I don't know," he admitted.

"Aren't you concerned?"

"Jesus said almost the same thing on the slopes of Mount Hermon near Caesarea-Philippi, and several times since then."

"It could happen as He says, you know. Caiaphas is determined to kill Him."

"That could not happen to the Son of God!" Simon said harshly, for Mary had touched on something that troubled him. When Jesus predicted His death, the disciples had always assumed that He was speaking in the form of a parable whose exact meaning they did not understand, as was often the case with His teachings until He explained them. But Simon had not been able to escape the gnawing fear that Jesus might be predicting exactly what was going to happen in Jerusalem. Such an occurrence was so foreign to his conception of Jesus that Peter would not let himself even think it might be true.

"Why does He go ahead of us as if He were eager to reach Jerusalem?" Peter added.

"Even knowing what was to happen, Jesus would obey the will of God."

"That God's own Son shall be put to death?" Simon asked incredulously.

"Jesus said that quite plainly just now," Mary reminded him.

"It is a parable. The meaning is different. It is something we cannot understand."

"Has He ever given you a parable before without explaining it?"

Peter shook his head. "No doubt He means that He will be rejected again in Jerusalem. After His rejection, He will rise in glory as the Messiah."

Mary put her hand on Peter's arm. Perhaps because she had known what it was to feel despair almost beyond caring, a despair Jesus had lifted from her that day on the shores of the lake, Mary could understand him better than the others. "Aren't you telling yourself this because you don't want to believe Jesus means exactly what He says?"

Peter jerked his arm away and got to his feet. "This is what comes of wasting time with women's fancies," he said angrily. "Jesus is the Son of God. Do you think He would allow Himself to be killed by men like Caiaphas and Pontius Pilate? If I believed that, I would lose faith in God Himself."

Mary shook her head gently. "Perhaps acceptance needs even greater faith than Jesus has required of us before, Simon," she said. "If the time comes, pray God we shall have that faith."

V

In another part of the camp, others were discussing Jesus' words. Judas of Kerioth and Simon, who was called Zelotes because he had formerly belonged to the radical Zealots, had been cheered when they had reached the road leading from Galilee to Bethabara and on to Jerusalem. The presence of such a large crowd of Jesus' own Galilean followers promised well for the establishment of the kingdom in Jerusalem. It was true that a great number in the group were women, but, the disciples were sure, many men who could bear arms could be found in Jerusalem if they were needed. Once Jesus proclaimed Himself King, thousands would flock to His standard if Caiaphas and the Roman authorities dared oppose Him. They were convinced that Jesus would then be forced to use His miraculous powers to destroy any opposition.

Judas particularly was pleased by the large crowd, many of them well-to-do. As keeper of the purse he had had no trouble during the early days in Galilee. People had flocked by thousands to be healed and, grateful for the miraculous cures, had been happy to contribute to the common fund from which Jesus and the disciples drew their support. Since Jesus had refused to be crowned king in Galilee, however, the number of gifts had fallen off sharply. At times Judas had almost been without money to provide food and shelter for the group, and he resented the fact that Jesus would not feed His own disciples in the same miraculous fashion that He had fed the five thousand.

One thing had sustained Judas through it all. He fully expected to be appointed keeper of the treasury in the kingdom which the Messiah would establish shortly in Jerusalem. The prospect of the honor and power that would be his then—and Judas was hungry for power—more than compensated for the discomforts of the present.

As for Simon Zelotes, his ambitions were strictly political and entirely disinterested. He hoped to see established in Israel a kingdom exceeding in glory even that of David and Solomon. With His miraculous power, Jesus would drive out the Romans and their Herods, welding Israel into one triumphant nation under God. Pontius Pilate's slaughter of the Galileans led by Barabbas a short time before had demonstrated that only a divine power could thrust out the Romans. But Jesus possessed this power, Simon knew, and He had only to use it to bring about the desired miracle.

These had been Simon's thoughts—until Jesus spoke tonight, prophesying His own death in Jerusalem. Now as he and Judas stretched out on their sleeping pallets, the Zealot voiced his fears.

"What do you think the Master meant tonight, Judas?" he asked.

"That the priests will reject Him in Jerusalem," Judas said.

"Only that?"

Judas shrugged. "And that He will rise in triumph, of course."

"Are you sure?"

Judas turned and looked across to where Jesus was lying sleeping. "The Master knows the Sanhedrin condemned Him to death. Would He be as eager as He is to go up to Jerusalem were He going to die there?"

"I suppose not," Simon admitted. "But if He is prophesying—"

"Are you a woman, to worry needlessly?" Judas demanded irritably. "Jesus must proclaim Himself Messiah in Jerusalem at the Passover. This is His last chance."

"And if He does not?"

"Then blood will be spilled, His and probably ours."

"Like those who followed Barabbas?"

If it comes to that, it is better for one to die than all of us," Judas said cryptically.

"But—"

"The Son of God must triumph over His enemies," Judas said. "If we believe anything less than that, our cause is lost."

VI

Salome, the mother of James and John, had been happy on the trip to Jerusalem. She could see that her sons were favored by Jesus, and as she walked along the road with the other women, an idea began to form in her mind.

Early one morning, as the camp was stirring itself for the coming day's journey, Salome called her sons to her and told them what she had been thinking. They listened eagerly and when she suggested going to Jesus that very morning when He would be amenable and refreshed by sleep, they agreed.

Jesus was standing beside the road with several of the disciples, waiting for camp to break, when Salome approached with James and John. "Master," she said, "I would ask a certain thing of You."

"What do you wish?" Jesus asked.

"Grant that these my two sons shall sit, the one on Your right hand and the other on Your left, in Your kingdom."

A look of pain came over Jesus' features. He loved the sons of Zebedee and had called them, with Simon and Andrew, His first disciples. In coming with their mother to ask that they be given precedence in His kingdom, they were guilty of the very sins of pride and covetousness which He had denounced again and again.

"You do not know what you ask," He said. "Are you able to drink the cup that I shall drink of? And be baptized with the same baptism that I am baptized with?"

"We are able," James and John spoke in concert, eagerly.

"You shall indeed drink of My cup," Jesus told them gravely. "And be baptized with the baptism that I am baptized with. But to sit on My right hand and on My left is not Mine to give; it shall be given to them for whom it has been prepared by My Father."

Peter and some of the others were angry at the sons of Zebedee for their presumption, but Jesus quieted them when they would have spoken out against them.

"You know that the princes of the Gentiles exercise dominion over them," He said. "And they that are great exercise authority upon them. But it shall not be so among you. Whoever will be great among you, let him be your minister. And whoever will be chief among you, let him be your servant, even as the Son of Man came not to be ministered unto, but to minister and to give His life as a ransom for many."

Without explaining further, Jesus stepped out on the road and the day's journey began. Behind Him He left a welter of emotions. Some were troubled because once again He had spoken of His death in Jerusalem. Others were angry at James and John and argued among themselves.

At a time when all should have been vitally concerned with what Jesus had revealed to them about the future, those dearest to Him failed to understand, failed to forget their own desires. None offered to comfort and strengthen Him against the coming ordeal.

26

*For the Son of Man has come to seek and
to save that which was lost.*

Luke 19:10

The weather was like summer when Jesus and the festive party of Galileans and Peraeans crossed the Jordan at Bethabara. Spring was already well advanced in this region but actually the climate of the Jericho Plain was so warm that even in winter heavy clothing was not worn. The air was full of fragrance, for irrigation had brought fruitful abundance. There were palm trees everywhere with the fragrant balsam, flowers of all sorts, groves of olive and fruit trees, and fields of growing vegetables. Often referred to as the Eden of Israel, the region could hardly have been better named.

A little south of the road from Bethabara to Jericho was one of the most memorable of Israel's historic spots. When the people had crossed the Jordan on dry land to attack Jericho and Canaan, Joshua had commanded that twelve stones be removed from the river bed and carried to their first encampment at Gilgal beyond the river, symbolizing the twelve tribes of Israel who made up his forces. Here they had set up a monument to God who held back the waters of Jordan until they could cross. At this same Gilgal, Saul had won a great victory over the Amorites and here his new authority as king of Israel had been acknowledged and his regime inaugurated with great celebration. Later the people of Gilgal had fallen into idolatry, however, and the stones themselves had been taken away to Shiloh.

Jesus did not point out to the procession that followed Him these glorious events in the history of Israel or draw the obvious parallel between what had happened to Gilgal and was happening in Israel at this very time. Instead He went on before His band of followers until Jericho came into sight.

Heavily walled and with four forts guarding its ramparts, the city occupied a commanding position on the plain. Although it had played a glorious part in the story of Israel, Jericho was now almost as much a heathen city as a Jewish one. The Romans loved its winter climate, as did Greek merchants and rich Jews who could afford to spend part of the year there. Herod's palace and its luxurious gardens were more splendid than anything in the whole region, and there was also a theater and amphitheater for the entertainment of the worldly-minded.

The streets of Jericho were always crowded but never more so than at the approach of the Passover. Essenes from their nearby community overlooking the Dead Sea, hawk-faced Nabateans from the eastern frontier, Jews from every section of Palestine, a few Samaritans, soldiers, sycophants from Herod's court, Roman officials—people from every walk of life jostled each other in the streets. Priests were a common sight, for the course assigned to this region required fully half the entire coterie of priests in attendance at the temple. Everywhere there were the tax collectors, since Jericho was an important center for the collection of tribute, levied not only on the lush products of the Jordan Plain itself but also as a customs duty on any goods brought into Judea from across the Jordan.

Jesus was well known in Jericho, having often taught only a few miles away at Bethabara. The people knew of His miracles of healing, and they had heard of His new doctrine which was like that of John the Baptist, but gentler and more attractive. The priests knew Him as one whose death had already been decreed by the Sanhedrin and who, in going to Jerusalem now, was insuring His own execution. And the agents of Herod knew Him as a Galilean troublemaker they had long sought to trap. But now, when he had ample opportunity to arrest Jesus, Herod hesitated. The wily tetrarch of Galilee knew how anxious Caiaphas was to destroy the Nazarene; it would be simpler to let Caiaphas execute Jesus and take whatever blame might follow.

Great crowds greeted Jesus upon His entry into Jericho; wherever He passed, people gathered in the hope of seeing Him perform some miracle. Others followed Him merely out of curiosity to see this man who, in going up to Jerusalem now, was defying the authority of the high priest and the Sanhedrin. Jesus, however, had no intention of stirring up turmoil in Jericho; He wished to pass through as quickly as He could.

||

B artimaeus had been blind for many years following an attack of the eye inflammation that was so heavy a scourge among the people of the region. After his blinding it had seemed that his world had ended and he at first prayed God to destroy him. Then, as he had grown accustomed to living in a world without light, he found his other senses beginning to sharpen in compensation for his loss, and soon he was able to achieve a certain degree of security.

Begging was almost the only occupation open to a blind man, however, so Bartimaeus resigned himself to it. Jericho, he found, was a paradise for beggars. The constant flow of people through the city, as well as the presence of the Romans, furnished a liberal source of alms. Bartimaeus early discovered, too, that the location of his begging post played an important part in the returns he received, and in regard to this matter he was fortunate, for through the generosity of a kinsman he was able to locate on the heavily traveled road leading from Jericho toward Jerusalem.

Great numbers of pilgrims went up to Jerusalem during the Passover season, and Bartimaeus was at his place, begging early and remaining late, crying out his condition, as was required of him, and receiving the alms of the passersby.

According to custom, when a procession of travelers or the entourage of a person of importance went through a town, the population lined the streets and roadways to bid them welcome and farewell. The Galilean who accompanied Jesus on the journey were of no particular importance to the relatively sophisticated dwellers of Jericho, but Jesus had become a center of controversy and therefore of interest. Many people were curious to see this man whom the high court and the chief priests had vowed to destroy.

From the noise that accompanied it, Bartimaeus realized that the procession was of unusual size. Edging closer to the roadway and crying out his plea for alms, he plucked at the sleeve of a bystander.

"Who is coming?" he asked eagerly, sure that such a commotion must mean the passage of at least a nobleman, perhaps one who would be generous.

"It is the Nazarene prophet with a group from Galilee," he was told.

"Jesus of Nazareth?"

"Yes."

Bartimaeus felt excitement rising within him. The story of how Jesus had raised Lazarus from the dead was well known in Jericho, for Lazarus and his sisters were large landowners in Bethany, less than a day's journey to the west. Even more important to Bartimaeus was the account which had reached his ears of how Jesus had given sight to Joachim of Jerusalem who had been blind from birth. Remembering these miracles, Bartimaeus was sure that, could he but draw Jesus' notice, he too would be cured by the Nazarene's miraculous power.

"Jesus, Son of David, have mercy on me!" he shouted.

Some of the Galileans who walked at the head of the party tried to silence him, for Jesus was purposely not pausing in Jericho where He might be accused by Herod's agents of causing a disturbance.

Bartimaeus had no intention of being silent, however. "Jesus, Son of David!" he cried again. "Have mercy upon me!"

A cry for mercy was one Jesus had never refused. Nor did He refuse now. Pausing, He directed that the supplicant be brought to Him.

Bartimaeus heard the words and did not wait. Leaping up in haste, he lost the upper part of his robe but did not stop to pick it up. Stumbling through the crowd, clad only in his loincloth, the blind man reached Jesus and fell at His feet.

"What do you want Me to do for you?" Jesus asked him.

"Lord, let me receive my sight."

There was no begging in Bartimaeus's request, no flattery, no fawning. It was a simple statement of Bartimaeus's faith in Jesus' ability to heal him. And the faith stirred an answering chord in Jesus' heart.

"Go your way," Jesus told Bartimaeus. "Your faith has made you whole."

So overwhelmed by the sudden burst of light and beauty from which his eyes had been shut away for so many years, Bartimaeus for a moment could only kneel in the roadway, dazed and half stunned by this miracle which had brought sight to him again. Jesus, pausing only long enough to heal him, was almost out of sight before Bartimaeus recovered from the suddenness of his cure.

When he did recover, he snatched up his robe where it had fallen, and throwing it around his body, joined the procession that followed the Master.

III

Zacchaeus was a small man, not only in body but in spirit. Though the office of tax collector or publican was the most despised in all of Israel, it gave a clever man a chance to grow rich and was a means of gaining power over others. Where a bigger man would have spurned this office, Zacchaeus, seeing its particular opportunities, had actively sought the post.

The collection of taxes was let by a contract under which the contractor guaranteed to produce a specified amount of revenue to the government. Whatever he was able to extract from the people over and above that enriched—within certain official limitations—his own fortunes. By shrewdly taking advantage of every opportunity his office afforded, Zacchaeus had become chief of all the tax gatherers in Jericho. In this position he wielded much power, power which greatly expanded the size of his small soul.

Zacchaeus was returning from one of the tax collection stations on the outskirts of Jericho when he heard the tumult that marked the passage of Jesus through Jericho after the restoration of Bartimaeus's sight. Always curious, Zacchaeus could not let such a procession pass without seeing for himself what person of importance was its center. The press of people made it impossible for anyone of such short stature to see over the heads of the crowd, but this did not deter the publican. Noting a sycamore fig tree nearby, he quickly scrambled into its lower branches from where he could see everything that went on.

The Galileans who accompanied Jesus knew many people in Jericho, for some of them came to Jerusalem every year at this season and both going and coming the City of Palms was a logical stopping place. As the procession went by, cries of greeting and warm salutations were being uttered all around Zacchaeus, but there were few persons to give him more than a civil nod. The people of Jericho could not afford to antagonize the tax gatherer, for that could mean a rise in taxes the following year, yet at the same time they took no pains to greet him.

For the first time since he was a small boy unable to play vigorous games with other boys of his age, Zacchaeus felt utterly alone. He had the power and riches for which he had worked all his life. But he was ignored in the salutations being exchanged below him; he missed the warm cheerful voice of a friend raised in a greeting that was not to curry favor but to express a spontaneous liking.

Little Zacchaeus in his tree, though taller than all the rest by his own efforts, suddenly sensed the narrowness of his own soul and his own life. He could have estimated almost to a single denarius the worldly goods possessed by many of the Galileans accompanying the Nazarene prophet, and his own fortune probably exceeded all theirs combined. And yet they had something he did not have. They loved Jesus of Nazareth and were joined together in the natural and happy bondage of that love, something Zacchaeus's own riches, his own power, had never brought him.

Sitting there, a forlorn figure in the sycamore tree, Zacchaeus was suddenly alone, bitterly and utterly alone with the realization that his own life, for all his cleverness and his efforts to impress others, was even smaller in its scope than he was in body. It was a shattering moment of awareness, and Zacchaeus would gladly have given all his wealth to be one of the happy Galilean fishermen who followed the Nazarene teacher to Jerusalem.

But now from the black depths of his despair, Zacchaeus heard a voice calling out his name. Absorbed in his own misery, he did not at first recognize its source. Then he heard his name repeated again and looked down to see that Jesus of Nazareth stood beneath the tree, looking up at him with eyes that were warm with a light Zacchaeus had not seen in another's face for a long time, a light of understanding and love.

"Zacchaeus, make haste and come down," the gentle voice said. "Today I must abide at your house."

Zacchaeus did not pause to consider that the Nazarene was under sentence of death by the Sanhedrin in Jerusalem. Or that Herod Antipas, who could influence the Roman authorities to take away Zacchaeus's commission as tax gatherer, was reported to be seeking the prophet's destruction. Nothing mattered save the genuine warmth and love he heard in Jesus' voice. Without hesitating, he scrambled down from the tree and ran to kneel at Jesus' feet, but Jesus blessed him and lifted him up.

Walking beside Jesus and not at all concerned now by his slightness of stature, Zacchaeus almost skipped in his happiness at the prospect of having such a guest in his home. As he walked, secure in the peace and serenity of mind the Nazarene's greeting had brought him, he poured out his heart, knowing instinctively that Jesus would understand and forgive his many faults.

This was not the attitude of the crowd that followed as Jesus and His immediate party turned aside to the tax gatherer's house, however. They knew Jesus was supposed to be a holy man, one who told even the haughty Pharisees what they should and should not do. And yet here He was, going to the house of the worst publican of all.

Jesus had never paid any attention to such grumbling, nor did He now. One of His most faithful disciples, Levi (or Matthew), had been a publican and had left his tax gatherer's table to follow Him. Jesus did not now tell Zacchaeus what he should do to atone for his past misdeeds. From the depths of his misery in the sycamore tree, the publican had sent forth an unspoken plea for love and understanding, and Jesus, with the greatness of heart that set Him apart, had heard and understood.

The change in Zacchaeus had begun to take place when he realized his need for the kind of riches that faith in Jesus could give him. The process of redemption for Zacchaeus begun then, even before Jesus had spoken to him, would go on now to its logical conclusion. Had evidence of this been needed, it could have been found in Zacchaeus's own words as they approached the threshold of his luxurious home.

"Behold, Lord," the publican said humbly. "I hereby give half of my goods to the poor. And if I have taken anything from any man, I return him fourfold."

The new Zacchaeus was speaking, the one who had been reborn in the sycamore tree, and Jesus recognized that the change was complete.

"This day has salvation come to this house," He said. "For the Son of Man is come to seek and to save that which was lost."

IV

Jesus had beard the grumblings of the crowd when He singled out Zacchaeus for His favor. On the threshold of the publican's house He turned to address those who were gathered outside, teaching them in the form of a parable.

"A certain nobleman went into a far country to receive for himself a kingdom and to return," He said. "And he called his ten servants and delivered them ten minas and said to them, 'Occupy yourselves till I return.'

"But his citizens hated him and sent a message after him saying, 'We will not have this man to reign over us.' And it came to pass, that when he returned, having received the kingdom, he then commanded these servants to whom he had given the money to be called that he might know how every man had gained by trading.

"Then came the first, saying, 'Lord, your mina has gained ten minas.' And he said to him, 'Well done, good servant. Because you have been faithful in a very little, you will have authority over ten cities.'

"And the second came saying, 'Lord, your mina has gained five minas.' And he said likewise to him, 'You will be also over five cities.'

"And another came saying, 'Lord, behold here is your mina, which I have kept laid up in a napkin, for I feared you because you are an austere man. You take up what you do not lay down and you reap what you do not sow.'

"Then the king said to him, 'Out of your own mouth will I judge you, you wicked servant. You knew that I was an austere man, taking up what I did not lay down and reaping what I did not sow. Why then did you not give my money to the moneylenders, that at my coming I might have required my own with usury?' And he said to them that stood by, 'Take from him the mina and give it to him who has ten.'

"But they said to him, 'Lord, he has ten minas.'

"'I say to you, that to every one which has shall be given; and from him who has not, even what he has shall be taken away from him. But my enemies, who do not wish that I should reign over them, bring hither and slay them before me.'"

The disciples, particularly Judas and Simon the Zealot, were pleased by this parable of a king who came back to be crowned in his own household. They felt it meant that Jesus intended to assume the authority of a King in Jerusalem, using His miraculous powers to destroy any who opposed Him.

It was a truly joyous group that took the road to Jerusalem now, one which could not doubt Jesus' own eagerness to reach the Holy City, for He pressed on ahead of the others, and by late afternoon they reached Bethany. Most of the party continued around the Mount of Olives to secure the select camping sites afforded by the western slope overlooking Jerusalem and the temple. Jesus remained in the house of Mary, Martha, and Lazarus in Bethany, a spot He had come to love almost as much as the beautiful hills and fertile fields of Galilee.

27

Look, the world has gone after Him!

John 12:19

The arrival of the large group of pilgrims that had accompanied Jesus could hardly pass unnoticed in Jerusalem. As soon as it became known that He was at Bethany, crowds began to flock to the suburb to see Jesus and also to see Lazarus, who had been raised from the dead only a few weeks before. Simon Peter and the rest of the disciples were pleased by the size of the crowds, for they would help swell Jesus' following when the time came for His triumphal entry into the city.

Caiaphas had been busy, plotting how to seize Jesus without stirring up a riot in the city which would bring the Romans upon the scene. Word had gone out through the entire area that anyone knowing the whereabouts of the Nazarene should at once notify Abiathar, captain of the temple guards. By taking Jesus outside the temple, Caiaphas hoped to avoid stirring up the multitude which had made His arrest impossible on other occasions there.

Had Jesus come directly into Jerusalem from Jericho, this stratagem might have succeeded, for the number of guards at the gates had been doubled. But by remaining at Bethany, a town where He had many followers, and then arriving in Jerusalem on the eve of the Sabbath, Jesus foiled Caiaphas' well-laid plan. To have arrested Jesus on the Sabbath would have been an act of desecration at which pious Jews would have risen up in horror. And to have taken Him when surrounded by such a large group of His Galilean followers would surely have meant a bloody conflict that would have brought Pontius Pilate into action. The memory of the abortive Galilean revolt was fresh in everyone's mind; a second revolt coming so soon after it would be interpreted by the procurator as a failure on the part of the high priest and the Sanhedrin to control their own people. It was quite within Pilate's authority, and in keeping with what they knew of his temper, to remove them summarily from office.

Frustrated and angry at the turn of events and not knowing what move Jesus would make next, Caiaphas was forced to wait until the Sabbath was over to call a meeting of the Priestly Council, or Lesser Sanhedrin.

It was a solemn-faced group that met in the palace of the high priest as soon as the setting sun marked the end of the Sabbath. Caiaphas, angry that Jesus had been able to come as close to Jerusalem as Bethany without being harmed, was determined that He should not enter the city itself. At any other time Nicodemus would have enjoyed the discomfiture of the high priest, but now he was too concerned with the danger to Jesus to take comfort from Caiaphas's troubles. Elam, as chief of the Pharisees, was coldly furious with both Caiaphas and Abiathar. He knew how much the hold of the Pharisees over the people could be weakened if, as before, Jesus denounced them to the crowds which would surely gather when word came that He was inside the city.

"You Sadducees have failed, as I knew you would," Elam accused Caiaphas. "How many times will you bungle the job of destroying this man?"

"Your agents followed Him through Galilee trying to convict Him of blasphemy," Caiaphas retorted. "It would have been simpler to stop Him there."

As usual, old Annas tried to be the peacemaker. "It serves no good purpose to quarrel among ourselves," he told the two. "The Nazarene has still not entered the city."

"And He will not do so," Caiaphas said. "Abiathar has guards at every gate. They will arrest Him if He tries to enter."

Nicodemus spoke for the first time. "I think neither of you realizes what has happened in this part of Judea since Jesus raised Lazarus from the d—"

"That was a trick!" Elam interrupted. "I have witnesses who will swear that Lazarus never was dead!"

Nicodemus shrugged. "Which will Pilate believe, the witnesses or the physician who pronounced him dead and saw him laid in the tomb? Remember, four days passed before Lazarus was raised."

"Are you saying we should crown the Galilean king because of that?" Elam sneered.

"King? No. I doubt if Jesus wants that."

"What does He want then? If you are so much in His confidence, surely He has told you."

"Perhaps for the people to return to the true worship of God," Nicodemus said. "Most prophets have been sent for that reason."

"Do you think Him truly a prophet?" the rabbi Jochai inquired.

"It would be simpler to name Him such and show Him the respect that is due a prophet."

"And let Him undermine our interpretation of the Law?" Elam demanded passionately. "If the people lose respect for the Law, they will drift into heathen ways. That happened once before and it could happen again."

"The Nazarene must die; the Sanhedrin has already decided that," Caiaphas said.

"How will you take Him then?" Elam demanded. "He is always surrounded by Galileans and you know what that name means to Pontius Pilate after what Barabbas's band tried to do."

"Not all His disciples are Galilean," Caiaphas pointed out. "One is of Judea, a native of Kerioth."

"Does that make Him a traitor?" Nicodemus asked.

Caiaphas flushed at his tone. "I have it upon good authority that Judas and perhaps one other among the Nazarene's disciples are not wholly satisfied with His activities. If Jesus became king, Judas could expect to control the treasury. But if he is convinced the Nazarene will not be king, perhaps—perhaps might he not want to save his own life?"

"Have you already negotiated with this one called Judas?" Nicodemus asked angrily.

Caiaphas ignored the question. On at least one other occasion he had suspected that Nicodemus had warned Jesus of his plots, so he now dismissed the gathering. But when Nicodemus had left, he called the others back.

"Have you a plan, Caiaphas?" Elam asked.

"In coming to Jerusalem for any of the feasts," Caiaphas said, "the Nazarene has so far followed the same course. He goes to the temple with a few of His followers and teaches from the porch like any other rabbi."

"He has no right to the title of rabbi," protested Jochai. "I have found none who can testify that the Nazarene studied under any great teachers. It is obvious that He follows neither Shammai nor Hillel."

"Exactly," said Caiaphas. "If Jesus dares to come to the temple, you will challenge His right to teach there, Jochai. But I don't think He will get that far."

"Why not?" Elam inquired.

"The Nazarene does not usually come to the city during the first days of any feast. He will probably remain in Bethany at the home of Lazarus. Our first task, then, is to seize Lazarus for harboring one under sentence by the court. And this time," he added grimly, "we will be sure that Lazarus is dead and that no trick can be used to make it appear that he has been raised from the dead."

"Do you think Jesus might give Himself up to save Lazarus?" Jochai asked.

Caiaphas permitted himself a smile. "The Nazarene must save Lazarus or deny His own teachings."

"The plan sounds feasible," Elam admitted. "And if Jesus is taken?"

"The court has already passed sentence on Him. It needs only to be reaffirmed, and this does not require the entire court."

Elam nodded with satisfaction. He knew from experience how arguments before the Sanhedrin could become involved. It would be much simpler to handle things with only a picked group present. Even if Nicodemus and Joseph of Arimathea were known to sympathize with

Jesus, they could easily be voted down. Then only Pontius Pilate's approval for the execution would be necessary, and the procurator had never been known to question the desires of the Sanhedrin on a religious matter.

"It is a good plan," the Pharisee agreed. "If the Nazarene lets Lazarus die and saves Himself, the people will realize that He is not the Messiah. And if He gives Himself up, we have Him without conflict."

There were no dissenting votes to the plan and Caiaphas instructed Abiathar to put it into operation. What the high priest did not know, however, was that even as the Priestly Council plotted together, Jesus had already decided to leave Bethany with a great party of Galileans and others. He was coming to enter Jerusalem and to teach boldly in the temple itself.

II

Jesus' decision to enter Jerusalem that day, the first of the Passover week, had been announced in Bethany by Lazarus and the disciples. Shortly after sunrise, people began to gather at the house of Mary, Martha, and Lazarus to accompany Him.

On the outskirts of Bethany beside the road leading into Jerusalem lay the small village of Bethphage, meaning "House of Figs," a name given to both the village and the surrounding area because of the large groves of fig trees there. Peter and John had been dispatched to this village with instructions from Jesus to find an ass and its colt which had not been ridden and to bring them both to Him on the road between Bethany and Bethphage. On the way the two disciples spread the news that Jesus would enter Jerusalem that very day in defiance of the high priest and the Sanhedrin. The story traveled rapidly through the village and soon a crowd had gathered beside the road along which Jesus and His party would pass.

Word had also been sent ahead to the large group of Galileans and others who had accompanied Jesus from Peraea and who were now camped on the western slope of the Mount of Olives. According to the plan worked out by Peter and John as leaders of the disciples, this group would join the procession just before they reached the city gates, swelling its numbers so impressively that not even Caiaphas would dare molest Jesus.

Jesus was halfway between Bethany and Bethphage when Peter and John met Him with the ass and its colt. Folding their robes to make cushions upon which Jesus could ride, they placed Him upon the back of the colt. When Jesus had mounted the colt, the procession was ready to begin once more.

As he rejoined the disciples, Peter passed Mary of Magdala, walking with the other women. The tall fisherman's face was happy and filled with pride.

"You were wrong, Mary!" he greeted her. "Do you see the colt that Jesus is riding upon?"

Mary smiled for she was very fond of the impetuous fisherman. "It shows Jesus is not afraid to go into Jerusalem. I knew that all the time."

"Don't you know what His entering Jerusalem on a colt means?" Peter exclaimed.

"You forget that I was almost a heathen for a long time," Mary reminded him. "Until Jesus freed me."

"Zechariah prophesied exactly what is happening today," Peter said. "I know the words by heart."

"Then tell them to me," she prompted.

Peter scratched his beard. "Let me see. Yes, this is the way it goes:

> *"Rejoice greatly, O daughter of Zion;*
> *Shout, O daughter of Jerusalem:*
> *Behold your King comes to you.*
> *He is just and having salvation;*
> *Lowly, and riding upon an ass,*
> *And upon a colt, the foal of an ass."*

Judas and Simon Zelotes were walking nearby, listening to Peter and Mary. Now the Zealot spoke. "You neglected the most important part, Peter, where the prophet says:

> *"And I will cut off the chariot from Ephraim,*
> *And the horse from Jerusalem.*
> *The battle bow shall be cut off,*
> *And He shall speak peace to the heathen.*
> *His domain shall be from sea to sea,*
> *And from the river even to the ends of the earth."*

Mary looked ahead to where Jesus rode at the head of the procession with the people going before Him, singing and shouting to announce His triumphant passage. "I hope you are right, my friends," she said fervently. "With all my heart, I hope you are right."

She did not remind them of another prophecy from the greatest of the prophets, Isaiah, which she remembered from her childhood, a prophecy which had applied to Jesus on other occasions, and which she hoped from her soul did not apply to Him now: "He is despised and rejected of men."

III

The news that the prophet of Nazareth, He whose actions now seemed to declare Him the Messiah, was coming boldly into Jerusalem set the city in a ferment.

"Who is this?" people demanded of each other. "Who dares defy the will of the high priest and the Sanhedrin?"

No one knew the answer, but many wanted to see Jesus. They had all at one time or another secretly nursed the impulse to speak out against the burden of tribute levied upon them for the support of the luxury-loving priests. They had resented the even heavier burden of the Law as interpreted by the Pharisees and rabbis who worked in close cooperation with the Sadducees. Many were driven now by mere curiosity, but many others had been healed by Jesus on previous visits or had heard Him teach, and believed in Him. Still others had seen the miracles—granting sight to blind Joachim, healing the man by the pool of Bethesda, raising Lazarus from the dead—and they had come to believe that the gentle Nazarene was indeed the Son of God.

Thus for various reasons a great crowd of people streamed out through the gates on the Bethany road to meet Jesus and escort Him into the city. They were insuring for themselves a place where they would be able to see the most dramatic and exciting event of the week, the clash between Jesus with His Galilean followers and the high priest's forces which sought to destroy Him.

Meanwhile, the head of the procession escorting Jesus from Bethany was just reaching the junction with the main caravan road between Jericho and Jerusalem. The most southerly of the three routes entering the city on this side, it was a rough but fairly broad track cut into the slope of the Mount of Olives. Washed by the winter rains, the path was rocky and filled with loose stones, making travel slow. On the left was the steep declivity of the mountainside while on the right loomed the shoulder of the Mount of Olives.

At Bethphage the road was lined with fig trees which grew in the rocky soil and produced well under the influence of the *moreh*. By now Bethany was out of sight behind the shoulder of the mount, and the stream of people pouring out of Bethphage to join the procession filled the rocky track and prevented anyone from passing.

At Bethphage they had already entered the outskirts of Jerusalem, although the main part of the city was still out of sight around the shoulder of the Mount of Olives on the right. Here, they began to meet the vanguard of those coming out through the gates. The Jerusalem Jews were somewhat more familiar with the ancient writings than those from the provinces, for the city abounded in teachers and synagogues where the pronouncements of the prophets were read regularly during the sacred services. The significance of the way in which the procession was organized struck some of these immediately. For Jesus had chosen to enter Jerusalem in the manner which the prophets had said would characterize the coming of the Messiah, "upon a colt, the foal of an ass."

A shout of praise and wonder went up from these newcomers, to be caught up and echoed again and again along the line of people as word of its cause was passed back to them. And with that shout, Jesus' entry into Jerusalem became something other than the usual procession of a teacher with a considerable following.

"Hosanna to the Son of David!" someone cried.

Instantly a dozen answering cries arose. "Blessed is He who comes in the name of the Lord! Hosanna in the highest!"

These phrases were usually chanted by the people as a response in the sacred readings of the psalm which began with:

> O give thanks unto the Lord for He is good:
> Because His mercy endures forever.

Like a flame sweeping through a field of dry straw, a burst of fervor swept through the crowd, firing those who had come from Bethany and Bethphage with excitement over what, it seemed, had now become the triumphal entry of a king into the Holy City.

Progress was slow, for the crowd had now begun to break palm and olive branches from the groves and gardens that lined the roadway to cast them before Jesus. Some, in the sheer excess of enthusiasm, took off their robes and spread them on the rocky path to make a carpet over which He could pass.

As they marched, the people continued to cry, "Hosanna to the Son of David!" until Simon Peter, his tall form easily visible above the heads of the crowd, started to shout the verses of the psalm which, according to tradition, was chanted as a welcome to pilgrims coming to Jerusalem for the feasts.

"Save now, I beseech thee, O Lord," he intoned in a voice that carried easily along the procession and echoed from the shoulder of the mountain beside the road.

"O Lord, I beseech thee, send now prosperity," the people answered in unison.

"Blessed be He who comes in the name of the Lord," Peter chanted.

"We have blessed you out of the house of the Lord," the people replied.

"God is the Lord, which hath showed us the light."

"Bind the sacrifice with cords, even unto the horns of the altar," the people answered.

"Thou art my God and I will praise thee."

"Thou art my God, I will exalt thee."

Then, as was the custom, the entire body chanted in unison the concluding verse, "O give thanks unto the Lord for He is good. For His mercy endures forever."

As they rounded an outthrust crag, a breathtaking vista of the city momentarily lay before them. The temple in the northerly part of Jerusalem was still hidden behind the slope of the Mount of Olives but the sacred Mount of Zion was clearly visible in the warm spring air. Terrace upon terrace ascended the slope of the mount, surrounding the luxurious palaces of the high priest, the Maccabees, and the richer men of the city. Upon the summit was the great palace of Herod, located where the palace of David had risen almost a millennium before. Even the turreted battlements of the fortress, tangibly threatening, could not detract from the rich beauty of the gardens, the green brought forth by the spring rains for this most sacred of all seasons.

This was the real Jerusalem, the monument to a God who had

made the people His very own through the ages, a place of worship and thanksgiving for His mercy and His divine love. Seen thus, hardly anyone could doubt that Jerusalem would endure forever, in spite of venal priests, in spite of injustices, intolerance, cruelty, in spite of the deliberate forgetting of God's laws.

The long procession was now passing over the ridge that marked the highest part of the road before beginning the descent of the Mount of Olives to the gates of Jerusalem itself.

As it moved, it gathered new recruits, more and more people joining the throng to swell the shouting that floated across the Kedron Valley to the guards at the gate through which the procession must pass.

It was too late for Caiaphas to stop Jesus now. The entire complement of Abiathar's guards would have been thrust aside by the sheer numbers of the throng which now accompanied the Nazarene.

As the road began to descend, the view of Jerusalem was for a moment cut off, and as if the removal of the threat posed by the momentary glimpse of Herod's citadel had released them, the disciples led by Simon Peter cast off all restraint.

"Blessed be the King!" they shouted boldly now. "The King who comes in the name of the Lord! Peace in heaven and glory in the highest!"

Some Pharisees who owned estates along the road had come out to see the cause of the clamor. Horrified that the disciples had dared to name Jesus King, an act of treason, they called out to Him: "Master, rebuke Your disciples!"

Jesus drew the animal He was riding to a halt in order to answer the Pharisees.

"If these should hold their peace," He said, "the stones would immediately cry out."

At His tone and His words, the Pharisees fell back in horror, but when the people heard Him thus announce His own kingship, a great shout burst from them again as they hailed Him for the Son of David so long expected by the Jews as their Savior.

"Behold, the whole world has gone after Him!" one of the Pharisees said in amazement.

Moving again, the procession followed the path as it climbed slightly, following a short but rugged section of roadway until it came out upon a broad ledge of solid rock almost like a floor. Here the full glory of Jerusalem burst before their eyes.

Seen across the deepest part of the Kedron Valley, the effect was that of a great golden city rising from an abyss, a truly spectacular and inspiring sight. Dwarfing even the beauty and magnificence of the city itself was the broad area of the sanctuary with the temple courts opened out around it like the pages of a book. The sun shone with its fullest brilliance and the great golden dome blinded the eyes like the glory of God itself. Even the plume of black smoke rising from the altars of sacrifice could not detract from the beauty of the scene as, clearly heard across the intervening depths, came the clear tone of a Levite's trumpet, calling the devout to worship.

The breathtaking beauty of the city, bursting on them so suddenly, momentarily stilled the clamor of the crowd. In the silence only one voice was heard, a voice torn by anguish almost beyond bearing.

"O Jerusalem! Jerusalem!" Jesus cried as tears ran down His cheeks. "If you had known, at least in this day, the things which belonged to your peace! But now they are hid from your eyes. The day shall come when your enemies shall cast a trench about you and compass you around and keep you in on every side. And shall lay you even with the ground, and your children with you. They shall not leave in you one stone upon another, because you knew not the time of your visitation!"

Jesus' voice broke on the last word and He turned His eyes away, reaching blindly for the rope as He started His colt moving again.

28

My house is a house of prayer,
but you have made it a "den of thieves."

Luke 19:46

Pontius Pilate was not in a pleasant mood. For more than six years he had ruled in Judea for the Emperor Tiberius, longer than any procurator before him, more than long enough, in his opinion, for any one man to be assigned to such an outpost of hell. It was not so much that the climate or even the country itself was bad. Caesarea on the seacoast was tolerable enough, and the winter palace of Herod Antipas in Jericho from which he had just come was quite comfortable, as was the lovely villa Herod had placed at his disposal at Tiberias on the Sea of Galilee. There were many good things, in fact, to be said for the land. What made life so burdensome in this part of the world was the people, their eternal contentiousness, their constant vying with each other for control, and the various contrasting shades of nationality represented among them. In fact, all Jews seemed alike in only one respect: a hatred for Rome.

Other captive peoples had shown their good judgment, in Pilate's opinion, by accepting Roman rule for what it was, the strongest civilizing influence the world had ever known. Rome had almost finished pacifying Gaul, and great universities, population centers with a real culture of their own, were springing up all over that pleasant and prosperous land. Even the barbarians to the north occasionally had the good sense to accept Roman rule philosophically and absorb from it what they could—while, it was true, preparing for new resistance.

But at least they fought battles like soldiers and died bravely on the battlefield.

The Jews were different, and even after years as ruler of Judea, Pilate admitted that he had never come really to understand them. The priestly class, under Caiaphas and Annas, were as luxury-loving and greedy as any Roman official. Those impulses Pilate could understand, but the self-righteousness of the Pharisees and the absurd attention to ritual was another matter. Those he would never comprehend, but he had noticed that when it came to the consummation of a shrewd business deal, they were as ruthless as any, rarely practicing what was taught in their ancient writings.

Then there were the fanatics, like the followers of the fellow Barabbas who was a prisoner in the dungeons of the Antonia in Jerusalem. One thing alone had saved Barabbas, the accident of Roman citizenship. Even a brigand could carry his case to Rome, though the emperor nearly always supported the decisions of his provincial governor.

If ever there was a senseless rebellion, that was it, Pilate thought as he rode from Jericho to Jerusalem this fine spring morning. Caiaphas had been angry because his own guards for the temple had not been able to handle the situation. Knowing Caiaphas, Pilate was sure that if he had been able to keep the swiftly rising revolt in hand, Barabbas would have been spirited away from the temple and the dagger of a sicarius would have found its way between his ribs before he had had a chance to demand a Roman trial. Caiaphas had handled situations like that before and Pilate admired his thoroughness—up to a point.

The forces with Barabbas had been small, only a few turbulent Galileans. Success could have come only through arousing enough people to join him once the fighting began. Considering that the city teemed with robbers and those who hated Rome, enough might easily have joined Barabbas if the affair had lasted sufficiently long to make the people believe Roman power was unable to control the situation. It was this possibility which had moved Pilate to order his small complement of Roman soldiers out of the Antonia and into the temple itself when the first outcry of revolt was raised. Revolution, he had learned by experience, was much like a forest fire. Stamp out the first blaze and nothing follows, but let the fire make only a little headway and it quickly flames out of control.

Pilate smiled now as he remembered Caiaphas's shocked protest when the Galileans were cut down on the floor of the temple. The desecration, as they called it, had been a good lesson for Caiaphas as well as for the rebels and the rest of the population, a warning that Pontius Pilate had no intention of letting things get out of hand. Or of letting Caiaphas take too much upon himself either, lest he become too ambitious. Pilate had once, in a short-lived attempt to understand them when he had first been assigned to Judea, read a history of the Jews. He had quickly learned that there was a vast difference between many of the basic concepts of their religion and the way they had been put into effect during the history of Israel. Once he had discovered that fact, he had realized the Jews were like any other subject people, to be constantly watched and ruthlessly put down if they dared to rebel.

It would have been more comfortable to have remained in Jericho during this spring season when the sun there was warm and the gardens at their height. But Pontius Pilate had learned that the religious festivals were always times of tension in which malcontents flocked to the city, often with the intention of stirring up confusion through which they might profit by thievery and rapine, as Barabbas had hoped to do. At times like these, a strong hand was needed in Jerusalem and this required Pilate's presence there. Once the period of tension was over, he could journey on to Caesarea and the games which would be beginning in the arena.

Pilate had been riding in the midst of the column near the heavily curtained animal-borne litter that carried his wife, Claudia Procula. It was only a few miles to Jerusalem now and he was anticipating the bath awaiting him and the cup of spiced wine his body servant would bring him. Except for the accursed smell of burning flesh that hung over the city at this season, the Antonia was not really uncomfortable. It was not so luxurious as Herod's palace, where he could have stayed, for the Antonia was actually a fortress guarding the very heart of Jerusalem. But his own quarters were passable enough and were on the other side of the building, away from the smoke of the sacrifices, though not wholly from the stench of burning meat. And it was just as well to be where he could keep his eyes upon the temple during the next six days.

Pilate's reverie was interrupted when the horse in front of him was suddenly reined in as they were passing around the Mount of Olives in the neighborhood of the fig groves of Bethphage. Lurching forward in the saddle, when his horse stopped suddenly, he almost fell on its neck and he righted himself with a curse.

"Sir," the decurion riding ahead of him apologized. "Pelonius stopped the column without warning."

Pilate spurred his horse along the road past the line of legionnaires who were now standing at rest. The centurion Pelonius, who commanded the detachment and had been riding at its head, was standing up in his stirrups now, shading his eyes as he looked ahead.

"The road is blocked, sir," Pelonius called back, hoping to anticipate and prevent one of the sudden fierce outbursts of temper for which Pilate was famous. "By pilgrims."

Pilate reached the head of the column and reined in his own mount. He could see Pelonius had spoken the truth. As far ahead as the gates of Jerusalem itself the road was filled by a procession of pilgrims on their way to the city, just such a procession as they had been passing all morning on the way from Jericho, but many, many times larger.

"I have never seen so many on the road before, sir," Pelonius said. "They seem to be with that man riding the ass ahead of them."

From their elevation on the mountainside, Pilate and his party could look down upon the procession winding down the slope toward the Kedron Valley just beyond the low, terraced hill called Gethsemane.

"Have you any idea who they are?" Pilate asked the centurion.

Pelonius removed his helmet and wiped sweat from his broad face with his arm. "I recognize a few people in the procession, sir," he said. "They are Galileans, followers of a Nazarene called Jesus."

"The one Herod was speaking of last night?"

"Yes, sir. They think He is a prophet."

"Galileans, eh?" Pilate was estimating the number of people in the procession and comparing it with the number of legionnaires now standing at rest behind him. If he knew Galileans—and he should by now—fully half that group wore daggers under their cloaks and probably some of them had swords hidden as well. To try to force a way through the procession could easily end in a melee whose outcome was far from certain.

"There are a lot of them, sir," Pelonius said, voicing Pilate's own thought.

"Are you afraid of a motley band of fishermen and farmers?" the procurator asked.

"N—no, sir."

Pilate gave a sharp bark of a laugh, a sound of merriment and disdain. "Then you are a fool, Pelonius. They could cut us to pieces and no one would ever know who killed us. Rest the column and let them go ahead of us into the city."

Pelonius's face cleared. "Yes, sir."

As Pilate rode back along the column, the rich curtains of the mule-borne litter parted and Claudia Procula looked out. She was a beautiful woman, with her proud Claudian heritage evident in the delicate loveliness of her face. Whatever his faults, Pilate loved her greatly and, understanding his weaknesses as well as his strength, she loved him.

"Is anything wrong, Pontius?" she asked.

"A group of pilgrims blocking the trail."

Her eyes widened with surprise. "And you are letting them go on ahead?"

Pilate laughed again, but the sound was not so harsh now. "A lot of your Galileans are among them." Procula loved Tiberias and the Galilean region best of all. "Frankly, I have to ambition to get my throat cut."

"They are going to the Jewish Passover."

"So Pelonius says," Pilate agreed. "He recognized some of them, followers of a man called Jesus of Nazareth."

"I heard the servants at Tiberias speak of Him," Procula said. "And once I listened to Him in Capernaum. He is a good man, Pontius. Thousands of people in Galilee follow Him."

"Half of them must be with Him now by the looks of that procession." Pilate turned in the saddle to look about him. "You know, I never bothered to study this countryside before, Procula. From the looks of these vineyards, it must be prosperous. I wonder if we are getting all the taxes we should from the owners."

Claudia Procula laughed. "Be careful. You might even come to like Judea."

"By the gods, no!" Pilate protested. "If I know Herod, he owns these vineyards or has an interest in them. His greedy fingers try to take everything else."

"Including Judea for his tetrarchy," Claudia agreed. "Herodias drank too much again last night and talked more than she realized."

"Herod would like to see me in trouble," Pilate agreed. "But after all these years I know how to handle that fox. Besides he doesn't seem to be as sure of himself as he used to be."

"The palace servants say he's been afraid since he killed a prophet named John," Procula said. "My maid had it from Herod's own body servant."

"Guilt can warp a man's judgment," Pilate agreed absent-mindedly. "But I can't understand being concerned over the death of one fanatic."

"In Israel a prophet is a holy person," Procula explained. "The Jews believe he is sent by their God as a warning."

Pilate looked at her sharply. "Surely, you don't believe any of this heresy, my dear?"

Procula shook her head. "If I were to choose anything of what you call heresy, it would be what I hear of the teaching of this man Jesus of Nazareth. He teaches that all men should love and respect each other."

Pilate laughed. "If I were to try loving and respecting these Galileans ahead of us," he said, "I would end with a knife in my back." He reined up the horse's head as the order to march came from Pelonius at the head of the column. "Good, we are moving again. Close the curtains, my dear. The hoofs stir up much dust."

"I am glad you did not spur through the pilgrims, Pontius," Procula said softly.

Pilate answered with his short bark of laughter. "Don't think I am softening. I only want to live long enough to shake the dust of this accursed country from my feet."

II

The rocky slope of the Mount of Olives, except where it had been cleared and dug up for vineyards or fig groves, was covered by thickets of the tough burnet bush with its murderous thorns. The *moreh* had already turned the entire hillside green and here and there an occasional bush was precociously putting forth a few of the brilliant red blossoms that resembled nothing so much as drops of blood.

During the winter a few clumps of the burnet had died and the wood of these was now sere and gray against the green that covered the hillside. The green bushes served no useful purpose except to spread upon the hillside a scarlet blanket that for a few weeks in the spring was incredibly beautiful. The dead bushes were much prized for fuel and gathering them was a slow, painful task.

It was the task to which old Jonas, thrust out of Elam's household many years ago, had been forced in order to make his living. Each day he trudged up the mountain to gather the thorny limbs, carefully piling them into a pack which he could carry on his back. Dry now, they weighed little but were a trial to him because of his hump; more than once the cruel thorns had pierced through the worn piece of leather he used to protect his skin, causing painful wounds. He could carry barely enough to bring in sufficient money for his meager needs. Like thousands of beggars, lepers, and other unfortunates, Jonas lived in a warren of hovels built against the outer walls of the city.

In spite of his friendship with Zadok, the bright-eyed cripple whose hovel adjoined his, Jonas had been bitterly lonely at first. Zadok went into the city each morning to beg, swinging himself along on his powerful arms and dragging his body behind him. Zadok had been born without legs. Often it was after dark when the beggar returned to his hovel, boasting of the alms he had obtained during the day. But on the hillsides there had been no one to talk to, for the woodgatherers were too busy to have time for idle chatter.

For a while Jonas had considered following Zadok's suggestion that he pretend some affliction more striking than the hump on his back, his stiff and painful joints, and his age; perhaps some dramatic infirmity such as being seized by devils whenever a crowd gathered, inciting the pity of onlookers so that they would give generous alms. It would have been an easy way to make a living, but Jonas had refused to beg; he had always earned his keep, and when he could no longer do that he was determined to he down and die.

And then one day, Jonas had found an old mule limping through a field outside the city. Its coat was ragged and crusted with dirt and it had not been fed lately so that the hollows between its ribs stood out painfully. But it had come to Jonas when he called it and had nestled its gray muzzle into his palm. With that gesture of need, of desire for companionship, Jonas had felt his loneliness fade. To be needed, if only by a grizzled old mule which, like himself, had been thrust out because it no longer earned its keep, gave him a feeling of pleasure such as he had not known for a long time.

"What is your name, old fellow?" Jonas asked the mule. The animal only nuzzled his hand the more and lifted trusting eyes. Jonas's forehead creased in a frown.

"I had a brother once named Eleazar," he said to the mule. "Would you like that name?"

Jonas borrowed salve from Zadok for the animal's sores, he found patches of green grass among the rocks where Eleazar could graze while he gathered thorns, and soon the hollows between the mule's ribs began to fill out and his coat grew sleeker under Jonas's nightly currying.

Working at night, Jonas wove a light pannier of withes and with this strapped on Eleazar's back he was able to carry more than twice his former load of thornwood into the city. Now he bought grain for Eleazar and food for himself, although their combined efforts brought in little more than enough to supply their needs. Whenever stormy weather or the hot sirocco of summer made it impossible to gather the daily load of wood, both of them were likely to go hungry the next day.

But both—Jonas and Eleazar—were happy this bright spring morning as they came down a path winding along the slope of the Mount of Olives on their way to the city with a load of wood. It was only five days until the Passover and, if the weather held, Jonas could even hope to have a small coin or two left with which to buy a dove for the sacrifice. He was hurrying to the city this morning with his load of thorns in order to reach the establishments of the lime burners and the potters before they had laid in their supply of wood for the day. Eleazar followed him down the mountainside, patiently picking his way along the rocky hail. The mule had traveled these paths many times and needed no guidance.

Just above the point where the path debouched upon the caravan road, Jonas stopped short. A small crowd had gathered where the roadways met, held back from entering the main road to Jerusalem because it was filled completely by a happy, jostling procession of pilgrims, waving palm branches and shouting, "Hosanna!" as if they were escorting a king.

Jonas felt Eleazar's muzzle nudge him in the back and reached out to rest his hand upon the animal's neck. A Pharisee, by his rich dress, Jonas judged, one of the wealthy landowners of Bethphage who had estates here on the Mount of Olives, stood nearby, his face heavy with displeasure. Jonas moved closer and, though the Pharisee reminded him of his former master Elam, dared to speak.

"Can you tell me who these people are, noble sir?" he asked respectfully.

"Galileans!" the Pharisee exploded. "The Romans should not allow pilgrims like this to clutter up the main roads. I have urgent business in the city this morning."

Jonas, too, had business in the city. If he did not reach the potters and lime burners soon with his load of wood, others would be ahead of him. Then he would have to wait until morning to sell and a whole day would be lost. Still he could not agree with the Pharisee that everyone did not have the same right to the road.

"All men are equal before the Most High," he said.

"If you believe that, you are a fool," the Pharisee snorted. "Galileans are nothing but trouble." His angry gesture took in the slope of the mountain now dotted with tents and cooking fires. "Do they stay in the city and help to support honest innkeepers? No. And they steal food from the landowners."

"At least they make sacrifices in the temple," Jonas said mildly.

The Pharisee from Bethphage shrugged. "Twenty men to one lamb— as many as the Law will allow. Or a dove."

Jonas felt a sudden surge of anger. "Do you know what it is to be hungry?" he demanded. "You with your fine robe and your fat belly? Do you know what it is to sleep in a hovel with only a sackcloth for a cover and it full of vermin? Do you not—" He stopped short, aghast at his effrontery.

The Pharisee drew back his head and surveyed the old woodseller coldly. "You speak disrespectfully, little man," he said. "How do I know you have not been trespassing on my land to gather thorns?"

Jonas lowered his head. "I spoke in the heat of anger. These pilgrims will keep me from selling my wood today and I will lose a day's work."

"I am a tolerant man so I forgive you," the Pharisee said magnanimously. "Are these Galileans never going to clear the road?"

A sleek mule led by a handsome youth with dark hair and bright intelligent eyes had just come down the hill from above Bethany and joined the group. Riding on the animal was a slender girl of about eighteen who strongly resembled the boy. She carried a basket filled with exquisitely molded vases of rough pottery and when she saw Jonas, her eyes softened in a smile.

"There is Jonas, Jonathan," she cried to her brother. "And Eleazar!"

Jonas heard his name and turned. At sight of the girl on the mule and the boy leading it, the frown of worry was smoothed from the old man's face.

"Shalom, Veronica," he said. "And you, Jonathan." They were the son and daughter of Abijah, one of the finest potters in Jerusalem. He often sold burnet wood to their father for his kilns.

"Eleazar is growing younger, Jonas," the girl said. "And so are you."

The old woodseller smiled and rubbed the mule's neck. "He thanks you, Veronica, and so do I."

The people gathered by the roadway turned to look at the girl and her brother and words of greeting now came from all sides, for she was well known in Jerusalem. With her fresh, natural beauty, her slender loveliness, Veronica was like the spring morning itself. Nothing in her demeanor would have told anyone that she had been unable to walk for years, or that often she had to remain in bed for months at a time while the inflamed bone in her leg throbbed with almost unbearable pain.

"We have been to Bethany to buy vases," Veronica explained to Jonas. "They have been selling faster than father can make them."

"No wonder," he said, "when you paint such pretty scenes on them."

The Pharisee turned to look at the girl. "Are you the one who paints vases for the potters on the street below the temple?"

"Yes, sir."

"You deserve success since you work so hard and do such good work."

Veronica's eyes sparkled. "No work is hard when you love it." She looked at the procession which showed no sign of ending. "Did you ever see such happy people?"

"They are keeping honest folk from their work," the Pharisee growled.

"Who are they?" the girl asked.

"Galileans!" Again he gave the word all the scorn he could put into it. "Escorting some prophet into Jerusalem, they say."

"A prophet? What is His name?"

"They call Him Jesus of Nazareth."

"The one who raised Lazarus from the dead?" Veronica asked excitedly.

"So He claims," the Pharisee admitted grudgingly.

Veronica looked down at the drawn and twisted leg hidden under her skirts. "They say people who only touched His garment have been healed," she said a little wistfully.

"Many so-called prophets heal foolish people who only think they are sick," the Pharisee said loftily. "It does not last; I have seen many such."

"But in Galilee Jesus fed five thousand people with only a few loaves and fish," she insisted.

"Then He should be rich by now," the Pharisee sneered.

Veronica shook her head. "I heard them talking of Jesus in Jerusalem at the Feast of Dedication. He helps the poor and those who are sick and crippled and have no money, and He doesn't take anything for Himself."

"A man with such powers would be a fool to use them without being paid," the Pharisee said disapprovingly. "After all, the laborer is worthy of his hire. What sort of world would this be if everybody gave everything away?"

Jonas had turned to examine the load of wood on his mule's back. A small sore had been rubbed on the animal's shoulder by the pannier, and he gently lifted up the wooden frame and placed his knitted cap under it to protect the irritated skin, though the hot sun would now beat down upon his own unprotected head.

"Forgive me, Eleazar," he said in a low voice. "I was in a hurry to get to the city and did not lash the load properly." He straightened up painfully, for his joints had grown stiffer through the years. "It will be better now," he promised the old animal.

"Jonas," Veronica said concernedly. "Your back is troubling you again, isn't it?" She looked toward the procession and the slender man with the brown beard who was riding, an ass in the midst of it. "You should go to the Nazarene while He is in Jerusalem and let Him heal you."

"First I must sell this load of wood so Eleazar can have some grain," Jonas said. "I can see the Galilean another time."

"But you will go to Him?" Veronica insisted.

"Maybe tomorrow when I have sold this load of wood," Jonas promised. "He does look like a good man."

"Galilean rabble!" the Pharisee snorted. "Cluttering up the roads! I shall report this to Caiaphas."

Veronica was still looking at the old woodseller with concern. Characteristically in her sympathy for him, she gave no thought to what the Teacher of Nazareth might do for her.

III

A biathar was waiting with the guards at the gate nearest to Bethany, but he quickly saw that he had no more chance of stopping the procession than he would have had in holding back with his bare hands the source-waters of the Jordan. Shouting "Hosanna!" and still strewing palm leaves and even their own garments upon the path before Jesus, the crowd ushered Him into Jerusalem as the King He rightfully was, now that at last He had allowed Himself to be acclaimed the Messiah.

As Jesus rode along, the tears He had shed for Jerusalem when it had first burst into view from the Mount of Olives were still wet upon His cheeks and His face was ravaged with pity and sorrow, His eyes bleak. Only a few people noticed His mood, however, excited as they were by the tumultuous welcome He was receiving.

Peter, seeing Jesus' face, was sobered and felt again the doubt about this final visit to Jerusalem that had troubled him. Mary of Magdala, who always watched the Master, noticed Jesus' mood and her heart was torn with concern. The mother of Jesus, pleased naturally by the acclaim that had come to her son, saw it and experienced a deep sense of foreboding; there was ample reason for her concern, too, for plainly visible across the Kedron Valley and a short distance to the right of the temple itself were the four towers of the Antonia. Behind it, on the western edge of Jerusalem, loomed the three towers of Herod's own fortress with the newly added stories of the upper levels plainly distinguishable from the old. Both were grim reminders that the power of Rome ruled here, a power which any king named by the people must either acknowledge or overthrow if he were to live.

Judas and Simon the Zealot were much too pleased by the public acclaim and the proof of Jesus' power over the multitude to be concerned by His sorrow or the threat of Rome. They felt He would surely use His power now to seize the reins of government. James and John too were vastly pleased by the tumultuous welcome and what it meant to their own ambitions to be among the highest in the kingdom of God, even now being inaugurated here in Jerusalem.

At the Passover season every possible precaution was taken to keep Jerusalem ritually pure. The narrow streets were cleaned daily, but the Pharisees carried their fear of defilement even further, walking only in the middle of the streets and leaving the outer edges to the heathen and the *am haarets* who troubled themselves little about such things. Even at the gates, the Pharisees were careful to pass through by way of the steps and a higher passage, while the defiled used the ordinary way.

Jesus was not concerned with Pharisaic scruples, however, nor were many of those in the crowd with Him. Since He was going directly to the temple, the center of religious and political life for all of Israel, He had chosen the eastern entrance, often called the Golden Gate. In using it He was giving direct affront to the scribes and Pharisees, for according to custom decreed by the rabbis, this gate could be entered only after proper attention to the ritual cleansing.

On the Porch of Solomon, where Jesus always taught, a group of children was listening to one of the rabbis. When Jesus arrived they left their teacher and flocked around Him and, as the crowd that had followed Jesus, they too began to shout, "Hosanna to the Son of David!"

One of the chief priests who was nearby heard the greeting of the children and his face went pale with anger. It was one thing for the people to acclaim Jesus the Messiah on the roads and in the streets, but quite another for it to be done here in the temple itself. Such an act was an affront to the priests, and he immediately reprimanded Jesus for allowing Himself to be named the Messiah. Jesus, however, silenced him sternly.

"Have you never read, 'Out of the mouth of babes and sucklings You have perfected praise'?" He demanded.

The priest did not answer; Jesus was quoting the words of David himself in the psalm that began:

> *Out of the mouth of babes and sucklings,*
> *You have ordained strength because of Your enemies,*
> *That You might still the enemy and the avenger.*

Helpless, the priests and temple guards left Jesus unmolested. They could not seize Him without stirring up the mass of people that had surged into the Porch of Solomon to hear Him, and such a disturbance would bring the Roman soldiers once again into the temple. Meanwhile, Jesus taught the crowd and healed many of the sick, the lame, and the blind. When it was nearly nightfall, He and the disciples left the city and returned to Bethany.

29

He who loves his life will lose it, and he who hates his life in this world will keep it for eternal life.

John 12:25

Darkness had already fallen when Jonas led Eleazar out through the Sheep Gate and tethered him in front of his tiny shelter built against the wall of Jerusalem. The area was a honeycomb of such structures, all having a common back wall provided by the city. In them dwelt beggars, cripples, lepers—a small city of the poverty-stricken drawn together by their common misery.

As he had feared, Jonas had not been able to find a buyer for his load of dried thorns. The Galileans had cost him a day's work, a loss he could ill afford. Before attending to his own meager wants, however, he carefully removed the load from Eleazar's back and took off the leather sheet that protected the animal's skin from the sharp thorns. He could not leave either the mule's load or the one he had borne on his back outside the hut, for they would certainly be pilfered before morning. When he finished stowing the bulky loads of wood inside the shelter, there was little space left for him to sleep, and he made his bed on a pallet spread across the door of the hut.

An old crone who lived a few huts away hailed Jonas.

"Why didn't you sell your load today?" she called.

"A prophet was on the road with His following and I had to wait for them to pass," he explained. "When I got to the lime kilns, the fires were out and no more wood was wanted."

The crone came up and fingered one of the branches projecting from the pack. "Nothing makes a hot cooking fire like burnet wood," she said wistfully, and Jonas knew what was in her mind. Carefully pulling out a branch, he gave it to her though it meant that much less money when he sold the wood the next day. The crone took it happily but almost immediately pricked her finger on one of the murderously sharp thorns.

"A plague on all thorn bushes!" she cried.

But she did not throw it away. In the warrens against the walls there was seldom wood for even a small cooking fire and Jonas knew she would nurse every twig. As for him, the cold night air would stiffen his joints and by morning he would hardly be able to drag himself about the city to seek a market for the wood.

As Jonas applied some salve to the sore spot on Eleazar's shoulder, his neighbor, Zadok, came swinging along on his powerful arms, dragging his short stumps of legs as he went. The cripple's thin face was alive with excitement and his black eyes were aglow.

"Don't come near me, half-man!" the old crone shrieked from the entrance to her hovel.

"Away with you, witch!" Zadok spat at her. "Zut!"

"Monster!" the old woman cackled, bouncing up and down on the vermin-infested pallet that was her bed. "Zadok is a monster!"

"I'm no more a monster than you are, old hag!" Zadok called to her and pretended to start into her hovel. She retired inside shrieking, in a routine they followed every day.

Swinging himself around in front of his own hut, Zadok lowered his body to a sitting position in the dust. "You should have been begging today, hunchback," he said. "The pickings were good."

"Vulture!" Jonas's smile took away any offense from the term. The cripple was almost his only friend in the world. "I had other things to do."

Zadok's quick gaze took in the size of the piece of bread Jonas had removed from his torn and patched robe and was beginning to munch. "I see you bought grain for the mule again," he observed, "and nothing for yourself."

"There was no money. I was too late to sell my wood."

"There is great excitement in the city." Zadok drew a packet of food from his own robe. "The Nazarene prophet, Jesus, has come to Jerusalem."

"I saw Him on the road. He and His followers kept me from getting to the gate until it was too late to sell my wood."

Zadok nodded, his head bobbing up and down on his scrawny neck. "Galileans make a lot of noise," he said. "Did you see the prophet?"

"Only at a distance."

"What did you think of Him?"

"He appeared gentle and thoughtful."

"Gentle and thoughtful!" Zadok spat the date seeds into the dust. "Not that one! He is turning Jerusalem upside-down."

"How?"

"His disciples were openly naming Him the Messiah and King in the temple and when one of the chief priests spoke to Him about it, Jesus flogged him with words."

"The Nazarene didn't look like a troublemaker," Jonas said.

"I saw it all with my own eyes," Zadok replied indignantly. "They say the high priest has sworn Jesus shall not leave Jerusalem this time alive. But Caiaphas will have to catch the Nazarene away from His Galileans. One of them is a giant; he could break me in two with his bare hands." He bobbed up and down in his excitement. "The Romans know how to handle troublemakers. So maybe we'll have a crucifixion this Passover."

"I hope not," Jonas said. "The apprentices of the lime burners and potters would want a holiday and I would not be able to sell them any wood."

"But I could make a fortune begging in the crowd," Zadok said happily. "I might even get a chance or two to snatch a purse."

II

Jesus slept at Bethany that night but the next morning was up early and on the way to Jerusalem. His manner was as it had been on the road from Jericho, as if He had much to do and little time in which to do it. He had not paused to eat before leaving Bethany, and on the walk around the Mount of Olives and across the Kedron Valley to the city gates, He began to feel hungry.

The region around Bethphage, lying beside the road into Jerusalem, was famous for its figs, and seeing a tree that was already in full leaf, though those around it were still bare, Jesus left the road. The fruit of the fig often appeared before the leaves so that on a tree in full leaf, He had expected to find fruit. But when He reached into the leafy branches He discovered that for all its brave show of leaf, the tree was barren.

The parallel between the fig tree and Israel was inescapable. In spite of all the outward show of obedience to the Law which its leaders professed, they were inwardly like the branches of this tree, barren of any useful fruit.

The disciples had followed Jesus, and coming up to Him now, eager to quench their own hunger with fresh figs, they heard Him say, "No man shall eat fruit of you hereafter forever." Then without pausing to explain, He continued purposefully on, entering the Golden Gate again as He had done the day before.

This time Jesus did not go directly to the Porch of Solomon but entered the temple market beneath the royal porch that formed the southern portico. Here the stalls for sellers of sacrificial animals occupied the entire southern wall of the sanctuary area and, lining the inside aisle of this same section, were the booths of the money-changers, each man sitting behind the heavy chest that held his stock of coins.

The yearly tax required by the temple and all gifts had to be paid, according to religious law, in the Tyrian shekel. All other coins, whether the Roman denarius, the Persian doric, the mina, or any of the myriad coinages then in use, had to be changed into the approved shekel of Tyre. This was the province of the money-changers who were allowed by law to make a small charge for their services. The Law did not set the rate of exchange, however, so they did not scruple to bilk the pilgrims who flocked to Jerusalem from all parts of the world. The moneychangers shared a portion of their profits with the priests for the privilege of setting up their cabinets in the temple.

Lines of waiting customers were standing at most of the booths when Jesus entered, and the heavy smell of smoke and burning flesh from the altars on the upper levels hung over them like a pall. Jesus paused and His eyes swept the length of the market where a babble of voices rose as the constant haggling over prices and exchange rates went on. As He watched, His eyes began to smolder with anger at the commercial prostitution of this edifice which had been dedicated to the glory of His Father. Striding forward purposefully, moving so quickly that even long-legged Peter increased his pace to keep up with Him, Jesus reached the first booth. Stooping, He thrust His hands beneath the table, overturning it and scattering coins, coupons, and other articles upon the floor.

The disciples were aghast. They had never seen Jesus in this guise. But no one tried to hold Him back as He strode on and seized another of the tables, upending it too and sending it crashing to the floor. Nor did He respect the money-changers. Stepping across to where one of them was haggling over the value of a coin with a pilgrim from Alexandria, He tumbled the heavy chest to the floor and sent the piles of coins spinning.

And now the disciples were infected by Jesus' forthright actions and themselves started overturning the booths around them. The sudden commotion brought the temple guards but they were unable to deal with so unusual a situation and hastily summoned one of the chief priests. That portly sybarite came in his rich vestments and the crowd opened a path for him to Jesus where He stood, panting a little, His eyes still flashing with anger.

The rage in Jesus' eyes and the authority He radiated disconcerted even the haughty priest. Before he could speak Jesus lashed out at him, His ringing tones carrying to the farthest corner of the temple area.

"It is written, 'My house is a house of prayer,'" He accused the priest. "But you have made it a den of thieves!" The priest gave no answer and after a moment, the anger in Jesus' eyes died away. Abruptly He turned and, with the disciples hurrying after Him, strode around the lower level of the east portico and Solomon's Porch where He had taught on other occasions. By now word had spread throughout the temple that the prophet of Nazareth had overturned the tables of the money-changers. No one doubted that the final test of strength between Him and the authorities was near.

III

Jonas's steps lagged as he approached the end of the street of the lime burners. Everywhere the story had been the same, and he could not expect to be more successful in the street of the potters. As he entered the courtyard of Ashar, he saw that here too the lime kilns were cold.

"Ashar," he called toward the open door of the house fronting upon the court where the kilns were. "It is Jonas. I have burnet wood for sale."

"I am not buying today, Jonas," a man's voice came from inside the house. "Come back tomorrow."

"I must sell this wood so I can gather more." Jonas was desperate. Eleazar's grain sack, as well as his own larder, were empty except for the single Tyrian shekel he had put aside for the Passover offering. He would go hungry himself rather than touch it, but he could not endure seeing the patient animal's hunger.

"I am on my way to the temple," the man's voice was impatient. "A new prophet is teaching there; all Jerusalem is going to hear Him."

In desperation, Jonas called, "You may have the wood for half price."

"Put it against the wall of the farther kiln, then," Ashar said. "I will pay you tomorrow."

"I have no money," Jonas pleaded. "To me it does not matter, but Eleazar—"

Ashar appeared in the doorway of his house, wearing a fresh robe, his beard carefully combed. "Stack it carefully," he said impatiently. "Here is the money." From the purse hanging at his belt, he counted out a few coins and tossed them toward Jonas. The little woodseller got down painfully on his old knees to retrieve the money from the dirt.

"The Most High will bless you, Ashar," Jonas said as he hobbled with the mule over to the kiln and began to stack the thornwood carefully. "Even if you did get the wood at half price," he added, but under his breath, for Ashar was a good customer and he did not wish to offend him.

The street of the potters lay just ahead and when Jonas had finished unloading, he led Eleazar along it, hoping that someone wishing to fire his kiln that night would commission him to bring in a load of thornwood before dark. But the potters' kilns were cold too. It seemed that what Ashar said was true; everyone in Jerusalem had gone to hear the prophet of Nazareth.

Near the end of the street, in the shadow of the great aqueduct which Pontius Pilate had built with the temple monies to bring water to Jerusalem, was the pottery yard of Abijah, Veronica's father. Abijah's wheels were stilled too, and his kilns cold this morning. Veronica, however, sat in her customary place beneath the great spreading limbs of an aloes tree (more familiarly known as the "Shoot of Paradise" or "Paradise Wood" because it was believed to be the only tree originally in the Garden of Eden which had not been lost).

Veronica had finished painting the small vases she had brought from Bethany yesterday, and the colors had been fired during the night. Now the vases were arranged on a bench beside her, delicate and lovely. Some of the painted scenes were of thornwood blooming on the hillsides, others represented the flowers that grew so luxuriously in the well-cared-for garden of her rich kinsman, the merchant Joseph of Arimathea.

Veronica had put down the paints and the tiny brushes she used in decorating the vases. Now her slender fingers were busy sewing a head veil of fine transparent cloth that lay upon her lap. With her full skirts spread out, no one would have known she was crippled. When she saw Jonas plodding along leading the mule, she called to him. "You and Eleazar must be thirsty, Jonas. Come and drink."

From its resting place between the roots of the great tree, Veronica took up an olla, or water jar, made of porous pottery which allowed a little of the fluid to seep through and evaporate, thus cooling the rest.

"I see you sold your wood," she said as she poured a cup of water for the old man.

"To Ashar"—Jonas gulped down the cold water gratefully—"for half price."

"Bring me the bowl." Veronica pointed to a shallow pottery vessel among those for sale. "I will pour some for Eleazar. Poor beast, he looks thirsty."

"At least he will not be hungry now," Jonas said as he placed the bowl so the mule could dip his muzzle into it.

"But if you got only half price for your wood, you will have nothing for yourself."

"It is no matter," the little woodseller told her. "I can get along."

"Miriam," Veronica called over her shoulder to the door of the house behind her. When a serving woman appeared, she said, "Bring out a loaf and some cheese and wrap it so Jonas can take it with him."

"But you mustn't—" the woodseller started to protest.

Veronica shook her head. "Jonathan heard the Nazarene Teacher in the temple. He says those of us who are favored by the Most High must share with others."

"I—what have I to share?"

"You gave your love to Eleazar when he had been cast out," Veronica reminded him.

"Have all your family gone to listen to the Nazarene?" Jonas asked.

"I sent them," Veronica said. "He has a wonderful message. For all of us."

"I have no time."

"I saw how painful it was just now when you stooped to get the bowl," the girl said. "Jesus has healed many. Perhaps He might heal you."

"First I must buy grain for Eleazar," Jonas temporized, not wishing to admit that he was too proud to beg for help. "Perhaps later I will go to hear the Nazarene."

Veronica put her hand on the old man's arm. "Please go, Jonas," she begged. "I know how much you suffer."

The mule had finished drinking and the old man stowed away in his robe the package of bread and cheese. Painfully he hobbled out of the yard and down the street toward the gate and his hovel against the wall.

Veronica picked up her needlework again. Busy at it, she did not notice she had a visitor until a warm, pleasant voice said, "May I drink from your water jar?"

Veronica looked up quickly and saw a lovely woman, with dark masses of lustrous hair the color of deeply burnished copper, standing beside her. The woman's face seemed vaguely familiar, though at the moment Veronica did not know where she had seen her before.

"Of course," she answered, and reached for the olla, but Jonas had placed it just out of her reach and she could not quite touch it.

A quick flush stained Veronica's cheeks. "Will you pour for yourself, please?" she said. "I cannot walk."

The woman moved gracefully and filled the cup. "I should have known you were crippled when I saw you riding on the mule beside the road."

Now Veronica knew where she had seen her before. "You were with Him," she said. "With Jesus of Nazareth."

"I am called Mary of Magdala," the woman said. "I serve Jesus and help care for those who follow Him."

She seated herself on one of the gigantic spreading roots of the aloes tree and picked up one of the small vases. "You paint beautifully, my dear," she said. "Some day you must come to Galilee and paint the flowers there."

"My uncle, the merchant Joseph of Arimathea, has promised to take me to Galilee," Veronica said eagerly. "I hear it is beautiful."

"More beautiful even than Joseph's own garden," Mary agreed.

"Do you know him?

"We are old friends."

"Is He really the Messiah?" Veronica asked.

"Yes, Veronica, He is the Messiah."

"Then He will rule over all Israel, and drive the Romans out."

Mary did not speak for a moment and Veronica saw a faraway look in her eyes. "Many who follow Jesus think He will be king," she said finally. "Perhaps some follow Him for that reason. But His real kingdom is in the hearts of those who love Him. Can you understand what I mean?"

"I think so," Veronica said. "It must be something like Jonas, the little man you saw here just now. He loves his mule, Eleazar. He often goes hungry so the mule can have grain to eat, and I know he would give his own life for Eleazar."

"As young as you are, my dear," Mary said, and now her voice was infinitely sad, "I think you are wiser than any of us." Then her voice changed. "How long have you been crippled?"

"For many years," Veronica said. "At first it was painful; my leg was inflamed. Lately there has been only a little pain."

"But you cannot walk?"

Veronica shook her head. "No."

"Doesn't it make you sad?"

"It did at first, but not anymore. You see, I sit here and all the world passes by, so I really have no need to go anywhere. I have my painting and my family. The Most High has blessed me beyond what I deserve."

"Jesus will heal you if you have your brother take you to Him," Mary said.

For a moment Veronica's eyes glowed at the thought of being whole again, then she shook her head gently. "So many others need Him more than I do; it would be selfish of me to trouble Him. Jonas's hump gives him pain all the time and Zadok the cripple can use only half his body. I know hundreds who are far worse off than I am."

Mary's eyes were bright with tears as she put her hand on Veronica's arm. "You are such as Jesus would have make up His kingdom, Veronica," she said. "I was greedy and vain until the Master forgave me for my many sins, but the things He teaches you have found out for yourself. God will surely bless you."

As the beautiful woman with the red hair rose to her feet, Veronica said eagerly, "You will come to see me again, won't you?"

Mary nodded. "I suspect we shall all be busy here in Jerusalem before long," she said. "I may need your faith to guide me when the time of trial comes."

Alone now, beneath the aloes tree, Veronica sat and pondered the strange words of the beautiful woman from Galilee, her needlework for the moment forgotten.

IV

The Jews were not the only ones to visit Jerusalem at the Passover season. With so many people thronging the city from all parts of the Roman Empire, a great deal of business was transacted during the week of the religious festival. Merchants from various cities congregated at this time, to buy, sell, and contract for each other's products. It was for this purpose that a group of Greeks from the Decapolis cities beyond the Sea of Galilee and the Jordan had come to Jerusalem. Jesus had not taught long in that area, but the healing of the demoniac in Gadara, when the swine had rushed into the lake, together with His words on His brief appearances there had aroused considerable interest.

To the Greeks, the teachings of Jesus had a natural appeal. In many ways they were distillations of the ideas propounded by the old Greek philosophers, describing a way of life that represented an ideal approach to the relations between men and men, as well as between men and their God—by whatever name they called Him.

Since Bethsaida was on the border of the Decapolis area and not far from Hippos, one of its leading cities, the disciple Philip was known to some of the Greeks visiting Jerusalem at this time. These sought him out while Jesus was teaching in the temple and requested that they be allowed to see the Master personally and speak with Him.

The question posed a problem for Philip. Jesus had on several occasions stated publicly that His primary mission was to "the lost sheep of Israel," yet He had healed the daughter of a Syro-Phoenician woman, the servant of a centurion in Capernaum, and others who were not Jews. Outside Jerusalem, Philip would hardly have hesitated to bring to Jesus what the Jews considered heathens. But with Caiaphas seeking a way to destroy Jesus, any traffic with Greeks might be seized upon and built up into a structure of false accusations. The Greek merchants were so obviously sincere in their desire to talk to Jesus, however, that Philip finally sought out Andrew and told him of their request. Since Jesus was just finishing His discourse and preparing to leave Solomon's Porch for the day, the two brought the Greeks to Him there.

The petition of the Greeks was simple and flattering. They had been listening to Jesus teach and now they wanted Him to come into the Decapolis cities and remain there for some time, making that region His headquarters. Jesus heard their request thoughtfully. When they finished speaking, He did not answer for a moment but looked out across the broad, many-columned portico and the city beyond with the shadows of a waning sun falling upon it.

He was deeply moved by this invitation. He had not been misled by the clamorous welcome of the crowd ushering Him into Jerusalem. He knew the attitude of the city's leaders had not changed. He was still under sentence of death by the Sanhedrin, and the agents of Caiaphas followed Him constantly, seeking to arrest Him the moment He was not surrounded by a crowd. He had no illusion about how quickly the fickle acclaim of the masses could turn into denunciation; He had had an example of that in His own city, Nazareth, and again in Capernaum when He had refused to let Himself be crowned king after feeding the multitude.

The offer of the Greek ambassadors represented a way out of His present danger. The Decapolis cities belonged neither to the domain of Herod Antipas nor to that of Pontius Pilate, but ruled themselves with a considerable degree of independence, though under the control of Rome. In the Decapolis Jesus would be free of the constant nagging of the Pharisees and scribes, and the ever-present threat of death at the sentence of the Sanhedrin. From there He could go on to teach in the great centers of the Roman Empire where His words were certain to bear fruit, for the Greeks, having put aside the old mythical gods, were actively seeking a new faith now.

In a way, then, the presence of the Greeks represented for Jesus a chance to begin His mission anew. Yet He never seriously considered accepting the offer, grateful though He was to those who made it. His mission had been stated with complete clarity in this very temple when He was twelve years old. He was about "His Father's business," the task to which He had devoted His life.

When He spoke, there was a light of dedication in His eyes that even the disciples could not remember seeing there before. "The hour is come that the Son of Man should be glorified," He said, speaking not only to the waiting Greeks but to the disciples and the crowd which still gathered around them. "Truly I say to you, except a corn of wheat fall into the ground and die, it abides alone. But if it dies, it brings forth much fruit. He that loves his life shall lose it; and he that hates his life in this world shall keep it unto life eternal.

"If any man serves Me," He continued, speaking more directly to the disciples, "let him follow Me and where I am, there also shall My servant be. If any man serves Me, him will My Father honor."

Now, for the first time, He admitted His own very human reluctance for what lay ahead; He acknowledged the temptation posed by the offer to escape that fate by carrying His mission into the country of the Greeks. "Now My soul is troubled and what shall I say? Father, save Me from this hour? But for this cause I came into the world." He bowed His head then, as if in submission to a will higher than His own and His next words were barely audible, spoken only for Himself and His Father in heaven. "Father, glorify Your name."

Later some said a clap of thunder shook the temple at just that moment. Others claimed they heard a voice from heaven say, "I have both glorified it and will glorify it again," as if Jesus were being answered. That

He heard something, perhaps intended for His ears alone, seemed certain, for He spoke again, still softly, "This voice came not because of Me but for your sakes." Then His own voice rose so that all could hear. "Now is the judgment of the world. Now shall the prince of this world be cast out. And I, if I be lifted up from earth, will draw all men to Me."

It was a prophecy of His own death, but the people who heard it, even the disciples, did not yet understand.

Jesus said no more but left the temple and once again, as was His custom every evening, took the road to Bethany. The people who had listened to Him scattered through the city, but already their first burst of enthusiasm was beginning to cool. Jesus had entered Jerusalem in the manner of a king, but two days had passed and He had not proclaimed Himself king. The dramatic clash expected between Him and the temple authorities had not taken place, though He had dared to overturn the tables of the sellers and the chests of the money-changers.

Expecting excitement and conflict, the people were disappointed, and being disappointed, they began to lose interest in the one who, for the moment, at least, had captured their allegiance on His triumphal entry. Like the disciples, they could not understand His talk of being lifted up, and as they discussed it with neighbors and friends that evening, some voiced the conviction that the Nazarene prophet could not be the Messiah for He had not taken His rightful place by force as leader of the people.

Render to Caesar the things that are Caesar's,
and to God the things that are God's.

Mark 12:17

Jesus ate the evening meal at the house in Bethany and retired early to His pallet. Judas and Simon Zelotes asked Simon Peter to join them in the yard and several of the other disciples followed them. The night was cool so they gathered in a nearby stable, with the smell of hay and the warm aroma of the animals rich in their nostrils. Judas was the first to speak.

"When will the Master proclaim Himself?" he demanded.

"When He is ready," Peter said. "We can only wait."

"What if He leaves again without taking over the reins of power?" Simon the Zealot asked.

"We can only obey and follow Him," said Peter.

But he was troubled. The doubts raised in his mind by Mary of Magdala had been largely dispelled by Jesus' eagerness to reach Jerusalem and His allowing Himself to be acclaimed as the Son of David (another term for the Messiah) on the day of His triumphal entry into the city. Two days had passed without any further action on Jesus' part, however, and Peter's old doubts had begun to return.

In his heart, Peter was close to Jesus, but he was a vigorous man and his nature rebelled against believing what his instinctive kinship with the Master told him was true. Like the other disciples, he expected Jesus to establish a temporal rule in Jerusalem that would lead inevitably to His being proclaimed in all of Israel. He believed that the Master could maintain that rule, even against Rome, through the power He wielded as the Son of God. Yet deep in Peter's mind there was the uneasy doubt that Jesus had not been referring to a temporal kingdom.

"Obey!" Judas repeated angrily the word that Peter had used. "Must we obey when He lets the temple guards take us all prisoner? And when the Romans nail us to crosses?"

"Surely the Master has revealed His plans to you, Peter," Simon the Zealot said. "He selected you as our leader after Him."

"I have not asked Him about His plans," Peter admitted. "And He has not told me."

"But you will ask Him?" Judas insisted.

"When the Lord wants us to know the future, He will reveal it to us," Peter said stubbornly. "You must have faith in Him."

"I will have faith when I see Him use thunderbolts to destroy the enemy," Judas said heavily. "Caiaphas and Pontius Pilate are scoundrels, and so is Elam the Pharisee. If Jesus does not act soon, they will think up some way to throw us all into prison."

"It would be folly to arouse the crowd," added Simon the Zealot, "unless Jesus is going to lead us and use His miraculous powers."

Judas started to speak again, then closed his lips firmly. Had Peter been looking, he might have been warned by the look of calculation in Judas's eyes, but he said nothing more and the impromptu meeting dispersed.

Peter did not return immediately to the house with the others but took a winding path through the garden. He was not to have the solitude he sought, however, for before he neared the house, a familiar voice spoke to him from the shadows.

"Simon." It was Mary of Magdala. "What were you men discussing?"

"Nothing that concerns women," he said a little shortly.

"Does it concern Jesus?" Mary was not offended at his tone for they were old friends. She knew Peter well and understood why he was troubled.

"Why—yes."

"The Zealot and Judas want the Master to name Himself king at once, don't they?"

"Yes," Peter admitted reluctantly.

"And you?" Mary came out of the shadows now and stood beside him.

"I don't know," Peter admitted. "One part of me says He must name Himself king. The other part doesn't know what to believe."

"He is not going to be king, Simon—at least not in the way they think. He told you that again yesterday."

"It was a parable."

"You know better. Jesus was telling us what is going to happen here in Jerusalem. Raising Lazarus should have convinced everyone that He is the Son of God sent to save the world. It didn't convince them, and now He sees that the only way to make the world know He is the Son of God is to let them kill Him and He will then rise from the dead. When He triumphs over death personally, not even Caiaphas will be able to deny that He is the Messiah."

"You are dreaming, Mary," Peter said, but without much conviction for she had expressed almost exactly his own doubts. "Why should He allow Himself to be killed when He has the power to destroy Jerusalem if He wishes?"

"Jesus has no wish to triumph through the power of God. He must triumph through the faith of those who love and follow Him."

Peter felt himself wavering, yet refused to be swayed; the idea was preposterous. It could even mean that if Jesus were killed, all of them could be killed with Him. And who among them, save the Master, possessed the power to rise from the dead? "Say no more," he said harshly. "And do not talk of this to the others. You will only make them doubt."

"You love Him, Simon," Mary said sadly. "If you do not understand, no one else will." She turned and went into the house, leaving Peter to his thoughts.

The morning was bright and clear. A crowd gathered early to escort Jesus into Jerusalem and it was easy for Simon Peter to tell himself that his doubts of the night before had been foolish, as foolish as Mary's fancies. Jesus was the Son of God with all the infinite power of His Father at His command. Possibly He was waiting for the last days of the Passover week to announce it.

Peter's spirits rose with every step toward the city, especially when he saw the fig tree which Jesus had cursed the previous morning. The free was now dried up from the very roots as if these had been cut, proving once again that Jesus did possess the power of life and death.

"Master," Peter called to Jesus, who was walking a little ahead of him on the road. "The fig tree You cursed has withered away."

Jesus stopped and turned to face the disciples. "Have faith in God," He told them, "for truly I say to you that whoever shall say to this mountain, 'Be removed and cast into the sea,' and shall not doubt in his heart but shall believe that those things which he says shall come to pass, he shall have whatever he says.

"Whatever things you desire," He continued, "when you pray, believe that you will receive them and you shall have them. And when you stand praying, forgive if you have aught against anyone, that your Father also which is in heaven may forgive you your trespasses. But if you do not forgive, neither will your Father which is in heaven forgive your trespasses."

He said no more then, but continued on into the city and the Porch of Solomon from which, as a recognized rabbi, He had always taught.

II

Caiaphas was a clever man. He had been angry when the crowds, particularly the stalwart Galileans who followed Jesus everywhere, made it impossible to arrest the Nazarene publicly. But having vented his anger upon the luckless Abiathar, he was able to consider other ways to combat the threat to his own regime posed by the Nazarene's presence in Jerusalem.

At all seasons of the year Jerusalem was filled with the priests and Levites who came to serve in the temple, swelling the large corps permanently stationed there for the ritual worship. Caiaphas had at his disposal, therefore, a great number of spies and when, by the third day of the Passover season, they reported that the size of the crowds which followed Jesus had dwindled, the high priest could at last devise a plan of attack. Jesus was safe from arrest only when He was surrounded by crowds. Caiaphas now intended to destroy their loyalty, leaving Jesus alone and relatively defenseless.

The right to teach was jealously guarded in Israel by the people as well as by the rabbis themselves. Since Jesus was not a product of any of the current rabbinical schools, having gained His title of teacher largely from His earlier experiences in Galilee, Caiaphas decided to attack His eligibility to speak from Solomon's Porch where there was always a large audience, particularly during the religious festivals.

On questions concerning the Law and its interpretation, the rabbis were considered the highest authority, subject only to review by the Sanhedrin in individual cases. Most of the leading rabbis of Jerusalem also sat in the Sanhedrin, so the court rarely reversed its pronouncements. In determining rabbinical authority, it was believed that authoritative teaching had to be based on earlier interpretations. Rarely did any teacher dare to put forth a new truth or a new interpretation of an old one, unless he could find ample authority in the old for the new. Thus rabbinical teaching had been stifled for centuries by ancient interpretations of the Law.

The nature of rabbinical authority was accepted without question by the people. If Caiaphas could succeed in proving that Jesus lacked the authority to be a teacher, the crowd itself would turn upon Him and eject Him from Solomon's Porch. To arouse the people, the high priest sent with the rabbi Jochai a number of the chief priests who were to discredit Jesus publicly.

Jochai and the priests who made up the delegation were members of the Sanhedrin and well known to the crowds in the temple. When they approached the spot where Jesus was speaking, the people parted respectfully to let them through. Jesus wore the homespun robe and sandals that were his usual garb. The contrast of His simple dress with the rich garments of the priests and the fringed robes and phylacteries of the others might have been to His disadvantage but for the quiet air of royal authority that He radiated.

Jesus recognized at once the purpose of the delegation but waited courteously for them to question Him. Jochai was the first to speak.

"By what authority do You do these things?" he demanded.

The question was cleverly worded. In demanding to know by what authority Jesus taught, they appeared to be questioning only His authority as a rabbi. Without waiting for an answer, Jochai added, "Or who gave You this authority?" implying, as the Sadducees had often tried to do before, that Jesus was an agent of Beelzebub.

Jesus answered with a question, always a disconcerting method of attack in any debate. "I will also ask you one thing," He said. "Which, if you tell Me, I will likewise tell you by what authority I do these things. The baptism of John: whence was it? From heaven or of men?"

Jochai and the priests withdrew a little way to discuss the question before answering. "If we say, 'From heaven,'" one of the priests pointed out, "he will say, 'Why did you not then believe him?'"

"But if we say, 'Of men,'" Jochai went on, "people will stone us, for they believe John was a prophet."

After a while they came back to Jesus and said, "We cannot tell."

Then Jesus said to them, "Neither will I tell you by what authority I do these things." He did not stop at that, but added: "A certain man had two sons and he came to the first and said, 'Son, go work today in my vineyard.' He answered and said, 'I will not,' but afterward repented and went.

"And the man came to the second and said likewise and he answered and said, 'I go, sir,' but did not go. Which of these two did the will of his father?"

"The first," Jochai answered immediately.

"I say to you that the publicans and the harlots go into the kingdom of God before you," Jesus said sternly. "John came to you in the way of righteousness and you did not believe him, but the publicans and the harlots did believe him. And you, when you had seen it, did not repent afterward that you might believe him.

"Hear another parable," He told them. "There was a certain householder who planted a vineyard and hedged it around and dug a winepress in it and built a tower and rented it out to husbandmen and went into a far country. And when the time of the fruit drew near, he sent his servants to the husbandmen to receive the fruits of it.

"But the husbandmen took his servants and beat one and killed another and stoned another. Again, he sent other servants more than the first and they did likewise to them. But last of all he sent to them his son saying, 'They will reverence my son.'

"But when the husbandmen saw the son, they said among themselves, 'This is the heir; come, let us kill him and let us seize his inheritance.' And they caught him and threw him out of the vineyard and slew him. When the lord therefore of the vineyard comes, what will he do to those husbandmen?"

The priests could give only one answer: "He will miserably destroy those wicked men and will rent out his vineyard to other husbandmen who will render him the fruits in their seasons."

"But did you never read in the Scriptures," Jesus said, "the stone which the builders rejected is become the head of the corner?"

There was no triumph in Jesus' voice at having bested the priests and the rabbis in their attempt to discredit Him, only a great sadness at their failure to see the truth when it was revealed.

III

Caiaphas and his agents so far had sought to convict Jesus only of breaking the Law of Moses, a crime over which the Sanhedrin, which he and his party dominated, had complete authority. But when the chief priests and leading rabbis failed to trap Jesus, Caiaphas decided upon another tack. This time he sent a group of students called the Herodians, brilliant young men from whose ranks would come the leading teachers and legal minds of the next generation, to try to maneuver Jesus into a statement that could be made the basis for charges against Him before the Roman authorities.

For this purpose, they chose a question which was hotly debated in the rabbinical schools: "Is it lawful to give tribute to Caesar or not?"

The question was not simply a point of debate, however. Conservative Judaism held that the right to coin money also involved the right to levy taxes and was in itself sufficient evidence of governmental authority. In accordance with this, the priest-kings of the Hasmonean house upon assuming power had coined money as a sign of their temporal, as well as religious, authority over the people. During the bloody reign of Herod the Great, few had dared defy the law requiring payment of a capitation tax of one drachma, or denarius, to the Roman authorities. But with the rise of nationalist spirit in recent years, the group whose most extremist members were the Zealots had begun to argue that paying tribute to Caesar was in fact acknowledging him as the highest royal authority, thus in a sense disowning Jehovah. The questioner sought to trap Jesus into making a statement resisting Roman authority, for which He could be thrust into prison, or offending a large section of the crowd who, whether or not they openly supported the radical Zealot cause, were certainly in sympathy with it.

Again, with His understanding of the motives behind the question, Jesus easily avoided the trap they had so carefully prepared for Him.

"Why do you tempt Me, you hypocrites?" He said scornfully. "Show Me the tribute money."

One of the students took a coin from his purse and handed it to Jesus, who held it up for the crowd to see. "Whose image and superscription is this?" He asked.

The question could bring only one reply, "Caesar's."

"Give to Caesar therefore, the things that are Caesar's," He told them. "And to God the things that are God's."

The students were so taken aback by His answer that they had no more to say and withdrew to debate among themselves. But Jesus had not been merely evading the question. He had elevated it, as He so often did with questions of human conduct.

Rome had brought unquestioned benefits to the people of Israel, such as protection from hostile states, a marvelous system of roads, the famed impersonality of Roman justice in which every citizen had the right to carry his appeal even to the emperor himself, the Roman ingenuity for building cities with streets and sanitary facilities, the keeping of adequate records, and the protection of individual rights against preemption by others. For these benefits, the people should pay through taxation.

God, too, had brought them benefits, principally that of life itself and, if they proved worthy of it, life eternal. He had bestowed upon them the bountiful gifts of the world in which they lived, the *moreh* that brought new life to the soil in spring, the sun that drew the seedlings from the earth and caused them to grow into strong healthy plants, the seasons with their ever-changing pattern of growth and dying. For these things, too, they should pay tribute to the God whose divine love had created them.

Thus, Jesus had given the only logical answer to the question of the students, but since it pleased neither faction among them, they found no comfort in it and refused to understand its deeper meaning.

31

O Jerusalem, Jerusalem, the one who kills
the prophets and stones those who are sent to her!

Matthew 23:37

The week had been a bad one for Jonas. Many of the lime burners and the potters had closed their establishments and gone with their workers to the temple to hear the Nazarene prophet. It had taken Jonas most of the previous day to sell the wood he had been carrying into Jerusalem when he was stopped by the procession of Galileans. Now with the day almost gone, he had been able to get only half price for that morning's load.

As he threaded his way through the crowd that jammed the street before the temple, Jonas saw Veronica on her mule with a basket of the exquisite little vases she painted. He started toward her but a portly man with a white beard and a heavily fringed robe almost knocked him down.

"Shalom, Elam," Jonas said breathlessly as he clung to Eleazar's neck for support. It was indeed his former master, and the Pharisee's face was black with anger.

"Oh, it is you, Jonas." Held back momentarily by the press of the crowd, Elam could go no further and acknowledged Jonas's greeting with a grudging nod. "I am in a hurry to visit the high priest," he added impatiently.

"Why are you so angry?" Jonas inquired mildly. Although his former master had cast him off when his usefulness as a servant seemed to be ended, he held no rancor against him.

"Who wouldn't be angry?" the Pharisee exploded. "Don't you hear Him?"

"My ears are not as good as they used to be," Jonas admitted. "Hear who?"

"The Nazarene! The cursed agent of Beelzebub!"

A sudden hush had fallen over the busy street and in the midst of it Jonas heard a voice ringing out from the temple with almost a note of sadness in it in spite of the words themselves.

"Woe to you, scribes and Pharisees, hypocrites!" the voice of the unseen man said. "For you shut up the kingdom of heaven against men and you neither go in yourselves nor suffer them that are entering to go in. Woe to you, scribes and Pharisees, hypocrites! For you devour widows' houses and for a pretense make long prayers. Therefore you shall receive the greater damnation."

Elam's face was suffused with anger and he was breathing heavily. "The man must be destroyed," he choked. "He is making us a laughingstock before the people."

As if the unseen speaker had heard and was answering, the words of condemnation rolled out over the heads of the silent crowd again. "Woe to you, scribes and Pharisees, hypocrites! For you pay tithe of mint and anise and cummin but have omitted the weightier matters of the Law—judgment, mercy, and faith. These you ought to have done, you blind guides which strain at a gnat and swallow a camel, and not leave the other undone."

"We Pharisees keep the whole Law!" Elam shouted indignantly. "We tithe and we fast and we give to the poor. What right has this—this madman—to call us hypocrites?"

Jonas did not answer, for the habit of obedience to Elam was with him still. But to himself he could not help admitting that so far the Nazarene had been describing his former master perfectly.

"Woe unto you, scribes and Pharisees, hypocrites!" the denunciation continued. "For you make clean the outside of the cup and the platter, but within they are full of extortion and excess. You blind Pharisees! First cleanse that which is within the cup and the platter so that the outside of them may be clean also."

"He speaks truth—that one," a man in the crowd said to another. "Look at the Pharisee there." He pointed toward Elam. "See how he flinches."

"You lie!" Elam shouted, but when the men around the speaker began to move toward him, he tried to push his way through the crowd to escape them.

"I am going to the high priest," he shouted at them. "He must silence this—this Galilean!"

Before the men could reach Elam, Jonas managed to place himself and the mule in their path so that they were blocked from his former master. Meanwhile, as if in answer to Elam, the voice from the temple porch continued. "Woe unto you, scribes and Pharisees, hypocrites! For you are like whited sepulchers which indeed appear beautiful outwardly, but are full of dead men's bones and of all uncleanness. You also outwardly appear righteous to men but within are full of hypocrisy and iniquity."

A murmur from the crowd drowned out the speaker's words for a moment, and Jonas pushed forward in order to hear, holding Eleazar's lead rope in his hand. When once again the voice of the Nazarene came to his ears, it was now a cry of pain more poignant than any Jonas had ever heard.

"You serpents! You generation of vipers! How can you escape the damnation of hell? O Jerusalem! O Jerusalem! That kills the prophets and stones them who are sent to you! How often would I have gathered your children together, even as a hen gathers her chickens under her wings, and you would not! Behold, your house is left desolate, for I say to you, you shall not see Me henceforth till you say, 'Blessed is He who comes in the name of the Lord."

The voice stopped speaking and shortly afterward the Nazarene and His disciples appeared at the head of the temple stairs, moving in a compact group. As Jesus passed, Jonas was startled to see how ravaged His face had become since He had seen Him a few days before on the road leading into Jerusalem. The group passed several paces from where Jonas stood and he heard one of the disciples comment on the richness of the temple buildings.

Jesus did not pause but His voice was heard by hundreds who stood in the street or followed Him down the steps. "Truly I say to you," He declared, "there shall not be left here one stone upon another that shall not be thrown down."

Then He was gone and the crowd swirled after Him.

With the street somewhat less jammed than before, Jonas was now able to see Veronica again and he moved toward where she sat on her mule, the basket of vases in her lap.

"Shalom, Jonas," she said, and when he brought Eleazar alongside she reached out to scratch the old animal's ears. "I see you sold your load today."

"Only two this week, and both at half price."

"I haven't done much better," she admitted, looking down at her vases. "There is so much excitement over Jesus that nobody wants to buy. The merchants are grumbling everywhere that He will ruin their business if He stays in Jerusalem any longer."

"He sounded just now as if He were leaving for good.

"You heard how He overturned the chests of the money-changers and the booths of those who sell animals, didn't you?"

Jonas nodded. "The people are excited now, but I have seen them this way over others who called themselves prophets. When the Nazarene leaves, it will be the same. The Pharisees will oppress us with the Law and the publicans will collect the temple tribute, with something to spare for their own purposes. Nobody helps the poor, Veronica, nobody but themselves."

"I think Jesus will help them. You heard what He said just now about the Pharisees?"

"Yes. But the only difference between Him and the others is that He doesn't seem to be afraid to say what we all think."

Veronica laughed, and just then Jonathan came running down the steps of the temple. "The guards are dispersing the crowd," he cried. "We must get out of the way."

Jonas pulled on the lead rope to get Eleazar away from the commotion that now was boiling around the steps of the temple. Veronica waved to him as she and Jonathan disappeared down the street.

Abiathar's burly figure appeared at the head of a party of guards, pushing a rabble of beggars and others down the steps. "Get back, you vermin!" he shouted. "Don't keep honest people from the temple!" Cries of anger and indignation sounded on every side but the crowd moved under the impetus of the temple guards, no one wanting to be the first to feel the prick of a sword point.

"He must be going to arrest the prophet," Jonas said half to himself and half to the mule. "I knew Elam would not let Him go unpunished."

Zadok came swinging his deformed body along the street with his powerful arms and spitting vituperation at the guards. His eyes were bright and his sallow face was flushed with excitement.

"Abiathar is driving out the beggars because they listened to the Nazarene!" he cried. "Put me on the mule, Jonas, before the crowds trample me under foot."

Jonas tugged at the cripple's body until he could get his hands on Eleazar's back and swing himself up. "Are they going to arrest the prophet?" he asked.

Zadok shook his head vigorously. "Not now. The people would tear the guards to pieces. But they will take Him right enough. After what He said about the scribes and the Pharisees! Abiathar will do it at night; that is Caiaphas's way."

The guards had reached the street level now and were driving the beggars and onlookers before them. "Off with you!" Abiathar shouted. "The temple is no place for thieves and beggars! Clear the streets!"

"The Nazarene was talking about you, Abiathar!" Zadok screeched from his vantage point on Eleazar's back. "You whitewashed tomb filled with dead men's bones!"

The captain of the guard wheeled, sword in hand. "You'll feel my sword, impudent scoundrel," he roared, then saw who it was that had spoken. "So it is you, half-man? I should have known."

"Take a word of advice from a friend, Abiathar," Zadok called. "Leave the Nazarene alone or the Galileans will gut you the way they do the fish!"

"You don't scare me, you freak," Abiathar said contemptuously. "We'll take care of the Galilean in good time." He looked at Jonas. "You there, woodseller. Keep better company if you want to stay out of trouble."

The crowd had scattered now. "I might as well ride home with you, Jonas," Zadok said. "Beggars will get little more today."

As they moved through the streets, the cripple chattered happily, for his nimble tongue was rarely silent long. "Abiathar is worried. I could see it in those pig's eyes of his. And that means Caiaphas is worried too. This Nazarene is a brave man—and a foolish one—to speak out against all of them at once. Now the Pharisees will join the priests in seeking to kill Him."

They reached the beggars' warrens outside the gate without incident. Across the Kedron Valley Jonas could see a small party of men ascending the slope of the Mount of Olives toward the public garden called Gethsemane. It was common knowledge that the Nazarene spent the night at the house of Lazarus surrounded by the Galileans who served as his bodyguard, but the lovely garden of Gethsemane was not far off the road to Bethany. Zadok went into his own hovel while Jonas busied himself rubbing Eleazar down with a piece of cloth and a little oil. The old mule's coat was getting thin from age and his skin tended to become irritated. While he worked, Jonas talked, half to the mule and half to himself, as he often did when the two were alone together.

"Only two loads of wood sold this week, old friend," he said. "We'll both be hungry at this rate."

Eleazar twitched an ear as if he were listening intently.

"Everything the Nazarene said was true," the woodseller continued. "The Pharisees *are* self-righteous and the priests are fat and prosperous from what the sellers and the money-changers pay for letting them cheat the pilgrims. But nobody ever does anything for people like us."

The rubdown completed, Jonas poured a measure of grain and gave it to the mule. "I'll be glad when the Passover is over and the Prophet goes back to Galilee," he continued. "Though I can't help wishing He would heal Veronica and let her walk again." He glanced toward the doorway of Zadok's hovel and saw that the legless man was sitting there, munching bread and goat's-milk cheese with a few dates. "They say He raised Lazarus from the dead, so He might even be able to heal Zadok."

The cripple popped out of his hovel, his eyes wide with indignation. "I heard that, hunchback," he said. "Keep your prayers for yourself, or for those that are asking for help."

"I only said it would be nice if Jesus of Nazareth would heal Veronica—and you, too."

"Why should I want to be healed?" Zadok snapped. "What do I want that I don't have?"

"But—"

"I have what money I want. People give it to me so I won't put a curse on them. I have food and a house to live in."

"But if you could be whole—"

"Then I would have to work as you do, or go hungry because I was too proud to beg. That way I would be nobody, but as I am, everybody knows Zadok the half-man. Even Abiathar is afraid of me."

"I never thought of that," Jonas admitted.

"That's why the people will never really follow the Nazarene," Zadok said. "He wants to change everything and most of them are satisfied with things as they are."

II

Judas of Kerioth was troubled as he followed Jesus and the others across the bridge spanning the Brook Kedron that flowed between Jerusalem proper and the Mount of Olives. Its waters were turbulent from the winter rains and heavily tinged with red from the blood of the sacrifices which were sluiced off through an opening beneath the great altar and directed by way of a tiled drain down beneath the temple and into the stream. The others, he knew, were excited by the forthright way in which Jesus had attacked His enemies that afternoon, but Judas was not sure that the Master's actions had been what they all considered them to be, a prelude to the final assumption of authority tomorrow or the next day. These were the only remaining days before the Passover itself, when any such action would be unthinkable.

Judas could not forget that last anguished cry of Jesus, "You shall not see Me henceforth, till you say, 'Blessed is He who comes in the name of the Lord.'" If this meant that Jesus would not return until the chief priests and the Pharisees named Him the Son of Man and welcomed Him to the city, then, Judas was convinced, the cause was already lost.

That Jesus could still be proclaimed Messiah and King in Jerusalem, Judas did not question for a moment. But it would have to be with such a blinding manifestation of glory and power that even the high priest could not deny His identity any longer. And Judas had seen no sign that Jesus intended any such thing. Nor did he see it now as the Master came to the Garden of Gethsemane where He loved to stop and pray for a while in the early evening before passing around the shoulder of the mountain to Bethany. Jesus was still sad as He gathered those He loved most around Him, and Judas had never seen His face so ravaged by pain and grief as now.

Simon Peter asked the question that was foremost in the minds of all of them. "Tell us what shall be the sign of Your coming and of the end of the world?" he asked, meaning the world of Rome and Israel as it existed then and the new glory of the kingdom in which Jesus would rule as Christ and King.

"Take heed that you are not deceived," Jesus answered somberly. "For many shall come in My name saying, 'I am Christ, and the time draws near.' Do not follow after them, but when you shall hear of wars and commotions, be not terrified, for these things must first come to pass. The end is not by and by, but nation shall rise against nation and kingdom against kingdom. And great earthquakes shall be in divers places and famines and pestilences and fearful sights and great signs shall there be from heaven.

"Before all these," He warned, "they shall lay their hands on you and persecute you, delivering you up to the synagogues and into prisons, to be brought before kings and rulers for My name's sake. And it shall turn to you for a testimony.

"Settle it therefore in your hearts not to meditate before what you shall answer," He advised them, "for I will give you a mouth and wisdom which all your adversaries shall not be able to gainsay nor resist. And you shall be betrayed both by parents and brethren and kinsfolk and friends. Some of you they shall cause to be put to death, and you shall be hated of all men for My name's sake, but not a hair of your head shall perish. In your patience possess your souls and when you shall see Jerusalem encompassed with armies, then know that its desolation is nigh.

"Then let them which are in Judea flee to the mountains," He continued, "and let them who are in the midst of it depart, and let not them that are in the countries enter into it. For these will be days of vengeance that all things which are written may be fulfilled. There shall be great distress in the land and wrath upon this people. And they shall fall by the edge of the sword and shall be led away captive into all nations and Jerusalem shall be trodden down of the Gentiles, until the time of the Gentiles be fulfilled."

The disciples could not believe He was speaking other than in the form of a parable, for Jerusalem with the shining golden dome of the temple lay in full view across the Valley Kedron, the softened rays of the setting sun giving it a beauty which it possessed perhaps at only one other time, with the coming of the dawn. It was incredible that this lovely city, which they devoutly believed He would tomorrow choose as His own, could be destroyed and that they should undergo the tortures He had described.

Now His voice changed and He began to teach them with a true parable.

"Behold the fig tree and all the trees," He said, the sweep of His hand taking in the wooded slope of the garden and the green of the olive and fig trees. "When they shoot forth you see and know of your own selves that summer is near at hand. So likewise when you see these things come to pass, know you that the kingdom of God is near at hand.

"Then shall the kingdom of heaven be like ten virgins who took their lamps and went forth to meet the bridegroom," He told them. "Five of them were wise and five foolish. They that were foolish took their lamps but no oil with them, but the wise took oil in their vessels with their lamps. While the bridegroom tarried, they all slept and at midnight there was a cry, 'Behold, the bridegroom comes! Go out to meet him.'

"Then all those virgins rose and trimmed their lamps and the foolish said to the wise, 'Give us of your oil, for our lamps are gone out.' But the wise answered saying, 'Not so, lest there not be enough for us and you. Go to them that sell, and buy for yourselves.'

"While they went to buy, the bridegroom came, and they that were ready went in with him to the marriage and the door was shut. Afterward the other virgins came; saying, 'Lord, Lord, open to us.' But he answered and said, 'Truly I say to you, I know you not.'

"Watch therefore," He counseled them, "for you know neither the day nor the hour wherein the Son of Man comes. Then shall the King say to them on His right hand, 'Come, you blessed of My Father, inherit the kingdom prepared for you from the foundation of the world. For I was hungry and you gave Me meat. I was thirsty and you gave Me drink. I was a stranger and you took Me in. Naked and you clothed Me. I was sick and you visited Me; I was in prison and you came to Me.'

"And the righteous shall answer Him saying, 'Lord, when did we see You hungry and fed You? Or thirsty and gave You drink? When did we see You a stranger and take You in? Or naked and clothed You? When did we see You sick or in prison and came to You?' The King will answer them, 'Inasmuch as you have done it to one of the least of these My brothers, you have done it to Me.'

"Then He shall say also to them on the left hand, 'Depart from Me, you cursed, into the everlasting fire, prepared for the devil and his angels. For I was hungry and you gave Me no meat. I was thirsty and you gave Me no drink. I was a stranger and you did not take Me in, naked and you did not clothe Me, sick and in prison and you did not visit Me.'

"Then shall they also answer Him, 'Lord, when did we see You hungry or thirsty or a stranger or naked or sick or in prison and did not minister to You?' And He shall answer them saying, 'Inasmuch as you did it not to one of the least of these, you did it not to Me.' And they shall go away into everlasting punishment, but the righteous shall go into life eternal."

For a moment after He finished speaking, Jesus' eyes were fixed upon the beautiful city where the lights of evening were now beginning to wink into being. Finally He rose to His feet and said almost matter-of-factly, "You know that after two days is the feast of the Passover and the Son of Man is betrayed to be crucified."

Without saying more, He left the garden and started along the path that joined the road leading to Bethany. The disciples were somber as they followed Him. Although they did not understand His words, they could not help but know from His manner that He had been warning them against some awful tribulation which was soon to occur, something very different from their own plans for the remaining days of the Passover season.

III

It was already growing dark when they left the garden and no one noticed that Judas did not immediately follow the party but remained behind. In the now empty and silent garden, he was alone as he considered Jesus' actions that day and the words He had just spoken concerning His coming death.

As keeper of the purse, Judas had been largely concerned with the mundane affairs of Jesus' ministry; he had never really understood its spiritual aspects. Like others, he had been thinking in terms of an earthly kingdom in which Jesus would rule Israel as the Messiah, with political, as well as spiritual, control over the nation. And to a man who had grown up in the little Judean village of Kerioth, the prospect of controlling the purse strings for the entire kingdom had seemed almost breathtaking in its implications. He had seized upon it eagerly when given an opportunity to become one of the disciples, and on occasion had not hesitated to help himself to the common purse.

Now Judas saw his hopes crumbling, destroyed by Jesus' refusal to assume His rightful place as ruler of Israel. After the way Jesus had humiliated the chief priests, the scribes, and the leading Pharisees before the people that day, it was a foregone conclusion that the anger of Caiaphas and his followers would be vented not upon Jesus alone but also upon His followers, including Judas himself.

To the small-souled man of Kerioth, there was only one logical course: to divorce himself from Jesus in such a way that he could be sure at least of saving his own life.

Still Judas hesitated, held by a small thread of loyalty to the leader who had lifted him from obscurity. He knew that the whole party was to dine that evening in Bethany at the home of a man called Simon who had been a leper until cleansed by Jesus. Judas had yet to hear from Jesus' own lips that He would not become King of the Jews. Sometime during the evening, the man of Kerioth determined he would demand an avowal of this, or its denial.

The guests had already gathered when Judas reached Simon's house in Bethany, but a place had been held for him at the table where Jesus, as the honored guest, reclined with the other disciples, His host, and Lazarus. The house was filled, for Simon was wealthy and had invited many guests. Most of those present believed they were taking part in a coronation feast for the next King of the Jews and it was a joyous and festive occasion.

Sensitive always to Jesus' thoughts and feelings because of her great love for Him and her instinctive womanly understanding, Mary of Bethany did not join the other women who, with her sister Martha, were serving at the feast. She had brought with her her most treasured possession—a jar of fine pottery such as the potters of Jerusalem fashioned, filled with an ointment made of spikenard, a rare and precious essence. Lazarus had brought it for her on his return from a journey some time ago, and she had treasured it ever since.

The disciples and Lazarus were seated together around one table with the other guests occupying tables in other parts of the large room. The women were constantly going and coming as they served, and Mary went unnoticed as she approached Jesus with the jar of ointment in her hand. But when Mary opened the jar and, pouring the ointment into her hand, knelt and anointed Jesus' feet, the rich fragrance quickly filled the room, calling attention to the scene.

Kneeling before Jesus, Mary let down the lustrous masses of her hair to wipe His feet. At the startling act, a sudden silence filled the room. The fragrance of the precious spikenard now spread to the kitchen and the women within crowded to the door to see what had happened. The silence was broken by the angry voice of Judas of Kerioth.

"Why was this ointment not sold for three hundred pence and given to the poor?" he demanded sharply.

A murmur of agreement came from some of the disciples, and even Lazarus looked at his sister in amazement, unable to understand why she had used such a rare jar of ointment to anoint Jesus' feet.

"Let her alone," Jesus said sharply. "She has kept this against the day of My burial. The poor you have with you always, but Me you will not always have."

Jesus' eyes were fixed upon Judas as He spoke. The man of Kerioth was sure now that Jesus knew of his small thefts from the common purse. He dropped his eyes to hide his guilt while a deep sense of shame and a rising anger at being publicly reprimanded burned within him.

Judas said no more, but his anger had burned away the slender thread of loyalty that held him to Jesus, and his active mind began devising a way in which to make sure that his own life would be saved when Caiaphas and his agents took Jesus to destroy Him. Two courses were open. One was to leave Jerusalem at once, but Judea was his home and as a known follower of Jesus he would certainly be hunted down and arrested. The other appealed both to his greed and his consuming desire to repay Jesus for the public reprimand. Judas chose the second course.

IV

Caiaphas had called a meeting of the Priestly Council in the private audience chamber of his palace for the morning after Jesus had dined with Simon, he who had been a leper. The higher temple officials were there, together with the heads of the various courses of priests then serving in the ritual of worship. Jochai represented the rabbis, Elam the Pharisees. Neither Nicodemus nor Joseph of Arimathea had been invited to this meeting, since Caiaphas wished no one to cast doubt upon the wisdom of the course he had decided to follow. Abiathar was not present, having been sent to watch for the coming of Jesus and His party to the temple.

Surprisingly, Caiaphas came into the chamber with a pleased look on his face and rapped upon the table for order. At the sight of his obvious satisfaction, the others turned to him eagerly to hear what had caused it.

"The Nazarene has condemned Himself at last," Caiaphas announced. "Yesterday, when He was leaving the temple, Jesus was heard to say of it, 'Do you see these great buildings? There shall not be left one stone upon another that shall not be thrown down.'"

"He did blaspheme against the temple!" Elam cried. "I heard it myself as I was coming down the steps."

"Many others heard Him, too," Caiaphas confirmed. "And will swear to it!"

"To blaspheme against the temple is the same as blaspheming against the Most High," Jochai agreed. "The man has condemned Himself out of His own mouth."

There was a chorus of assent and the room buzzed with excited conversation until Caiaphas held up his hand for silence. "I have called you here to decide how best to take the Nazarene prisoner," he said.

"Why not announce publicly that He blasphemed against the temple and said it would be destroyed?" Elam suggested.

"The merchants will surely be against Him when they hear of it."

"And the artisans," another agreed. "There is hardly a person in Jerusalem whose welfare is not closely connected in some way with the temple."

"We can depend upon the Jerusalem Jews to denounce the Nazarene," Caiaphas said. "They have already suffered loss because of the way He has stirred up the crowd, but we must first take Him by stealth somewhere outside the temple."

"If the Galileans are with Him, blood will be shed," Jochai warned. "It must not be in the temple."

"Why not when He leaves the city?" one of the priests asked. "It is known that He spends each night at Bethany."

'That would seem to be the best course," Caiaphas agreed, "except for one thing. He must be taken quickly. Tomorrow is the day of unleavened bread and tomorrow night the Passover will be eaten. We are pressed for time."

"Send guards to arrest Him at Bethany," Elam suggested. "Pilate will surely give you whatever Romans you need."

"The Galileans surround Him there," Caiaphas objected. "Some of them probably hold Roman citizenship and Pontius Pilate must be kept out of this matter until the Sanhedrin formally asks him to approve the sentence of death. It will be better to take Lazarus, as we had planned before. I believe Jesus will give Himself up when we do that."

There was a knock upon the door of the room and the guard stationed there opened it to admit Abiathar. The burly guard's face wore a pleased look and the high priest's face took on a similar expression as Abiathar whispered into his ear.

"Our problem is solved!" Caiaphas announced triumphantly. "One of the Nazarene's own disciples is outside. He has offered to betray Him!"

"It may be a trick," Elam warned.

"This man is a Judean, of Kerioth," Caiaphas said. "I spoke of him before, you will remember. I have had my eye on this man for some time."

Abiathar ushered Judas into the room. The traitor tried to appear completely at ease, even in the presence of the high officials of Jerusalem, but there was a wary look in his eyes. "Who are you?" Caiaphas demanded brusquely.

"Judas of Kerioth. Formerly a disciple of Jesus of Nazareth."

"Why are you not with Him in Bethany then?"

"I can no longer follow a false prophet and a blasphemer," Judas said in a tone of unctuous self-righteousness.

"You followed Him until today." Caiaphas's voice was scornful. "Why do you want to leave Him now?"

"I want no part of a blasphemer."

"Or of His punishment?" Caiaphas shot at him.

Judas weighed his words carefully, conscious that if he did not drive the hardest bargain now, he might condemn himself. "You wish to seize Jesus," he said boldly. "But you fear the crowds. I can tell you where to take Him when only a few will be with Him."

"Where?"

"There are some details to be considered first."

"Your price?" Caiaphas suggested.

"My price, yes," Judas said, more sure of himself now.

"What do you ask?"

"Amnesty for myself," Judas said. "And whatever such a service is worth to you."

Elam started to speak, but Caiaphas forestalled him. "The Nazarene has blasphemed against the temple. That alone is enough to insure His death."

"If you can take Him without stirring up a revolt, and bringing in the Romans," Judas agreed.

"Very well," Caiaphas told him. "Betray the Nazarene to us so we can take Him easily and you will be spared whatever punishment His followers receive."

Judas breathed more easily. At first Caiaphas's manner had made him feel he could not hope to win that much. Now he took courage and determined to try for more.

"Such a service deserves a greater reward," he suggested. Caiaphas looked at him contemptuously and for a moment Judas quaked with an inner fear, sure he had pushed the cruel high priest too far. Then Caiaphas turned to the clerk at the table beside him. "Give this man thirty pieces of silver, the price of a slave," he said. 'But no more."

"But—" Judas began.

"I said no more," Caiaphas told him sharply. "The Galilean is losing favor with the crowd and we could soon have taken Him whenever we wished. Thirty pieces of silver or nothing."

Inwardly seething at the cheapness of the price and at Caiaphas's scorn, Judas nevertheless recognized that the high priest could be bargained with no more. "I will do as you ask," he said and added righteously, "After all, it is right to bring a blasphemer to judgment."

"And right for a traitor to be paid no more than what he is worth," Caiaphas agreed sarcastically. "When can we take the Nazarene?"

"Tomorrow. Jesus will eat the Passover somewhere in Jerusalem, I do not know where yet. It will be late when He leaves and only a few will be with Him. I will bring you word myself."

"See that you do," Caiaphas said. "And if you betray us, you will die beside your false Messiah. Be sure of that."

A new commandment I give to you, that you love one another;
as I have loved you, that you also love one another.

John 13:34

Zadok was bursting with news when he reached home that night. "They say Caiaphas is sure of destroying the Nazarene now," he told Jonas. "One of His own disciples has betrayed Him."

"If they love Him, how could they do that?"

"Men love many things, hunchback," the cripple said philosophically. "But most of all money. Caiaphas paid the fellow well, of course."

"I could never betray a man who has been kind to me."

"That's why your ribs are showing, my friend," Zadok said. "If you would steal and beg as I do, you would not have to work." He crunched a date and spat out the seed. "By the way, have you done anything wrong lately?"

"No. Why?"

"I saw Abiathar as I was leaving the temple area. He asked about you."

Jonas paled a little. His conscience was clear but that meant little. The captain of the temple guards was a cruel man who made the beggars pay him well for the best places near the temple. But he could have no reason to trouble Jonas, or so the woodseller tried to assure himself.

"Abiathar is coming to see you in the morning," Zadok added. "He said to tell you not to go up to gather thornwood before he comes."

"Why would he want to see me?"

"You've done something wrong. What else? If I were you, I would take Eleazar and run away to Emmaus for a few days. Or to Bethany."

Jonas straightened himself painfully. "I've broken no law. I will not run away."

"Whatever happens is your own fault then," Zadok said virtuously. "I warned you."

Jonas did not sleep well that night. In his dreams a giant Abiathar pursued him and brutally beat Eleazar. By morning he was fully expecting the worst, but when the captain of the temple guards appeared, he held himself as proudly erect as his painful back would let him.

"So?" Abiathar said heavily. "Even beggars like you dare to look your betters in the eye now, Jonas. You must have been listening to the Nazarene."

"I have no time for anything but work," Jonas said. "With the lime burners and the potters no longer firing their kilns."

"They'll fire them again soon enough. You are the one who gathers the thorn bushes on the hillside outside the gate, aren't you?"

"Yes. But I have paid the tribute—"

"Be silent and listen," Abiathar said, "I have a mission for you."

"A mission?" Jonas repeated, startled.

"Gather an armful of green thorns on the hillside outside the gates for me today and I will pay you a shekel." A shekel was considerably more than Jonas ordinarily earned in a day.

"The green ones will not burn," he protested.

"Did I say anything about burning?" Abiathar laughed at the blank look on the little woodseller's face. "Bring the thorns to the palace of the high priest before midnight. There will be another shekel for you if you are prompt."

"But why green thorns?"

"For a crown," Abiathar said and laughed hugely again at the little man's mystification. "A crown of thorns—for a king of Israel!"

||

John Mark had been busy ever since Peter and John had come to tell his mother that Jesus would eat the Passover supper that evening in the upper room of their house on the outskirts of Jerusalem. Mark's days were usually spent at the scribes' school where he was a brilliant and promising student, but since this was the day of the unleavened bread at the end of which the Passover meal would be eaten, there had been no school.

Instead of coming into the city on the day after His dramatic denunciation of the scribes and Pharisees, Jesus had remained at Bethany with His disciples. Jerusalem buzzed with rumors all day long. Some said Caiaphas and the Sanhedrin had a definite plan for taking Jesus; others that His followers would use up in revolt if Abiathar attempted to arrest Him. On one point there was general agreement now. Some sort of clash between Jesus and the authorities was inevitable; things had gone too far.

Mark, his mother, Mary, and his Uncle Barnabas had become followers of Jesus during His first visit to Jerusalem as a Teacher. They had many friends and relatives in Galilee and so had known of Him before He had appeared in the city. Since then they had been staunch believers in Jesus as the Messiah, and awaited the coming of the kingdom of God which He would inaugurate on earth. Barnabas was not one of the Twelve, but he had been one of the seventy and was particularly close to Simon Peter.

There had been errands for Mark to run all afternoon. The task of preparing the Passover feast for such a large company was not an easy one and the neighboring women had been called in to help Mary. Many things still had to be purchased at the last moment, though, and Mark had been busy running back and forth between his house and the shops. He did not mind, for it was a great honor indeed that Jesus had chosen to celebrate the Passover in their home in Jerusalem rather than the luxurious one of Mary, Martha, and Lazarus at Bethany. Besides, Simon Peter had asked him that morning to keep watch outside the house during the supper lest the agents of the high priest learn where Jesus was and try to arrest Him.

One rumor had been particularly rampant in Jerusalem that day, and Mark had heard it at several of the shops. It was said that one of Jesus' own disciples had betrayed Him to the high priest, but this Mark found hard to believe. It was incredible that any of the Twelve who were closest to Jesus would betray Him to Caiaphas and thus insure the Master's death.

Barnabas had gone with Peter and John to the temple to purchase the paschal lamb early that morning. After it had been slaughtered on the altar there, they had brought the carcass home and it had been roasting all afternoon. Now the savory smell of the meat and the fragrant herbs and other delicacies which his mother was preparing filled the house and drifted out into the yard where John Mark watched for the arrival of the honored guest.

The youth had bathed and put on a new robe, one he had been saving for the ceremony when he would complete the year at the scribes' school and go on to another level of study. Now he waited in the shadows of a large sycamore tree beside the house, which was on a secluded side street. He was to warn his mother when the guests appeared so that she could be ready to greet them.

It was dark when, from his vantage point in the shadow of the large tree, Mark heard the voices of people approaching. He did not call out yet, for it might be only a group of neighbors returning home for the feast or even the temple guards who, if it were true that Jesus had been betrayed by one of His disciples, might have learned where He was to eat the Passover and be coming to take Him.

Then Mark heard the booming voice of Simon Peter among those approaching and, knowing now that the expected guests were arriving, ran to tell his mother and his Uncle Barnabas. Jesus was at the head of the group with John on one side and Simon Peter on the other. Reaching the house they took the stairway leading directly to the upper room where the meal had been prepared.

Reluctantly Mark went back to the tree. He would much rather have been with the men, listening to the talk, but Peter had commanded him to watch, and he would not betray the tall fisherman's trust. Then the thought came that he could accomplish both things by climbing into the tree whose spreading branches were near one of the open windows of the upper room. Scrambling up, he perched himself there just as Jesus and the others came through the door.

III

The traditional Passover meal consisted mainly of the lamb which had been slaughtered in the temple that morning, its fat and entrails burnt upon the altar. It was served along with unleavened bread, thin wine, and the bitter herbs which symbolized the persecutions in Egypt from which the Children of Israel had been delivered by God's mercy at the request of Moses.

The meal began at the setting of the sun when a trumpet blast from the highest point of the temple announced the Passover. A rather rigid routine was customary, beginning with a benediction which was followed by a cup of wine and then the formal washing of hands by the company. Thirteen different steps were observed in all, ending with the singing of the hallel at midnight in a psalm of thanksgiving.

The low table had already been prepared and the cushions upon which Jesus and the disciples were to recline were in place. In the street outside, the disciples had been wrangling among themselves over who should occupy the place of honor at the right hand of Jesus and the controversy continued into the house. Peter naturally felt that he should be the privileged one because Jesus had designated him at Caesarea-Philippi as the stone upon which He would build His church. John and his brother James were also particularly beloved by Jesus, and felt that it was they who should occupy the places of honor. Judas, as keeper of the purse, always sat close to the Master so that he could receive any instruction which Jesus wished to give him from time to time.

Jesus stopped the argument almost as soon as they entered the room. "The kings of the Gentiles exercise leadership over them and they that exercise authority upon them are called benefactors," He said. "You shall not be so, but he that is greatest among you, let him be as the youngest. And he that is chief, as he who serves. But who is greater, he that sits at meat or he that serves? Is it not he that sits at meat? Yet I am among you as He who serves.

"You have continued with Me in My temptation," He went on warmly, "and I appoint to you a kingdom as My Father has appointed to Me, that you may eat and drink at My table in My kingdom and sit on thrones judging the twelve tribes of Israel."

Subdued now by the rebuke, however gently delivered, the disciples took their places, with John at the place of honor and Judas on the left hand. Peter sat directly across the table from John. Jesus had treated Judas like the others all day and the man of Kerioth was sure that his visit to the high priest had not been noted and that no one knew of his intention to betray the Master.

At the beginning of the meal, Jesus pronounced the benediction and the ritual cup of wine was then passed. After that, when the time came to wash their hands, Jesus took off His robe and, taking up a towel and a basin of water placed at the entrance of the room for that purpose, knelt first before Simon Peter who reclined at the end of the row of cushions surrounding the table on three sides. The tall fisherman was ashamed now because he had argued with James and John over who among them should have the highest place at the feast and protested against Jesus abasing Himself thus.

"Lord," he asked humbly, "do You wash my feet?"

"You do not know what I do now," Jesus told him. "But hereafter you shall know."

"You shall never wash my feet," Peter still protested, not understanding what Jesus meant by the action or the words.

"If I do not wash you," Jesus told him quietly, "you have no part of Me."

Contrite now, Peter knelt before Him. "Do not wash my feet only," he begged, "but also my hands and my head."

Jesus shook His head slowly and kneeling, washed Peter's feet and dried them with a towel. "He who has bathed needs only to wash his feet and is every whit clean," He said. "But you are not all clean."

Judas felt a sudden stab of fear. Could Jesus have somehow learned of his plan to betray Him?

Jesus said no more. He washed the feet of the other silent disciples, put on His robe again, and then sat down with them. Judas's fears began to fade.

"You call Me Master and Lord, and you speak well, for so I am," Jesus said as the meal progressed. "If I then, your Lord and Master, have washed your feet, you ought also to wash one another's feet, for I have given you an example that you should do as I have done to you.

"I do not speak of you all," He continued. "I know whom I have chosen. But that the Scriptures may be fulfilled, he that eats bread with Me has lifted up his heel against Me."

Judas suddenly pushed away the dish before him. If he could have escaped without betraying himself, he would have done so, but Jesus went on speaking in the same matter-of-fact tone. "Truly I say to you, that one of you will betray Me."

John was beside Jesus, and Simon Peter beckoned him to ask the Master who it was that would betray Him. When John asked the question, Jesus did not immediately answer but reached out and dipped a piece of bread first in the bitter herbs and then into the savory juices from the meat.

"It is he to whom I shall give the sop," Jesus said in a low tone which only a few of them heard but which was perfectly audible to Judas.

The giving to another of the bread dipped in herbs and the juices of the lamb was an act of humility quite in keeping with Jesus' early action in washing the disciples' feet. And as He passed the sop to Judas Iscariot, He said quietly, "That which you do, do quickly."

His face frozen with fear and shame, Judas took the sop mechanically and put it into his mouth, but the taste of the herbs was like gall and pushing himself away from the table, he rose and plunged from the room into the night.

Because Judas carried the purse and paid for whatever was bought, most of the disciples, assuming that he had gone on some matter in connection with the meal, were not alarmed when he suddenly left the room. The paschal supper was at its height now, but when Jesus spoke again the gravity in His voice stilled their merriment.

"Children, yet a little time will I be with you," He said soberly. "You shall seek Me but as I said to the Jews, 'Where I go you cannot come.' So now I give a new commandment to you, that you love one another as I have loved you. By this shall all men know that you are My disciples, if you have love one for another."

"Lord, where are You going?" Simon Peter asked.

"Where I go you cannot follow Me now," Jesus told him. "But you shall follow Me afterward."

"Why can I not follow you now?" the tall fisherman insisted. "I will lay down my life for your sake."

"Will you lay down your life for My sake?" Jesus asked with a note of infinite sadness in His voice. "Truly I say to you, the cock shall not crow until you have denied Me three times."

IV

From his perch in the sycamore tree, John Mark had watched wide-eyed as Jesus and His disciples took their places at the table. Though he could not hear very much that was being said, he could understand the significance of Jesus' act in washing the disciples' feet, for he had heard the Master say more than once that he who would be greatest in the kingdom of God must become the servant of all. Mark had known too, that something was wrong when he had seen the look on Judas' face as he plunged from the room.

Mark remembered now the rumors in the city that one of Jesus' own disciples would betray Him, and he could not help wondering if it was Judas. The man of Kerioth was still visible, hurrying along the street and, acting upon an impulse, Mark slipped quickly from the sycamore tree and set out in pursuit.

Earlier one of the sudden black thunderclouds that sometimes drenched Jerusalem at this season, as an aftermath of the winter rains, had swept over the city. Now the sky was clear and the stars were shining. The rain had washed away the filth of the day from the streets, and the city seemed unusually fresh and clean as if it, too, had bathed and put on fresh raiment for the Passover.

Through the narrow, almost deserted streets of the Lower City, Mark followed Judas across the depression of the Tyropean Valley. As the streets began to climb into the more fashionable area of the Upper City, the way grew steeper, but Judas hardly slowed his pace and at times Mark had to trot to keep him in sight. Knowing every part of Jerusalem intimately, for he had lived there all his life, Mark was fairly sure where Judas was going. When the imposing structure of the palace of the high priest loomed up in the darkness ahead, he knew he had done right in following the man of Kerioth. For Judas went boldly to the gate leading into the outer court and knocked upon it for admission.

The city was quiet, for on the Passover night all remained indoors to eat the paschal meal, coming out only a little before midnight to sing the hallel together in thanksgiving once again to the God who had made Israel His own. From the courtyard of the palace, however, there came the sound of voices and when Mark crept close to the gate through which Judas had been admitted, he was able to see that a group of the temple guards were assembled there, along with perhaps two dozen Roman legionnaires.

Being careful not to let himself be seen, Mark worked his way through a section of hedge until he was near enough to hear and see at least part of what was going on. He was able to make out the burly form of Abiathar talking to Judas, and in the light of what he had seen in the upper room and the sudden flight of the man of Kerioth, Mark was almost certain that he knew the trend of the conversation.

His suspicions were confirmed when one sentence came loud and clear enough for him to understand it.

"The Garden of Gethsemane," Judas was saying. "He will go there after the singing of the hymn."

Mark remained no longer. He knew Jesus often went to the beautiful garden on the slope of the Mount of Olives when He left the city in the evening, stopping to pray there before going on to Bethany. What more logical place for Him to go tonight after the Passover meal was finished? Knowing Jesus would be accompanied only by the disciples and a few others, Judas had betrayed the garden to Abiathar as the place where he could capture Jesus without stirring up a riot.

The very simplicity of the plan made its success almost inevitable. Only if Mark could get back to his home before Jesus and the others left for the garden was there a chance to save the Master from capture.

Indeed the hour is coming, yes, has now come.

John 16:32

In the traditional ceremony of the Passover, near the end of the meal the youngest always asked the meaning of the celebration. This was the time for the oldest present to retell the story of how God had led the Children of Israel up out of bondage in Egypt. When the time came tonight, however, Jesus took a wine cup and filled it. "Take this and divide it among yourselves," He directed the eleven disciples who remained about the table. "For I say to you, I will not drink of the fruit of the vine until the kingdom of God shall come."

While the cup was being passed from one to another, He also took bread and, breaking it into pieces on the plate, gave it to them to eat.

"This is My body which is given for you," He told them. "This do in remembrance of Me. The cup is the new testament in My blood, which is shed for you."

The disciples were troubled, for Jesus had never carried out this ceremony before and they did not understand its real meaning.

"Let not your hearts be troubled," Jesus counseled them. "You believe in God, believe also in Me. In My Father's house are many mansions. If it were not so, I would have told you. I go to prepare a place for you and if I go and prepare a place for you, I will come again and receive you to Myself, that where I am, there you may be also. Where I go you know, and the way you know."

"Lord," Thomas protested, "we do not know where You will go, so how can we know the way?"

"I am the way, the truth, and the life," Jesus said simply. "No man comes to the Father but by Me. If you had known Me, you should have known My Father also, and from henceforth you know Him and have seen Him."

"Lord, show us the Father," Philip begged, "and it will suffice us."

"Have I been so long a time with you and yet you have not known Me, Philip?" Jesus asked sadly. "He who has seen Me has seen the Father. How then can you say, 'Show us the Father'? The words I speak to you I speak not of Myself, but the Father who dwells within Me, He does the works."

Jesus rose from the table, for the Passover was ended now and there remained only to sing the hallel as the final act of the ceremony. But before going out, He stopped to pray. "I pray not for the world," He said looking up to the heavens, "but for them which You have given Me, for they are Yours. Now I am no more in the world but these are in the world and I come to You. Holy Father, keep through Your own name those whom You have given Me, that they may be one, as We are. While I was with them in the world, I kept them in Your name. These that You gave Me I have kept, and none of them is lost but the son of perdition, that the Scripture might be fulfilled.

"Now I come to You and these things I speak in the world, that they might have My joy fulfilled in themselves. I have given them Your word, and the world has hated them, because they are not of the world, even as I am not of the world. I pray not that You will take them out of the world, but that You will keep them from evil. Sanctify them through Your truth.

"Neither pray I for these alone," He continued, "but for them also who will believe on Me through their word. That they all may be one, as You, Father, are in Me and I am in You. That they also may be one in Us that the world may believe that You sent Me. O righteous Father, the world has not known You, but I have known You, and these have known that You have sent Me. And I have declared to them Your name, and will declare it: that the love wherewith You have loved Me may be in them and I in them."

As He finished speaking the prayer, the sound of voices singing the hymn floated through the windows from the city outside. Jesus led His disciples out and there they joined their own voices in the hymn of praise. Only when it was finished, did He turn His steps toward the Garden of Gethsemane.

II

The Lady Claudia Procula, wife of Pontius Pilate, stood on the balcony outside her bedroom high up in the fortress of Antonia. Another Passover season was almost gone and she was thankful. Now with the ritual feast drawing to a close in the last moments before midnight and tomorrow, a day of quiet, it did not seem likely that there would be trouble in Jerusalem.

The scrape of a sandal told Procula that her husband had come out on the balcony. Lately Pilate had been moody as the months dragged on with no indication when the Emperor Tiberius in Rome would send him from Judea to a new and more responsible post. Pilate had been drinking more than usual too, but tonight she noted happily that he appeared to be almost sober. When he came up to the marble balustrade surrounding the balcony, Procula put out her hand and laced her fingers with his in the darkness.

"It's almost over," she said. "I came out here to listen to the people sing."

"It is better for them to sing than to shout against Rome," Pilate agreed.

"There's been little shouting this time. At least I haven't heard it."

Pilate laughed. "The Jews were too busy shouting against each other. The Galilean we saw on the road from Jericho has Caiaphas and his Priestly Council thoroughly upset."

"Why? He was only a Teacher."

"The Nazarene has courage, even if He lacks judgment," Pilate said. "He denounced the scribes and Pharisees in the temple."

"Has the high priest been to you about Him?"

Pilate shook his head. "Caiaphas has to get rid of the fellow, but he's afraid of Him. People cheer the Nazarene on because He attacks the scribes and the Pharisees and the priests. They might riot if Caiaphas arrested Him, so He is trying to destroy Him without any public notice. He doesn't want my soldiers in the temple again."

"You did handle that rather ruthlessly."

"I am the governor of Judea, my dear. And I am supposed to be ruthless—with rebellion." He chuckled. "I'll admit I went a little further than usual that time just to teach Caiaphas a lesson. He's too ambitious to suit me, and I wouldn't put it above him to foment some sort of a disturbance occasionally just to keep the people from looking too closely at how he operates the temple and its revenues."

"What about the Galileans?"

"They rebelled, so they would have been executed anyway," Pilate said. "But I think I may choose to be lenient with that fellow Barabbas. The people expect me to release a prisoner to them tomorrow; it's an old custom here. From what we've been able to drag out of Barabbas, the whole thing was started to create a safe opportunity for theft. If I let him go, the people will be impressed with Roman justice, but Caiaphas will still remember I didn't hesitate to act swiftly when the occasion demanded."

Procula did not speak for a moment and Pilate said, "Are you troubled, my dear?"

"I was thinking in a way I would hate to leave all this."

"Hate to leave Judea!" Pilate said incredulously. "Are you mad, Procula?"

"It is beautiful, you know."

"Only because it is night and everybody is waiting for an angel to fly over or something like that. By day Jerusalem is a miserable, quarrelsome city."

"But they have such confidence in their God," Procula protested, "and that they are His chosen people."

"Why would any god choose a people as quarrelsome as the Jews? The whole thing is nothing but a myth, Procula. The Jews believe in their Jehovah the same way the Persians believe in Ahura-Mazda and the Egyptians in Isis and Osiris. Every country has some sort of myth about a particular god."

"But the Jews have something much more beautiful than that," Procula insisted. "My maid, Nerva, heard Jesus of Nazareth teaching in the temple the other day. She was telling me what He said, Pontius. And I remember that He said much the same thing when I heard Him for a few moments in Galilee. It was beautiful and sensible."

"So are the philosophies of Plato, or Aristotle, my dear. But Plato and Aristotle were men of education and greatness of mind, not teachers from a village that even Jews themselves despise."

"It isn't the man, Pontius. It's the truths He teaches. Besides, many people believe Jesus is the Son of the Jewish God."

"That's what's troubling Caiaphas," Pilate agreed. "If the Nazarene were really the Son of that God, Caiaphas would have to obey Him." Pilate chuckled again. "It seems that Jesus doesn't believe in thieving tax gatherers or corrupt priests. Did you hear what He called the Pharisees the other day?"

"No."

"Whited sepulchers, full of bones and rotting flesh. To a Jew nothing could be more degrading. And I never heard a better description of old Elam."

"Hush, Pontius," Procula said. "They take this matter of defilement seriously. You know that."

Pilate had turned moody again. "A few more months in this sepulcher they call Judea and I'll be thoroughly defiled, too."

The sound of voices singing rose on the still night air. "They are singing the hallel," Procula said softly. When the hymn was finished, she turned to her husband, her eyes wet with tears. "It's beautiful," she said.

Pilate's eyes, however, were fixed on a line of lights moving along one of the streets between the palace of the high priest and the gate leading to the Garden of Gethsemane. The line of torches was double and almost straight.

"Soldiers are marching down there," he said. "And Romans, by the looks of those torches."

"Who could it be?"

"I always reinforce the temple guards with Roman soldiers during the religious festivals.... That looks like the whole detail."

"Are you going to investigate?"

"Caiaphas will let me know what's happening soon enough," Pilate said with a shrug. "If there has been disorder and he puts it down, so much the better. The people won't blame us. If he fails, I can always send more men to take care of things."

"But what could be the trouble? There's no sign of disturbance in Jerusalem."

"Whatever it is, we'll hear about it tomorrow," Pilate said.

As Procula stepped into her room again and closed the door against the night air, the soft notes of the hymn could still be heard over the city, drowning out the distant tramp of marching men.

III

Jonas was utterly weary as he plodded down through the depression of the Tyropean Valley and began to climb the sloping street of the Upper City, leading to the palace of the high priest. He had almost failed to carry out Abiathar's commission to bring the green thorn bushes from the hillside beyond the walls. Only fear of punishment had driven him now to complete it.

Zadok had been ill that morning, having gorged himself on some sweetmeats stolen from a shop when the proprietor was not looking. No one else would have anything to do with the legless man, and since Zadok insisted that he must go into the city early the next morning, Jonas had been forced to stay at home to care for him. It had been late afternoon before Zadok had improved enough for Jonas to leave him. Then the storm had driven him to take shelter in a cave housing a winepress on the hillside, and while he sat and waited for it to subside he had pondered on Abiathar's strange words about the crown of thorns. He could not find the answer, but the effort to solve the puzzle helped to pass the time. When finally, just before sunset, the storm stopped, Jonas had barely time before darkness fell to gather the thorns and make them into a pack to carry on his back.

On the way he made the mistake of stopping by his hovel to pour Eleazar his evening measure of grain, and found Zadok, now ravenously hungry, demanding food. In order to pacify the cripple, Jonas was forced to go out and buy food, so that it was late when he was finally able to start across the city with the thorns for Abiathar. He was almost afraid to go, knowing the captain of the temple guards would be displeased with him for being so tardy. But at the worst he probably would receive a thrashing whereas if he failed to deliver the thorns he would be thrown into the prison for stealing, since Abiathar had already given him the shekel.

To Jonas's great pleasure, Abiathar was not at the palace. The guard on duty knew nothing of the commission to gather the thorns, and Jonas had no choice except to wait for Abiathar if he were to get the rest of his promised reward. A few guards were also waiting in the courtyard, warming themselves around a small fire they had built. When Jonas approached, they did not order him away, so the little man settled with his back against a tree in the warm glow of the fire.

IV

Across the Brook Kedron, its waters still red from the many hundreds of lambs sacrificed on the great altar that day, Jesus and His disciples ascended the slope of the Mount of Olives to the gate of the beautiful garden called Gethsemane. As He walked, Jesus spoke to them of what was to come.

"All of you shall be offended because of Me this night," He told them. "For it is written, 'I will smite the shepherd, and the sheep shall be scattered abroad,' but after I am risen again, I will go before you into Galilee."

Peter, impulsive as ever, spoke up in protest. "Even if all men should be offended because of You," he said, "yet I will never be offended."

Troubled by Jesus' recent references to His own death, Peter had been carrying a short sword hidden under his robe for the past several days. He was not accustomed to weapons other than a club or his powerful fist, but was determined to protect Jesus if trouble arose.

Jesus looked at him with the warm light of understanding and affection in His eyes for He understood equally Peter's weaknesses and his strength. "Before the cock crows this night, you shall deny Me three times," He told the tall fisherman.

Peter protested all the more vehemently that he would follow Jesus even to death and the others added their own protests. When He came to the gate leading into the garden, Jesus told the rest of the disciples to stay behind, taking with Him only Peter, James, and John, the three who were closest to Him. When they were a little distance inside the garden, He said to the three, "My soul is exceedingly sorrowful, even unto death. Tarry here and watch with Me."

Leaving the three behind, Jesus went to the very center of the garden and began to pray. "O My Father, if it be possible, let this cup pass from Me." Then the waiting disciples heard Him say, "Nevertheless not as I will, but as You will."

Jesus continued to pray and while the three waited, their eyes grew heavy for it had been a long day for them. When the Master returned after a little while, He found all three asleep.

"Could you not watch with Me one hour?" He asked reproachfully. "Watch and pray, that you do not enter into temptation. The spirit indeed is willing, but the flesh is weak."

He went a little deeper into the garden alone to pray once again and this time the disciples heard Him say, "O My Father, if this cup may not pass away from Me unless I drink it, Your will be done."

Peter, James, and John were again asleep by the time Jesus returned to them. He did not wake them but went back to pray once more and after a few moments returned and roused them.

"The hour is at hand when the Son of Man is betrayed into the hands of sinners," He told them. "Rise, let us be going. Behold," He said, "he is at hand who betrays Me."

Still half asleep, Peter and the other two hardly understood Him. But now from the direction of the gate where the other eight disciples waited came a sudden sharp challenge and the sound of feet running through the trees and much shouting. Wide-awake now, they could see the light of torches coming toward them up the slope through the garden and hear the clank of weapons and the tread of many feet. The three looked at each other in consternation and sudden fear. The presence of soldiers here could have but one meaning. Caiaphas had sent them to take Jesus prisoner.

V

John Mark was panting and his body was drenched with sweat. He had hardly noticed the strains of the hallel floating over the city, and when he reached his home he ran up the outside stairway to the upper chamber without stopping. When he stepped inside, however, he found that only his mother and several of the neighboring women were there, busy putting the remainder of the food away and cleaning up after the supper.

Mary looked up in surprise when Mark burst into the room. "I looked for you beside the sycamore tree just now, Mark," she said. "Did you go with Jesus and the others to Gethsemane?"

"I was following Judas," Mark gasped. "To the palace of the high priest. Where is the Master?"

"They sang the hymn here together and then left for the garden on the Mount of Olives. Jesus went there to pray before going on to Bethany."

"Judas knew the Master was going to the garden!" Mark said. "He has betrayed Jesus to the high priest so the guards can arrest Him!"

Mary caught her breath. "Are you sure, son?"

"I heard him tell Abiathar he could take Jesus in the Garden of Gethsemane because only a few would be with Him. I must go and warn the Master!"

"Your robe is wet with sweat," Mary protested, her first concern for her son. "You will be chilled by the night air!"

"I must go, mother!" Mark insisted. "If I can get to the garden first, they may be able to flee to Bethany. Or at least we will have time to arouse some of the Galileans camped on the Mount of Olives."

Mary hurried to a closet and took out a length of linen cloth. "Wrap this dry cloth around you then and leave the robe here," she said. "And be careful, Mark!"

For already the boy was gone, wrapping the length of cloth about him like a Roman toga as he ran.

The cooking fires on the slopes of the Mount of Olives, where those camped there had roasted the paschal lamb before their tents that afternoon were dying away now and in the darkness only an occasional glow showed where they had been. The moon was hidden behind a cloud, and Mark, as he ran through the streets, stumbled more than once and fell several times, for he was almost exhausted. Each time, conscious that every moment counted, he pulled himself to his feet and kept on going.

At the city gate, he was forced to stop, for the column of guards with Abiathar and Judas in the lead was just then passing through on the way to the Garden of Gethsemane. He darted through the gate after the guards, hoping to pass them and still reach the garden in time to warn Jesus. But one of the soldiers saw what he was trying to do. Thrusting out the handle of his spear, he tripped Mark and the youth fell to the ground, half stunned.

"You'll not warn the Nazarene of our coming, boy," the guard called to him as he passed with the others.

Painfully, Mark stumbled to his feet. The column had passed him now and he had no choice except to fall in behind it.

Up the slope the guards marched. At the gate of the Garden of Gethsemane a little knot of men had gathered. Mark recognized a number of Jesus' disciples and for a moment he thought they were going to resist the passage of the guards. But when Abiathar drew his sword and a dozen men behind him bared their spears, the little group melted into the darkness.

There was no sign of Jesus or Simon Peter and Mark hoped, as the column of guards marched through the gate, that they might somehow have been warned and made their escape. But then in the light of the torches borne by those at the head of the column, he saw them standing a little way inside the garden itself. Jesus was in front, as if He were protecting the others, with Simon Peter just behind Him and James and John a pace farther back. There was no sign of fear in Jesus' eyes or in His manner as the column on an order from Abiathar divided to surround Him.

Mark saw Abiathar turn to Judas and speak but could not hear what was said. He could see that Judas hesitated, however, but when Abiathar growled again, the betrayer stepped forward and, pretending to embrace Jesus, said, "Master," and kissed Him.

Immediately—for Judas's act had been the signal—the guards moved forward and seized Jesus. James and John had drawn back before the naked swords in the hands of the soldiers, but Simon Peter stepped forward. Mark, to his surprise, saw that Peter was bolding a sword. With an awkward movement the disciple slashed out at one of the guards who was holding Jesus by the arm. The man parried the blow easily, however, and Peter succeeded only in slicing the ear of one of the bystanders. A blow from another soldier's sword knocked the weapon from Peter's hand, and when he saw the blade thrusting forward to cut him down, the tall disciple turned and, as the others had done, ran away among the trees into the darkness.

"Have you come out as against a thief with swords and staves to take Me?" Jesus demanded scathingly of His captors. "I was with you daily in the temple teaching and you did not take Me." Then Mark heard Him say almost as an afterthought, "But the Scriptures must be fulfilled."

Jesus was standing alone, all the disciples having been driven away by the weapons of the guards. The one who had tripped Mark on the road saw him and called out, "The boy here tried to bring word of our coming. He must be one of them."

At the cry one of the guards seized the linen cloth Mark had wrapped about his body but, stricken with terror, the boy twisted himself free and fled in nothing but his loin cloth, leaving the linen garment behind.

The underbrush tore at Mark's body as he stumbled through the grove, driven by a fear greater than he had ever known. When the absence of any sound behind him assured him that he was not being pursued, he slowed to a walk and tried to think clearly. He saw now that he was not far from the wall surrounding the garden, and going to it, climbed on the rocks so that he could see the slope below him and the path that led from the garden to the city. As he watched, he saw a man plunge down the path, running and stumbling as if he were pursued by a thousand demons, although there was no one following. For a moment Mark dared hope Jesus had somehow broken away from His captors. But as the bend in the path brought the man only a few paces from where Mark stood on the wall, he recognized Judas of Kerioth.

For a moment the face of the man who had betrayed Jesus was revealed in the light of the moon which had now come from behind the clouds. And at the utter terror mirrored there, Mark could not keep back a cry of astonishment. Only one certain of destruction, Mark sensed, would be in the grip of such fear. Judas of Kerioth had realized, too late, that he who betrayed the Son of God could not escape retribution.

The clank of military gear warned Mark that Abiathar and the guards were leaving the garden, and he drew back along the wall into the shadow of a tall tree. Slowly the column came into sight, two lines of soldiers with Jesus walking in their midst, His hands secured by fetters and naked spears menacing Him on every side. The youth was sick with shame that he had run away, for he saw that Jesus was now entirely deserted.

When the procession had disappeared down the road leading to Jerusalem, Mark climbed down from the wall and made his way back along the path toward the center of the garden. So far as he had been able to tell, his linen garment had not been carried away by any of the guards. He hoped it might have fallen to the ground and still be in the garden, for he was already shivering in the chill night air.

The place was empty now and Mark found the cloth lying where it had been torn from him. Grateful for its warmth, he wrapped it about his shaking body and started down the path again in the wake of those who had taken Jesus prisoner. Near the gate, he heard crashing sounds in the underbrush and drew back quickly from the road, thinking that some of the guards might have been left behind to look for Jesus' disciples. But when a tall figure stumbled from the trees into the road and stood looking about him dumbly, Mark gave a cry of recognition. It was Simon Peter.

"Simon!" Mark called.

The big man stiffened and started to lumber toward the underbrush beside the road, but Mark ran out into the open where he could be seen. "It is John Mark!" he called. "Your friend!"

The disciple seemed in a daze, but Mark's words and familiar voice finally penetrated his mind. Slowly he turned and the youth saw that, in addition to the wounds from brambles on his cheeks and arms, Peter's face was ravaged by suffering and shame.

Sensing that Peter had been driven almost out of his mind by the shock of what had just happened, Mark approached him slowly. "You know me, Peter," he said. "It is John Mark."

"Mark." Peter looked at him dazedly. "Where is the Master?"

"Abiathar has taken Him prisoner. Judas betrayed Him."

"But Jesus gave Judas the sop."

"I heard Judas tell Abiathar that Jesus would be in the garden here with only a few of you."

"Where have they taken Him?"

"To the palace of the high priest, I think," Mark said. "The guards came from there."

Peter seemed not to understand. Mark took him by the hand. "Let us go to the palace, Peter," he said. "Maybe we can help Jesus."

The words seemed to penetrate the shocked mind at last. "Yes. Yes, we must help Jesus," he said almost mechanically.

"This is the way," Mark said, starting to lead the tall fisherman down the path. "I will take you there."

And so the two of them, the boy and the man who both had tried to help Jesus, together left the garden the Master had loved.

VI

For the mockery that was to be called a trial, Jesus was first taken to the Palace of Annas, the former high priest who was still the most influential figure in the priestly hierarchy. Annas had held the high priesthood himself for only six or seven years, but had managed afterward to have several of his sons, as well as his son-in-law, Caiaphas, succeed him. By dexterously using the vast temple revenues to further his power, as when Pontius Pilate had been allowed to use temple funds for the great aqueduct, Annas had managed to keep himself and his family on good terms with the Romans and had thus kept the highest religious office under his control. He did not now intend to allow Caiaphas, who sometimes failed to reason before acting, to bungle the matter of Jesus' death, and had ordered the Nazarene to be brought to him as soon as He was taken.

Annas first asked the prisoner to implicate His disciples, thinking Jesus might seek to save Himself and incriminate others, thus making the charges which were to be leveled against Him even heavier. But Jesus refused to answer any questions about the disciples even though they had all fled when He was betrayed by Judas and then had been taken. So the old high priest switched to matters of doctrine, where the chief charges against Jesus lay.

"Why do you ask Me?" Jesus answered him. "I spoke openly to the world and always taught in the synagogue or in the temple, where the Jews go. I have said nothing in secret. Ask them who heard Me. They know what I said."

At His words, Abiathar struck Jesus across the mouth with his fist, almost knocking Him to the ground. "Do you answer the high priest so?" the captain demanded indignantly.

A trickle of blood flowed from Jesus' lip where the captain's fist had driven the flesh against a tooth, but He did not falter or cringe.

"If I have spoken evil, bear witness of the evil," He challenged Abiathar. "But if I have spoken well, why do you strike Me?"

They continued the questioning but realizing at last that it was futile, they took Him to the palace of Caiaphas where the Priestly Council had been waiting since the end of the Passover to pass judgment upon Him.

With Jesus now in his hands, Caiaphas ordered Abiathar to let the

Roman soldiers who had aided in the arrest return to the Antonia. Until it was time to ask Pilate's approval of the death sentence, he meant this to remain a strictly Jewish matter. The fewer Romans involved, the better.

Abiathar and several guards took Jesus into the inner court of Caiaphas's palace. The rest remained outside where Jonas and some others were warming themselves by the fire. Jonas had been startled to see Jesus a prisoner, but the connection between the green thorns he had gathered that afternoon and what was happening here did not occur to him.

As on the other occasions when he had condemned Jesus and sought a way to capture Him, Caiaphas had been careful not to invite Nicodemus and Joseph of Arimathea to the Priestly Council, sometimes called the Lesser Sanhedrin. It was only the inner circle, who had long ago decided that Jesus must die, who were waiting. Jesus was now brought before them by Abiathar and left standing alone in the center of the audience chamber.

Caiaphas, Jochai, Elam, Annas, and several of the chief priests, scribes, and Pharisees were seated behind the long table. They could not have claimed to constitute a legal meeting of the Sanhedrin, though all were members of the high court. Their only purpose here was to give a semblance of legality to what had already been decided, so that there would be no trouble when they brought Jesus before Pilate and asked for His death.

For this preliminary hearing, Caiaphas had prepared carefully. A number of witnesses had been brought in and coached to swear they had heard Jesus speak blasphemy. But now, before the pitying look in Jesus' eyes as they perjured themselves, the witnesses began to stumble in their carefully rehearsed stories and contradict each other. Some claimed to have heard one thing, some another, and Caiaphas was white with fury before he finally managed to get three of them to agree on the same story, that Jesus had blasphemed against the temple by saying He would destroy it and build another within three days. The charge was flimsy enough, and Caiaphas realized now how badly his case might go if he went to the Romans with so makeshift a body of evidence and Pontius Pilate examined it at all closely.

Finally, in exasperation, the high priest addressed Jesus. "Do You answer nothing?" he demanded. "What is it these men witness against You?"

The confusion of the witnesses had already proved that Caiaphas had no real case, but Jesus did not point that out. When He did not answer, the furious high priest shouted, "Are you the Christ, the Son of the Blessed?"

For the first time since He had been arraigned before the Priestly Council, Jesus spoke. "I am," He said calmly. "And you shall see the Son of Man sitting on the right hand of power and coming in the clouds of heaven."

"What need do we have for further witnesses?" Caiaphas exclaimed triumphantly, and tore his robe in the conventional gesture of indignation. "You have all heard blasphemy. What do you think?"

Like puppets the Council gave the prepared answer. "He is guilty of death."

Jesus showed no visible reaction to the verdict, but continued to stand before His accusers, observing them with a look of compassion on His face as if He pitied them for their part in this scurrilous travesty of a legal trial. Before that gaze, some of them began to fidget, but at a signal from Caiaphas, Abiathar and the guards struck Jesus again and spat upon Him. Then, as if to find a relief from their own shame and guilt at what they had done, the members of the Council also began to vilify Him.

Even before Caesarea-Philippi, Jesus had predicted this very scene with the words, "The Son of Man shall be delivered to the chief priests and to the scribes, and they shall condemn Him to death."

One part only of that prophecy remained yet to be fulfilled, the phrase "And shall deliver Him to the Gentiles."

That, according to Caiaphas's plan, was the next thing to be done.

VII

Jesus had already been taken into the palace of Caiaphas when Mark and Peter arrived. A crowd was beginning to gather outside the gate of the courtyard and, knowing the city as he did, Mark noticed that it consisted largely of beggars and other rabble, with a sprinkling of merchants and artisans, including money-changers and sellers from the temple. They were making little noise. In fact they appeared to be waiting, as if for a signal.

Peter still seemed to be in a trance and did not resist when Mark led him to the opening in the hedge through which he had watched Judas betray Jesus to Abiathar. By creeping through the hedge, they, and a few others who had pushed their way through the gate, were able to enter the outer courtyard where the guards waited around the fire for the deliberation of the Council to be made known. It was a cold night and as they approached the fire to warm themselves, a servant girl from the palace who had been talking to one of the guards came to Peter and looked up into his face.

"You were with Jesus of Galilee!" she cried accusingly.

Peter drew back sharply, and only Mark's hand on his arm kept him from bolting with the same overpowering surge of fear he had experienced when the guard had disarmed him in the garden. A deep-seated terror took control of him for a moment, driving out all sense of loyalty and duty.

"I know not what you say!" he shouted loudly and drew back into the shadows of the porch where his size would not make him so conspicuous.

Another of the high priest's servants saw Peter there a few minutes later and, thinking to curry favor with her master by denouncing one of those close to Jesus, cried, "This fellow was also with Jesus of Nazareth!"

"I do not know the man!" Peter shouted, half out of his mind, not only with fear for himself but also from the sorrow and bitter disappointment that the man he had believed to be the Son of God had failed to use divine power for His protection.

The violence of Peter's denial drove the girl away, and he continued to sit in the shadows, with Mark beside him, shivering in the cool night air but not daring to approach the fire where someone else might recognize him. In spite of his shock and his bitter disappointment that Jesus had allowed Himself to be taken, there still burned in Peter the faint hope that at the last moment the Master would smite His enemies with the sword of God, not ineffectually as Peter had tried to do in the Garden of Gethsemane, but with the power that had raised Lazarus from the dead and had fed the five thousand on the shores of Galilee.

The courtyard was becoming crowded now, as more and more of the crowd outside pushed their way through the gates. A money-changer from the temple, eager for a chance to belittle any who followed Jesus, saw Peter in the shadows and, sure that he recognized him because of his size, came up to question him.

Peter answered only in monosyllables, but it was impossible to hide the rough accent of Galilee in his speech.

"Surely you are one of them," the money-changer said. "Your speech betrays you."

"I know not the man!" Peter shouted with a curse and shambled from the courtyard with Mark at his side. Hands reached out to seize him, but with his great strength he put them off. Cursing his tormentors, he reached the street and continued on until he was beyond the edge of the crowd massed now at the gate, waiting for the decision of the Council to be announced.

Only when the voices of his tormentors no longer pounded in his ears did Peter become conscious of another sound, the distant crowing of a cock announcing the first rays of dawn. And as if the words were being spoken in his ear once again, he heard the voice of Jesus saying, "Before the cock crows this night, you shall deny Me three times."

Shame and guilt engulfed Simon Peter now and great sobs shook his body. He wept, not so much for the Master he loved, who was a prisoner waiting sentence, as in thought of the rock of strength he could have been to Jesus had he not yielded to the fear for his own safety. Distraught and sobbing, Peter hardly realized that John Mark was taking his hand and leading him away from the palace of the high priest toward his own home in whose upper chamber Peter himself had that night eaten the last supper with Jesus.

VIII

As he watched Jesus being led in chains into the palace of the high priest, Jonas could not help comparing the Nazarene's present estate with that less than a week ago when He had entered Jerusalem in triumph. In spite of the misery which the past week had brought him, the hunchback felt only sorrow for the Nazarene. Strangely enough, now that he had seen the Teacher closely, he could not shake off the feeling that somewhere he had known Jesus before, although he had no memory of the exact circumstances.

It was unfortunate that the Galilean prophet had tried to oppose Caiaphas and the priests, Jonas thought sadly. Unless, of course, He was the Messiah—and that was impossible. No Jew would dare treat the Anointed

One as Jesus was being treated for he would surely know that the wrath of God would destroy anyone committing such a blasphemous act. But even the best men, Jonas knew, could hardly hope to oppose such powerful adversaries as the chief priests and the Romans. And Jesus was a man.

Jonas had heard Simon Peter deny that he knew Jesus, but he had not blamed him. The Galilean's was a lost cause, and nothing could be gained now by His disciples destroying themselves with Him. Peter had been only acting wisely, Jonas thought, in denying any connection with his former master.

The night was cold and, small as he was, Jonas had gradually been pushed away from the fire as the crowd filled the courtyard. He wished Abiathar would come out soon and pay him the other shekel so that he could go back to his hovel and sleep. He could not afford to lose the coin, for there would be no thorn-gathering on the day after the Passover and the next day being the Sabbath, he would lose two days of work. Even the two shekels he had earned would barely buy food for Eleazar and himself over that period.

The sun had already risen when the door to the inner court of the palace swung open and Abiathar came out. Pushed from the fire by the crowd, Jonas had been working his way gradually toward the porch and the door leading to it. When Abiathar opened it, he was only a few paces away.

"Abiathar," he called, his teeth chattering from the cold. "I brought the thorns. Where is my shekel?"

"Don't bother me, woodseller," the captain said impatiently. "I will give it to you later." He strode to the gate of the courtyard and looked over it at the crowd that had been gathering there. At the sight of him a shrill voice among them cried, "Death to the Galilean blasphemer!"

With a start, Jonas recognized the voice. It was Zadok's.

Hearing the cripple call out and seeing the way the rabble pressing against the gate seemed to be looking to Abiathar for instructions, Jonas was sure now that he was watching something already rehearsed. For how else would the crowd know what charge was being made against Jesus when none of them had been inside the court?

"Be still!" Abiathar ordered, and at once the tumult that had begun to rise subsided. "There will be time enough for that."

"You've kept us waiting overlong, Abiathar," a man in the crowd called. "When do we condemn the Nazarene?"

"Hold your tongue!" Abiathar shouted. Turning, he strode back to the porch and threw open the door to the inner court. Jonas could see Jesus now, with the blood congealed upon His cheek from the cut in His lip. He stood straight and silent before the Council and the guards while they spat at Him and reviled Him. Once again the hunchback was seized with the conviction that he had known the Nazarene a long time ago. If he had not needed the other shekel so urgently, he would have left at once. He wanted no part of this attack upon a man of whom he had never heard evil spoken, except by those whose sins He had attacked so forthrightly.

Two guards came out, leading Jesus between them; He stumbled a little as they jerked Him along by His bound hands. Even in degradation, with spittle upon His face and His robe, the Nazarene had an oddly royal dignity about Him, and when He first appeared, the crowd waiting in the courtyard and outside the gate fell back and for a moment was silent.

Then Zadok's shrill voice cried, "Blasphemer! He blasphemed against the temple!" Others took up the cry again, it seemed to Jonas, as if by signal. A great tumult and shouting eddied about Jesus and the guards as He was taken from the courtyard.

"'Where are they going?" someone shouted at the guards. "To Golgotha?"

The "place of skulls," Golgotha, so-called for the shape of the rock formation there, served as the scene of executions for the city, required by Mosaic Law to be outside its walls. Here those convicted of any capital offense were either stoned to death or crucified according to Roman custom.

"That will come later," the guards called back in answer to the question. "You know the Law; only the Sanhedrin can pass sentence of death."

Jonas understood where Jesus was being taken now: to the house of the Sanhedrin located by the sanctuary area. The sun had already risen over the hills toward Jericho so that it was fully light, and as Jonas looked out over the crowd, he was not surprised to catch sight of Zadok swinging along in their midst, dragging his body expertly between his arms while he chattered steadily to those around him.

Moving through the crowd, Jonas came up beside the cripple. "What brings you here?" he demanded. "You are supposed to be sick."

Zadok still looked a little pale and there was sweat on his forehead. "I wish you had brought Eleazar," he said.

"You have no business here at all," Jonas told him severely.

Zadok grimaced. "Would you have me give up my location to another beggar?"

Jonas knew that Abiathar assigned places in the proximity of the temple, the area where the beggars were most likely to receive the largest alms. In return, the favored ones shared a part of their gain with the burly temple captain. The arrangement was no more reprehensible than that by which the sellers in the temple sold tickets for only the choicest lambs and then delivered an animal of lesser quality to the altar, dividing the profit with the priests.

"Why would Abiathar take your place away?"

"Word went out last night to the beggars and others who profit from the temple that Abiathar wanted us here this morning to shout against the Nazarene," Zadok explained. "He is paying me extra to call for the prisoner's death."

"But that is unjust!"

Zadok shrugged. "Caiaphas wants it done. That's all the justice you need in Jerusalem. Call for the Nazarene's death when the time comes, Jonas, and I will put in a good word for you with Abiathar."

Jonas shook his head. "The Galilean is a good man. I wish Him no harm."

"Neither do I," said Zadok matter-of-factly. "But I have to live and since Caiaphas means to destroy Him anyway, it's no harm to do as Abiathar wishes."

"Why does he need you to shout against the Galilean?" Jonas asked. "After all, the Sanhedrin can sentence Him."

"The Nazarene cannot be executed unless Pontius Pilate approves the sentence," Zadok reminded him. "Caiaphas cannot have much of a case against Him, but if Pilate believes the people are stirred up against the Nazarene, he will be easy to convince. After all, what is one dead Galilean to a Roman governor if he can serve to prevent a riot? With enough of us who have something to gain from it shouting for the Galilean's death, how will Pilate know that most of the people believe Him to be a prophet?"

Zadok's explanation was so logical that Jonas could find no flaw in it. But he could still feel sorry for the prisoner and be glad he was going to have no part himself in the death and degradation of this innocent man.

Crucify Him! Crucify Him!

John 19:6

One thing remained before Caiaphas and the Priestly Council could demand that Pilate put Jesus to death. The formal sentence of the Sanhedrin had to be passed upon Him once again, and for this purpose something resembling a meeting of the whole court had to be held. By arranging it for early in the morning and sending out notices only a short time before, Caiaphas had insured that most of the members who attended the meeting of the court would be those who, like himself, wished to see Jesus destroyed.

Consisting legally of seventy-one members, although the number was less than that from time to time, the Great Sanhedrin ordinarily met in the building just outside the sanctuary area reserved for it. Since only twenty-three members were required to constitute a quorum, Caiaphas had experienced little difficulty in summoning mainly those whom he could be sure would vote as he wished.

Jesus came before the judicial group shortly after the sun had risen. He had been reviled, spit upon, and struck repeatedly. The blood from some of the wounds caused by this maltreatment showed on His face and body. Yet none of it had been able to destroy the regal bearing which had characterized Him from the moment when He had faced His captors in the Garden of Gethsemane. Now, as He was brought before those who could sentence Him to death, there was no sign of subservience or pleading in His manner. Instead, the look in His eyes was still one of compassion, compassion for these men who, in order to destroy Him, were prostituting the function of the most noble court in all of Israel.

Caiaphas took charge of this hearing as he had the meeting of the

Priestly Council in his palace. He was determined that nothing would be introduced which might prevent the carrying out of his plan for destroying Jesus.

"Are You the Christ? Tell us," he demanded contemptuously.

Jesus broke the silence which had characterized Him during most of the arraignment so far.

"If I tell you, you will not believe Me," He said quietly. "If I also ask you, you will not answer Me, nor let Me go. Hereafter the Son of Man shall sit on the right hand of the power of God."

"Are you then the Son of God?" one of the judges asked Him.

"You say that I am," Jesus answered.

"What need do we have of any further witnesses?" Elam demanded from his seat near the center of the half-circle occupied by the members of the court. "We ourselves have heard from His own mouth."

The taking of the vote was simply a formality. It was quickly done and Abiathar, at Caiaphas's order, led Jesus from the house of the Sanhedrin to present Him to Pontius Pilate for approval of the death sentence.

II

To the camp of the Galileans on the slope of the Mount of Olives overlooking Jerusalem, and to those of Jesus' followers who had waited in Bethany for His return after eating the Passover in the city, word of the Master's arrest in Jerusalem and His condemnation by the Sanhedrin came shortly. Mary of Magdala had been looking after the mother of Jesus and she now undertook the sorrowful task of taking Mary of Nazareth into Jerusalem in the vain hope that she might be able to plead with the authorities for the release of her son.

They set out at once, but could make only slow progress; word of the dramatic events that had taken place during the night had already sped through the countryside around Jerusalem and people were beginning to move toward the city in great numbers. Many were saddened by the arrest of one they had come to respect and love as a great Teacher, if not as the Son of God. Others were drawn only by the excitement and the prospect of that most thrilling of public events, an execution.

On any other occasion, Mary Magdalene would have been happy at the natural beauty all around her as she hurried with the mother of Jesus along the road leading to the city. The hillsides were already beginning to break out in a riot of color from the spring flowers that would soon be completely covering them. Daffodils were already in bloom, with here and there clumps of sea-leek as well as the star-shaped blossom of the "flower of Sharon." Now and then a cluster of "cuckoo flowers" could be seen, making against the white and green a splash of lilac. The burnt thorn grew everywhere, but only an occasional clump as yet showed its tiny bloodlike blossoms.

Many of the pilgrims who had come to Jerusalem for the festival were already folding their tents preparing to leave. With luck they could reach Bethabara and the caravansary at the ford of the Jordan that day and spend the Sabbath there on the next. Only black coals where the paschal lambs had been roasted the afternoon before and the litter that accumulates around a campground remained to show where those who had already departed had spent the days of the festival.

Many of the tents had still not been struck, however, for the news from Jerusalem was more exciting than the festival had been. People were hurrying from the camps and filling the road into the city, shouting eagerly as they walked. Mary, in her eagerness to learn what had happened to Jesus, would have liked to go faster, but His mother was not so young as she, and their pace was slow. Besides, something had blocked the traffic between Bethphage and Jerusalem and there the flow of people had slowed almost to a halt. The two Marys were not able to see the cause until they rounded a curve in the road. The line of travelers was being diverted from the path around an olive tree whose branches overhung the roadway there. Swinging from one of the limbs with his girdle tight about his neck was the body of a man who had obviously hanged himself.

Mary did not need a second look to recognize Judas of Kerioth.

The Jews traveling into the city shunned the body, making a wide half-circle around it. Mary could see at a glance that Judas was beyond help; his protruding tongue and eyes, the bluish pallor of his skin, the complete absence of movement in his body as it swung on the tree—all these indicated death some time before.

Anyone could see what had happened. A tall rock stood beside the road, and Judas had obviously stood upon it while tying one end of the girdle to the limb and the other around his neck before stepping off. He had slowly suffocated from strangulation, kicking and jerking while his body turned and turned again upon the improvised gibbet.

A small knot of people stood to one side looking at the body. As she passed, Mary recognized Simon Zelotes who, alone among the disciples, had been a close friend of Judas Iscariot. The Zealot's face was drawn and his eyes were haunted with fear.

"Simon," Mary called to him and Zelotes turned like a hunted thing that hears an unexpected sound, ready to flee.

"It is Mary of Magdala, Simon," she called. "The mother of our Lord is with me."

People were staring now and Simon came to them rather reluctantly as they stood with Joanna the wife of Chuza, Salome the mother of James and John, and several others.

"What has happened to Jesus, Simon?" Mary asked.

The Zealot spoke rapidly and in a low voice, looking about him nervously all the while. "Judas betrayed Him to the high priest. For thirty pieces of silver."

Mary caught her breath. "Then Jesus has really been arrested?"

"And condemned by the Sanhedrin."

A sob broke from Mary of Nazareth. "Did no one defend Him?" Mary Magdalene asked.

"Peter tried, but was disarmed. We were all driven away by the swords of the guards and forced to flee."

As clearly as when He had spoken of it only a few days before, Mary remembered how Jesus had prophesied His death in Jerusalem, foretelling it exactly as it was happening now.

"Where is the Master?" Mary asked.

"For fear of being recognized, I could not get closer to where they have Him," Simon answered. "Someone said the temple guards were taking Him to the Antonia—to Pontius Pilate."

Mary looked up at the body of Judas still hanging from the limb. She had never liked the man of Kerioth. He had been moody, given to sharp words and bursts of anger when he did not get his way. But she could feel no hate for him now, even for what he had done to Jesus. Perhaps alone among the close followers of the Master, she understood that this thing had to be done, she could not have said exactly why; it was a part of God's plan for bringing to pass His kingdom on earth.

"What of him?" Mary inquired of Simon, indicating the dangling body.

"I will cut him down later," Simon said, "after the crowds have passed. He was paid thirty pieces of silver for betraying Jesus, but I heard in Jerusalem that he took it to the temple early this morning and gave it to the priest as a gift."

Mary took some coins from her purse. "See that his body is buried somewhere," she said. "If you need more money, I will give it to you."

"God will bless you, Mary," Simon said humbly. "A man who came from Jerusalem just now said the priests are going to buy the potters' field with the thirty pieces of silver Judas gave them. If so, he could be buried there."

III

Pontius Pilate had not been pleased when he was notified that the Sanhedrin was sending him a prisoner for confirmation of death sentence. So far the Passover had been uneventful. As usual he had assigned two dozen legionnaires to Caiaphas to help keep order. But from what Pelonius, the centurion in charge of the troops assigned to the Antonia, told him, Caiaphas had used the Roman troops to arrest the Nazarene prophet. Pilate did not doubt that this was the person who was now being sent to him for sentence.

At any other time Pilate would have approved the sentence of the Sanhedrin with hardly a glance at the condemned man, since in Judea Rome customarily left the handling of religious affairs to the Jewish court. But irritated at Caiaphas for using the Roman troops to arrest one of his own people on a religious charge, Pilate was determined to look into the matter further. He had thought the high priest had learned his lesson when the Galileans led by Barabbas had been killed on the floor of the temple recently; now it seemed that the haughty son-in-law of Annas needed a further reminder that Rome ruled here.

The sound of voices shouting outside the paved praetorium in front of the Antonia warned Pilate of the arrival of the prisoner, even before the centurion Pelonius came to tell him of it. The Jews would not come into the Antonia itself, since to enter a heathen building would cause them defilement at this, one of their holiest times. Pilate let them wait until he had finished breakfast. Only then did he show himself upon the elevated terrace overlooking the courtyard.

Pelonius was an old hand at handling this sort of situation. Pilate noted with approval that he had drawn up his troops on either side of the court with weapons ready in case there was trouble. The crowd had surged to the gate of the court, and from their midst Abiathar and another guard now emerged, dragging between them the slender form of the Nazarene. It was the first time Pilate had seen Jesus since the afternoon they had both arrived simultaneously from Jericho. He was surprised now by the courage evident in Jesus' manner and the lack of any fear in His eyes.

Behind Jesus and His guards, Elam and several of the leaders of the Sanhedrin, including some of the chief priests, approached Pilate to present the case of the high court against the prisoner. They were careful, however, not to come close enough for the shadow of the covered terrace to fall upon them and defile them.

"Free the prisoner and step back," Pelonius commanded Abiathar curtly. Jesus had been brought to the foot of the steps leading to the terrace where Pontius Pilate stood with a lictor bearing behind him the fasces of authority signifying that this was actually a court of law.

"What accusations do you bring against this man?" Pilate demanded coldly of the Sanhedrists.

"If He were not a malefactor," Elam said unctuously, "we would not have delivered Him to you."

"Take Him and judge Him according to your Law then," Pilate said sharply.

"It is not lawful for us to put any man to death," Elam protested.

Pilate stepped back and motioned for Jesus to come closer. "Are you the king of the Jews?" he inquired.

"Do you say this of yourself," Jesus asked gravely, "or did others tell it to you concerning Me?"

Pilate was pleased by the question. He was no groveling wretch, certain of death and begging for His life, but a man who held Himself proudly and spoke without fear. "Am I a Jew?" Pilate asked. "Your own nation and the chief priests have delivered You to me. What have You done?"

"My kingdom is not of this world," Jesus said quietly. "If My kingdom were of this world, then My servants would fight so that I should not be delivered to the Jews."

"Are you a king then?" Pilate inquired.

"You say that I am a king," Jesus said. "To this end I was born and came into the world, that I should bear witness to the truth."

"What is truth?" Pilate said with a shrug, and turned to address Elam and the Sanhedrists who stood some distance away, still carefully avoiding the shadow of the building.

"I find no fault at all in Him," the governor announced.

Abiathar was watching. At the words, he gave a signal to the crowd which pressed against the gates, and immediately, as planned, they set up a howl of indignation.

Caiaphas had not accompanied Elam and the others. It was not in keeping with his high office to demand personally the death of any man. He had foreseen the possibility that Pontius Pilate might hesitate, however, and by having the crowd protest against the procurator's decision if it went against that of the Sanhedrin, he hoped to remind Pilate of what a disturbance here in Jerusalem over the Nazarene could mean.

Pilate hesitated, but before Elam could break into the tirade that was upon his tongue, the centurion Pelonius, standing behind Pilate, said, "This man is a Galilean, sir. And the tetrarch Herod is still in Jerusalem."

Pilate's face cleared. Here was a way out; let Herod take the blame since the Nazarene was a subject of his.

"Take Him to Herod," he ordered. "A man should be judged by His own ruler."

IV

As a sop to the religious sensitivity of the Jews living in his tetrarchy, Herod Antipas usually came to Jerusalem for the Passover. He was not devout himself; in fact, like his father before him, Herod was a Jew by adoption and had assumed only a thin veneer of Jewish faith. But he was ambitious and had hopes of one day adding Judea and the enormous tax revenue of Jerusalem to his domain. For that reason, it was expedient to show himself here at this time and pretend to a certain amount of piety.

Herod had been relieved that morning when word came that

Caiaphas had arrested the Nazarene Teacher who had stirred up Galilee not so long before. Of late he had no trouble from Jesus, but most of the time the Nazarene had remained in the domain of his brother Philip. Herod would still be pleased to hear of His destruction, however, and since the Nazarene had many followers it was best that the blame for His death should fall upon the high priest and Pontius Pilate, so that Herod could claim his own hands were clean.

Herod was dismayed when word was brought by one of the servants that Pilate had sent Jesus of Nazareth under guard to the palace of the Hasmoneans for Herod to judge. But he did not let himself be troubled long. This fellow was reputed to perform miracles; He would no doubt, Herod told himself, be eager to do everything He could to impress the tetrarch of Galilee in the hope of gaining favor and perhaps a lighter sentence.

Herod sent his servants around the palace to gather his guests into the audience chamber to which he now ordered Jesus brought. Elam and the priests who would present the charges of the Sanhedrin against Jesus were admitted to the room. And as soon as Herod entered, Elam began to deliver a tirade of false charges against Jesus. The tetrarch listened a while and then raised his hand for silence.

"What do You say to these charges?" he demanded of Jesus, who had not yet spoken.

When Jesus did not answer, Herod frowned with annoyance. He could almost believe the man was pitying him; certainly the Nazarene's manner and His refusal to speak fitted the assumption: But how could a man under sentence of death by the Sanhedrin pity the powerful tetrarch of Galilee?

"Do you not defend Yourself?" Herod demanded angrily. "If these charges are true, You should be stoned—or crucified."

Jesus still did not answer and Herod turned to the chamberlain who stood beside his chair. "Bring me a—" He started to say "whip," but then he stopped and a sly smile stole over his face. "No. The King of the Jews must be properly honored. Bring me a robe of purple. It is not right that a king wear such a garment as He does. And bring sandals for His feet."

The guests realized what Herod had in mind and began to laugh. It had been a long time since Judea had had a king, and the last had been the ill-fated Archelaus. Herod would give them one now and the joke would be on the leading citizens, men like Elam and the other rich Pharisees in the audience chamber who had always fought the ambition of Herod Antipas to rule over the province.

The chamberlain quickly brought a robe of Tyrenian purple which he draped about Jesus' shoulders. Another servant took off the worn sandals and laced on fine leather footgear from Herod's own wardrobe.

"Now you look like a king, Nazarene!" Herod said. "Go back to Pontius Pilate and tell him I have named You King of the Jews."

Elam started to protest, but the tetrarch cut him off. "Neither you nor Pilate shall make me a scapegoat," he said. "You state that this man claims to be King of the Jews, so I have made Him king for you. If you do not want Him, depose Him and get another."

Elam and the other Sanhedrists now had no choice except to bring Jesus back to Pilate and report that Herod had refused to take jurisdiction over Him.

V

By the time Mary Magdalene reached the Antonia with Mary of Nazareth, Jesus had already been taken to the nearby palace of the Hasmoneans for the interview with Herod. Since Mary of Magdala lived in Galilee and was a close friend of many influential members of Herod's court, she decided to go at once to Herod on Jesus' behalf. But before she could arrange for Mary of Nazareth to be cared for by some of the Master's followers in the crowd, word came that Herod had sent the prisoner back to Pontius Pilate.

Shortly Jesus appeared, followed by a jeering crowd and wearing the purple robe which Herod had put upon Him in derision. At the sight of the blood and the bruises on His face where He had been beaten by the guards, Mary Magdalene could not help crying out. She would have run to throw herself at His feet, had not the press of the crowd prevented her.

While Jesus was in the house of the Sanhedrin, Jonas had gone back to his hovel outside the gate to feed Eleazar, and since, if Abiathar paid him the shekel, he might be able to buy grain when the shops opened, he took the old mule back with him. Now, as he led the patient animal through the crowd, he saw the beautiful woman of Galilee standing with tears upon her cheeks and recognized her as the one he had seen in the train of

Jesus when he had waited beside the Jericho road during the Nazarene's triumphant entry into Jerusalem.

Appreciating the irony in Herod's action as a joke upon the high priest, the crowd laughed uproariously when they saw Jesus wearing the purple robe of a king. But Pontius Pilate was annoyed when Jesus was presented to him again with word that Herod had refused to order the Nazarene's death. "You have brought this man to me as one who perverts the people," he told Elam and the Sanhedrists sharply. "I have examined Him before you and found no fault in Him touching the things of which you accuse Him. Neither has Herod. I will therefore chastise Him and release Him."

Elam stepped forward. "Noble Pilate," he said, "we have a custom that on this day, you release one prisoner to us. Will you follow that custom again at this season?"

"Do you wish me to release the King of the Jews?" Pilate asked contemptuously.

"There is Barabbas," Elam reminded him. Since they had returned from the palace of the Hasmoneans, Abiathar had been quietly giving instructions to the rabble pressing against the gate of the praetorium. At the mention of Barabbas's name, the beggars and thieves at the front of the crowd set up a sudden clamor.

"Release Barabbas!" they cried, drowning out those who called for Jesus to be released instead.

Pilate looked at Jesus and was struck once again by His regal bearing in spite of the indignities which had been heaped upon Him. Behind Him, Pilate saw that Claudia Procula had come to the edge of the terrace; she was looking at him with a light of pleading in her eyes and he knew that she was silently begging him to be merciful with the Galilean.

"Take Him and scourge Him," he ordered the centurion Pelonius "Then bring Him back to me."

Turning on his heel, Pilate left the terrace without giving the crowd any indication of what his final decision would be. Calling a servant to bring him wine, he sank down upon a bench and put his head between his hands. But still he heard the cries of the crowd outside, clamoring that Barabbas be the one to be released.

When Pilate felt a familiar soft hand upon his cheek he reached up and pressed Claudia Procula's fingers against his face. "Please have nothing to do with this righteous man, Pontius," she begged. "I suffered much because of Him in a dream."

"I wish this were all a dream," Pilate said fervently. "And that it were over."

"Why didn't you let Him go?"

"If I let the Nazarene go free, Procula, Caiaphas will have the Sanhedrin protest my action to Rome. And you know how much I want to get away from this cursed land."

"Could they make trouble for you because of a just decision?"

Pilate nodded wearily. "In this case, yes. The man was openly named King of the Jews by His followers; many heard them and He did not deny it. Just now He explained to me that He means a spiritual kingdom. But how could I ever convince Tiberius of that?"

"What will you do then?"

"Caiaphas has stirred up a crowd of beggars and thieves to demand the Nazarene's death. I recognized some of them at the gate just now. But there are many in Jerusalem who believe He is a prophet. If I have Him scourged, part of the rabble will be satisfied. Then the rest can demand that He be released instead of Barabbas."

From the open window that gave upon the courtyard, came the shouts of the soldiers as they started to scourge the prisoner. The scourge was a whip with several thongs, each loaded with acorn-shaped balls of lead, sharp pieces of bone, or spikes. Stripped of His clothes, His hands tied to a column or stake with His back bent, the victim was lashed with the flagels by six lictors who plied these instruments of torture almost to the point of the prisoner's death.

Scourging was not a pretty sight, and Claudia Procula drew the curtains across the window to shut away the sound, but not before she saw the plaited lash with its weighted ends fall upon the slender back bared to it, the cruel thongs cutting into the flesh. She gave a soft cry of pain and protest, for she had seen before what scourging could do to a man, shredding the flesh upon his body and, if one of the leaden balls at the end of the lash happened to strike his eyes, sometimes bursting them from their sockets.

No cries came from the victim and no entreaties for mercy. Presently Pilate went to the window and shouted for the scourging to stop and the prisoner to be brought back to the praetorium. Shortly Jesus appeared there again, His face bloody from the wounds inflicted by the lash and the leaden weights. The soldiers had dropped His robe to His waist to scourge Him and had not raised it, so the crowd could see how cruelly lacerated the upper part of His body was from the scourging.

Even the group of hardened thieves and beggars at the gate were silent at what had been done to the prisoner. They knew the same fate would come to any one of them judged guilty of a capital crime before they were put to death. In the silence, Pilate's voice was loud.

"Behold!" he shouted. "I bring Him out to you that you may know I find no fault in Him." With a gesture he indicated Jesus who stood at the foot of the steps leading up to the terrace, still holding Himself proudly in spite of the agony from His many wounds.

"Behold the man!" Pontius Pilate cried again.

The crowd was still silent. Then Elam, realizing that in a moment Pilate might release Jesus and that the Sanhedrin could make no complaint for he had already been cruelly punished, shouted, "Crucify Him! Crucify Him!"

Immediately others took up the cry, and the beggars and the thieves at the gate, knowing that Abiathar would punish them if they did not follow his instructions, added their voices to the din.

"Take Him and crucify Him!" Pilate shouted. "I find no fault in Him."

The Sanhedrists had no intention of allowing Pilate to taunt the crowd into executing Jesus without official Roman approval, however. For that they could themselves be punished during one of the unpredictable moods which often seized the procurator.

"We have a Law!" the Pharisee shouted. "And by our Law He ought to die, because He made Himself the Son of God!"

Pilate turned to Jesus. "Will You not speak to me?" he almost pleaded. "Do you not know I have the power to crucify You or to release You?"

Jesus' lips were swollen, but when the words came they were clear and distinct. "You could have no power against Me," He said, "unless it were given you from above. He that delivered Me to you has the greater sin."

Pilate hesitated, wishing to free Jesus but afraid still of the effect a protest to Rome by the Sanhedrin might have on his career. Elam, watching Pilate and sensing what was in his mind, spoke directly to the harried governor.

"If you let this man go, you are not Caesar's friend," he said. "Whoever makes himself a king speaks against Caesar."

In his heart Pilate believed Jesus innocent, yet if he released Him, a charge would surely be brought by the Jews that he had failed to approve the death sentence for one who sought to be a king in Judea, in itself a capital offense. And that, Pilate knew, would mean the end of his so far distinguished career as a Roman governor.

To a man of Pilate's ambitions there was only one answer. "Shall I crucify your king?" he asked Elam and the other Sanhedrists again.

"We have no king but Caesar," they answered, by their own words committing the ultimate sin of blasphemy according to their Law.

Pilate turned to an aide who stood behind him. "Bring me a basin of water," he said wearily. When it was brought, he washed his hands and dried them on a towel, holding them up for the crowd to see.

"I am innocent of the blood of this just person," he said. "See you to it."

From the crowd came the answering shout, "His blood be on us and on our children."

"Have Barabbas released," Pilate directed Pelonius. "And turn the Nazarene over to them to be crucified."

As Pilate went back into the palace, moving like a man whose shoulders were weighted down by a heavy burden, Abiathar stepped up to Jesus. Placing upon Jesus' head a chaplet plaited from the green thorns that Jonas had brought to the palace of Caiaphas the night before, he drove it down with a blow from a reed which he then thrust into Jesus' hands as a scepter.

"Hail, King of the Jews!" he shouted derisively. As blood started to drip down Jesus' face from the wounds of the thorns, the crowd surged forward to drag Him from the praetorium into the street leading to Golgotha, the place of execution.

In all the tumult, no one heard the cry of grief and pain that was torn from Jonas by Abiathar's act. At last the little hunchback realized why he had been sent to gather the thorns on the hillside yesterday. In his ignorance he had made possible this final degradation of the innocent man who was now being driven out to be killed.

This is Jesus, the King of the Jews.

Matthew 27:37

It was not often that Veronica was able to leave her father's house, for Jonathan, busy with his studies at the scribes' school, was not available to lead her mule and all the others were occupied with their work. Once a year she looked forward to a holiday, a visit to the home of her mother's kinsman, Joseph of Arimathea, with its lovely garden and its beautiful trees and flowers. In Jerusalem no one worked on the day following the Passover celebration, and Veronica had been planning for a long time to make the trip across the city to Joseph's home on that day.

Joseph was rich and Veronica would not have thought of shaming him by visiting his home in anything but her best garments. During the year, she had been saving to buy a head veil like one she had seen in the pack of a merchant who had paused one day to buy some of the small vases she painted with scenes of the Jerusalem area. The veil was of a wonderfully fine fabric, a type of cloth that had been woven for a thousand years in the Phoenician city of Byblos on the sea-coast to the north, a material prized, she had been told, even by the women of Pharaoh's court in Egypt. Of an almost gossamer thinness, the cloth of Byblos shone with a luster of its own.

Ever since she had seen the head veil, Veronica had begun to lay aside whatever money she could to buy one for herself. Only a few weeks ago the merchant had appeared again and had agreed to take what she had saved in partial payment for a length of the cloth, letting her have it then and collecting the rest when he came again. Since that time, Veronica's nimble fingers had been busy whenever she had a free moment, binding the cut edges of the cloth with a fine, even stitching and making the whole into what was, she was sure, the loveliest head veil in all of Jerusalem. Only yesterday, while watching the paschal lamb roasting upon its bed of coals in the courtyard, she had finished the stitching. Now, as she rode out into the bright morning sunlight on the way to visit Joseph of Arimathea, her hair was covered by the veil, the fabric only a little more lustrous than the golden hair.

Veronica tried not to reveal her pride in the lovely veil, for it was not good to be proud of one's possessions when so many others did not have things equally valuable. But this was the first thing of much value that she had ever bought with her own work, and she could not help feeling that the passersby were admiring the beautiful veil, although in truth they were admiring as much her own fresh loveliness.

Veronica's conscience did prick her a little, for she knew many poor people who could have bought food with the money she had paid for the cloth. Still she had also saved for her usual gift to the temple. She and Jonathan had even sacrificed a dove this year in addition to the paschal lamb provided by the family, so she could tell herself she had done what the Law required. The head veil made her happy and she was sure the Most High would not hold it against her if she chose a little happiness when so much of her life had been filled with pain from her crippled leg.

One thing only marred Veronica's happiness, the news that Jesus of Nazareth had been arrested during the night and was even now before Pontius Pilate for sentencing. She knew Pilate's reputation as a ruthless man, but she still dared to hope he would be just and recognize in the Nazarene the qualities of gentleness and kindness to others which she had heard so many people say were the essence of His teachings. It was rumored that Jesus and His followers had sought to make Him king in Judea and overthrow the rule of Rome, but Veronica found that hard to believe. From the glimpse of the Nazarene she had had that day on the road to Jerusalem, He had seemed to be a kind and deeply pious man, not the sort of revolutionary who occasionally stirred up Jerusalem as Barabbas and his followers had done.

The home of Joseph of Arimathea lay at the northern edge of the suburb which had grown up west of the sanctuary area on some rising ground, not far from the traditional place of execution called Golgotha. The Roman term was Calvaria, which had the same meaning, namely, the skull. From their home at the edge of the Tyropean Valley near the great aqueduct, Veronica and Jonathan had to pass through much of the suburb lying between the Place of the Skull and the fortress of Antonia. So it was that their route soon joined that along which Jesus was being driven by the soldiers and the rabble stirred up by Abiathar.

When they came to the way leading to Golgotha, their progress was stopped by a great crowd lining the roadway on both sides, waiting for the procession headed by the condemned man to pass on its way to the place of crucifixion. Since they could go no farther, Jonathan was forced to halt the mule, but, not being able to walk, Veronica remained upon its back. Many people were weeping, but for the most part the crowd was made up of the merely curious, who delighted in anything sensational, even if it were a public execution.

"Jonathan," Veronica begged. "Let us go back. I don't want to see Him."

Jonathan would have obliged his sister, but the press of the crowd around them made it impossible to move, except into the roadway. And this area was kept clear by guards from the temple.

"The crowd is too great," he told Veronica. "We'd never get through now."

Just then a rising clamor of voices warned that the condemned man was approaching, and soon the head of the procession came into view, moving slowly because the crowd pressed in on both sides, eager to get a close look at the doomed man who wore a crown of thorns upon His head.

First came a dozen Roman legionnaires, clearing a way through the crowd with the butts of their spears. Behind them Jesus staggered, carrying upon His back the heavy crossbeam, called the patibulum, to which His arms would be nailed.

Crucifixion was the most horrible form of death, not simply because of the immediate pain but because the condemned man would hang upon the Cross sometimes for days before he died from exposure or loss of blood. Originally devised centuries before by Egyptians as a punishment for escaped slaves, it had been adopted by the Romans for the most heinous of crimes because of its spectacular lesson to would-be lawbreakers. Death by crucifixion was a stigma, the most degrading form of execution, and the ultimate humiliation that in itself identified the victim as belonging in the lowest class of criminals.

Veronica could not repress a cry of indignation and sympathy when she saw the doomed man approaching. With the heavy beam of the patibulum upon His back, He was barely able to stagger along and had fallen repeatedly into the dirt. His face, already wet with blood and sweat, was caked with dust and Gis tortured eyes looked out at His tormentors as if through a mask. Behind Him two other men, identified by the crowd as dangerous thieves who had been sentenced to death by crucifixion, also stumbled along with the patibula strapped to their backs. But they were strongly built and fared better than the gentle Nazarene.

Veronica did not try to hide the sobs that shook her slender body or the tears that poured down her face. Around her women were weeping everywhere, and she recognized the beautiful woman of Magdala among those who followed close behind Jesus, supporting an older woman whose face was also ravaged by grief.

Jesus stumbled to His knees a few paces away from the girl and the guards had to jerk Him to His feet, cursing Him for not being able to stand. When He was just opposite Veronica, His knees buckled once more and He fell again, burying His face in the dust of the roadway because, with His arms held by thongs around the patibulum, He had no way of protecting Himself.

The Romans on either side of Jesus pulled Him to His knees, but this time the centurion Pelonius brought the procession to a halt and came back to look closely at the prisoner as He swayed in the grip of the soldiers. It was obvious that, if they released Jesus, the weight of the patibulum would only force Him to fall again.

"Loosen the beam from Him," Pelonius ordered. His eyes were surveying the crowd and now lit upon a heavy-set man who stood nearby. "You there," he called. "What is your name?"

The big man looked startled. "Simon. Simon of Cyrene."

"Take the beam and carry it for Him," Pelonius ordered.

Simon did not hesitate but stepped forward. The soldiers had already loosened the thongs and lifted the patibulum from Jesus' back. Now they raised it so that Simon could slip his arms through the thongs and ease the timber upon his broad shoulders.

With the weight removed from Him, Jesus straightened His body and looked around Him. Veronica could have touched Him from where she sat on the back of her mule. As she looked into the Nazarene's eyes, she was amazed to find no resentment mirrored there, only pain and suffering and, she was sure, a look that seemed to be one of compassion even for those who were torturing Him. Obeying an impulse she did not stop to question, Veronica, while the soldiers were adjusting the patibulum to the broad shoulders of Simon the Cyrene, quickly removed the veil from her head and handed it to Jesus.

He took the lustrous cloth in His two hands and pressed it to His face, wiping away the sweat, blood, and dirt that was caked there. As He handed the veil back to Veronica, stained by the print of His face almost as if its outlines had been painted upon the cloth, He smiled gently at her in thanks.

Veronica felt as sudden warm feeling of happiness and security flood her body, though just why the smile of this man to whom she had never spoken should do this, she did not know. But before she could say a word, the soldiers had jerked their prisoner by the arms and He had moved on, holding Himself erect now that the weight of the beam no longer pressed upon His back.

Veronica stared at the cloth with the print of Jesus' face upon it. She felt no sorrow that the beautiful veil was ruined. She knew she would never try to remove the stains from the gossamer fabric, for the cloth, stained as it was, was now far more precious to her than it had been before. What she had seen in Jesus' eyes when He had looked at her, the memory of His smile, was something she knew she would treasure all her life in the print of His features upon the veil.

"Veronica! Veronica!" A shrill voice calling her name brought the girl suddenly out of her reverie. She saw Jonas, his face set and white, his eyes like those of a hunted creature, leading Eleazar as rapidly as he could through the crowd with Zadok on the animal's back. The hunchback stumbled in his haste, like a man walking in his sleep, and seemed oblivious to the screeching of the cripple.

"Stop him, Veronica!" Zadok pleaded. "Stop him or I will be killed!"

Jonas showed no sign of having heard or even of recognizing the girl or her brother who had always been his friends. Zadok's face was livid with fear and he called Veronica's name again as the mule came abreast of her.

Without thinking, she slipped from her mount, and moving over to Eleazar, quickly seized Zadok about the waist and helped him swing to the ground where he lay in the roadway, panting with relief.

"Jonas—Jonas has been like one possessed—ever since he saw Abiathar place the—the crown of thorns on the Nazarene's head!" he gasped.

"Why?"

"Jonas gathered the thorns. Abiathar paid him a shekel to do it. Now he says he must ask forgiveness of Jesus. Before He goes to the cross."

He mopped his brow. "You saved my life, Veronica." Then his eyes grew wide and he swung his body up with his powerful arms and backed away from her.

"What is it, Zadok?" Veronica asked. "Is anything wrong?"

"You walked!" the cripple said incredulously. "You walked and lifted me from Eleazar's back!"

Veronica looked down at her feet and saw that they were standing firmly upon the road. To reach Zadok, she had taken three steps and yet had been conscious of no pain. She had not even limped. Instinctively, she swayed a moment and reached out toward Jonathan and the mule for support, but they were still several paces away, her brother still engrossed in watching the crowd that now swirled in the wake of Jesus toward the place of execution.

"I did walk!" she whispered, and moved her crippled leg tentatively, then when she felt no pain or unsteadiness, stepped bravely upon it. "I am well, Zadok!" she cried. "I have been healed!"

The beggar looked at her narrowly. "How did this happen?"

"Jesus—and the veil!" She held up the cloth with the Nazarene's face still outlined upon it in blood, sweat, and dirt. "It is why I felt so different when I took the veil from Him! It had healed me as soon as I touched it!"

"Maybe He really is what they say," the beggar said slowly. "The Messiah."

"You can prove it, Zadok!" Veronica cried, holding out the veil to him. "Touch it and you can be healed as I was!"

But the deformed man now backed farther away in fear. "Keep it away from me!" he screeched, swinging himself off through the crowd with his powerful arms as if a demon were in pursuit.

Veronica turned to look about her at the crowd that was already thinning out as the people fell in behind the Romans and their prisoner to follow them from the city. Jonathan saw that she was not on the mule and with a cry of concern started toward her. Then he stopped as, her eyes shining, Veronica walked to him.

"You don't need to carry me again—ever!" she told Jonathan happily. "I have been healed by the Messiah, the Son of God."

II

Even with his tortured hump, Jonas had never experienced physical agony to compare with the mental pain that had seized him when he saw Abiathar place the chaplet of green burnet upon Jesus' head and press the cruel thorns into His flesh. Until then he had felt only pity for the Nazarene, the same sort of pity he would have felt for any good man who was being unjustly executed. Now his own sense of guilt engulfed him, and an overpowering need to beg forgiveness filled him with an urgency he could not deny.

That Jesus would not forgive him, once he was close enough to beg it, did not once occur to Jonas. He had heard others tell of the Nazarene's teachings and knew that the one thing in His doctrine which appealed most to those burdened by the consciousness of their own sin was the promise of forgiveness if they came to Him and asked it. Certain that his own burden would be lifted once he came near enough to the Nazarene to beg forgiveness, Jonas seized Eleazar's lead rope more tightly and pressed on in the wake of the crowd that had poured out of the courtyard of the Antonia to follow Jesus and the Roman soldiers.

The condemned man was well ahead of Jonas by now and with the people jostling him on all sides, he could make only slow progress leading Eleazar. To Zadok's screams and imprecations he had paid no attention; the half-man, he knew, was quite capable of caring for himself. Though he could have made more rapid progress by dropping Eleazar's lead rope, it did not occur to Jonas to abandon the faithful mule. Eleazar was a part of him; he would as soon have cut off his own right arm as leave the animal to the mercies of the crowd.

Through the gate leading to the hill of Golgotha, the procession poured, Jonas squeezing through and protecting the mule as best he could with his body. As the crowd burst through the narrow opening, it fanned out like water pouring through a cleft in a dam. In spite of all he could do, Jonas and Eleazar were thrown against the wall. In the press, Jonas dropped the lead rope and had to push his way through to try to seize it again, losing valuable time once more. But with the people spreading out as they streamed through the gate, he was sure he could move faster and could reach the Nazarene before it was too late.

"Jonas! Jonas!" The voice was so weak that he did not recognize it at first, but the sound of his own name was enough to stop him.

"Jonas! Help!"

He placed the voice now; it came from against the wall where a man lay, his white robe already stained with a spreading blot of red where he had been wounded. In the same instant, Jonas recognized his old master, Elam.

"Help!" Elam begged weakly. "Help, or I die!"

Jonas hesitated and looked toward the crowd that was still streaming through the gate in the wake of the condemned Galilean. If he stopped now, all chance of reaching Jesus was lost. And yet the spreading stain on Elam's white robe meant that the Pharisee must be badly wounded and would probably die unless someone came to his aid.

Among the crowd no one showed any sign of stopping, so Jonas came to kneel beside Elam. The Pharisee's face was pale with the fear of death and loss of blood; his eyes, as he looked up at Jonas, were like those of an animal brought down in the hunt and not yet dispatched.

"A sicarius," Elam gasped. "He stabbed me—took my purse. Tear my robe and bind my wounds. Then carry me to a physician."

Jonas gave one last look toward Golgotha. He could see the procession beginning to climb the hill upon which stood, stark specters of death against the spring sky, the three uprights upon which three men would soon be dying. He knew he could never ask forgiveness of the Nazarene now. The burden of his guilt must rest upon his soul forever. But he could not let Elam die.

Turning, he began to rip the Pharisee's robe to make a bandage for the two knife wounds in his side.

III

It was about the third hour when the procession taking Jesus to be crucified reached the hill of Golgotha. With the shadows of the uprights falling almost across them, Mary of Magdala, with Mary the mother of Jesus, and Mary the wife of Cleopas, stopped at the foot of the hill to watch while Simon the Cyrene carried the patibulum to the center upright and laid it down. Jesus, His head lifted proudly and showing of sign of fear, walked up the hill to where the soldiers waited. On either side, the thieves who were to die with Him were already being dragged to their crosses, screaming for mercy.

As a final gesture of humanity, it was customary to give a condemned man wine with myrrh to bring on insensibility, but when Pelonius offered it to Jesus, He refused with a shake of His head, choosing to bear the full pain of the death He had chosen for Himself. Nor did He struggle when they seized Him and threw Him down upon the patibulum, binding His arms to it with heavy cords. Then while one of the four soldiers in charge of the execution spread out both His hands in turn upon the wooden beam, another drove through His palms the nails that would hold Him suspended there.

A great sob broke from Mary of Nazareth when she saw the first nail driven home into Jesus' flesh and she turned away, unable to watch any longer the agony of her son. Her own heart breaking with pity for Jesus, Mary of Magdala comforted the older woman as best she could. She had seen some of the disciples among the crowd now gathered at the foot of the hill, but did not speak for fear of identifying them to members of the Sanhedrin who had also come out with the crowd to witness the execution of the death sentence they had voted. When John appeared beside her and helped Mary of Nazareth to a rocky outcrop where she could rest, Mary Magdalene moved up the hill until she was as close to the foot of the cross as the soldiers would permit.

With Jesus' hands securely nailed to the crossbeam, the soldiers lifted it and, carrying the timber with His body dangling from it by the nails and the cords, hoisted it into place against the center upright.

The pain must have been agonizing, but Jesus did not cry out as the patibulum was fastened into place and then, to complete the crucifixion, heavy spikes were driven into the lower portions of the upright through Jesus' feet. Finally, across the upright beam a board was nailed upon which had been painted with brush and ink in large letters:

THIS IS JESUS, THE KING OF THE JEWS

As Jesus hung there upon the cross, those who had sought to destroy Him shouted insults for a while. Finally, they began to drift away, leaving only the soldiers whose task it was to watch until the three condemned men were dead, the small knot of women with John and Mary of Nazareth, and a scattering of disciples and followers of Jesus who chose to maintain the deathwatch there.

At the foot of Jesus' cross soldiers began to throw dice to see who would win the garments of the three prisoners to be sold for money to buy wine.

Woman, why are you weeping? Whom are you seeking?

John 20:15

Through the early hours in the morning, Peter had remained hidden in John Mark's home. Overcome with grief and guilt at having thrice denied the Master he loved, Peter could at first do nothing but wring his hands and moan in sorrow. Mary, Mark's mother, had begged him to eat, for she could see that he was close to breaking from remorse and sorrow, but Peter had refused. All that morning he prayed without pause, trying to remember the things Jesus had taught him since that day so long ago when the Master had come to the shores of Galilee and said, "Follow Me, and I will make you fishers of men."

As he prayed and recalled the times when he had sat at the feet of Jesus and listened to the great truths of the doctrine He had come to earth to preach, Peter now at last began to understand that Jesus had not come into the world to establish an earthly kingdom in Israel. And he could see that he and the other disciples had refused to listen to Jesus because of their ambition for earthly glory. The Master had opened for them—had they but been able to realize it—the gates of a vast and endless spiritual kingdom which all might enter merely by acknowledging Him and living according to the simple precepts He taught, dwelling there with Him through eternity.

||

About the sixth hour a strange pall of darkness fell over Jerusalem like an ominous cloud. Thunder rolled across the hills and lightning slashed the sky, sometimes appearing to seek out the pinnacle of the temple as if to destroy it.

When Mark's mother and those around her came to Peter for reassurance in the face of this strange phenomenon which none of them could understand, he finally found the strength to put aside his own fears, as he had not been able to do the night before in the courtyard of Caiaphas. And he discovered that comforting others took away much of his own fear and uncertainty.

The darkness had been over the city for nearly two hours by the time John Mark returned from the praetorium. His first words confirmed the conclusions at which Peter had arrived during the morning, now that he was able to understand the meaning of what Jesus had been telling the disciples for the past several months.

"Jesus is crucified on Golgotha!" the youth cried. "Between two thieves!"

For a moment Peter's heart was so filled with pain that he could not speak. "Where are the other disciples?" he asked finally.

"John took Jesus' mother away with him," Mark said. "Mary Magdalene and some other women are watching at the foot of the cross. The others have scattered."

Peter said no more but began to ready his robe and sandals.

"They will recognize you if you go out now," Mark protested. "You were the only one who tried to resist last night."

"They must recognize me," the big man said simply. "Because I am going to the hill and demand that I be crucified beside Jesus. With my head down, for I deserve no better."

Mark was horrified. "You cannot help the Master now!" he protested.

"But I can help myself," Peter said, "by atoning for my guilt in deserting Him and denying Him."

"I will go with you," the youth offered.

"No," Peter told him. "This is a journey I must make alone."

The darkness which had engulfed the city was already beginning to lighten when Peter strode through the gate leading to Golgotha, his powerful body proudly erect, his face calm with purpose.

When he approached the foot of the hill, he saw that while two dying men still hung on the outer crosses, the center one was empty. As he stood looking up at the cross in perplexity, a group of Roman soldiers passed him going down the hill, carrying the garments of the executed men over their arms.

Slowly Peter climbed the hill until he stood at the foot of the center upright, looking up at it.

"You knew Him well, didn't you?" a voice said beside him, and Peter turned to see a Roman centurion standing by. It was Pelonius who had commanded the detail of troops charged with the execution.

"I knew Him and loved Him," Peter said simply.

"I saw you with the Nazarene when He entered Jerusalem almost a week ago," the Roman said. "He must have trusted you, for you walked beside Him."

A great sob broke from Peter and he pointed to the bloodied patibulum lying upon the ground at the foot of the upright member of the cross. "Nail my arms to that," he begged, "and let me too die here."

The Roman shook his head. "I have crucified many men," he said, "but none such as this one. Even on the cross He said, 'Father, forgive them for they know not what they do.' He was a righteous man. You can serve Him better by continuing to teach what He taught than by a needless sacrifice of your life."

Peter looked again at the empty cross and once again he seemed to hear a gentle but familiar voice saying: "You are Peter, and upon this rock I will build My church. And the gates of hell shall not prevail against it."

The centurion was right. To let himself be crucified now would be to deny Jesus once again by ignoring the Master's own words about him. His task was clear. To rally those who had followed Jesus. To go back to Galilee, to Peraea, if need be, and carry on the work Jesus had begun.

"Where have they taken Him?" he asked.

"The merchant Joseph of Arimathea asked Pilate for the body," Pelonius said. "He and the lawyer Nicodemus took it away a short while ago. I heard them say they were laying the Nazarene in Joseph's own tomb in his garden."

Peter knew the place, for both Joseph and Nicodemus had been followers of Jesus. It was not far away.

"I will go there," he said. "They may need my help."

"Be careful how you show yourself," Pelonius warned. "The Pharisees know Jesus said He would rise again, so they asked Pilate for a guard to keep the tomb sealed."

Peter nodded. "I will be close by."

"The Nazarene was a righteous man," Pelonius said.

III

Jesus had died around the ninth hour. Joseph and Nicodemus had come for His body as soon as they could make the necessary arrangements. They were forced to move rapidly because the Sabbath began at sunset and they wished to lay Him in the tomb before then. Toward the end, one of the Roman soldiers had thrust a spear into Jesus' side to make sure that He was dead. Joseph and Nicodemus had time only to wrap the bruised and lacerated body in cloths soaked in myrrh to preserve it against the real preparations for burial, which could be made now only after the Sabbath, and to lay it in the empty tomb hewn from a rocky outcrop in Joseph's garden. This done, they had helped close the door of the tomb, swinging on hinges pivoted in the stone, the guards sent by Pontius Pilate at the request of the Sanhedrin rolling a great stone against the door of the sepulcher to seal it.

Through the night and the day of the Sabbath, Mary Magdalene with two other women kept watch in the garden near the tomb. The disciples did not come nearer, for with Roman guards present, there was danger of their being recognized and arrested. Simon Peter, finding in work some surcease from his grief, was busy bringing together the rest of the disciples and planning for their departure to Galilee after the proper burial of Jesus' body had been completed. As he worked, Simon was more and more inspired by the growing conviction, which had begun to crystallize as he stood looking up at the empty cross, that he was doing what Jesus wished him to do.

With the coming of sunset, the Sabbath was officially ended and Mary went into the city to buy the spices with which to prepare Jesus' body for proper burial the next morning. The soldiers guarding the sepulcher had refused to let them open the tomb that night, for their orders were to keep it intact until the third day on which Jesus had said He would rise again. The women had therefore remained in the garden during the night in the shelter of the building where Peter and the others were, planning to come early to the tomb and pay their last tribute to the Master by anointing His body properly for burial and watching the door close for the last time.

John had taken Mary of Nazareth away long before death had come to Jesus on the cross. Distraught with grief, she was in a state of collapse and he had made himself her guardian while she rested and recovered from the shock of seeing her son nailed to the cross.

Mary of Magdala had been weary from the night and day of watching and the trip into Jerusalem to buy spices. She slept soundly but in the hours before dawn found herself suddenly awake. The other disciples and the women who had also remained in the shelter were still asleep, for it was not yet dawn. Without awakening Peter or any of the others, Mary arose from her pallet and left the house.

She could not have told why she took the path through the garden to where Joseph's sepulcher had been hewn from the rock, nor did she know what she expected to find there. So it was that when she came into the clearing before the tomb and found the great stone rolled away and the door open, she could think only that the authorities must have taken Jesus' body away for some final act of desecration.

Without going nearer, she turned and ran back to the shelter where the others were sleeping. She aroused Peter and John. "They have taken the Lord out of the sepulcher!" she told them.

With Mary of Magdala, Peter and John went at once to the sepulcher. When they saw the stone rolled away and the tomb opened, it did seem that Mary had given the explanation. For the guards, too, were gone, which almost certainly meant that they had taken the body out during the night.

John bent down and looked into the tomb but all they could see, spread out on the empty stone shelf where it had lain, was the linen cloth with which Nicodemus and Joseph had wrapped Jesus' body. Peter came from behind John and, stooping because of his great height, went on into the tomb to see for himself that it was indeed empty. John then followed Peter's lead, and together they examined the rock-hewn chamber carefully for some sign of what had happened. But nothing gave them a clue. Except for the linen cloths which had been soaked in the aromatic spice and wrapped about the body, nothing remained.

The two disciples were as puzzled as Mary had been when she first came into the garden. Only one explanation came to their minds at the moment; the high priest must have ordered Jesus' body secreted somewhere lest the disciples abduct it from the tomb and claim that Jesus had indeed risen from the dead on the third day as He had predicted. Since they had no idea where the body had been taken or what had been done with it, they could do nothing but wait.

Simon and John returned to the shelter to awaken the others and tell them of this unexpected turn of events, but Mary of Magdala remained behind and, falling to the ground in front of the empty tomb, began to weep at this needless act of desecration upon the body of a man who had already died the most shameful of deaths.

Kneeling there, it suddenly seemed to Mary that the tomb was illumined for a moment and she saw two men in white sitting inside. When one of them spoke to her, saying, "Woman, why do you weep?" the vision and the voice were so real that she answered, "Because they have taken away my Lord, and I know not where they have laid Him."

The sound of her own voice in the silence that lay over the garden and the empty sepulcher startled her. When she felt a hand touch her shoulder, she drew back sharply.

A man stood beside her, only half visible in the dim light of early dawn. Kneeling, Mary could not see His face, but she recognized by His dress that He was not a soldier.

"Woman, why do you weep?" He asked. "Whom do you seek?"

Thinking that the man must be Joseph's gardener or a servant, Mary spoke quickly as she got to her feet.

"If you have borne Him from here," she said, "tell me where you have laid Him and I will take Him away."

"Mary!" The gentle voice spoke only her name, but at last she knew who it was that stood beside her.

"Master!" Mary's throat filled with happiness and she could say no more.

"Touch Me not," Jesus warned her, "for I have not yet ascended to My Father. But go to My disciples and say to them, I ascend to My Father and your Father; and to My God and your God."

Her eyes swimming now with tears of joy, Mary turned blindly toward her beloved Master but He was no longer there. The garden was empty with only the tomb and the wide-open door and the memory of His voice as He had spoken to her. Jesus had fulfilled His final prophecy. He had indeed been crucified and on the third day He had risen from the dead.

"Peter! John!" Mary cried as she ran toward the shelter where the others still were. "It has been fulfilled! Jesus has risen! Jesus has risen!"

IV

Dawn was breaking over the hills beyond the Mount of Olives when Jonas led Eleazar out through the gate on the way to the hillside to gather thornwood. It was the morning after the Sabbath and he had gone hungry through the previous day, having spent all his money to buy grain for Eleazar after depositing Elam safely at the Pharisee's home. Troubled by grief and shame still because of the part he had played in the execution of the Nazarene, Jonas had hardly noticed his own hunger. But as he plodded along behind the mule now, letting the patient animal pick its way up the familiar path, he found himself staggering with weakness.

The guards at the gate had been excited. Jonas had heard one of them telling the other that the body of the Nazarene had been stolen from the tomb during the night, but he was too distraught and too weak from hunger to pay much attention to their gossip. Hardly anyone was on the road this morning, and when he turned off along a path that wound up the hillside, he and the mule were alone. He had noticed a number of dead thornwood bushes in this area when he had gathered the green thorns for Abiathar several days before. At this season, there were not many dead thorns left, so it took longer to gather a load unless one was lucky enough to find a cluster of them.

Eleazar took the familiar path ahead of Jonas, the lead rope tied to his pannier for there was no need to guide him here. Jonas walked along behind, his head down, still sick with the grief that had assailed him when the crown of thorns had been pressed down upon the Nazarene's head. That he had saved Elam's life did nothing to mitigate his guilt and shame.

Suddenly Jonas realized that a man had fallen into step beside him. He had not seen the stranger appear nor heard footsteps overtaking him, but had been trudging along with his eyes to the ground and could easily have failed to see anyone approaching.

"Shalom," Jonas greeted the stranger courteously.

The man did not speak but when Jonas raised his head, he found himself looking into deep-set eyes in which shone such a kindness and warmth that he felt an answering feeling rise within him.

"I did not observe you on the road, sir," Jonas said. "You see, I am sad because I gathered thorns here for the crown they put upon the head of the Nazarene."

The stranger smiled as if He understood and somehow Jonas did not find it odd that He still had not spoken a word.

"I tried to reach the Teacher and beg His forgiveness," Jonas went on, "but I was kept back when Elam was stabbed. If Jesus had forgiven me, I would not be sad now."

Just talking to the stranger who walked beside Him without speaking seemed to bring peace to Jonas's troubled mind. And when the other man reached out to put His arm across the great hump on his back in a gesture of friendly assurance, the little woodseller felt an inexplicable warmth flood his soul. Most startling was not the stranger's gesture nor its effect upon Jonas, but the fact that now he distinctly remembered having had this same sensation once before.

It had been a long time ago when, cold and afraid, he had looked up in the sky above the courtyard of an inn in Bethlehem and had seen the brilliant star hanging there and felt its warmth drive all fear and pain from his body. The feeling was as distinct and as comforting now as it had been on that night more than thirty years ago.

The stranger's arm was like a protecting mantle about Jonas there on the hillside. When the little woodseller turned his head, he could see the other's hand where it rested upon his shoulder and, as plainly as if he had seen them himself on the hill of Golgotha, Jonas detected the print of the nails which had fixed the outstretched hands to the patibulum.

"You must be the—" Jonas stopped for he was alone. In fact, there was not even the print of a sandal in the dusty track beside him to mark where the stranger had walked.

Standing in the roadway, Jonas shook his head slowly. "I have been dreaming." he told himself finally. But the feeling of peace that flooded his soul and the touch of the stranger's arm which it seemed he could still feel about his bent and gnarled shoulders were not a dream.

"The Nazarene claimed He would rise from the dead," he said, unconsciously speaking aloud. He did not finish the sentence for it was incredible that the man to whose shameful death he had contributed should have risen and come here today to comfort him in his grief. Such a thing could not happen to Jonas the woodseller. He was not even a follower of Jesus nor had he ever spoken a word to the Nazarene—unless it had been just now.

Noticing that Eleazar had gone on ahead and was out of sight around a turn of the path, Jonas hurried to catch up with the old animal. As he rounded the hill and saw stretching before him the broad patch of burnet where he had gathered the green thorns he stopped with a feeling of awe and joy. Now, at last, he knew who had comforted him a few moments before on the road. What he was seeing could only be a sign that Jesus of Nazareth had indeed risen from the dead and had forgiven him his own part in the shameful death of the cross.

In the center of the patch of thorns, exactly where Jonas had gathered those for the crown, a mass of the green burnet had bloomed overnight with thousands of blossoms shaped like drops of blood making a scarlet slash of color across the green hillside that was like a burning beacon in the dawn.

Long, long ago, Jonas had been allowed to give the first gift to a child who, the shepherds had said, was announced to them by the angels as the Son of God. Now, many years afterwards, he knew he had also given the last gift, a crown for the King who would rule forever in the hearts of men.